Dear Reader,

Welcome to another month of Duets! And allow me to introduce myself as the new editor for the line. I'm committed to bringing you the funniest, most romantic books each month from all your favorite authors. I also love to hear from you—our readers—so please drop me a line at the address below.

We have a very special treat for you in Duets #23, as Lori Foster has penned a sexy, funny story about a hero who is holding out for marriage in *Say Yes*. Then Cathy Yardley launches the first of our MAKEOVER MADNESS books with *The Cinderella Solution*. Haven't we all flipped through the pages of our favorite magazine studying makeovers and wondered what would happen to our life if we took on a completely new image?

Then men and women unexpectedly forced to live together is our theme in Duets #24. Diane Pershing traps her hero and heroine together in their job and house. Lois Greiman puts hero and heroine into the same living space and adds a healthy dose of animals. Laughs and romance fill both homes.

Enjoy our romantic comedies!

Birgit Davis-Todd
Senior Editor, Harlequin Duets

Harlequin Books
225 Duncan Mill Rd.
Don Mills, Ontario
M3B 3K9 Canada

"Are we going to do a lot of...this, when you move in?" Sara asked breathlessly.

Gavin's brain shut down. "Aw, hell." Reminded of his plan, he shoved himself away from her. How did that saying go? You won't buy the cow if the milk is free? Not that he liked comparing himself to a cow. A bull, maybe...

"Sara, if this is going to work, you're going to have to stop making it so easy on me."

"Me? What about you? You're the one who started the kissing."

"Yeah. But you didn't have to go all soft and hungry on me."

"I'm not going to let you blame me for this, Gavin! You're the one who climbed into bed with me."

"But I'm not the one who tried to crawl on top of you in the middle of the night."

She sucked in so much air, she choked. "I would *never...!*"

Nodding, he said, "Yes, you would. *You did.*" Then he added in a low voice before she could get too worked up, "But I didn't mind at all."

For more, turn to page 9

"I wanted you to see these viciously sexy outfits," *Charlie said.*

"No," Gabe said. Seeing her in plain white bra and matching panties was viciously sexy enough, thanks very much!

She laughed and ignored his protest.

When she had finished modeling her creations his heart was beating as if he'd run a marathon. Finally she slipped back into her jeans and shirt.

"So? What did you think?" she asked eagerly.

What did he think? He thought she'd shaved ten years off his life with that sensual torture! "I thought it was very...nice."

"Nice?" She frowned at him. "I'm looking for devastatingly sexy. Come on, Gabe, work with me!"

"Fine," he said, sighing deeply. "You were incredible. You would make a Buddhist monk pant like a dog. If God had made anything better he would have kept it for himself. Satisfied?"

She grinned. "Now, *that's* what I wanted to hear."

For more, turn to page 197

HARLEQUIN DUETS

ISBN 0-373-44089-8

SAY YES
Copyright © 2000 by Lori Foster

THE CINDERELLA SOLUTION
Copyright © 2000 by Cathy Yardley

LORI FOSTER

Say Yes

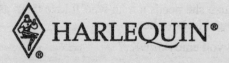

HARLEQUIN®

TORONTO • NEW YORK • LONDON
AMSTERDAM • PARIS • SYDNEY • HAMBURG
STOCKHOLM • ATHENS • TOKYO • MILAN • MADRID
PRAGUE • WARSAW • BUDAPEST • AUCKLAND

Dear Reader,

When I was six years old, I won a drawing contest in the city newspaper. The prize was a complete Worldbook Encyclopedia set. (And lucky for me, a rubber finger puppet!) My parents made me a deal. I'd give them the encyclopedias until I graduated, and they'd buy me anything I wanted. I wanted a baby pig.

At a nearby farm we found the most adorable little spotted piglets running around playing. But there was one especially homely pig, just sorta gray, sorta fat, sorta shy. I chose him. And named him after Monnie, my grandma.

He got fatter and uglier as time went by, and finally I gave him to a local farmer who promised to keep him as a stud pig. Monnie was happy till the day he died.

I've always loved animals—the tailless cat, the bird with a broken wing, the snake a neighbor wanted to kill, the dog who shed too much. Every animal I've come into contact with has added something to my life.

This story is about a woman who loves pets just as much as I do—especially the dysfunctional or ugly ones.

Of course she needs a man who'll love them as well, so I found him for her.

I hope you enjoy *Say Yes!*

Lori Foster

P.S. You can write Lori at P.O. Box 854, Ross OH 45061, or send an e-mail to lorifoster@poboxes.com

To my computer-guru buddy and good friend
Jen Sokoloski. Without you, Jen, my computer and all
that goes with it would likely still be a mystery. <g>
Thank you for all your help.

And to Linda Keller, my best friend.
Thank you so much for listening, talking,
sharing, giving—for being you.

1

IT WAS THE LOUD, SHRILL scream of rage that drew Gavin Blake's attention, along with the frantic shrieks that followed. Gavin stared down the middle of the narrow street, blinking hard to make certain he wasn't hallucinating. But no. There was his usually calm, very friendly neighbor Sara Simmons, her dark curly hair bouncing out behind her as she ran hell-bent after Karen, his used-to-be girlfriend. He hadn't seen Karen in months, not since their breakup, and the sight of her now wasn't what fascinated him. No, it was gentle, sweet, *passive* Sara—who at the moment held a rake which she wielded with all the force and efficiency of a massive war club. And each time she swung it, punctuating her efforts with low, threatening growls, Karen wailed in fear.

A disbelieving smile twitched on his mouth as he heard Sara issue a rather lurid, improbable threat. So far as Gavin could tell, Sara hadn't even touched Karen yet, but it was a close thing. Karen's shirt was open, but her efforts were all centered on escaping the woman bent on retribution, not on covering her half-naked chest. As they neared the entrance to the garage where Gavin stood, he tried to get himself out of the way. But Karen made eye contact, and evidently, even though they were no longer involved, she decided he might be her savior.

Hah! Sara behaved very much like a woman scorned—or a woman who had caught her fiancé intimately involved with another woman. And knowing Karen as he did, that assumption wasn't unrealistic. He'd learned some time ago that Karen would never be a faithful, devoted, loving partner. Which was why he'd ended the relationship and sent her on her way months ago.

But as the two women ran straight for him and he saw the fury—and the hurt—in Sara's eyes, Gavin knew for a certainty Karen had been up to her old tricks. He decided to stay out of the matter and let Sara do her worst, knowing she wouldn't actually hurt Karen. But the women had other ideas.

They tried to use him as a maypole.

He dropped the file he'd been holding and saw the approved plans for another subdivision scatter across the garage floor. He struggled to maintain his balance with Karen trying to shield herself behind him and Sara trying to go straight through him. He bent to retrieve a floor plan being mangled under furious feminine feet and was promptly shoved away and onto his backside. Having just come from the office, he was unfortunately wearing dress pants. He started to grumble, but then Karen made a dive for the house, and Sara followed, climbing right over the top of him.

There was another loud screech, and Gavin couldn't help but grin. He'd known since first meeting Sara that she was a passionate little thing, filled with energy and an abundance of emotion. But this was the first time he'd seen that emotion really set free. The jerk she'd planned to marry would never have made her happy. Gavin supposed, in a way, he owed Karen his thanks for showing Sara just how big a jerk Ted really was.

Then he heard the sound of breaking glass and decided he'd have to intervene after all. Knowing Sara, and he'd come to know her very well since she'd moved into one of the houses he built, she'd hate her loss of control once she calmed down.

He wondered briefly if she'd allow him to console her.

Coming up behind Sara, he was just in time to duck the rake as she took another swipe at the cowered, screeching Karen. Gavin snatched it out of her hands, and when she rounded on him, he pulled her close in a careful bear hug. "Just calm down, honey."

He tried to keep the satisfaction and good humor out of his tone. Little by little, the enormity of the situation was sinking in, and he was starting to feel damn good. He'd now see the end of Sara's fiancé—and without a guilty conscience. He'd held back, keeping his personal interest to himself, unwilling to involve himself in a set relationship, even though he knew the relationship was doomed. Sara was much too good for Ted, she just hadn't seemed to realize it.

But with these new crimes against him, Sara would surely send Ted packing. Finally they would both be free of ties, and he'd be able to pursue her the way he wanted to.

Sara growled, and he had to admit, the menacing sound was very effective. "Let me go, Gavin."

No way. She felt damn good in his arms, too good. He looked down at her rigid expression, her bright eyes, and had to fight to keep from kissing her. This was the first time he'd ever been able to actually hold her, and he liked it—a lot. She growled again and he saw that slightly crooked front tooth, the one that always taunted him, made him want to touch it with his tongue. He tightened his hold just a bit more, relishing the feel of her small body tucked up against his, and breathed in her gentle fragrance. Sara always smelled of sunshine and softness and woman. He lowered his mouth to her ear.

"I think you've made your point, honey. Karen understands the error of her ways."

She struggled in his arms. "You don't know what they... They were in my *house,* in my bed!"

He did know. The house meant everything to Sara, but very little to Ted. In fact, Sara had bought the place herself, no small feat for a woman alone with a moderate income. And not a day went by that she didn't tell him what a wonderful job he'd done building that house. She made him feel as if he'd given her the moon.

"It won't happen again, Sara. I promise."

He had a hell of a time controlling his elation. And when Sara peeked up at him with energy and emotion blazing in her blue eyes, he couldn't help himself. He smiled.

Very slowly she looked around. A lamp lay broken on the floor and Gavin saw her wince. When her gaze landed on the shattered picture, she closed her eyes as if in pain. Color flooded her smooth cheeks.

Behind him, he heard the sounds of Karen slinking away. No doubt she planned to make a strategic retreat. Gavin ignored her. In the three months she'd been gone, he hadn't missed her once. "Sara? Are you okay now?"

"Let—me—go."

Cautiously, making certain she wouldn't bolt after Karen again, Gavin lowered his arms. She stood there, her eyes still closed, her cheeks pulsing with heat. She said in a strangled whisper, "I'm sorry."

Gavin touched her cheek, swamped with tenderness and a real healthy dose of desire. "Hey, don't worry about it. After a boring day in the office, I needed a little excitement."

She drew in a long, slow breath, then opened her eyes, but didn't look at him. Instead she surveyed the damage. "I didn't mean to break anything."

"Karen would probably disagree."

Her gaze shot to his face and her hands curled into

fists. "I don't want her anywhere near me ever again."

She was such a ferocious, impassioned little thing when duly provoked. "Don't worry. I think Karen has learned her lesson. Besides, I wasn't the one who invited her here."

She scowled. "No. Ted apparently did."

"What will you do?" He was very curious, but he held no sympathy for Ted. In fact, he wanted to rub his hands in glee over Ted's folly. The idiot.

Sara lifted her chin, then slowly stepped around the broken glass on the floor. "I'll take care of Ted." Gavin watched her stiff posture as she walked away, and he wondered if he should accompany her home so she wouldn't have to face Ted alone. Then he thought better of it.

Ted didn't stand a chance.

Besides, Sara was private, with a streak of dignity and pride a mile wide. She wouldn't want an audience when she gave Ted the boot. He knew Sara—not as well as he'd like to, but probably better than Ted would ever know her. At least he knew enough to realize how important old-fashioned values were to her. Possibly because they were important to him as well.

She'd talk to Ted, listen to his lame excuses, then toss him out on his miserable can. She'd be hurt for a while, but she'd get over it, just as she'd get over Ted. Gavin was willing to give her some time.

And then it was finally going to be his turn.

HOUSE FOR SALE BY OWNER.

Stunned, Gavin slowed his truck until he came to a complete stop. Sara had been avoiding him. The friendly talks in the yard had ceased, as had her spontaneous visits to the construction sites. It used to be that Sara couldn't keep away when she saw the crew working on another house on her street. She loved the process of seeing a house built, of everything coming together to make a home, almost as much as he did.

But lately, her pride and embarrassment had caused a wall he was damn tired of beating his head against.

And now she wanted to sell? Like hell.

Cursing to himself, he put the truck in Park and climbed out. He glared at the stormy, cloud-filled skies, then glared even harder at the For Sale sign. Stomping over to her yard, he ripped up the sign and threw it into the back of his truck, then brushed his hands off in a show of satisfaction. Try to sell, would she? Without a single word, without giving him the chance he'd been waiting for? Ha!

He'd been patient too long, that was the problem. He had a plan, and it was time he put it into motion. He wanted Sara, had wanted her for a long time. And starting right now, he was done with waiting.

SARA WAS NAKED, she was wet, and she was frustrated.

She was also alone.

Water sloshed over the sides of the large Jacuzzi tub when she jerked awake. The vivid fantasy she'd

conjured in her mind evaporated. She realized it was
the loud clapping of thunder that had startled her from
the luxury of her bath—and the man she'd been
dreaming of.

Disgusted, she shook her head. She'd made a point
of avoiding Gavin since that awful, fateful day. She
shouldn't be dreaming about him, either. She was
tired, that's all, too much overtime at work wearing
her down. She'd counted on a leisurely soak in her
Jacuzzi tub to ease away her weariness and her aches
and pains. But since Gavin had built the house and
installed the tub, it was no wonder her thoughts had
chased after him again. Now the storm was here, and
her fantasy gone, so she supposed her bathtime was
over.

Water dripped onto the ceramic tile floor as she
threw a worn towel around her body. Sheesh. Even
in her imagination, she couldn't indulge a satisfactory
romantic interlude. Maybe she should give up on
dream men, just as she'd given up on the real thing.
Romances, even the imaginary kind, evidently
weren't meant for her. Besides, dogs were much more
reliable. Unfortunately, like the house, dogs required
upkeep. And as much as she wanted one, she wasn't
home enough to keep a dog company—or vice versa.

Still dripping, she stomped off to close the windows. Without the cooling breeze, the interior would
soon become unbearable, but she couldn't afford air
conditioning any more than she could afford a dog.

The evening had turned very dark, and she remembered her front door was open, with only the screen door latched. As she went to close it, she saw the threatening sky, felt a spattering of the rain as it blew in over her porch. She thought again how nice a pet would be, another living thing to keep her company on a dreary night like this. Granted, a dog wouldn't provide quite the same company as a man, but then, a dog required much less maintenance. Dogs weren't as messy as men. They were more loyal and friendly. Dogs never made promises they couldn't keep...

Suddenly she noticed her For Sale sign was missing. She'd only just put the thing in the yard that day!

Distracted from her daydreams by the possibility of vandalism, she clicked open the lock on the screen door and stuck her head outside, automatically breathing in the churning, moist night air.

"You planning to dance buck-naked in the rain?"

Squealing, she lurched backward and slipped off her wet feet before the familiarity of that deep, masculine voice could penetrate. She would have fallen if her backside hadn't smacked up against the gaping front door.

It took her a moment to regain her dignity—what was left of it—before she cautiously stuck her head outside again. A burst of white light splintered through the night, and she saw her one and only neighbor, Gavin Blake, standing to the side of her door. He was in the shadows, but she would recognize his body, his voice, his *presence,* anywhere. She shivered. *Boy, could she recognize him!*

But Gavin would forever be relegated to the role of her fantasy man. Nothing more was possible. Not after the incident.

She continued to stare, then blinked in surprise as her eyes adjusted. Soaked completely through by the storm, Gavin stood there in a soggy T-shirt and shorts, with a bottle of wine in one large hand.

Good grief! He was too darn gorgeous, too big and imposing and male. He was also the last person she ever wanted to see, other than in her dreams.

But…but there he stood.

Her stomach took a free fall and her heart shot into her throat. She squeezed her eyes shut, but when she opened them again, he was still there, still watching her. "A pet. I most definitely need a pet."

Gavin raised his brows, his dark eyes glinting in the shadows, his tone amicable. "Hey, I hadn't planned on anything so forward, at least not this soon, but petting's good. I'm into petting if that's what you really—"

"No!" Sara dodged his outstretched hand and ground her teeth together, feeling foolish. "I meant a pet, as in a dog that might have barked and let me know someone was here."

His gaze slid from her face to her towel-wrapped body. "Then I'm glad you don't have a dog."

With a gasp, she ducked into the house and shielded herself behind the front door. After a long, silent moment, she began to realize he wouldn't just go away, and that she'd once again made herself look ridiculous. She poked her head around the door.

Gavin chuckled. "I'm getting soaked standing here, babe. You going to ask me in or what?"

"Ah… No. Not a good idea." She knew her tone lacked conviction. She'd wanted him, *really* wanted him, for the longest time, but not now, not at this precise moment.

Not dressed only in a towel.

He looked down at his feet, as if considering the situation, then pulled the screen open and stepped inside. "Sara." His tone was chiding. "I've given you plenty of time. I hoped you'd be willing to talk to me now."

She couldn't hold his direct gaze, so she glanced at the bottle of wine in his hand. "What do you want, Gavin?"

"You."

Oh wow. Heat washed over her in undulating waves, and she took a hasty, nervous step back, bumping into the wall. She couldn't, wouldn't, look at him. Gavin cupped her cheek with a rough palm and lifted her face. His smile gentle, his voice low, he murmured with a good dose of sincerity, "I like you, Sara. I always have. From the very first day you looked at this house and proclaimed me a master planner and the best builder you'd ever come across, I knew we were destined to be very good…friends."

Teasing, she thought. *Only teasing.* But he *was* a talented builder, putting that little extra into a house to make it special. Gavin Blake was, at only thirty-three years of age, an extremely successful man.

Sara could still remember the first time she'd laid eyes on him. He'd shown her around the house himself because he'd been inside, adding some touches to the existing kitchen. He'd been enthusiastic, speaking about his work with the intensity of an artist, while looking every inch the rugged male in his ragged jeans and work boots. There had been a healthy sweat dampening his T-shirt, and he'd smelled *so* good. The cocky way he walked kept grabbing her attention. He was confident of his abilities, and with good reason. What he did was exceptional; he expected the same of the men who worked for him. He'd shown her all the perks his housing offered, all the ways he'd improved on the average plans to make his creations special.

And she'd fallen instantly in love…with the house. But she'd also felt a very real attraction for the man. Gavin had the sensitive hands of an artist, and her fertile mind had imagined those hands everywhere they shouldn't be.

Though she'd been engaged then, and he'd had a relationship of his own, it hadn't taken her long to realize she was planning to marry the wrong man.

But once she'd become free of Ted—the cheating slime—it had been too late. Gavin had witnessed the worst of her, and she was too embarrassed to see him again. And too realistic to keep trying for a romantic future that would only elude her.

But now Gavin was here, in the flesh.

"You used to come and talk to me while I worked." He leaned closer, his gaze drifting over her face. "I've missed you, Sara."

His suggestive tone shook her. She shifted from one bare foot to the other, her naked knees pressed together as she remembered their easy camaraderie, the swell of excitement she always felt whenever he was near.

Gavin watched her, his gaze straying over her shoulders and across the tops of her breasts. She knew her blush had spread, and that it was visible even in the dim light. Then his hand lifted from her cheek and he slid a rough fingertip over her lips. Her breath caught somewhere in the bottom of her lungs, making her dizzy.

"You never used to blush so much."

She thought she should move, but she didn't. She swallowed, then stated the obvious. "I never had good reason before."

"Ah." He turned to look outside, his hands propped on his lean hips, the wine bottle still held securely. "I assume we're talking about the... incident?"

Sara swallowed. It had been a fiasco and the most humiliating moment of her life. It wouldn't have been quite so horrendous, catching Ted with Karen, if she'd handled the situation with a modicum of grace, a little poise. But no. She'd had to go and do her impression of a berserk gardener, grabbing the closest weapon, which happened to be a plastic rake, and chasing a near-naked woman up the middle of the street!

Catching her bottom lip in her teeth, she groaned. The memory was not a humorous one for her, and now here she was, cowering behind a door, making a total fool of herself once again. She would have straightened her shoulders if it wouldn't have caused her towel to slip. "Just why are you here, Gavin?"

He stared at her, or more precisely her mouth, watching as her teeth worried her bottom lip. He was so tall—over six feet, making her five foot five seem very diminutive. And his wet T-shirt had turned transparent, clinging to his wide shoulders, taunting her with what it both hid and revealed. She could see the dark hair on his chest, appearing so very soft in stark contrast to his hard body.

She knew she didn't want to see what the rain had done to his cutoffs. She felt flustered enough as it was.

His tone was gentle, insistent. "It's been six weeks, Sara. I figured that was plenty of time for you to get over whatever ails you and get friendly again. You've been snubbing me ever since that day."

Her brow puckered at the misunderstanding. "I wasn't snubbing you. I...I wasn't at all sure, after the damage I did, if you'd want to talk to me again." That was a partial truth, because she'd sent him a note of apology and asked for the amount of the damages. She'd found the note stuck inside her screen door, with the message, Paid In Full, scrawled across it. It was sheer embarrassment that kept her away now.

He sighed, then shook his head. "Why don't we sit down and talk? I'm going to set you straight on a few things."

Without waiting for her agreement, he kicked off his wet tennis shoes and headed for her kitchen, giving her the perfect opportunity to make a fast break for the bedroom. She did, back-stepping the whole way just in case he turned. And with every foot that separated them, she pondered the possibilities of why he was here. A tiny flare of excitement stirred, but she ruthlessly snuffed it out. Gavin wasn't for her, and he never would be.

2

WHEN SARA ENTERED the kitchen a few minutes later, wearing a loose sundress that fell to her knees, she found Gavin leaning against the counter. He gave her a slow, thorough once-over, his gaze intent, his mouth tipped in a slight smile. Then he plucked at his wet T-shirt, pulling it away from his body. His voice was pitched low and deep when he spoke. "The storm took me by surprise. Do you mind if I take this off so I can get comfortable, too?"

Her mouth went dry. She tamped down the natural inclination to lick her lips, and shook her head instead. Heaven only knew what she might do if presented with such temptation. "I'm not sure if that's a good idea. There's not much for us to talk about."

"Of course there is." He peeled off the shirt with no thought for modesty or her overly rapt attention. She stared, anxious to catch every riveting detail of exposed male flesh.

She laced her fingers tightly together and held herself still as he shook out his shirt and laid it over the back of a chair to dry. Facing her, he adopted a no-

nonsense expression, a stern warning that she was to pay close attention.

The man was half-naked—he had her attention.

"I didn't care about the lamp, Sara. Or the picture." There was a pause, then he added, "I didn't even care about—"

Wincing, she cut him short. "I didn't realize I'd broken more than the lamp and the picture."

"You didn't." He sprawled into the chair, stretching out his long bare legs. He was muscled everywhere, the physical labors of his job keeping him in excellent shape.

She remained standing, too nervous to relax. It was a mixed reaction from the electric charge of the storm, sheer exhaustion, and Gavin's presence. The man had always affected her in one way or another, but since the incident, she'd done her best to repress her more emotional feelings.

Now they were swamping back in force.

Gavin cleared his throat, waiting until she met his gaze before continuing. "I was going to say I didn't mind that you'd chased after Karen."

She sucked in a breath, her shoulders going rigid. "Well, I should hope not! She was...was..." Sara searched for a more delicate word than those coming to mind. There weren't many. She finally settled on, "Unfaithful."

He smirked, one brow raised. "She was that. But then, unlike you, I wasn't engaged. In fact, if you'll remember correctly, Karen and I had broken up months before. She wasn't here because of me, Sara, she was only here to visit Ted.''

Sara made a grimace, knowing what he said was true. She certainly couldn't blame him for Karen's presence, not that she would have anyway. Blame had nothing to do with her avoidance of him. Humiliation did. ''Karen and Ted were the only ones responsible. I know that.''

He nodded. ''Good. Then there's no reason why we can't remain...friends. Is there?''

Put like that, what choice did he give her? ''No. I guess not.''

''By the way, whatever happened to lover-boy? I assume you sent him on his way?''

With a sound of disgust, she shook her head. ''I didn't have to. When I got back Ted was already more or less dressed and anxious to go. I found him peeking out the door, watching for you I suppose. He crawled out to his car, then slithered inside. He left skid marks in my driveway he was in such a hurry to escape. I think he was afraid you'd come after him.''

''More likely he was afraid of you.'' Gavin slanted her a look, his smile once again in place, though this time it looked more tender than humorous. ''You swing a mean rake, lady.''

Another wave of heat inched along the back of her neck, but she refused to look away from his probing gaze.

''Besides,'' he continued, ''I wasn't angry at Ted. I'd long since given up my claim on Karen, and in a way, he did me a favor. If he'd hung around, I might have even thanked him.''

Sara stared. "You've got to be kidding me."

"Nope." With no sign of amusement now, he leaned forward in his seat and reached for her hand. "Ted hung himself. He made certain you'd never be able to forgive him, to take him back. I wanted him gone, Sara, because I knew he wasn't right for you. He'd never have been able to make you happy.''

She had to agree with him there. Ted was not the man she wanted to be tied to for life, and in a way, she almost felt grateful, too, because his lack of morals had freed her before it was too late.

Feeling hesitant and uncertain, she asked, "It didn't bother you—not even a little—that he'd been having an affair with Karen?''

"It made me mad as hell that they hurt you. But for myself? No. Karen is free to do as she pleases, not that she ever felt any restrictions to begin with.''

He hadn't loved Karen. Sara was both relieved, and depressed. If tall, beautiful, outgoing Karen hadn't been able to gain his affections, a woman like herself wouldn't stand a chance.

But then, she'd always known that.

She pulled her hand away and tried to fill the silence. "I applaud your control. I'm afraid I was a little more sensitive about the whole thing.''

"I know." He gave her a teasing look. "I remember.''

Dropping into her own chair, Sara propped her elbows on the table and covered her face with her hands. It all seemed so ridiculous now, but at the time... "I still can't believe I barged through your house, swinging a rake and raving like a lunatic. It was so unlike me. I've never before indulged in such a fit, no matter what the provocation."

She heard a low choked sound, and peeked from between her fingers to see Gavin trying to contain his humor. "What?"

He shrugged, then mumbled around his chuckles, "I was just thinking of the strain you must have been under, keeping all that explosive emotion bottled up."

"I'm not an emotional person."

He sputtered, then lost the fight to keep from laughing. Dropping her hands, she scowled at him, but that only served to make him laugh all the more. At her. She felt renewed humiliation and jerked to her feet, her eyes narrowed on his face. "Go home, Gavin!"

He caught her wrist and tugged her close despite her resistance, trying to rid himself of his smile, and failing. "Ah, Sara. If you could have seen your face that day! It was damn impressive. Outrage and indignation and a good dose of evil intent... Hell, for a second there, you terrified even me. I thought about running for cover along with Karen! But with you shouting accusations and threats so horrid my ears rang, it didn't take me long to realize what had happened, and—"

"And you were amused."

He sobered instantly. "No." Squeezing her fingers,

he held her hand close to his side. "I was relieved. You were too good for that jerk and I was glad you realized it before you married him and ruined everything."

Feeling perverse, partly because she didn't understand him, and partly because he was still smiling, she said, "You hardly knew Ted."

"Wrong. I'd spoken with him several times, though not nearly as much as you and I talked. He was a worm. Believe me, Sara, you're better off without him."

She scowled, thinking of Ted's empty promises, and her empty house. Her own gullibility. She'd wanted to be wanted so badly, she'd been willing to be duped by Ted.

Now she merely felt like a fool. "He worked hard to convince me to marry him."

Gavin tilted his head, his eyes intent. "Whatever he told you was probably lies."

She knew that now. Ted hadn't really cared about her at all. Big surprise. "He said we'd make the perfect couple, that love was something that came over time. We were too old to be frivolous, to wait for the kind of relationship you see in movies and read about in books. He said he was as alone and lonely as me, and he convinced me he wanted the same things. A secure home, a lasting relationship. So we approached this wedding business in a logical, no-nonsense fashion. We discussed up-front who would be responsible for various things, and what was expected of each of us. We had the future all mapped out.''

Gavin was attentive, staring at her, seemingly fascinated.

She tried to ignore his hold on her wrist, the warmth of his palm and the way his scent made her toes curl. "Ted broke nearly every promise he made. I still wonder why he wanted to marry me in the first place.''

"What promises?"

Trying to act indifferent, she shrugged. "You mean apart from the promises to be faithful and act honorably and to stick around through thick and thin?"

Gavin watched her with compassion, and she hated it. She knew she sounded like a woman scorned, but a part of her still felt betrayed, not by Ted, because he didn't really matter, not anymore. But by her own foolish hopes for things that either didn't exist, or else weren't meant for her.

She sucked in a slow, calming breath. "Part of the deal was that I'd buy the house, and he'd furnish it.'' She lifted her free hand to indicate her almost barren kitchen. A small, aged Formica table and two chairs sat in the middle of the floor. They were ugly and looked totally out of place in the exquisite kitchen Gavin had constructed. The rest of the house was the same, the rooms either near-empty or "furnished" with used, mismatched pieces.

"As you can see, Ted left before furnishing anything. Even the backyard is barren, and I'd really

wanted a porch swing and a pet and a picnic table."
She sighed. "I'd thought this could be a real home.
Instead it's just an empty shell."

Gavin leaned back, one dark brow raised high.
"Let me get this straight. You were willing to hook
up for life with a bastard like Ted just for some lawn
furniture?"

Sara blinked. Put that way, it did sound rather foolish. Not that he understood it all. She had planned to
be a good wife, to do whatever it took to make the
marriage work. She'd wanted kids and Christmas,
family budgets and a family car. She'd even wanted
the struggles that came with maintaining family unity.

She'd gotten nothing but a severe dent to her pride.

She hadn't loved Ted, but she had liked him, and
she'd been willing to put every effort into making a
solid marriage.

But how could she explain all that to Gavin? He
was a man who never wanted for companionship, a
man who had his pick of women ready to stand by
his side. He would never consider accepting a woman
he didn't really want, just for something as base as
companionship.

"So everything wasn't perfect," she allowed, "I
thought we could manage. We would have grown
closer with time. We could have made it work." She
took a deep breath and mumbled, "I still think the
least Ted could have done was furnish a room or two
before he ruined everything."

Gavin shook his head. "You can get what you need

later, without his help. Be glad you didn't marry him. It would have been a disaster.''

He seemed so vehement. But then, that was one of the things that had drawn her to him, his self-assurance and confidence. ''You don't understand, Gavin. You've never had any desire to be married.''

''Why do you say that?''

Trying to refrain from making another scene, she wiggled her wrist free of his hold and sat down. She wished she'd kept her mouth shut, but now he was waiting for an explanation.

No way did she want Gavin to know just how fascinated she was with him, or the extent of her emotions. She'd suffered such enormous guilt when her feelings toward him had turned...lecherous. She'd never suffered sexual frustration in her life, but when it hit, it *really* hit. Like a tsunami.

It was doubly difficult because her feelings for Gavin had begun as respect and friendship. More than anyone else, more than Ted or any other man she'd known, even more than her parents, Gavin made her feel accepted and liked. She was comfortable around him. She supposed it was only natural that her fertile mind had started to meander into forbidden topics. So she'd felt guilty.

Right up until she came home and found Ted in bed with Gavin's girlfriend. *Ex-girlfriend,* she reminded herself. And then all hell had broken loose. Or, to be more accurate, she'd broken loose, reacting like a demented ogress.

Gavin was watching her, and she had to tell him something. Trying to pick her words carefully, she said, "Karen told me once, when I'd first moved in, that you weren't the marrying kind. She claimed you liked a lot of—" she cleared her throat "—*variety*. She was bragging, because you supposedly cared enough about her to ask her to move in. She said you wanted only the best."

Gavin didn't react the way she expected over the invasion of privacy. He seemed intrigued, and his cocky grin spread wide over his face. "You discussed me with Karen?" At her noncommittal shrug, he propped his elbows on the table, laced his fingers together, and leaned toward her. "What else did she say to you?"

"Oh, this and that." Actually, thanks to Karen, she knew things about Gavin she shouldn't have known, intimate details that made it more than difficult to be around him, and twice as tough to control her imagination.

At least she didn't have to worry about guilt anymore, since she was now free. And alone. She didn't even miss Ted, which was almost sad since she'd once been engaged to him. But long before she'd caught him with Karen, she'd had doubts about marrying him. He didn't have the same respect for marriage, didn't have the same commitment that she did. To her, marriage meant a lifetime, not until the convenience wore off. Few people seemed able to suffer that small stipulation. Her parents hadn't understood. Neither had Ted.

So along with shedding Ted, she'd rid herself of the idea of marriage. She'd simply given up. Obviously there was something about her that made a long-term commitment impossible. She'd come to the conclusion she needed something shorter term.

Like a blazing, red-hot affair.

She glanced up at Gavin, afraid he might be able to read her mind. But no, he just looked thoughtful. She sighed. Such a gorgeous man, so proud and confident, sometimes arrogant, always fair. But Gavin was more a fantasy man, the perfect male to manifest in a dream, with the reality a million miles away.

Yet…they *were* both single now, and he was sitting right there in her kitchen chair, wearing nothing more than damp jean shorts and a healthy dose of male charisma, insisting they should be friends, which could possibly mean…what? Sara blinked, realizing she'd been quiet too long while contemplating short-term, sizzling, erotic plans.

His wicked grin had turned smug. "So you talked about this and that, meaning…?"

The best defense was a good offense, and she was tired of acting like a ninny. "Gavin, are you actually fishing for compliments?"

"Would you give me any?"

"No." She grinned at his feigned hurt, feeling some of the old camaraderie return. "You certainly don't need me to bolster your ego. You surely know how attractive you are."

He went perfectly still, and his voice turned husky and suggestive. "You really think so?"

She pulled a wry face. "I'm not blind, Gavin. And you don't wear humility worth a darn."

"You never acted the least bit interested. Whenever we talked, it was about the house, or what you intended to do to the yard." He lowered his brows over his dark brown eyes. "Or about your upcoming wedding." He said the last in a disgusted tone, as if the very idea turned his stomach.

"I was engaged! Did you expect me to flirt with you?" Besides, she thought, even after she'd gotten rid of Ted, she knew she wasn't in Gavin's league, not by a long shot. Where he was tall, dark, gorgeous—basically perfect—she was basically plain. Her dark curly hair was always unruly, her eyes a medium shade of blue. There was nothing remarkable about her, other than her slightly crooked front tooth, which certainly didn't fall under the category of sexually appealing traits. She was a very ordinary woman, and he was an extraordinary man.

So why was he here?

Gavin came to his feet, pacing away from her, then back again. He seemed unsettled and she didn't know what to expect. Then he stopped before her.

Crossing his arms over his bare chest and staring down at her, he said, "So we're both available now, right?"

"Uh…"

"And you've already admitted you like me."

Had she actually come right out and said that? She didn't think so. It wasn't likely she'd take another chance on rejection. "I've always liked you, Gavin. You're a nice guy, and you're unbelievably talented…"

"There, you see." He nodded, apparently more than satisfied with her comments.

"But—"

"No buts." He shocked the rest of her thoughts right out of her head when he gripped either side of her chair and leaned down until their noses almost touched. His voice emerged whisper soft, his eyes staring into hers. "I like you, too, Sara. And I want to see you."

Completely frozen, Sara simply stared back. What he said, how he said it, seemed unbelievably seductive. She told herself not to be foolish, not to misunderstand, but she felt her stomach curl up and squeeze tight. For a moment, she thought she might swoon in excitement. Or maybe throw up in sheer nervousness. It was a definite toss-up.

His gaze dropped to her mouth, lingering for a long moment, but to her extreme disappointment, he moved away. "I came today to celebrate. And to convince you to stop hiding from me."

After sucking in two huge gulps of air, she managed to speak without croaking. "Uh, celebrate what?"

"Your freedom. We can start with a toast. I'll pour the wine." He went to the cabinets, and before she could stop him he opened the top drawer, then the next, looking for a corkscrew.

Sara groaned, knowing what he would find, knowing she would be mortified; she resigned herself to the inevitable. She was almost getting used to it.

There was a moment of stunned silence before Gavin turned to face her, a pair of her pale bikini panties dangling from one long finger. He wore an expression of mixed chagrin and incredulous disbelief. "Do you always keep your underwear in the kitchen drawers?"

She would definitely throw up.

There wasn't anyplace adequate for her to hide, though she did consider crawling beneath the table. Of course, he'd still be able to see her, and she'd still have to come out sometime. She didn't think he would just go away.

She dropped her face to the table and covered her head with her arms. "I told you I don't have much furniture." It sounded like an accusation. "The only drawers in the house are the ones here in the kitchen."

Her words were muffled, but she assumed by Gavin's rough chuckles he'd understood her. When she heard him opening and closing other drawers she jumped out of her seat to stop him. He had a silk camisole in one hand, a garter belt in the other and a look of profound masculine interest on his face. The feminine garments looked very fragile and soft in his big hands. Sara snatched them away, glaring at him despite her embarrassment.

He made an obvious, rather measly effort to hide his reaction. "Damn, I'm glad I came today. I'm learning all kinds of things about you." He reached out and stroked the garter belt with a knuckle, his tone dropping to an intimate level. "I had no idea you wore such racy lingerie."

Her face felt so hot, her vision blurred. "Don't you dare laugh at me again, you big—"

The sky exploded with a splintered streak of neon light and the house shook with the accompanying thunder. They both jumped, and in the next instant were left in complete darkness. Sara held her breath, stunned into silence.

Gavin reached out and felt for her, his fingers landing first on her throat, then skimming across her collarbone before curling over her shoulder. "Sara?"

"Lightning must have hit a power line." Her voice lowered to a whisper in deference to the fury of the storm.

"Probably."

They stood there in the dark, and Sara could hear him breathing, could feel the heat of his body as he slowly, relentlessly pulled her closer. She could smell his wonderful, delicious, toe-curling scent. Her heart knocked against her ribs and she cleared her throat. "Well. So much for drinking wine. What do we do now?"

It was a loaded question, unintentional of course. But Sara saw the amused flash of Gavin's white teeth. "It just occurred to me," he whispered. "If your underthings are all in here, and you changed in the bedroom, what are you wearing beneath that dress?"

She managed a horrified gasp just before he lowered his head. She knew he was going to kiss her, and she didn't voice a single complaint.

She may have even met him halfway.

3

HE WAS RUSHING IT.

Gavin knew he should pull back, give her time to adjust to his intentions, but he couldn't quite get his body to agree with his mind. She was so soft, so sweet against him. And it seemed as if he'd wanted her forever. Hell, it had been forever. A lifetime, in fact.

She was breathing in quick, gasping pants. Touching her mouth with his own, he stifled the small, arousing sounds and gently kissed her. It took all his control to keep the contact light. The feel of her full breasts pressed to his chest tested his resolve.

So many times in the past he'd brushed against her, or shook her hand, or patted her shoulder. Casual touches that left him wanting so much more. He'd teased himself by visiting with her so often, especially whenever she spoke about Ted. Even if the man hadn't turned out to be a jerk, Gavin would have hated him because he had Sara.

He smiled to himself, thinking what a challenge she was, how complex and complicated her personality could be. She'd surprised him more times than he could count.

When she suddenly opened her mouth on his, then grabbed his ears in both hands and kissed him with an intensity he hadn't expected, he wasn't only surprised, he was stunned. And thrilled.

He slid his arms around her narrow waist, marveling at how feminine she was, how perfect she felt to him and with him. Her mouth was hot and damp and clinging to his. When he slipped his tongue just inside her mouth, she groaned. The small sound made him shake. He could have kissed her forever.

But the idea of her underwear continued to plague him, and without even meaning to, he allowed his hands to wander until he cupped her lush backside and discovered for a fact she was naked beneath the dress.

He shuddered again and his body reacted. He pressed her forward against his groin, his hands kneading, rocking her into his hips. His control slipped, but she didn't seem to mind. Things were happening fast, but that suited him. Giving her time, waiting for her to get over her embarrassment, had nearly used up all his patience.

Just remembering all the lonely, frustrated, lust-filled nights he'd suffered through recently filled him with renewed purpose, and he slanted his mouth over hers until she accepted his tongue completely. He explored her with a leisurely thoroughness, fascinated by that small crooked tooth, touching it with his tongue. And then...

She pushed him away. Gavin tried to reorient himself, but the room was dark, and all he could see of Sara was her outline and the gleam of her wide eyes, watching him. He could hear her breathing, as harsh as his own, and knew, even without the benefit of light, she was surely blushing again.

"I want you, Sara."

She started to step back, but he reached out and caught her. His hand landed first against a plump breast, but he quickly altered his hold to her upper arm. They both breathed hard.

Sara trembled, and even that excited him. He'd never known a woman like her, with her honest reactions and sincere emotions. She couldn't hide her feelings, even when she tried. There wasn't an ounce of guile in her entire being. That alone made her unique.

"Why?"

Her tone dripped with suspicion. Because it was dark and she couldn't see him, he gave in to the urge to grin. He was happy, dammit. After allowing her six long weeks to recover from her embarrassment and any lingering feelings she might have had for her damn philandering fiancé, he was finally with her.

He'd wanted her from the day she'd walked into his house and proclaimed him a genius. It was the first time a woman had noted anything about him other than a physical attribute. He was proud of the houses he built, and so was his family. But no other female had taken the time to realize the extent of his natural talent when it came to his work.

It hadn't merely been the compliment that had done the trick, though. It had been her exuberance, her expressive nature. She was aware of life and the world around her in a way he'd never considered before. She took pleasure in such simple things, in the house he'd built, in her yard work. And he'd watched while she made plans to turn that house into a home with a family...*for another man.*

God, it had eaten him alive, kept him awake at night, and generally filled him with a morbid kind of desperation. She was meant for him, he knew that. And it wasn't just her enthusiasm for him and his work. It was everything she did. Sara was the type of woman children would instinctively trust. Men would gravitate toward her because she was secure and comforting. She drew him with her honesty and her optimism and her generosity...and that lush little body of hers that constantly tempted him to touch. He couldn't discount the body.

He looked at Sara and thought of home and hearth, Christmas and...rumpled sheets on a rainy night. Sara, naked and warm. He groaned. It was an eclectic mix of emotions she stirred, volatile in their power. But knowing he couldn't overwhelm her with his full plans or feelings yet, he said simply, "You're beautiful."

There was no reply, just a telling silence. He sighed, knowing well enough she didn't believe him. "It's true, Sara. Ted probably didn't tell you often enough, bastard that he was, but you're very easy on the eyes.''

She cleared her throat, and he waited with a half smile, anxious to see what she would say.

''I'm short.''

Ignoring her resistance, he pulled her close for a quick hug, his chuckles rumbling in the quiet of the kitchen. Her head tucked neatly under his chin, his arms looped at the small of her back, he pretended to measure her against him, then nodded. ''You're perfect.''

''Gavin...''

He knotted his hand in her curling hair and tugged until she tilted her face up. Between small, nipping kisses that she greedily accepted, he said, ''You're also very sweet and sexy. It's been hell staying away from you.''

''I had no idea—''

He didn't let her finish, kissing her again until her hands came to his bare chest and smoothed over his skin. Her touch was shy and curious and he knew he'd lose control again if he didn't put some space between them. Damn, now *he* was trembling like a virgin on prom night.

She'd been hurt by Ted, and he didn't want her on the rebound. He didn't want her doing anything she might regret later. And he didn't want her only for an affair.

When he made love to Sara, it had to be because she wanted him as much he wanted her, which was one hell of a lot. Her confidence was a bit low now, and she was obviously gun-shy about getting involved with anyone again. But he could be patient. Being with Sara would be worth the extra effort.

Whispering, because she was still pressed close, her lips nearly touching his, he asked, "Where do you keep the candles and matches?"

"In the cookie jar."

"Ah. Of course. Where else would they be?"

Sara straightened away from him, and he could imagine her fussing with her uncontrollable hair, her nervous hands busy. She moved toward the counter and he heard the *clink* of a glass jar. "I keep them here because the drawers are all full and... Well, I know it doesn't make any sense, but I just couldn't quite bring myself to put my panties in the cookie jar."

"I do understand."

She went still, then asked with a touch of renewed suspicion, "Are you laughing at me again, Gavin?"

He tried to make himself sound appalled. "I've never laughed at you."

"Hah!"

He ignored that. It was obvious he'd have his work cut out for him. "Find a corkscrew, too, and we can take the wine to the other room and get comfortable." He felt her hesitation before she began opening cabinets and rustling through drawers. Very cautiously, she handed him two glasses in the dark, then took his arm to lead the way. It was an unnecessary measure on her part. He knew this house as well as she did, knew exactly where the family room was. And the master bedroom. But he would never refuse her touch, no matter how platonic.

He hadn't been inside much since she'd moved in, though, and he had no concept of the placement of furniture, what little there was. She led him to a couch, then sat beside him.

"I'm sorry I can't offer you a better seat, but the sofa is it." She struck a match, then held it to the candle.

Gavin looked around the room. There was a portable television sitting on a crate, the sofa arranged against the back wall, and one end table next to it with a lamp. The oak moldings along the floor took on a soft sheen in the candlelight. So did Sara.

She turned toward him, her mouth open to speak, and caught him staring. There was a moment of complete stillness, their gazes locked, and then she jerked to her feet, flustered. "I forgot to get anything to put the candle in. I'll be right back."

"Oh, no, you don't." He wrapped his fingers around her narrow wrist and tugged her back into her seat. "We can use one of the glasses, and share the other."

"But it'd be just as easy—"

"I've already kissed you, Sara, very thoroughly." He kept his tone soft and quiet, his gaze holding hers. "Your tongue was in my mouth. Surely sharing a glass can't bother you that much."

Her eyes were huge, locked with his. "It…it's not that."

"Good." He didn't give her time to form more excuses, and he didn't want her alone in the kitchen, building up her defenses. He opened the wine and filled the glass, then handed it to her. "Here's to your narrow miss at unhappiness, and my escape from monotony."

Quiet and still, she searched his face, her brow drawn in concentration. After a few cautious sips of the wine, she handed the glass back to him. "You really aren't at all upset with me for attacking your house?"

The question overflowed with uncertainty, and Gavin took her hand in his again, rubbing his thumb over her knuckles. "Seeing the look on Karen's face was worth it. You surely did impress upon her the hazards of poaching."

She'd been a stunning sight that day, a virago with a rake, female fury at its finest. He smiled. All he really remembered feeling that day was relief, because he knew Sara would never tolerate infidelity. Ted and Karen, with their lack of morals, had provided him an unhindered chance to attain something he'd wanted very badly.

He honestly couldn't say he regretted the incident, but it prodded him like a sore tooth that Sara had been hurt. The thought of her mooning over another man filled him with territorial and possessive urges that would shock a liberated woman.

Deliberately he took a large swallow of the wine, then handed the glass back to her. She needed to relax just a bit, to take down a few of those walls that kept her so rigid. He wanted Sara to be as he first remembered her—filled with unrestrained excitement and bubbling enthusiasm.

With his arm along the back of the couch, Gavin made himself comfortable, stretching out his legs and making certain his thigh pressed close to Sara's. She was familiar with him as a friend and neighbor. He wanted her familiar with him as a man. *As a lover.*

She didn't move away. When she looked at him again, he dropped his hand to her shoulder in the natural way of offering comfort.

"Quit fretting, honey. You've got plenty of time to find the right man for you, someone who better suits you, someone who'll appreciate you, someone who…"

She shook her head, denying him long before he finished praising her. "No way. I went that route and it was a far cry from matrimonial nirvana. I've given up on the idea of marriage forever. It's nothing but a hoax, anyway. I've decided to stay blessedly single. I'd rather have a pet instead of a troublesome man."

Gavin's heart and breath both froze. He wheezed out, "Excuse me?"

"You know. A little friendly furry pet to keep me company."

"Ah…somehow I don't think it's quite the same."

"Yeah, well. It's a sure bet an animal would be

more fun than a husband. More loyal. Steadfast. As long as you're good to an animal, they won't ever leave you."

That was *not* what he wanted to hear. He chewed his upper lip, contemplating her stubborn expression. He hadn't calculated on quite this attitude. For as long as he'd known her, Sara had talked about getting married and settling into domestic bliss. "I can see where you might be a little more reserved now, but it'd be ridiculous to judge every man by Ted."

"I wouldn't do that! I'm not dumb." Then she said in disgust, "But it's not just Ted. I've never seen one really successful marriage. I'm not sure there is such a thing. But I do know I don't intend to waste my life looking for a husband. Ha! No sir. Not anymore. Pets are less mess, and they're guaranteed to be more trustworthy." She punctuated that statement with another long drink, finishing the glass and promptly refilling it. "It was past time for me to reevaluate and alter my thinking. I did, and I decided marriage is a waste. At least it seems to be for me."

Now *he* needed the drink.

But Sara had become vehement in her speech, and in-between stating her newly revised plans, which from what he could tell meant avoiding any kind of human commitment, she practically guzzled the wine. Her cheeks were flushed and her eyelids were getting heavy. Bemused, Gavin sat back to watch her.

She made a face with each drink she took, until finally the glass was empty again. She obviously wasn't used to drinking and didn't care for the taste. He didn't want her flat-out drunk, only relaxed. So he snatched up the bottle before she could take it, then pried the empty glass from her hands.

"I understand why you're bitter, Sara, but good marriages do exist."

Flopping back against the couch, she rolled her eyes, then directed her gaze at him. She was sprawled against his side, effectively caught in the curve of his arm. She crossed her legs and swung one small foot. Her words were low and cynical. "Sure they do. Maybe one out of every hundred. And even those aren't really happy, they're just making do. I don't like the odds. Now, a cute little puppy—I could handle that. You make certain they have food and water, clean paper to piddle on, and you can cuddle with them all you want. Done. There's nothing else to it. You love them and they love you. Unconditionally."

It was such a change in attitude for her, he was temporarily thwarted. He wanted to get married, dammit, wanted to settle down for the first time in his life, and now the woman he wanted was dead set against marriage. After all the empty relationships he'd had, he didn't intend to get involved in another. He'd just have to find a way to put Sara back on the straight and narrow.

A good example couldn't hurt. "My parents have been happily married for forty years."

A strange look crossed her face, and her smile wobbled.

"What?" Gavin felt a little uncomfortable with her intense study. She seemed to be contemplating the wonders of the world. "Sara?"

She shook her head, and one lock of curly dark hair fell across her eyes. "Nothing. I just hadn't thought of you that way."

He smoothed the hair back behind her ear, enjoying the intimate contact, the tender touching. It beat the hell out of a handshake any day.

He coasted his fingertips over her fine, soft skin, then continued to cup her cheek. He liked the feel of her, warm and soft and so damn feminine. He liked having her so close and comfortable with him. He could build on that. Friendship was a great start to deeper things. "What way, Sara?"

"You know. With a family."

"Oh?" He touched her ear and the curve of her chin, the sensitive skin beneath it. "You thought I was found under a rock?"

She smiled. "No."

"So how did you think of me?"

She gave his simple question a great deal of consideration before answering. "The eligible bachelor. A playboy, maybe. But definitely not a family guy." She frowned, then snuggled against his palm. "Do you have any brothers or sisters?"

She looked very content, curled up by his side. He wanted to kiss her again, but held himself back. He wanted her to know about his family. He wanted her to *meet* his family. "No brothers. Three sisters. All older than me."

She giggled, something he'd never heard her do before. Usually her laughs were deep and throaty and full, not teasing. "You were the *baby?*"

He tried to look indignant and failed. "That's right. And it was pure hell fighting for any rights in that house. Do you have any idea how much time three teenage girls can spend in a bathroom?"

"No." She looked away, then reached up to cover his hand with her own. "I was an only child."

"Hey." The way Sara pouted was more enticing than a hot kiss. Damn, he hurt with lust. He looked away from that tempting mouth and stared at her ear instead. It was a cute ear, but it didn't send him into a frenzy of lust. "I'll gladly give you my siblings. All three of them." He forced a laugh. "Actually they'd love you. So would my mother."

"I don't know, Gavin. My own mom isn't all that fond of me."

He felt something freeze inside him at the sincerity in her eyes. Lust was forgotten. "That can't be true."

She nodded her head in sharp response. "Yes, it is. She and my dad fought all the time. They were divorced, with joint custody, but they both had busy lives and I...well, I guess I just interfered."

Frowning, Gavin asked, "So you got shuffled between the two of them?"

"Yeah. Dad kept me more than Mom, but even then, it was never for more than a few months. But at least he tried. Once, he even bought me a puppy, to keep me company while he was gone to work, he said. But then a few weeks later, I had to leave because he got a new girlfriend, and Mom had a fit about the dog and…and Dad gave it to a guy who owned a farm. The pup had plenty of room to run around and play, he said.''

Oh God. Gavin could feel her pain, could see it in her eyes. He couldn't begin to imagine how a small child, especially one as tenderhearted and sweet as Sara, might have reacted to such a blow. She must have been crushed.

So many things were starting to make sense. He said very quietly, his eyes on her face, ''You really cared about the dog, didn't you?''

She wouldn't look at him. ''Of course I did. He was a cute little thing, always running by my side, sleeping in my bed at night. We'd take long walks together, and play together down by the stream. I loved him. But what was really awful was that he loved me, too. He thought I'd always be there for him, but there wasn't anything I could do when Dad took him away. I begged, but Mom only offered to let me get a fish.'' She peered up at him. ''Fish aren't nearly as messy, you know. But they are pretty hard to cuddle.''

He'd never guessed Sara might have had a less than perfect upbringing. She was always so filled with optimism. He'd just assumed, with her so determined to marry, that she'd come from a background similar to his. But he realized now her need for a marriage, a home, even a pet, wasn't because she'd seen the wonderful side of that life, but because she hadn't. Ever. She'd been shuffled around and she wanted now to find some stability.

He supposed it made sense, the way she'd reacted to her upbringing. His parents had shown him the better side to marriage, his sisters, too. But still, when they'd all wanted to see him happily settled, he'd rebelled. They wanted him to do one thing, so he fought to do another. It was a response borne more of stubbornness than logic, but being the only son in a family of females had bred that stubbornness. Fighting for your independence in the midst of a gaggle of coddlers was a hard habit to break.

"Is that why you were so anxious to get married? You wanted a home of your own?"

Without his encouragement, she raised her small hand and smoothed it over his chest, tangling her fingers in his body hair. The wine had helped to lower her inhibitions, and she seemed very intent on exploring the different textures of his body. She apparently enjoyed touching him, feeling him. And heaven knew, he wouldn't discourage her from it. But now her gestures had new significance. He wondered how often, if ever, she'd been coddled and held.

Her gaze came up to meet with his, and he caught his breath. Damn, she was so sexy, and she didn't seem at all aware of it.

"I think I wanted to prove to my parents how easy

it could have been if they'd only tried. Neither of them spent near the energy on their relationship that they gave to their jobs.''

They evidently hadn't spent much energy on their daughter, either. Gavin leaned down and kissed her forehead, wanting to crush her close, but also wanting her to continue talking. "Sara... I understand how you must have felt. But trying to prove a point to your parents isn't a good reason to marry the wrong person.''

"I know. Ted was *nothing* like a pet. Well, maybe a whiskery little rat.'' Her brow puckered as she considered that, then qualified, "One with mange.''

She said it so seriously, and he agreed so completely, Gavin couldn't stop himself from kissing her again. He meant it as a tender touch, a form of teasing comfort, but Sara didn't cooperate. She cupped his face in her hands and licked over his lips, making small, soft sounds deep in her throat that drove him crazy.

He loved her enthusiasm, but he wanted so much more. "Sara...''

"You taste so good, Gavin. I knew you would.''

Oh Lord, he'd put himself in a hell of a position.

He knew it was the wine and her own vulnerability making her speak so boldly. Sara was generally rather reserved and circumspect in her behavior. But then, she'd been engaged, and he knew she would never have betrayed a commitment.

He'd never understood why the house meant so

much to her. Now he did. It symbolized all the things she hadn't had as a child. And he had built it for her. His chest puffed up and he felt like crowing. Surely that had to count for something in her eyes.

Her soft hands moved across his shoulders, his chest...his belly. He caught his breath and heard her laugh. Then he caught her hands. Much more of that and he'd forget his good intentions.

"You're awfully hairy," she whispered. "Probably not as hairy as a puppy, though. And you smell much better than a dog would."

"Thank you."

She smiled at him, their noses only half an inch apart, and her eyes nearly crossed. He shook his head, thoroughly exasperated with her, but mostly with himself. He'd had such grand plans, self-centered plans, and now he'd have to alter them a bit to give her the time she needed. He felt the weight of responsibility, and knew he'd never do anything to hurt her.

As he came to a few decisions, he watched her sway in her seat. She seemed to be trying to keep him in focus. "You're awfully serious, Gavin."

"And you're awfully drunk. You sure as hell can't hold your liquor."

"I know." She didn't sound sorry, only accepting. "Ted used to say I was too prissy. It irritated him that I wouldn't drink with him. But I knew if I did, he'd take advantage of me."

He wished Ted was here now. He wished he'd gone

to see him six weeks ago, when he'd first cheated on Sara and hurt her. He hadn't then because he didn't want it to seem as though he'd coerced her final decision in any way. If she left Ted, it had to be because she chose to, not because he made her feel she should.

Pushing her back enough so he could catch his breath, Gavin asked, "Aren't you worried I'll take advantage of you?"

"No. Unfortunately," she said, in a mournful voice, "you're too honorable for that." Then she gave him a slow, exaggerated wink. "But maybe if you drink enough, I could take advantage of you?"

She swayed again as she said it, and nearly fell off the couch. Gavin caught her, then held her upright. "You'd like that, would you?"

"Oh, yes." She pushed his hands away and curled close again, snuggling the side of her face against his chest. "I probably shouldn't tell you this, but I've fantasized about you."

The air squeezed out of his lungs. He gasped and choked before he could manage to say, "Come again?"

Either she didn't notice his shock, or she chose to ignore it. "I think about what it would be like with you." She peeked up at him. "You know. *Intimately.* I was thinking about you just before the storm hit and made me leave my bath. They were *very* nice thoughts, Gavin."

"Ah, Sara…" He sounded like he might strangle on his own tongue.

She sighed. "Karen would tell me all sorts of private things, boasting, you know, and I'd want to smack her because she was living my fantasies."

Damn, he was hard. Really, really hard. It seemed every time he got his libido under control, she'd say something, or do something, or smile—Lord, he loved her smile—and then his body would react. He stayed semierect around her, though she was naive enough not to notice. But Karen had. He wondered if that was why she'd shared intimate details with Sara, to stake a claim of sorts. He shook his head. None of that mattered now, but the small woman curled against him deserved his better judgment, not his lust, which meant he couldn't do a damn thing about the opportunity presenting itself.

He muttered a curse and she heard him. Peering up to see his face, she traced his mouth with her finger and he swallowed hard. She looked so...*ready*. Damn, did she look ready.

And physically she might be. But emotionally, he figured Sara had a long way to go before she would really trust him and accept his feelings for her. Right now, she didn't seem to feel ready for anything more than a house pet. Damn, damn, double damn.

"Sara..."

"Don't you want to know what my fantasies are?"

"No!" She was trying to seduce him, and succeeding admirably. If sex was all he'd wanted, he'd be the luckiest man alive. But he wanted so much more with her. And allowing her to do something she'd regret tomorrow wouldn't aid his case. It'd make him damn happy for one night, there was no question about that, but in the long run, he'd lose out.

He held her at arm's length, trying to convince himself of his own thoughts. "Sara, why don't we talk about something else?"

She pushed against his rigid arms, trying to get closer again. "But—"

Her stomach growled, giving him the excuse to interrupt. "Are you hungry? What time did you eat dinner?" She continued to stare at him a moment, as if the change in topic had thrown her. Then she shrugged.

"I haven't eaten yet. I was too tired when I got home, and I just wanted to soak in the wonderful Jacuzzi tub you installed in my bathroom. But then the storm hit, and I knew I had to close the windows. And then you were here, so..."

Images of her lounging in the spacious, tiled tub— naked and thinking of him—played havoc with his better intentions. A man could only take so much. He cleared his throat and tried to calm his racing heart. "Why were you so tired? A hard day?"

"All my days have been hard lately. I've been working twelve-hour shifts during the week, then volunteering my weekends to the animal adoption center."

Gavin stared at her a moment before dropping his head into his hands. *Wonderful. He'd been pouring wine down an exhausted, hungry woman.* Then part of what she said really hit him. Twelve-hour shifts? He frowned at her, tilting her face up so he could better understand. "You've been putting in a lot of overtime?" She nodded, her eyelids drooping, and he asked, "Why?"

A look of sadness came over her face, and she seemed ready to cry. Gavin vowed then and there never to let her drink again. He'd always turned to mush around weeping women, and with Sara, he felt particularly susceptible.

"I love my house, Gavin."

She said it in a near wail, startling him. "Calm down, babe, and tell me what the problem is."

She threw her arms out, nearly slugging him in the eye. He ducked, then watched her cautiously in case she started to go off the couch again. "I can't afford to stay here. I have to sell my beautiful house."

"What?" He tried to sound surprised because he wasn't ready yet to admit to stealing her sign.

She went on in a rush, making broad gestures with her hands. "I used most of my savings on the down payment. Ted was supposed to buy the furniture, and then pay half on all the monthly bills. The utilities, the groceries, the taxes, the insurance, the…"

"I understand." He rubbed his forehead, frustrated. The house was rather expensive for a single person. His was only slightly larger and he knew how expensive maintenance could be.

He'd come to think of this house as Sara's. Long before she'd actually moved in, he'd made it special for her, added little things, put in extras. He'd known she would love the tiled tub, and she had. He'd thought of her reaction as he installed the beveled glass mirrors. Everything in it, from the time she'd chosen the plans, had been picked specifically for her. The idea of anyone else living in it just didn't feel right. It was almost...sacrilege. "There must be another solution besides selling."

"I've been trying to find one." Sara twisted around in her seat until she faced him. Her sundress had hiked up to her thighs, and one strap hung loose down her pale, smooth shoulder. Her hair, always a little unruly, drooped over one eye. Gavin hid his grin. She looked ready to fall asleep on him, but first, she needed something to eat.

"Come on, Sara." He hauled her to her feet, supporting her when she would have slumped back down again. "Let's go scrounge you up some food."

The candle had formed a small pool of wax in the bottom of the wineglass, and Gavin picked that up to guide them through the darkened house. The air had gotten hot and muggy; his skin felt damp with sweat. Sara snatched up the wine bottle before they left the room.

He led the way into the kitchen, hearing her hum beside him. "Am I going to find any other surprises in your kitchen cabinets?"

She dropped to a kitchen chair, then shrugged. "Who knows? I can't even remember where I've put everything."

"While I'm hunting up some food, why don't you tell me just how short you are on making ends meet." It was a personal question, but Sara didn't seem to mind. She propped her head up with one fist and regarded him as he searched through the refrigerator.

"It gets a little worse each month. I figure I can make it through the summer, then *pffftt,* I'm out of luck."

Gavin raised one brow. *"Pfffit?"*

"Yeah. I'll be flat broke."

"What about your family? They won't help at all?"

"Hah!"

No. Her family didn't sound like the type to pitch in. And Sara wasn't the type to ask for help. She was an independent little thing. Several times when she'd been doing things to or for the house, he'd had to force her to let him help her. Ted hadn't been anywhere around then, but he seldom was when work needed to be done and Gavin had enjoyed stepping in to fill the slot.

He remembered when he'd gotten his first apartment. His parents and his sisters had all come over with donations, things ranging from furniture to food to cash. And they'd all helped to paint and arrange furniture and prepare the apartment for him to move in. But Sara had no one. He couldn't imagine being so totally...*alone.*

He looked at Sara. Her eyes were closed, and she appeared so serene, so accepting, he wanted to protect her, he wanted to declare himself. But it was too soon. He had to get her used to having him around more, had to give her time to adjust and get over her ridiculous prejudice against marriage.

He found some lunch meat, cheese and pickles and set them on the table for sandwiches. He also poured two large glasses of milk. When he sat in the chair opposite her and began stacking meat and cheese on the bread, her eyes opened. She gave him that killer smile, the tip of her crooked tooth just barely visible. He faltered, then shoved the loaded sandwich at her.

Rather than starting on the food, she continued to watch him, and Gavin knew he had to divert her attention or he'd never make it through the meal. "I could give you a loan."

She bolted upright, nearly throwing herself off the chair. Outrage shone clearly in her expression. "Absolutely not!"

He'd known that would be her answer, but he wanted to help her. "Now, Sara—"

"Don't be ridiculous, Gavin. For Pete's sake, we're only acquaintances, despite my rather lurid fantasies. And I have to face facts. If I can't afford this place now, a loan isn't going to help. I'd only end up in the same situation, but then I'd owe you, too."

He stared, that part about "lurid fantasies" still singing through his brain.

"Gavin?"

She was right, but he wouldn't accept her moving. He could alter his plans a bit, but he wouldn't have them completely ruined. He wouldn't give up. He'd spent months mapping out his strategy, and he wouldn't let a little thing like finances get in his way. "Maybe…"

She held up a hand to stop him. "It's not your problem. Besides, I've been working on it, and though I'd rather not, I think I may have come up with a solution."

Thank goodness. Gavin nudged the sandwich toward her again, wanting her to eat. "What are you going to do?"

"I'm going to look for a roommate."

It was a viable solution, he supposed, but… "Do you really want another woman living here?"

"Heck no. Women tend to run a household, to be territorial about where they live. They want to add their own little touches, leave their mark. This is my house, and I don't intend to let someone else take it over. I'd rather go ahead and sell it first."

She gave him a drunken leer, then explained with a flourish, "I was talking about a *man*."

4

GAVIN STARED, feeling as if someone had just sucker-punched him in the gut. Was she trying to kill him? Sara with yet another man? *Hell no!* He'd only just gotten rid of Ted-the-despicable. He had no intention of going through that personal hell again.

She gave him a sleepy smile, unaware of how tense he'd become or the agony she caused. He watched as she folded her arms on the table, then rested her head there. She continued to watch him, and she continued to smile. She looked…adoring, and that made him uneasy. After a deep sigh, she said, "I've always thought you were the most beautiful man."

Ridiculously he felt a blush inching up his neck. Thank God it was too dark for her to see, even though her gaze was direct and very intent. "Eat your sandwich, Sara."

She chuckled at his brusque tone. "I'm not all that hungry."

He took a vicious bite of his own ham and cheese. The room was so silent, he could hear himself chew. He also heard her small, dreamy sighs. "Where, exactly, do you intend to find this *person* who will live with you?'' He couldn't quite bring himself to specify a male.

''I'm not sure yet.'' She gave an elaborate shrug. ''I suppose I'd want someone willing to pitch in, not just expect me to do all the work. And he'd absolutely have to be fun. I can't stand a sourpuss. And he'd have to like pets. I really do want a pet. Maybe a cute little floppy-eared puppy. There's always plenty of them at the shelter that need homes. Too many, in fact. We're nearly full now, and still, every day, someone drops off a litter and...''

''Sara?'' He couldn't bear it if she started crying again.

''Hmm?''

''You're digressing. Where do you intend to find this paragon who'll live with you?''

''I suppose I could ask around at the office on Monday. Or maybe I could run one of those ads.''

''No! No ads.'' Her eyes widened at his tone, and he shook his head, then paced away from the table. ''You don't know what kind of crazy might show up with an open ad.''

He couldn't exactly picture her questioning the men at her office, either. She worked as a secretary for a large corporate firm, and the people there were very stuffy. He knew, because he'd done some contracting for them. How Sara could thrive in that environment, he didn't know. All those suits and exacting regulations would have driven him batty. But for Sara, who always smiled and carried a cheerful disposition, it would be doubly difficult. He supposed it was just one more example of her ability to overcome the obstacles in her life. She'd evidently learned to adapt with her parents, and with her work. But there was only so much adapting a gentle, honest woman like her could do.

And that was why she wanted a dog.

Did she really think having a pet would fill her life? Did she think a dog could act as a buffer against the outside world? He was certainly no psychologist, but it seemed obvious to him Sara wanted to be loved, despite her new resolve not to marry. And since she'd given up on finding a man to fulfill that important task, she was willing to give the duty to a pet.

He snorted. She'd just have to settle for him, and that was that.

But how to convince her? He chewed his lip a moment, undecided, but he knew in his heart what he would do. He stared at the window and tried to keep his body inattentive to his plans. He cleared his throat. "I suppose there's only one solution."

He waited for Sara to ask him to explain, and when she didn't, he turned to frown at her. "Sara?"

His only response was a soft, snuffling snore.

Amused, he smiled at the picture she made. Her mouth was open, one cheek smooshed up by her arm, and even when he smoothed a hand over her hair, she didn't stir.

Well now. It was Friday. She didn't have to be at work tomorrow, and neither did he. All kinds of possibilities presented themselves, and this time he'd throw nobility out the door. All's fair in love and war, and with Sara, he had a feeling it would be a balancing act of each.

Unfortunately he'd have to start with the war.

THE SUN WAS BRIGHT when Sara opened her eyes. She stretched, then winced at the pain in her head. She felt lethargic and didn't particularly want to get up, which was unusual because she usually woke easily.

She swung her legs over the side of the bed, noticed she wore a badly rumpled sundress instead of her nightgown and then she remembered.

She'd gotten drunk last night.

She'd gotten drunk and hit on Gavin.

Mortified, she pressed a hand to her chest to contain her racing heart, trying to remember everything she'd said to Gavin. Though her head pounded from her overindulgence, it unfortunately didn't obliterate her memory. She recalled several damning tidbits of conversation that had slid silkily off her muddled tongue, and she knew for a fact she'd simply curl and die if she ever had to face him again.

He sauntered through her bedroom door carrying coffee and wearing a wide smile. "Good morning, sweetheart. Did you sleep well?"

She quickly closed her eyes. Death had to be imminent.

Any second now.

If she just waited…

"Sara?"

No such luck. Sara peeked one eye open and saw that Gavin loomed over her, his brow lifted in question. She blinked, caught her breath and her stomach began flip-flopping.

Gavin was still wearing his cutoffs, but now they were unsnapped and only partially zipped.

Partially was enough to make her eyes buggy.

In the full light of morning, he was simply breathtaking. And with a dark beard-shadow covering his lean jaw and his hair sleep-mussed, he looked good enough to be breakfast. He was also waiting for an answer to his question. "I, ah…"

"I slept great," he said. "Your bed is a little short for me, and it was hotter than hell with both of us snuggled in there, but then—" He gave her a wink. "—I could overlook the little discomforts."

Everything in her jerked to a shuddering standstill. Her heart stopped beating, oxygen snagged in her lungs. She was frozen, staring, mouth agape.

He had to be teasing.

Oh God, please let him be teasing.

There was no way he'd slept with her. Surely, even through a drunken haze, she would have remembered such a momentous occasion. She looked directly at him, refusing to flinch, prepared to dispute him and call him on his bluff. She opened her mouth, cleared her throat, and out came something that sounded vaguely like, *"Hmgarph?"*

Gavin set the coffee mugs on the nightstand, then

plumped the pillows behind Sara. "Here, lean back and get comfortable. I thought we'd have our coffee in bed."

"*Hmgarph,*" she said again, because his warm hands had closed around her calves as he swung her legs onto the mattress, settling her despite her stiff resistance.

How many times had she imagined something like this? Something like this...after something much more significant of a sexual nature. She'd dreamed such things, but she'd certainly never considered them actually happening. After all, Gavin was...well, he was Gavin. And she wasn't his type, not at all. She'd even been stretching the boundaries of fiction to imagine it in her dreams.

Yet here he was, and here she was, and all she could do was make nonsensical garbled sounds. If she could only understand why he was here, maybe she wouldn't be so nervous. It couldn't be for the most apparent reasons. Gavin couldn't be interested in her. After all, even Ted had found her so lacking, he'd quickly wandered. Her own parents hadn't deemed her interesting enough to want to have around. There was simply something about her that made people keep their distance. So surely Gavin wouldn't...

He scooted in with her, quite at his ease, his big luscious body taking up a lot of room. He casually handed her a mug of steaming coffee. His smile now was one of satisfaction and contentment. "Now, isn't this better?"

Better than what, she wondered, and drank half the cup in one gulp. Despite the heat of the drink, she shivered. It hit her suddenly how cool the room was. Before she could ask, Gavin offered an explanation.

"The electricity came back on about five this morning. It had gotten damn steamy in here, so I turned on your air."

That got her tongue temporarily unglued. "I can't afford to run the air conditioner."

What an inane comment to make, she thought, given the fact she was lying in bed with a mostly naked, utterly devastating man, who surely wasn't there for the usual reasons a man put himself in a woman's bed yet she didn't know why he was really there and couldn't seem to find the wits to ask him.

But her mind simply refused to focus on the real issues. It was too much to take in, and with her heart doing wild leaps around her chest, and her eyes busy exploring every inch of Gavin's hard body, her concentration was nil. Her brain kept screaming, *What happened?* but her heart kept whispering, *I'll bet it was good!*

Gavin took a long sip of his coffee before turning to her. "You can afford to be comfortable, Sara. Remember, you've got a roommate now to split the bills, so there's no need to suffer this heat wave."

Roommate? She remembered mentioning the half-baked idea to him, but she never claimed to have found anyone. She wasn't even looking, not since she'd decided she had no choice but to sell. She bit her lip, frowning.

Gavin reached up and rubbed his thumb across the edge of her teeth, freeing her bottom lip and halting her heartbeat in erratic midpump. "I love how you do that." His voice was a rough whisper, deep and compelling. "It makes me hot."

Sara felt like a zombie. A wide-eyed, speechless, sleep-rumpled zombie who could do no more than stare. She swallowed hard to remove the choking disbelief from her throat. "How I do...what?"

"The way you chew on your lip." His big thumb continued to caress her mouth, his eyes watching as she struggled to breathe. "It's so damn sexy. Especially with that little crooked tooth. When I kissed you last night, I felt that tooth with my tongue."

He thought her crooked tooth was sexy? Sara laughed, comprehension dawning. Of course. It was all a dream! She was probably still in the damn tub, and she'd drown herself before she actually woke up. It would be poetic justice.

"What's funny?" Gavin still looked at her lips when he asked that question, and Sara had to fight not to smile. She didn't want him to think she was deliberately flaunting her sexy tooth.

She laughed again, covering her mouth with a hand. How ridiculous that sounded, even in a dream. She shook her head. "I just realized I must still be asleep, that's all."

Gavin looked up to meet Sara's eyes. *Hot.* His gaze

was so hot, Sara hoped she never woke up. She liked having him look at her like that, as if he cared for her, as if maybe he loved her a little. It was a foolish notion, but if dreaming made it seem real, she'd willingly stay asleep.

"When I was younger, the schoolkids used to make fun of my teeth. Mom said she couldn't afford cosmetic dentistry, and Dad kept forgetting. Now that I'm older, it really just doesn't matter anymore."

Gavin's eyes narrowed just the tiniest bit, as if someone had just pinched him, then his gaze dropped to her mouth. "You have a beautiful smile, and the one tooth is only slightly turned, certainly nothing for kids to tease about. I'm glad you didn't fix it."

She chuckled again, finding his answer as bizarre as everything else that happened. She said, "A crooked tooth is a crooked tooth."

Very slowly, Gavin leaned across her and took her coffee cup, setting it on the nightstand with his. As he moved, his broad, hard chest crowded her back and she inhaled his sleep-musky intoxicating scent. She had only a moment to contemplate his motives, and then he kissed her.

Just as he'd said, his tongue pressed between her lips, warm and soft and damp, then probed along the edge of her teeth. *This was no dream.* Sara made that acknowledgment the same instant she decided she didn't care. It was too exciting, the way he teased her with his tongue. She opened her mouth wider, her hands moving against the firm contours of his chest.

The hair there was crisp, but soft, tickling her palms and curling between her fingers. And the heat—there was so much heat.

He gave a low groan and urged her closer, then tilted her into the bed until he was lying on top of her.

"Sara," he whispered, his lips moving over her cheek, her forehead, her mouth again. He lifted himself onto his elbows, caging her between his muscled arms. With one hand, he smoothed her wildly rambunctious hair away from her forehead, then gave her a tender smile. "You're not drunk anymore."

Sara blinked at the change of subject. Her mind was still back there with that kiss, with the damp heat and his talented tongue and... She shuddered. "No."

"Hungover?"

Since she'd never been hungover before, she wasn't sure. But it sounded vulgar, so despite her pounding head she rejected the idea. "Just tired. And a bit of a headache."

With a slow thrust of his hips, he reminded her of all the places they touched, how intimately they were entwined. "Good. That's good." His gaze lifted to lock with hers. "Now tell me about these fantasies."

Her eyes widened.

With the lightest touch, his mouth brushed over hers. "Last night, you said you fantasized about me. You even offered to tell me what those fantasies were."

Even the air conditioning couldn't counteract the

flustered heat she generated, and she hadn't even made it out of bed yet. "I...ah, I was drunk."

His tender smile curled her toes and made her thigh muscles tingle. "I know. But you didn't make it up, did you? Tell me now."

"I should never have said anything."

"I'm glad you did."

"I feel so ridiculous."

"I think you feel very soft and warm and sweet." He pressed against her to emphasize his words, and groaned deeply. "Oh, yeah. Very sweet."

His tone of voice, rumbling and deep, could be lethal. "Gavin..."

"Sara..." He mimicked her, then gave her another light, taunting, tell-me-all kiss. It was almost as if he couldn't stop himself. Sara was considering that possibility, her eyes still wide, when he said, "When do you want me to move in?"

She reeled. True, she was lying flat on her back, and Gavin's weight kept her securely stationed against the bed but still she reeled, at least mentally. Did he intend to keep her off balance all morning? "Uh...what are you talking about?"

His low sigh fanned her warm cheeks, her lips. "I can tell you're not a morning person." His kiss this time lingered, and left her bemused. "That might be a problem, babe, because I definitely am."

"Am what?" In truth, she *was* a morning person. But then, she'd never awakened before with a gorgeous man looming around, endearments tripping off

his oh-so-suave tongue, while flaunting his too tempting, mostly bare, exquisite body. So she understood
her vast confusion even if he didn't. It had very little
to do with her sleeping habits. "Gavin, will you make
sense?"

"All right." He kissed her once more, short and
sweet, then said, "I'm your new roommate. You do
remember asking me to move in last night, don't
you?"

When she only continued to stare, waiting for the
punch line, he added, "You were very convincing,
shooting down all my arguments, even threatening me
with that damn rake once. I had no choice. No choice
at all. You insisted I see things your way. And of
course, I did. Who could resist a begging woman?"

She narrowed her eyes, knowing she would never
beg, not even in a drunken stupor. The rake at-
tack…well, they both knew that was possible. But not
begging. "I haven't begged for anything since…well,
since I was kid."

His expression softened, the teasing gone to be replaced with tender understanding. "When you begged
to keep your puppy?"

She didn't want to talk about that, not now, not
when her emotions already felt so raw and exposed.
"You're only playing with me, aren't you?"

He gave a sigh of long-suffering affront. "I've
been a perfect gentleman, despite your provocation."
Then he glanced down at their layered bodies.

"Though I'll admit playing with you has entered my mind several times."

Good, she thought. Let's play, and you can quit trying to confuse me with things I can't accept. She thought it, but she hoped her silent encouragement wasn't too obvious.

He sat up, then pulled her up, too. She swallowed her disappointment as he moved to her side, trying to concentrate on what he had to say.

"It's all settled. I can get most of my stuff moved in over this weekend, if that's okay with you. Actually I was really relieved when you asked. I was only kidding about you having to beg me. This will work out perfect. It's been a real pain letting people through the house with me living there. I'm not a slob or anything, but I hated having to worry about every little thing I left out of place. And people have no respect for your privacy. They snoop through drawers and cabinets as if they already own the place. This way, with me living here, I'll still be close enough to supervise things, which is why I moved into the model home in the first place, but my privacy will be protected." He raised a brow in her direction. "That is, as long as you don't suffer a penchant for prying."

Her back stiffened. "I do not pry."

"You said you asked Karen personal questions about me."

"I didn't have to ask," she sputtered indignantly. "She gloated on and on about what a phenomenal stud you are. She practically shoved the information down my throat. I tried not to listen—"

"But she was insistent? How annoying for you." His smug grin set her teeth on edge and set her head to pounding. Now that he no longer touched her, she was beginning to see the situation with just a tad more clarity. Still, there was too much she couldn't remember.

"I have no recollection of asking you to move in. In fact, I never once considered such a thing." *Not seriously, anyway.*

"Well, why not? We've always gotten along well. Are you telling me you made promises while you were drunk that you've no intention of keeping?"

That was the rub. She wanted to grab this opportunity and take complete advantage of it and him. He was the most compelling man she'd ever met, with a strength and gentleness that formed a potent mix. This could prove to be a page right out of her fantasies. She thought of Gavin's skilled hands, his confidence and capability, and her stomach leaped in encouragement. *Say yes, say yes,* her body screamed.

But she'd made a vow to herself after her breakup with Ted. Never again would she leave herself open and vulnerable to humiliation. A woman should only have to suffer one such incident in her lifetime, and she'd had her quota. She would have to stay in control of any situation, especially those involving men. Right now, with Gavin, she certainly wasn't feeling any sense of real control; she was mired three feet under in deep, dark confusion. He seemed to want her, yet he kept pulling away. Not far away, especially given that he wanted to move in, but just enough to make her want him more, when she already wanted him plenty! It wasn't fair. It wasn't the behavior she was used to from men. Not that she'd been a highly sought after female, but the men she had known had made their intentions plain. Gavin was evidently willing to keep her guessing. But why?

When she remained quiet, Gavin prompted her with a slight nudge to her shoulder. "Well?"

Feeling trapped, she asked with a degree of obvious caution, "Did I make very many promises last night?"

His look was suggestive. "A few."

Her teeth sank into her bottom lip, and she saw his gaze drop to follow the action, the intensity of that gaze palpable. She immediately hid her teeth behind her lips, but not before their thoughts collided. They were each remembering last night, and the fact he thought she was sexy.

She had to give herself a few minutes to collect her composure, without his disturbing influence, before she made any decisions. Gavin had the power to hurt her much more than Ted ever could have. Ted had been a solution, but Gavin was a desire, a need, a dark craving. To have him, for whatever reason, and then lose him, could be devastating. "Why don't you meet me in the kitchen after I shower and change and we can...discuss all this."

"Hell of an idea." He was already on his feet, moving with an air of triumph. "I'll throw together some breakfast."

Her nervousness was enough to choke a cow, and her stomach rebelled at the mere thought of food. "I don't think…"

"Don't worry. I promise to go light." He was halfway out of the room before he added, "I'm an excellent cook, Sara, and I don't mind pitching in. I've even been accused of being fun on occasion, so you shouldn't have any complaints at all."

Gorgeous *and* an excellent cook? But what was all that nonsense about him being fun?

Sara heaved a sigh. She had no idea what was going on. One thing was certain, he had her interest. It was almost too good to be true, though she wanted it to be.

God, how she wanted it to be.

It was terribly risky, especially since she knew deep down that if she accepted Gavin, on whatever silly terms he spoke of, she might end up totally devastated.

Then again, since she was no longer looking for husband material, knowing exactly how futile that endeavor would be, Gavin might very well be the perfect roommate. She couldn't expect a man like him to commit himself to one woman. Commitment was no longer a requirement. Right? She nodded her head at her own question, but still wasn't convinced. As long as she had her fair share of his time…

Ground rules, that's what they needed. He should be hers exclusively for at least a while. She could glut herself on his masculine charms, then move on to newer game. Men did it all the time.

The thought of newer game actually sickened her. Lately all men had seemed a big turnoff, at least romantically. But not Gavin. Maybe that was because he was such a good friend, too.

She saved the uninteresting, disturbing thoughts of greener pastures for later and concentrated on the glutting part while she prepared for her shower. Now *that* was enough to get a woman wide-eyed and bushy-tailed in the morning. Everyone deserved a little fantasy time, and it looked like this might be hers.

Maybe this would all work out after all.

GAVIN'S PLAN WAS MOVING along rather smoothly. All he needed now were a few ground rules. He had to get Sara to commit, somehow, even if for a short while. He'd work on extending that time as they went along, teaching her to trust him, to trust her own feelings again, and eventually, she would be his. Only his.

It would have to be a unique role reversal, but he planned to hold out on her. She wanted him, that much was obvious. Not as much as he wanted her, which was impossible given his constant state of arousal. But he was more determined, and therefore it stood to reason he could control his reactions better.

At least, he hoped he could. He prayed he could. Damn, could he?

It wouldn't be easy. It would be his greatest challenge. More so than building an expansive house, more than doing a renovation, more than…

He grinned, thinking he had likened himself to a superhero, ready to leap tall buildings to rescue his lady-fair—by withholding sex. Actually, leaping a building might be easier than holding out on Sara.

She wasn't a woman who inspired higher levels of celibacy. Not when she went all soft and warm and willing every time he touched her.

But he wouldn't let her use him.

He chuckled out loud, pondering his course of action. He'd force her to be a *gentlewoman* and do the honorable thing, namely marriage. Teasing her would be fun, and a type of stratospheric sensual torture, because teasing her meant teasing himself and he was already on the ragged edge of lust. But with the promise of success, he could take it.

Hopefully Sara couldn't.

He had breakfast ready when she wandered in, looking refreshed and in control. Her cutoffs matched his own, but she wore a pastel T-shirt, where he opted to remain shirtless. He hadn't missed her fascination with his chest, and while he'd always been aware of the attention from other women, it hadn't mattered to him nearly as much as Sara's appreciation. He knew if she hadn't liked him as a man, she wouldn't have given his body more than a single, cursory glance.

But she *did* like him, and she did a lot of gawking, not just glancing. So if flaunting his body would help capture Sara, he'd flaunt away without an ounce of remorse.

"Feeling better now?"

She gave him a wary look, then nodded. He was pleased to see she was still uncertain how to deal with him. As long as he kept her off center his odds of success were improved. She didn't want marriage, so he was going to have to sneak it in on her.

"Breakfast smells good."

"Then your appetite has returned. I'm glad. You never did eat your sandwich last night."

When she looked puzzled, he decided to be benevolent and explain. "You fell asleep. I carried you to bed."

Her eyes widened. "Then...?"

"Nothing happened, Sara. Is that what you're wondering about?" He tried for a look of masculine affront. "I told you I behaved myself, though I swear it wasn't easy."

He loved how she blushed. Looking down to avoid his gaze, she pushed her hair behind her ears and fidgeted. Gavin waited, fighting to keep his amusement hidden.

"Last night is...something of a blur. At least parts of it are. Some things I remember clear as a bell, but others..." She hesitated, then forged on. "I have no memory of asking you to move in. None at all."

Guilt swamped him. She looked too confused, vulnerable, too. He considered confessing, maybe giving her some partial truths that would reassure her, when she shook her head.

"It doesn't matter. I'll be glad to have you."

Gavin felt his lips twitch, along with his heart and other numerous, masculine parts of his body. "Have me?"

Her eyes flared, and she stammered, "That is, I mean, I'll be glad to have you *here*."

He raised one brow, his skeptical gaze going to the kitchen tabletop.

"I don't mean *have you*, have you, I mean... You could come here..."

He opened his mouth but she quickly cut him off.

"No! I don't mean..." Slapping a hand to her forehead, she said, "I'd...I'd like you to move in."

He never said a word, giving her the chance to state her intentions outright. She had to make the ultimate decisions of what and who she wanted.

"It will have to be a complete partnership. I'll continue with the house payment myself. The rest of the bills we'll divide down the middle, even the groceries. And we'll have to share all the chores." Then she seemed to consider that. "Although, if you really do know how to cook, maybe we could work out a deal. I wouldn't mind doing the grocery shopping and cleaning up the kitchen if you'd fix the meals. It's the truth, I'm an awful cook."

"No problem. When I can't cook, we'll order in or dine out. What do you say?"

She looked suspicious again, so he tried a very sincere smile, which only deepened her frown. "That's fine, I guess, but there are a few more things we need to iron out."

She seemed entirely too serious, so Gavin handed her a plate of food, hoping to distract her from her thoughts. "Here, eat while we talk. You need some nutrition after your raucous night of drunken revelry."

She accepted the plate, then breathed deep of the combined scents of scrambled eggs, toasted English muffins and fresh fruit. "It really does smell delicious. I hadn't realized I was so hungry."

Gavin watched her taste everything, then nod approval. He said, "My mom and sisters didn't want to turn me loose when I moved out. It seemed one or the other of them showed up twice a week with home-made meals. I either had to learn to cook for myself, so they wouldn't worry, or be forever indebted to them. I chose to learn to cook."

Sara smiled around a mouthful of warm muffin. "They sound like very nice people."

"Yeah, and I'm spoiled rotten." He waited until she had another mouthful of eggs, then added, "You'll get to meet them next Saturday. They're coming to visit."

She sputtered and choked and coughed while he patted her back. "Are you all right?"

She wheezed a deep breath. "The damn muffin went up my nose."

Gavin bent down to look in her face. "No kidding?"

She took several more gasping breaths, a large drink of juice, then demanded, "What do you mean they're coming to visit?"

With a deliberate shrug of indifference, he said, "Mom always calls on Saturday morning. I knew she'd be worried if she couldn't reach me, so I phoned and gave her this number. One explanation led to another and now she wants to meet you. And whenever my mom interferes, my sisters are close on her heels."

"But…but…I can't meet your family!"

"Why not?"

He watched her search frantically for an answer, and finally come up with, "Because!"

"Because?"

She made an elaborate show of exasperation. "You know why, Gavin. What will they think?"

That I've finally met the woman I intend to marry. He didn't tell her that, of course. If he had, she'd have put a stop to his folks visiting real fast. She was so damn skittish about marriage and family and commitment now. But his family was the better part of him, a real selling tool to a woman like Sara. She wouldn't be able to resist any of them, and they wouldn't be able to resist her. He was certain of that.

Hoping to distract her once more so she wouldn't put up too much fuss, he leaned forward until his mouth was only a hairbreadth away from her lips. "You've got a whole week to get used to the idea."

Her eyelids fluttered, then closed as he kissed her. It was a very light kiss, soft and void of sexual intent.

For about three seconds.

Her soft moan shot his good intentions all to hell. When her tongue touched his lips, Gavin stumbled out of his chair and pulled Sara from hers, all without breaking the kiss. With only two steps he had her backed to the counter, trapped there with his body. She was so soft and sweet from her shower, so warm, he couldn't resist touching her.

Tangling his fingers in her dark, curly hair, he tipped her face to the side so his mouth could explore her throat. She hummed a small sound of pleasure, her hands gripping his bare shoulders, urging him closer. He felt the slight sting of her nails.

The distraction worked. In fact, he forgot why he was distracting her.

He kissed her again, wet and hot, his tongue sliding in, imitating what he wanted. What *she* evidently wanted, too, a truth that his carnal side relished. She wasn't drunk this morning, and she knew what she was doing. That thought kept pounding through his brain, driving him.

She groaned and arched into him. It was too much, and he lost control. He was hard, urgent, and he pressed his erection against her soft belly, hearing her groan again and feeling her cuddle him closer. One hand moved to cup her breast, and her nipple was stiff, ready. He started shoving her T-shirt up. He wanted to taste her, to have her nipple in his mouth, sucking, licking…

"Gavin?"

"Hmm?"

Breathless, she whispered, "Are we going to do a lot of…this, when you move in?"

His brain shut down for a single heartbeat. "Aw, hell." Reminded of his plan, he shoved himself away from her, jamming both hands into his hair. Immense frustration rode him, along with total disgust. He'd never get her to marry him if he was so easy. How did that saying go? Something about not buying the cow if the milk was free? Not that he liked comparing himself to a cow. A bull, maybe, but still…

He forced himself to take several deep breaths and face her. She looked aroused. Her lips were a little puffy, her shirt half untucked, her cheeks flushed.

But it was her eyes that grabbed and held his attention. They were bright and clear and filled with hot anticipation.

"Don't do that." His tone was cautious, and he backed up a step. Sara slowly followed. Her gaze remained glued to his, and as he watched, wary, she licked her lips. He felt like a meal set before a starving person.

It wasn't an altogether unpleasant feeling. "Sara…" he warned.

"I wasn't complaining, Gavin, when I asked if—"

"I know." He held up a hand to ward her off, both

physically and verbally. If she said much more, if she ... again, if she licked her lips just one more ... oner. Thankfully she stopped. He ... how to begin, what exactly to say. He needed her to know how much he wanted her. That was an important fact she had to understand with un-... ainty. But he also had to make her un-... wouldn't allow her to toy with his affec-... . There would be no simple fling. If she wanted the beef, she had to buy the bull. Period.

"What is it, Gavin?"

Trying to look stern, he folded his arms behind his back and paced. "You're just coming out of a bad relationship, Sara. People tend to react on the rebound whenever they've been hurt, and—"

"How do you know?" Then her eyes narrowed. "You're talking about your breakup with Karen, aren't you? You said she had stopped being important to you long ago."

Her tone was accusing, and he flinched at his poor choice of wording. "True. Karen didn't mean that much to me. But it was another example of a failed relationship, and I'm getting too old to keep involving myself in dead-end situations. Do you understand?"

She nodded, the movement slow and thoughtful. "But I didn't think you were looking for involvement anyway. And I've already learned all I need to know about these things. If you're afraid I'll get clingy, I promise I won't. I'm not looking for happily ever after. Not anymore."

So. That hadn't just been the drink talking. Having her reiterate her intentions so plainly pricked his temper. He didn't like the idea that she planned to use him for mere sex. For mere, mind-blowing, torrid, delicious sex. God, he was an idiot. A determined idiot.

Glaring, he said, "That's just it. We're both looking for different things now. And that means we should move slowly."

Her gaze skittered away, and she nodded. "I see."

Exasperated, he said, "No, you don't. I want you, Sara. A lot. That much should be plain."

Lifting her shoulders in a shrug, she said, "I suppose."

"Dammit! You're deliberately provoking me. No, don't try to look innocent." He saw her lips quirk in a small smile, then she frowned again. "Sara." He said her name as a chastisement. "We'll have to get together on this if it's going to work. Do you at least agree to that much?"

"If what will work?"

"Me staying here. We'll need some rules."

"Such as?"

"Such as..." He gestured with his hands, indicating the two of them. "We'll have to work on maintaining some decorum."

"You don't want to kiss me anymore?"

"Oh, yeah," he drawled, letting his gaze linger on her mouth. "I want to kiss you. But it'll have to stop there. We need time to get used to each other. Time to form some sort of understanding, without the past getting in the way.''

She raised one brow, waiting for him to elaborate.

''You're going to have to stop making it so easy on me.''

''Me? What about you? You're the one who started the kissing.''

He smiled to himself, preparing his trap. Give and take, that's what was needed. ''Yeah. But you didn't have to go all soft and hungry on me.''

''Hungry! I wasn't...''

''Yes, you were. And you made those sexy little sounds.'' He stepped closer again, one finger touching her warm cheek. ''I've kissed other women and not lost my head like that. So it must be you.'' He had to bite his lip to keep from laughing, she'd gone so rigid, her frown so fierce.

''I'm not going to let you blame me for this, Gavin! Why, you're the one who climbed into bed with me when I was drunk!''

''But I'm not the one who tried to crawl on top of you in the middle of the night.''

She sucked in so much air, she choked. ''I would never...!''

Nodding, he said, ''Yes, you would. *You did.*'' Then he added in a low voice before she could get too worked up, ''But I didn't mind. Not at all.''

''Gavin...''

''Are you going to help me move a few of my things here today?'' He threw that in just to change the subject before she could get angry enough to toss him out on his ear. Not that he'd let her toss him out, but accomplishing his goals would be easier if she didn't want to wring his neck.

After blinking several times, she glanced at the clock, then accepted the new topic with a vague show of relief. "I suppose I could help a little. But I have to go to the shelter this afternoon. I'm sorry, but they're counting on me. If I'd known everything that would happen, maybe…"

"No, that's okay. I can manage on my own." And without her help, there was no way he could haul his mattress and box springs down the street. Leaving the sleeping arrangements as they were suited him just fine, at least for the time being.

"If you're sure?"

It was obvious to Gavin she wanted some time alone, time to sort through all he'd thrown at her over the past twelve hours. "Positive." Then he nudged her plate at her to get her to finish eating. "It seems to me you're a damn picky eater. That won't do. I like to cook and I'll expect you to be properly appreciative of my efforts."

Sara lifted her chin. "I think that's one rule I won't have a problem abiding by."

"Good." He waited until she finished eating, then went to the side of her chair. Time for the next step. He could hardly wait for her reaction. Damn, but he was a genius.

She glanced up at him, her expression alert.

He tried to look serious. "Now, I was thinking, Sara. Maybe you ought to pick out that pet you want today. I know it's kind of soon, but since we'll both be living here, it shouldn't be a big problem or an expense to keep up with one cute little animal. I'll be glad to help out some, to look after it when you're not around, to take it for walks every now and then. What do you think?"

Her eyes widened, and the look of naked excitement that came over her features was worth any amount of nuisance. Gavin didn't look forward to a puppy's accidents, or the chore of housebreaking, but he had thought it an excellent way to start stepping in the right direction. Once she saw how supportive he could be of her pet, she'd realize he wasn't the least bit similar to Ted. And he'd been right.

She leaped from her seat, wrapped her arms around him and gave him a strangling hug. She talked nonstop about whether or not she wanted a large or small pet, male or female. Gavin silently congratulated himself when she rushed out the door, anxious to reach the shelter.

He rubbed his hands together. Things were moving along just as he planned. And as Sara had once told him, he was a master planner.

5

SARA GLANCED AT THE HOUSE, but saw no sign of Gavin. She didn't want him to witness her approach. Stealth wasn't her forte, but she felt certain if she could only initiate the idea of this particular animal slowly, everything would go better. No way would she give up her pet now that she had chosen. It had loved her on sight, and the feeling had been mutual. This animal was now hers. But that didn't mean she wanted to fight about it, either.

Her mind whirled with everything the day had brought her way. Throughout her stint at the shelter, her feet had barely touched the ground. She was truly happy. More than that, she was excited. First Gavin, and now her very own pet. And not just any old pet, she thought with satisfaction.

Lugging the heavy box from the back seat, Sara murmured soft soothing phrases to the animal within. Jess and Lou, the couple who owned the shelter, were thrilled when she made her choice. They were also endlessly amused.

That was nothing new, because Jess and his wife had a bizarre sense of humor, a humor that often escaped Sara. But in this instance she hadn't been nearly as obtuse as they'd assumed. And she hadn't minded their good-natured teasing, either, not when they'd supplied all the shots and a thorough checkup on the newly arrived animal for free.

It had been imperative that she take the pet, because if she hadn't, it was a certainty no one else would have.

She'd barely gotten through her front door, huffing with the effort to carry the large box and the weight within, when she heard Gavin approaching. The second she saw his face, she set the box on the floor and stepped in front of it, plastering a bright smile on her lips. "I'm back."

Gavin looked her over from head to toe as if he'd missed the sight of her. "So I see."

His voice was soft, and Sara only blinked when he leaned close and gave her a sweet, welcoming kiss. As he started to pull away, she tilted into him and the kiss intensified.

He seemed determined to keep her at a physical distance.

She was determined to make him relent.

He was in her house. He was available. She figured the least she should do, as an enterprising, healthy woman, was take advantage of the opportunity presented to her.

It was amazing the effect he had on her, she thought, deliberately wrapping herself closer. She hadn't known feelings like these existed until Gavin decided to move in. And since, she'd suffered constant frustration. If he didn't give in soon, she'd go crazy from unrequited lust. Damn his ridiculous ethics.

His hand had just started down her back, encouraged no doubt by her soft moan, when a loud, rumbling growl erupted from the cardboard box.

Gavin froze, his mouth still touching hers, but his eyes wide-open. ''What the hell was that?''

Uh-oh. Teatime. She winced just a bit, then whispered, ''My pet?''

His eyes flared even more and he took her shoulders, moving her aside and staring down at the box. ''What did you get? A mountain lion?''

''Well, actually...'' That was as far as Sara got before the box seemed to explode and a massive streak of mangy yellow fur shot out, like a marmalade cannon blast. The huge alley cat surveyed its surroundings in a single derisive glance, swishing its badly bent tail then giving a vicious shake of its monstrous, square head. A small, lopsided pink bow hung precariously over a damaged ear, an ear that was only half there.

Gavin's mouth hung open. ''My God.''

The cat gave him a look filled with disdain, then strutted past, sniffing the carpet and, for the most part, ignoring the humans.

''What the hell is that?''

Sara forced a cheerful expression, hoping to brazen it out, but her words were too quick and nervous to hide her concern. "My pet, of course. Isn't she beautiful? The man who dropped her off today said she was expecting."

"Expecting...what?"

"Kittens!" Sara glanced at the cat, who stared back without a single blink of its large pea-green eyes. Perhaps if Gavin believed the ruse, he'd be more inclined to accept the shabby monster. Surely no compassionate person could turn away an expectant mother. "Her name is Satin."

Gavin sent her a skeptical, slightly horrified look, and Sara rushed on. "She's had a few...mishaps, and being as old as she is, the shelter didn't really hold any great hope of finding her a home. I couldn't leave her there indefinitely, without hope, without prospects. I just couldn't."

The cat chose that moment to give them both its back, walking away with a hunter's stride and sticking its bent tail high into the air. Again, Gavin's mouth fell open, then quickly tightened in chagrin. "Ah, Sara? That cat's about as pregnant as I am."

She already knew that, but she wasn't ready for Gavin to realize it. It was her best excuse for bringing the beast home.

She swiveled her gaze back to him, her brows lowered in stern regard. "If you've gotten yourself into trouble, Gavin, don't look at me. You said our night together was innocent enough."

His smirk proved he wasn't fooled, or diverted. Walking to the cat, he said, "Come here, fella. Let's get that hideous bow off your head."

To Sara's amazement, the aloof cat halted his exit and waited in regal patience while Gavin knelt down and worked the bow free. He ignored Sara as he spoke with the cat. "Satin, is it? More like Satan, I'd say, given the looks of you. You've raised some hell in your days, haven't you, boy?"

The cat's purr was more of a scratchy growl, and the first Sara had heard. It was clear to her the animal hadn't led a pampered life. She'd taken one look at the poor creature and every nurturing instinct she owned had kicked in. The farmer who'd brought the cat in had hoped to escape the shelter's costs by claiming it to be a future mother. He'd dropped off the box and left again all within a matter of moments. But the second the cat had been cautiously lifted free of the cardboard confines, it was obvious he was a tom.

That hadn't deterred Sara. And while she'd pretended to believe the farmer's story, she had put up with her friends' amusement. What the heck? It had gotten the cat some pretty special treatment, and the truth was, she was almost embarrassed to admit she wanted the cat simply because he was alone and unwanted, a feeling she understood all too well.

She felt a strong affinity to a rather homely, bedraggled animal. And that wasn't something she wanted to explain, even to her friends.

Gavin stood again and faced her. "Have you had this animal checked? He looks like he could be carrying any number of diseases."

The cat rolled on the carpet, stretching and luxuriating in his freedom from the bow. Everywhere his big body touched, a patch of dull yellow cat hair remained. He desperately needed a good brushing.

"Jess is a vet, and he checked her...ah him, over. Other than a few scrapes—"

"And missing body parts."

Sara nodded. "Yes. Other than the missing ear, he's healthy. His tail is bent for good and his voice box is damaged, I'm afraid. There's nothing we can do about that. But I have vitamins for him, and a good cat food that should put some shine back in his fur and—"

Sara was cut off as the cat decided he wanted more of Gavin's attention and made a sudden, smooth lunge into his arms. Gavin had no choice but to catch the weight, which was considerable, Sara knew. He staggered, cursed, then reluctantly held the beast. There was a look of distaste on Gavin's face, but still, he scratched the cat's head with his free hand.

Amazed at the cat's show of affection, Sara laughed. "Oh, Gavin, isn't that sweet? He likes you."

"Yeah. Sweet." Gavin grimaced as the cat began

to purr again, all but drowning out any attempt at normal conversation.

Satisfaction filled her, and Sara nodded in approval of Gavin's attempt to treat the animal with kindness. "I think he feels indebted because you knew he was a male."

"Uh-huh. Right."

"Don't look at me like I'm screwy. It was obvious he didn't like that pink bow."

"We men feel strongly about that sort of thing."

"Wearing bows?"

"No. Having our masculinity questioned."

"Ah."

"Sara? Did you really believe this beast to be a..."

Before he could finish his question, she had the front door open and headed out. "I have a lot of stuff in the car yet. A litter box, a bed, the food. Will you keep an eye on Satin while I bring everything in?"

"Satin, hell. At least forget that name, will you?"

Chancing a glance at his face, Sara saw Gavin was resigned. She sighed in relief. "What should we call him?"

Looking at the cat as he considered her question, Gavin finally said, "With that vicious purr, Satan suits him well enough."

"He does look like the very devil."

To Sara's surprise, Gavin became defensive of the cat. "Just because he's not some prissy feline shouldn't matter. He's a good mouser, I bet." Then he added, "I had a cat like him when I was a kid. He'd go out every so often and either come home the strutting victor of a romantic rendezvous, or a bedraggled soldier from battle. Either way, there was always a female involved somehow." The cat rubbed his large head against Gavin's chest in agreement, leaving a blotch of fur behind.

"Well," Sara said on her way to the car, "his nights on the town will soon be curtailed. I'm going to have him neutered."

The cat gave a loud hiss and Sara looked back to see him racing down the hall. Gavin scowled at her, then went after the cat, calling in soft sympathy, "Here, kitty, kitty, kitty..."

Everything was working out, Sara thought. Only two days ago, she was alone, without a single soul who cared. Now she had Gavin—no matter how temporary that arrangement might be—and she had a wonderful new pet. Not only that, the two males had bonded already.

Now, she thought, feeling lighthearted and happy and half-silly, the only thing missing in her life was lawn furniture, and it no longer seemed so important.

GAVIN LOOKED DOWN at the cat twined around his bare ankles. "At least you enjoyed my dinner." He knew today had to make an impact; it was the first day of their "relationship." So he'd made, in his humble opinion, a stupendous dinner, topped by a killer dessert. Sara had eaten a fair portion, had even complimented him on his efforts, but other than that, her attention wasn't where he wanted it to be—on him.

Handing the cat another scrap of meat, Gavin considered his next step. Sara hadn't as yet asked how his moving in had gone. She'd been much too busy settling Satan and enjoying being a pet owner to concern herself with anything as mundane as the new man in her life.

Pushing back from the table, Gavin left his seat and walked to where Sara stood rinsing dishes in the sink. "Are you sure you don't want any help?"

"We had a deal, Gavin. You cooked, so I'll clean."

"I wouldn't mind helping…"

"You've done enough today." She turned, giving him a fat smile. "The meal was fabulous."

Without giving himself a chance to think about it, he leaned down and skimmed her cheek with his mouth. She smelled so damn good, even after working in an animal shelter all day. He nuzzled her hair, her ear. The catch in her breath was audible, and he leaned closer, caging her between his body and the counter.

Water dripped down his neck when her wet hands settled in his hair, holding him still so she could kiss him. But he darted away. Seeing the disappointment in her eyes, he hid his smile, and his own frustration. But he'd just decided what to do next. "I think I'll go take a shower, then, if you're sure you don't need any help.''

"Fine. Go.'' She returned her hands to the sudsy water, her stiff back showing her disgruntlement.

With a hidden grin, Gavin turned, and nearly tripped over the cat. Satan seemed to want to stay right on his heels, no matter where he went or what he did. He said to the cat, "Sorry, no shower for you. Stay here and visit with your new master.''

The cat answered with a grouchy, rusty roar, but he did stay.

Whistling, Gavin went into the bathroom and stripped down. Even with the door closed, he could hear Sara banging the pots and pans around, venting her own frustration no doubt. But that was fine with him. He wanted her so frustrated she wouldn't be able to resist him when he suggested making their relationship more permanent. He wanted her on the edge, willing to overlook her reservations on marriage in order to get her sexual needs fulfilled.

And to that end, he'd do what he had to do.

After quickly showering, he reached for a towel. Leaving the water running, he pulled the door open and yelled, "Hey, Sara?''

There was a moment of silence, then she stuck her head around the hall. She stared at him, her gaze dropping quickly from his face to his wet chest and then down his belly. She stared at the loosely draped towel wrapped low around his hips and mumbled a crackly, "Hmm?"

"I left my shampoo in a box by the front door." His smile was innocence personified. "Would you bring it to me, please?"

He watched her swallow, then drag her eyes back to his face. "Shampoo?" she asked, as if in a fog.

"Yeah. I've got a preference for my own, if you don't mind."

"No. No, I don't mind."

As he watched her hurry away, the cat slipped through the door and wove itself around and between his ankles, leaving his damp legs with clinging yellow fur. Gavin pushed the door wider and tried to nudge the cat out. Satan refused to budge.

"Go on, scat."

The cat hunched back, preparing to leap into Gavin's arms again.

"No!" Gavin backed away, holding the towel with one hand and shooing the cat with the other. He took three steps into the hall, hoping Satan would follow.

"Here you go."

The sound of Sara's breathless voice brought him back around. She held out the bottle of shampoo while staring at his legs. Gavin deliberately widened his stance, letting the towel part just a bit, then saw her eyes flare.

He saluted her with the bottle. "I appreciate it, honey. Thanks."

"Uh...you're welcome."

It was dirty pool to use her attraction for his body against her, but he would do it all the same. He started to stretch, raising one arm over his head and feeling much like a determined exhibitionist. He was just getting into the game, appreciating Sara's attentiveness, when he felt Satan's front paws land solidly against his backside, throwing him off balance. Gavin jerked forward, almost stumbling into Sara, then turned with a yelp when Satan began contracting his claws in his butt.

The problem, the way Gavin figured it, wasn't that the cat had inadvertently scratched him. It was that as he'd turned, Satan hadn't released his hold and as a result the cat's claws were now snagged in the towel, leaving Gavin bare-assed, with only the top corner of the towel preserving his frontal modesty. What was that about best laid plans?

Sara was no help at all; she was too busy ogling.

Gavin thought about abandoning the towel in favor of maintaining his consequence. Being hunched over with your backside exposed while you fought with an alley cat over possession of a towel wasn't a very dignified position, certainly not one to impress the woman of his choice.

A quick peek at Sara showed she wasn't impressed so much as stunned. "Dammit, Sara, get the cat."

She seemed to shake out of her speechless stupor,

and then leaned against the wall, folding her arms over her breasts. "Why?"

"So I can get the towel."

She waved a negligent hand, her gaze glued to his backside. "Just let him have it. That would be easier than untangling you both."

Her words were careless, but when she glanced up, the look in her eyes was pure dare. Now that his options had been severely limited and his plans had gone awry, Gavin knew he had little to lose. Unfortunately he felt embarrassed, which was stupid considering he'd been blatantly flaunting himself anyway. Not that he'd planned to flaunt to the degree of total nudity, but it was too late now.

He couldn't let her have the upper hand, not tonight. He needed to get things moving; the sooner the better. So he stiffened his resolve, gave her a narrow look to warn her of his intentions and released the towel.

To his relief, Sara gave up the game and fled. He'd barely straightened before she rounded the corner of the hall, her wild hair flying out behind her, her startled gasp still filling the air. He frowned down at the cat, who only blinked back. "Any more stunts like that and I'll put the damn bow back on you myself."

The cat quickly followed in Sara's footsteps. Gavin shook his head. "Onward to Plan B. And let's hope it's just a little more successful."

SARA MANAGED TO AVOID any prolonged time with Gavin for the rest of the evening. She took an extended walk with Satan, leading the cat off a thick leash. Then she took her own leisurely bath, soaking for a long time in the Jacuzzi tub until her toes were wrinkled and her muscles finally relaxed.

Still, her mind churned in chaos, playing the same scene over and over again. The picture of Gavin totally nude wasn't something she would ever willingly erase from her mind. The memory of it was enough to send a warmth of anticipation swelling through her body. So it was her own reaction that had her taking long walks and hiding in her tub.

She had literally run! It wasn't to be borne. What had overcome her, she didn't know, but part of it had been self-preservation, she was certain. If she'd stayed, she wouldn't have only looked. Oh, no. Even now, her fingers tingled with the need to touch. The man was too fine for words, too much temptation to resist. She probably would have attacked him. He'd been naked, so therefore unable to offer much defense.

She had no idea what he had hoped to accomplish with his striptease act, but she had no doubt it had been deliberate, though maybe not the part where he actually lost the towel. After all, there was no way he could have prompted Satan to interfere. But the man was up to something. The question was: What?

After she'd finished drying and brushing out her

impossible hair, she put on the gown she'd bought herself last Christmas. It was pretty, definitely the prettiest gown she owned, but it wasn't very comfortable. Not that comfort mattered right now. Pretty mattered; comfort ran an insignificant second.

She needed the fortitude of knowing she looked her best before she faced Gavin again. They needed to talk, to clear the air, and she had no wish to wait until morning, giving herself the long night to fret over her cowardly race down the hall. And besides, he might want to kiss her again…or more. She voted for more, not that he'd asked her opinion.

She tried to gather her thoughts and organize them into some semblance of sanity, but they jumped here and there, filled with anticipation and hope and frustration. And as she entered her bedroom from the master bath, her hands busy smoothing the starched fabric of her gown, she stopped in midstride. The sight of Gavin's large, masculine body sprawled across *her* bed in nothing more than leisure shorts with a magazine in his work-worn hands, swept her mind clean of even her insane notions.

He planned to sleep with her again?

She was at first shocked, then immeasurably optimistic. All day, even while picking out her pet, she had nurtured a small hope that Gavin would forget his reticence and let his basic instincts take over. She didn't understand why he kept hesitating. They knew each other well enough, better than many married couples, she thought, considering how much they'd always talked, and six weeks had already passed since her breakup with Ted, assuring she wouldn't react on the rebound, as he'd claimed.

Determined, she sidled toward the bed, waiting for him to acknowledge her presence. The epitome of nonchalance, he held one finger in the air to indicate he needed a moment more to finish the article he was reading.

Irritation was a nasty element to add to an already confused female brain.

"Excuse me." When he looked up, one brow raised at her waspish tone, she added, "What are you doing?"

"Reading."

He plainly thought she should have figured that one out on her own. Irritation turned to a tinge of anger. "Okay. Why are you reading in my bed?"

"Oh." He set the magazine down and scooted higher against the headboard. "I wasn't able to move my bed on my own—it's a king-size, you know. All I got transferred today were my clothes and personal items. By the way, I took the closet in the guest room. And since your stuff is in this bathroom, I thought I'd use the one in the hall."

"So...you're sleeping here tonight?"

"Where else?" He crossed his arms and tilted his head, his dark eyes sincere. "Your sofa is much too small. And I'll tell you, the thought of the floor isn't the least bit appealing.''

"So why not just sleep in your own house tonight?''

"Because all my clothes and personal items are here. Remember?''

He sounded so reasonable. She wasn't buying it for a minute. He was up to something. Only she didn't know what it was he wanted to achieve, and this time she knew better than to try to outmaneuver him.

Then it hit her. The man was in her bed—exactly where she wanted him to be. She didn't *want* to outmaneuver him.

Trying not to look as anxious as she felt, Sara pulled back the covers and slid into bed. She felt as stiff as the lace collar on her nightgown, and just as ridiculous. The touch of Gavin's gaze was a tangible thing, and very unsettling.

Without looking, she knew he would be smiling. He would be amused by her nervousness, maybe even a little smug at the effect he had on her. She didn't want to add to his confidence, but she didn't know what to do or how to act. Having anyone close, especially a man, wasn't a feeling she'd experienced much in her lifetime. And this man seemed to genuinely care for her to some degree. The feelings he evoked, those of lust and a craving for tenderness, would be visible in her eyes. She kept her gaze on the sheets, not wanting him to see just how confused she really felt. Then she couldn't help herself and looked at him anyway.

He wasn't smiling; there was nothing of a humorous nature in the way he watched her. Sara started to turn away again, but he captured her chin on the edge of his hand. "You're beautiful."

Staring, her chest tight with emotion, Sara bit her bottom lip. His eyes flickered, then narrowed on her mouth. With a harsh groan he turned away. "Lord, Sara, you make it so damn hard."

Her eyes widened and her mouth opened.

"Not..." He shook his head, laughing a little, groaning again. His eyes met hers, chagrined and filled with the tenderness she craved. "This is damn difficult. You're making me crazy."

"Gavin..."

"No. Don't you dare say it."

"Say what?"

"I don't know. But it's for certain whatever it is will push me right over the edge. Now give me a kiss good-night and let's get some sleep."

Only her eyes moved, searching his expression, hoping to see some sign that he was jesting. "Just like that? Go to sleep?"

Gavin reached past her to turn off the bedside lamp, then settled his upper body over her, his large hands holding her face. "No," he whispered, his mouth feathering her lips, his breath warm and soft. "The kiss first, then we sleep."

And what a kiss it was. Sara clung to him, feeling the wet touch of his tongue, the rough caress of his fingertips as he tunneled his hands into her hair. It was a kiss meant to prepare her, but not for sleep.

When it ended, she wanted to wail in frustration. But then Gavin pulled her against his side, settling her close and covering them both. His hand smoothed over her arm, and her cheek rested on his chest, the uneven tempo of his heart sounding in her ear.

She hadn't gotten the lust she wanted, but the tenderness was there, enough to wallow in, and for the time being, she decided it was more than enough.

6

WAKING WITH A WARM, SOFT body curled close had its advantages. And its disadvantages.

Gavin peered down at Sara's face and felt every masculine instinct he possessed surge to the surface. He wanted her, and his body reacted, painfully so. It was a wonder the sexual pulsing in his lower body didn't rock the entire damn bed. If Sara awoke, there would be no way for him to hide his desire.

But it also felt remarkably right to have her here with him, to breathe her unique scent first thing in the morning, to feel the comfort of her nearness. She slept like the dead. He had hardly slept at all.

The radio alarm buzzed, then loud music kicked on. Turning his head to see the clock, Gavin realized it was almost ten. He needed to rise, to begin a new day of plans. This morning, he intended to overwhelm Sara with his culinary expertise.

A wise person somewhere once claimed the way to a man's heart was through his stomach. Couldn't the same apply to a woman? He would prove to Sara how indispensable he could be, and when she softened toward him, and the attitude of marriage, he'd be ready.

The music hadn't disturbed Sara's sleep. Gavin turned to look at her again, feeling overwhelmed with compassion at her obvious exhaustion. Her cheeks were flushed with the warmth of sleep and there was a darkness around her eyes that showed the level of her fatigue.

She'd been trying so hard to keep it all together, the house, the job, the humiliation from the incident. He wished now he hadn't waited so long to approach her. All he'd done was give her time to chastise herself and build up her defenses. When he thought of her past, he knew she would have a difficult time taking another chance on love.

His thoughts were interrupted by a loud, rasping roar. Gavin looked down at the floor and saw Satan. The cat gave him a blank-eyed stare, then prepared to heave his heavily muscled body into the bed. Since Gavin didn't want Sara awakened yet, he forestalled the cat with a hand and carefully slipped his arm from under her head. She made a slight sound of protest and curled into his pillow.

It was a sunny day and Gavin felt enthusiastic about his chances of making headway. Satan followed him as he pulled on jeans and walked through the door, closing it quietly behind him.

The cat also followed him into the bathroom and wound around his feet, making his morning ablutions more difficult than usual. Satan had the uncanny ability of being right where Gavin wanted to step, each time he wanted to step. Walking had never seemed so difficult before.

He grumbled at the cat, stumbling along down the hall, but the sight that met him in the living room stopped him in his tracks.

There was so much cat fur floating around, the damn cat should have been bald. Gavin looked down, but no, Satan was as shaggy as ever. "Did you have to rub against everything?"

Satan showed his sharp, pointed teeth in what Gavin chose to believe was a feline grin, not a threat. "Okay, so you're telling me you need to be brushed? I'll have to brush the damn house first."

He let Satan out the back door, then checked to see if he had the ingredients for omelets. He'd been known to make a really mean omelet. One bite, and Sara would have to accept her good fortune in having him as a roommate.

Unfortunately, thirty minutes later when he had everything set on the table, the rich aroma of coffee in the air, steam rising from the egg dish, Sara refused to get up.

Gavin shook her shoulder again. "Come on, sleepyhead. I've got breakfast ready for you."

She snared a pillow and pulled it over her head. "Go away."

"Babe, I know you're tired." Gavin did his best not to sound impatient. She'd been in bed for over nine hours, and he knew for a fact she'd slept soundly because he'd laid awake, torturing himself all night by listening to her soft breathing. ''I've cooked you breakfast. You don't want it to get cold.''

She started to snore.

Gavin lifted the pillow in disbelief. Her eyes were closed, her features relaxed, and her lips slightly parted. A soft, very feminine snore escaped those lips.

Then Gavin saw that her nightgown had slipped down one shoulder and the slope of her breast was exposed. He swallowed hard. Last night, he'd felt that plump breast pressed against his side once Sara had decided to relax. In fact, it hadn't taken her long at all to decide she liked being held close to him, even lying half on top of him.

She'd stayed that way throughout the night, tormenting him, and reveling in the comfort of it. It had been so apparent that she'd never had such comfort before, Gavin hadn't minded staying awake. He'd do it again if she wanted him to. He had intentions of holding her every night from now on.

He gave up on trying to wake her when she rolled onto her stomach in the middle of the bed and sprawled wide enough to cover the whole mattress. He gave one gentle pat to her cute rounded backside and left the room.

This wasn't turning out to be the idyllic morning he'd planned. How could he woo the woman if she wouldn't wake up?

Satan came back in to keep him company while he ate his own omelet. He lingered over the meal, still hoping Sara would awaken. Every so often, he made an especially loud noise, scraping a chair across a floor, banging a plate on the table, but she slept on. Finally, when the eggs were cold, he gave Sara's share to Satan, who sniffed it repeatedly before concluding it might actually be edible. After cleaning the dishes, he located a brush and carried Satan outside.

The cat began purring even before he'd put the brush to his hide.

Another half hour passed before he realized there was no end in sight. Satan looked sleek and well groomed, his large head appearing more square without the benefit of excess fur to soften the effect, and his tail looked more bent for the same reason. But there were still hairs falling loose. His coat was so thick, that no matter how much Gavin brushed, he couldn't remove all the excess. Every time Satan stepped, he shed.

Several old scars were now visible through the smooth coat, however, and Gavin eyed the cat with respect. "You're a regular warrior, aren't you, boy?"

Satan stretched, arching his body high and spreading his considerable claws wide. His mouth opened in a yawn that displayed an impressive array of sharp teeth. All around the yard, hanging from the trees and clinging to the flowers, were clumps of yellow fur, some drifting loose to float in the air like dandelion fluff, rolling across the lawn with the sultry breeze. A small cloud hovered around the porch, the air filled with cat hair as if it were a fine morning mist. Gavin did his own stretching, being careful not to inhale the hair, then turned at a sound from the house.

Sara stood in the doorway, now dressed in loose shorts and a pullover top, a slight smile on her face. "You've been brushing the cat."

Gavin stood and looked down at the cat hairs now clinging to his own body. He had to fan the air so that he could see her clearly. "However did you guess?"

He knew he sounded sarcastic, but he was now a grubby mess, breakfast was over and there she stood, looking so damn desirable he wanted to carry her right back to bed.

The lengths he was forced to go to just to win her over. And she hadn't even had the decency to get out of bed.

"Satan looks very handsome."

"Handsome is not a word that will ever be applied to that monster, but I suppose he looks much better." Gavin studied her closely. She still appeared a little wiped out, as if she'd only just opened her eyes. "You okay?"

She flushed, then quickly nodded. "Yeah, fine. I'm sorry I slept so late. I don't suppose there's anything to eat?"

A sleepless night took its toll on his patience. "I had omelets and muffins and fresh coffee, but you refused to get up."

Sara bit her lip, then looked up at the sunny sky. "What time is it?"

"Almost noon."

That startled her. "Good grief. I'm sorry."

"It's my day off. I had hoped we could spend some time together."

"Oh."

She sounded less than enthusiastic. Then he saw her put her hand to her stomach. "Are you sick?"

"No, of course not." And she flushed again.

"What finally encouraged you to get out of bed?"

"The phone rang. It was…Jess. He wanted to know if I could come out to the shelter."

"Why? Isn't Sunday *your* day off, too?"

"Usually. But I…well, I already told him I'd stop by."

Gavin tightened his jaw. The day rapidly dwindled into a dismal failure. "For how long?"

"I don't know. But I told him I'd be there in about an hour."

"Dammit, Sara. Why today? Why can't it wait?"

She flinched, then lifted her chin. "You have no right to curse at me. This is one of the ground rules we should have covered. You don't tell me what to do, and I won't tell you what to do."

Gavin knew he'd lost his edge, knew he was pushing too hard, but he couldn't seem to stop himself. He'd been sexually deprived too long, dammit, especially considering all the provocation he'd suffered. He was a man on the verge of exploding, and he figured when it happened, his hormones would cover more ground than Satan's hair.

Trying for a moderate tone while his body screamed in frustration wasn't easy. He cleared his throat. Twice. "I really wish I'd known beforehand." *There.* That had sounded calm enough.

She frowned. "Are you getting a cold? Your voice is all raw and scratchy."

He stared at her, seeing the concern now in her eyes. If he wasn't so horny, the entire situation might have been humorous. Gavin drew a deep breath, and choked on a cat hair. "I'm fine," he wheezed, when she started forward. Then he waved her off. "Go on. I've got plenty to occupy me for the day, I guess. Satan shed all over the house. I'll stay here and clean it up. What time will you be home?"

"It's not your job to clean up my cat's mess."

He stared at her hard. "I'm the one that suggested you get a pet."

"Still..."

It was annoying the way she constantly looked at him as if waiting for him to turn on her. Did she think just because the cat had obliged him to do a little vacuuming, he'd get angry and walk out? After how hard he'd worked to walk in? He snorted.

But then she nibbled on her bottom lip, and he saw that sexy crooked tooth, and forgave her for doubting him. He cursed, then locked his jaw against the unbearable provocation she presented. "I asked you what time you'd be home."

She suddenly exploded. "I'll be home when I'm darn good and ready."

Gavin was stunned by her outburst, but evidently not as stunned as Sara. She gasped, stiffened up like a lightning rod, then turned and ran back into the house. Gavin stood there, wondering what in hell had brought that on.

When he heard her car driving away, he cursed again, this time rather viciously. Satan wrapped around his leg and roared his approval.

Well, hell.

Obviously he wasn't handling things right. He supposed, given his frustration from the night before, Sara might be under the same stress. He'd always thought it rather arrogant of men to assume women didn't suffer the same sexual discomforts as men. Frustration was frustration, whether you were male or female. *And she had wanted him.*

A slow smile spread over his face. Maybe he'd been looking at this all wrong. It was possible making love to her would reach her far better than anything else. It would prove how much he wanted her, and that was certainly important since Sara didn't seem to have a clue about her own desirability.

It would also offer that special closeness that always occurred between two people who really cared about each other. He was convinced Sara did care about him. She was merely being stubbornly cautious.

He'd have to be careful to maintain control, but he could do it. It wouldn't do to let her think their lovemaking was *only* sex. He couldn't let her use him without reaching for the commitment. He wasn't easy. No sir. Gavin Blake was not a man to be trifled with.

And he'd be certain to say all the right words, to treat her tenderly, to show his love.

With that determination, he decided not to wait for the night. As soon as Sara returned home, he would allow her to seduce him. He rubbed his hands together and grinned in heated anticipation. Satan, being a perceptive cat, grinned with him.

SARA DREADED SEEING GAVIN again. She was never her best at times like these, and having an extra person in the house had only complicated matters. As long as he didn't push her, she could probably maintain control. But if he insisted on cutting up at her, or trying to second-guess her, she might very well explode.

And speaking of exploding…the constant yapping from the back seat had become very wearying. The tiny dog, a mixed miniature breed of some sort, was the noisiest, most rambunctious little creature she had ever seen. And how one little minuscule animal could move so fast on only three legs she didn't know. But boy, this one could.

She was glad Jess had given her the excuse to escape the house, and she was even grateful that they'd given her the chance to look over the tiny dog. But dragging in another animal for Gavin's approval, especially when he'd been annoyed when she left…

The second she pulled into the driveway, she saw

his truck was still there. Everything inside her started to relax; though she dreaded another confrontation with him, she also drew comfort from knowing she wasn't alone, from knowing Gavin was inside. But then he stepped onto the porch, and his disconcerting gaze settled on her face.

Renewed heat rose in her like a tide.

He looked wonderful and strong and handsome; she looked like hell. Mother Nature had a hand in that and there was little she could do about her puffy features and tired eyes. But he didn't know that. Yet.

And she was certain he could hear the constant, annoying yapping from the back seat. She tightened her hands on the steering wheel.

Strolling down the sidewalk, Gavin flicked his glance from her face to the back of the car several times. Then he stepped around and opened her door when she didn't show any indication of doing it herself.

For the moment he seemed inclined to ignore the dog. "You weren't gone very long."

"Nope. Not long at all." Sara tried a smile, but it felt more like a grimace.

"Long enough to pick up another pet?"

"Well...you see, it's like this. The dog sorta looked at me, and...well, we bonded." Sara rushed on, wanting him to understand. "She's had an accident and lost a leg. But she's still plenty scrappy, and she gets around fine. She just needs some TLC. As busy as the shelter is, they can't possibly give her the attention she deserves.''

''But you can?''

His tone seemed mild enough, only curious, though he had to raise it to be heard over the racket the dog made. Sara wasn't at all certain of his mood. And she knew her own mood was precarious at best.

She stepped around Gavin and started to lift the cage from the seat. He pulled her aside to do it himself.

She drew a deep breath. ''I suppose this is one of those times when you think I should have consulted you first. But you see, there really wasn't any point. I couldn't very well leave the dog there.''

Gavin ignored her and started up the walk, holding the cage away from his body and wincing at the continued grating sound. ''It's not very big.''

''No. She's very fragile.''

He said with a touch of sarcasm, ''She doesn't sound fragile. Does it ever shut up?''

''Well...no. Not so far.'' Then she hastened to say, ''But I'm certain once she settles down, she'll get quiet.''

Gavin sent her a doubting look as he carried the dog through the house. ''You didn't bother to wonder what I would think, but did you stop to wonder how Satan might react to the dog? She wouldn't make much more than a snack for him. He might just mistake the dog for a squirrel or some other rodent. And in case you didn't know, Satan is real fond of catching rodents.''

Sara's eyes widened. "No, I hadn't considered that."

"Make certain the front door is closed tight."

Sara started to ask why, then saw that Gavin was about to open the cage, and the little dog was running in circles as if winding itself up for the event. She checked the door, and just as he released the dog, Satan strolled into the room to investigate. The dog shot out as if propelled by force and skittered to a frenzied halt directly in front of Satan.

Then the yapping began again.

Satan endured it with nothing more than a mild look of disgust before he turned away. When the dog made a grab for his tail, Satan turned, punishing the animal with a quick swipe of one paw, then sat back to judge the results.

The dog went instantly mute.

Keeping a wary, worried gaze on Satan, the dog began slinking very slowly over to Sara, its gait awkward due to the missing leg. Satan blinked once in dismissal and curled up in the center of the floor to sleep.

Sara picked up the dog and smiled. "There, you see. They get along fine."

Gavin seemed to be considering her. He watched her for so long, she began to squirm, and finally her temper ignited. "Will you stop it?"

He lifted one brow. "Stop what?"

"Stop trying to dissect me. I brought home a dog. This is still my home, Gavin. I can do as I please."

It sounded like a challenge, a rather nasty one at that, even to her own ears. She was immediately contrite, but it put her on edge having him study her that way.

Gavin dropped his gaze to the floor and his hands went to his hips. She could see his chest rising and falling and knew he struggled to control his own temper. She almost wished the dog would start barking again. It was too damn quiet.

And then Gavin started toward her. She backed up two steps before she caught herself. He took the dog from her arms and set it on the floor. It wandered cautiously, creeping on its three legs, over to where Satan slept.

Gavin tugged her close to his chest. "I don't want to fight with you today, babe."

His voice had been so low, so husky, Sara blinked in confusion. What was he up to now?

He nuzzled her neck and she felt her annoyance melt like a chocolate bar in July. Her heart started galloping. He was such a sexy man, and it was so unfair of him to keep teasing her like this. When his hands settled on her back, then coasted down to her bottom, she sucked in a quick breath and shivered. "Gavin..."

"Shh. You're so tense, honey. Relax, will you?"

Relax? She couldn't possibly relax. Not when he was touching her. At the best of times he could arouse her with only a look, but touching, too? She tried to step away, but Gavin tightened his arms.

"I want you, Sara."

Her mouth fell open, then she leaned back to see his face. "What?"

"I want you. Now."

She continued to stare at him, disbelieving, her anger building to the boiling point, then suddenly detonating. "Of all the rotten, mean, underhanded..." She shoved him away, seeing his face go blank in surprise. "Have you looked at me, today? Well, have you? Do I look the least bit attractive?"

Both Gavin's brows shot up. "Well...yes, you do. You always look nice."

She leaned forward, jutting out her chin. "I'm *bloated,*" she growled in a near demonic tone, as intimidating as Satan ever hoped to be.

"Uh..."

"And at the moment," she continued, "I'm feeling especially mean."

Just as the dog had reacted to Satan, Gavin backed up, keeping a wary eye on Sara. "I...ah..."

"I wanted you yesterday, Gavin, but *noooo*. You wouldn't give in." She began stalking toward him, and he continued to back up. "I also wanted you last night. Jeez, I practically begged you. But you couldn't relent then, could you? Oh, no. But now today, oh sure, *now* you want to!"

Gavin stared at her as if she'd lost her mind. "Sara, what in the world is the matter with you?"

"I can't *today,* you ass."

Ignoring her insult, he asked carefully, "What do you mean, you can't?"

Her face felt hot already, but she didn't care. What a dirty trick. Offering himself when she couldn't accept. Lord, men could be so obtuse. "Think about it, Gavin. It'll come to you."

Her tone had been laced with so much sarcasm, he shouted in return. "Think about what? You're not making any sense. You said you wanted me, well, I want you, too. So what's the problem?"

"I wanted you last night. I'll want you again in a few days. But not until then."

Gavin went still, his frown clearing as understanding dawned, and then slowly, he began to grin. "You're on your period? That's what this is all about?"

Sara punched him in the shoulder. It hurt, like smacking her knuckles against a rock. "Don't you dare laugh at me!"

"Honey—" He reached out for her but she dodged away.

"And don't try to placate me. I'm not in my best of moods at this time of the month."

He bit his lip. "Yeah? I'd already guessed as much."

"Oh, this is so unfair!" she wailed, and the little dog jumped up and chimed in, throwing her head back and howling in a high-pitched, excited whine. Satan decided he'd had enough of all of them, and lifting his massive head, he let loose with a loud, commanding roar.

That was evidently all it took, because Gavin started laughing, and then he couldn't stop. He looked at Sara between his bursts of hilarity, met her outraged gaze, and fell against the wall, holding his sides, roaring every bit as loud as Satan.

Disgusted, Sara stomped from the room. If he was enjoying himself so much, he could just do it without her. She heard him struggling to control himself as she neared her bedroom, and right before she slammed her door shut, he said to the animals, "Now look what we've done. You guys better start thinking of a way to apologize, or we'll all be sleeping outside tonight."

Sara thought that wasn't a bad idea at all.

GAVIN GAVE HER FIFTEEN minutes to calm down. No more, because he was afraid she'd go to sleep again. And no less, because after all, he wasn't a complete fool, despite his recent conduct.

He opened the door without knocking, very cautiously peeked inside and saw Sara curled up on the mattress, holding her middle.

Gavin walked quietly into the room. "I fixed you some warm tea and a sandwich. The tea always helped my sisters."

Very slowly, Sara turned on the mattress to face him. "Needless to say, I feel like a fool again."

"Nope, not this time. It's my turn." After setting

the food on the nightstand, he reached out and touched her cheek. "I am sorry, babe. Here I was making grand plans for a day together, and you weren't feeling at all well. I should have realized."

She narrowed her eyes and stared at him. "Grand plans?"

"Never mind. How do you feel now?"

"Men aren't supposed to be understanding about this sort of thing, Gavin."

"Are you kidding? I've got three sisters, and believe me, they forced understanding down my throat until I choked on it. I had no choice at all."

Sara moaned and turned her face away. "This is too embarrassing."

"Don't be ridiculous." Gavin caught her shoulders and hauled her upright, plumping the pillows behind her. "Here, drink your tea." Gavin watched her sip carefully. She still blushed, but of course, she had no way of knowing how he enjoyed taking part in her womanliness.

He regretted like hell that they wouldn't be making love after all. He'd damn near worked himself into a frenzy just thinking about it. Then she'd showed up with that silly dog and he'd almost forgot what he wanted.

But maybe this would work out better.

He wanted to break through all her defenses, and this was a surefire way to get to sleep with her, without becoming sexually intimate. They could talk, and he could hold her, and he could show her how much she meant to him, how special she was.

She watched him over the rim of the teacup, and he smiled. "The animals seemed to be getting along. They actually started playing a little. That is, if you can call Satan chasing that little squirt playing. The dog didn't seemed frightened, though, even if Satan did sound a bit annoyed."

Sara picked up the plate with her sandwich on it and broke off a piece of the crust. "About the dog, Gavin..."

"Does she have a name?"

"I don't know. When Jess and Lou found her, she didn't have a collar."

"Maybe you should name her, then."

Sara hesitated, then bit her lip. He could see her mentally girding herself, and he anxiously waited to see what argument she would present.

"Gavin, I know I said a lot about this being my house, and I could do what I want, but I didn't mean to say I wouldn't take your feelings into consideration. I want you to be comfortable here."

He couldn't help smiling inside. This was the closest she'd come to admitting she wanted him to stick around.

"After I left today, I regretted losing my temper. I sort of thought you might decide it wasn't worth the convenience and be gone when I got home."

"I'm not going anywhere, babe."

She looked dubious. "It's not like me to be so

emotional, but—'' She stopped when he started grinning again. ''Despite what you think, Gavin, I am not an emotional woman. At least, not in the normal course of things.''

''I wasn't exactly a prince this morning, myself. I had planned to finesse you with my great cooking ability, but I couldn't get you out of bed. I ended up feeding your very excellent omelet to the damn cat. Then Satan needed brushing, and it turned into a much bigger chore than I'd intended.''

Sara looked very chagrined. ''You fixed me a special breakfast?''

He leaned forward and kissed her. ''Don't worry about it. Satan showed appropriate appreciation of my efforts.''

''I'm sure it was delicious.'' She peeked up at him, then sighed. ''No man has ever cooked me breakfast before.''

He'd be willing to bet no man had ever played hard to get with her before, either! He merely smiled.

A few minutes later she had finished the sandwich and was once again yawning. Gavin removed the plate from her lap and stretched out beside her. She sent him a horrified look.

''Come here. I'll make you feel better.''

''A man of many talents?'' She looked uncertain, but she did lay down beside him. Gavin moved her around until she was situated against his body, spoon fashion. He laid his large palm over her abdomen and began to gently rub her. Sara groaned.

"Feel good?"

"Mmm."

She nestled closer and Gavin had to bite back his own groan as her rounded buttocks rubbed against his groin. He kissed her on the side of her neck, then whispered, "Now that I'm here, you'll be able to rest more." It wasn't a very subtle hint, but it was true. She'd realize her good fortune if he had to point it out to her every damn day.

"I don't want to take advantage of you, Gavin."

Her voice edged toward sleep. Gavin kissed her again, hugged her a little tighter. "You can't use someone who's willing, honey. I want to be here, with you."

"And with the pets?"

"Yeah. Even with the damn pets."

Her sigh was soft and dreamy and a bit hopeful, then she said, "I've never known anyone like you, Gavin."

He was counting on that being the case, because he knew, even if she didn't, he had been a goddamn *saint!*

7

He had made remarkable headway reestablishing their friendship in only a week.

But still, Sara blanched at the idea of meeting his family. They were due to arrive this morning, and while he felt they still had plenty of time, he couldn't go back to sleep.

He'd come to the conclusion, sometime around the middle of the week, that he was most assuredly a man of steel. Only a superhero could have withstood the magnitude of denial he'd forced on his body.

He'd slept, in painful celibacy, with Sara every night.

In some ways it had been unbelievably erotic, holding her, whispering in the dark of the night, discussing the past and the present. He hadn't yet been able to get her to talk about a future. And the more he learned of her childhood, the more he understood.

That was why, even though Mother Nature no longer conspired against him, he hadn't taken that small step beyond holding her to making love to her. Their relationship became more concrete by the day, but it was still a delicate thing.

Several times Sara had tried taking the initiative, but he always managed to put her off. He wanted to hold out for a declaration of her feelings. He wanted marriage and commitment. He wanted her to buy the cow...er, bull.

But with every day, it got tougher to cling to his high convictions.

And though Sara certainly seemed to like and trust him more now, she was no closer to declaring herself than she had been when he first moved in.

Instead he continually suffered the agonies of unrequited lust, and he honestly didn't know how much more he could take.

Hopefully his family, with all their loyalty and unity and open friendliness would have an impact on her. He glanced at the clock again, and decided he might as well shower and get dressed. But he was loathe to leave the bed, to leave Sara. The effect she had on him was alarming and confusing and so damn sweet. No other woman could stir all his senses the way she did. She left him aching with lust and hurting with tenderness.

He heard a small sigh and glanced back at Sara. He caught her staring.

Trying for a cavalier facade to hide his emotions, he gave her a cocky grin and a wink. "Morning, sweetheart."

Dropping her gaze to his mouth, she reached up and touched one finger to his lips. "Gavin?"

Those slumberous eyes, that gentle touch, were his

undoing. Gavin groaned, then accepted her kiss when she leaned up and pressed herself anxiously to him. Her body was sleep-warm and womanly soft. The encouraging sounds she made were low and lazy, still ruled by her slow wakening. When she slipped one bare thigh over his legs he discovered her gown had gotten twisted up high during their sleep.

The week of sleeping together had taken a toll on both of them, so rather than pause to think about what he was doing, Gavin helped to settle her hips over his. Her arms wrapped around his head, her mouth ate at his, kissing him in a way that crumbled rational thought and any resistance. Though what she did was enough to drive any man crazy, there was an awkwardness to her movements that told him she hadn't taken the lead very often. He reveled in that fact.

"Sara, honey..."

"Gavin, please! I don't want to wait anymore."

She kissed his mouth again, seducing him, holding him still for her assault. She was brazen, voracious, and he loved it.

His hands smoothed down her spine to her backside, lush and firm. Growling, he pushed the tangled gown aside and cupped her, feeling the silkiness of her panties and the warmth of her flesh. His fingers probed.

Sara straightened her arms, her head thrown back, her hips pressed firmly into his. Even with her eyes closed, she appeared stunned, excited and so sexy he no longer thought of long-term plans or goals. She needed him now, and that was enough.

Switching their positions, Gavin pinned her beneath him then began his own seduction. He pulled the tiny buttons open on her gown, baring her breasts. Her nipples were taut and full, and he carefully closed his teeth around one, hearing her harsh groan, feeling the urgency of her hands as she sank her fingers into his hair.

He suckled and tugged, licked and teased. Sara moved beneath him, trying to wriggle out of the gown without breaking contact. She only managed to get it tangled around her belly, but her arms and legs were free. Gavin leaned back to look at her.

Flushed with need from her brows to the tips of her toes, she was a beautiful sight. Her small hands knotted in the sheets on either side of her hips, and her legs were slightly sprawled. He grasped a handful of the gown in each hand. "Raise your hips."

Within moments, she was naked, the gown and her panties tossed aside. Gavin wasn't given a chance to enjoy the sight before Sara had grabbed him again, tugging him back to her. He kissed her throat, the sensitive skin below her breasts, her belly. She arched into him, gasping.

Then he felt the cat leap onto the bed. Beside the bed, the dog began yapping, wanting to join the cat, but unable to manage it.

Gavin tried to nudge Satan away with his foot. The

beast thought it was a fine game, and swatted at his big toe. The dog howled for attention.

"Scat, dammit."

Sara moaned softly. "What?"

It was ironic enough to be funny, but when Satan bit his toe, and the dog began her infernal yapping at top volume, his amusement vanished. Grumbling and cursing, Gavin got to his feet, then met Sara's confused gaze. "Sorry. I need to put the cat and dog out."

"Oh." She scrambled for the covers, but Gavin caught her hands.

"No. Don't move. I swear, I'll be right back." Sara hesitated, then relaxed into the bed, giving Gavin an uncertain smile. After one more long, sweeping look at her body, he hauled the reluctant cat into his arms and left the room, the dog following in his wake.

He refused to think about his decision. Sara was ready, he was sure of it. So what if she hadn't told him she loved him, or even hinted that such a thing was possible? The fact they couldn't resist each other had to count for something. It would be a good bargaining tool for marriage.

The cat kept giving him quizzical looks, and Gavin felt compelled to explain. "Don't take it personal, big guy. You two just happen to have rotten timing, that's all." He sat the cat down and opened the front door. After hooking the dog to her lightweight chain and watching her run out, he turned to the cat. Satan stared back, refusing to budge. Again, Gavin nudged him with his foot. Satan only blinked.

Narrowing his eyes, Gavin murmured, "Now where did Sara put that bow...?" With a disdainful snarl, Satan sauntered out. Chuckling, Gavin was just about to close the door when his mother and father pulled up to the curb. Behind them was another car, and then another.

It looked as though the whole Blake family had arrived. Nieces and nephews began tumbling out the open car doors, and one of his sisters waved. Closing his eyes, Gavin silently went through every curse he knew. It didn't help one iota. Talk about rotten timing.

It took his mother only a moment to reach him, and then he was smothered in a hug. He looked over her shoulder to the end of the sidewalk and saw Satan suffering a similar fate, only it was a group of four children who gathered around the cat. The dog was thrilled with her share of attention, and barked in canine elation. His father and brothers-in-law were slower in leaving their cars.

It was a regular family get-together—not quite what he'd planned, and certainly not how he'd planned it. He cleared his throat when he heard Sara singing along with the radio, then watched as his mother looked in that direction.

"Your new lady friend?"

"Ah, yeah. Mom...we weren't exactly up yet."

"Well, no problem." She patted his shoulder, her

smile impish. "You two can go ahead and get ready while we unload a few things."

Gavin groaned. "Tell me you didn't."

"You know I can't come empty-handed, son. It wouldn't be right. Especially now that you've—"

Sara's voice, slightly outraged, interrupted. "Gavin! Don't you dare change your mind again. You started this, now come back here and finish it!"

Horrified, Gavin stared into his mother's wide eyes, then winced as Sara's voice rang down the hallway again. "You don't want to be accused of being a tease, now do you?"

His mother raised one brow, indicating where her son had gotten the habit, and Gavin could only be thankful the rest of the family hadn't heard. They were taking their time reaching the porch, stopping every so often to admire one of the newer houses being built on the street.

Gavin floundered. "She's, ah..."

"Impatient?" his mother supplied, deadpan.

He shook his head, then walked to the hallway. "Sara!" He had to shout to be heard over the radio. "My mother is here."

The radio snapped off, and after a moment of heavy stunned silence he heard the telltale sounds of Sara rushing around the room. She flew into the hall, wearing only a sheet.

"Sara!"

Running toward him, she yelled, "Don't let her in

until I get a pair of panties out of the…'' She came face-to-face with Gavin's mother. "Kitchen."

The rest of the family chose that propitious moment to step through the door. Gavin didn't know what to do, and his family, more silent than he'd ever heard the lot of them be, didn't help by simply staring.

Sara turned and let her head hit the wall with a dull thud.

Then his mother asked in a subdued tone, "She keeps her underclothes in the kitchen?''

SARA WANTED TO DIE. She thought, *If this were the Land of Oz, I could just sink beneath this sheet and melt away.* But it didn't happen. It was all well and good to plan a free-spirited affair with a gorgeous, virile man like Gavin, but it was quite another to have to face his mother—*his mother, for God's sake*—wrapped in nothing more than a sheet, the evidence of the affair plain for anyone to see. Only there wasn't an affair, dammit, not yet, because they'd interrupted. Hopefully his mother didn't know *that.*

She felt more than embarrassed, she felt…guilty, and she wouldn't tolerate it. She was a grown woman, and she could darn well do as she pleased.

She sucked in a deep breath, plastered a serene smile on her face, then turned to face the fascinated masses.

Jeez, there were a lot of them.

A dozen sets of eyes were trained on her. She lifted her chin and said a very proper, "Excuse me," then strolled down the hall to disappear into her bedroom. A minute later, Gavin joined her.

She stood with her back facing the door, staring out a window, but she knew it was him. He didn't say anything, and finally she turned to look at him. He leaned against the closed door, his arms crossed over his chest, a pair of her panties dangling from his right hand.

Without a word, Gavin held them out to her.

Sara closed her eyes. "Why am I always being humiliated around you?"

He didn't answer. Sara supposed that was because there wasn't an answer. When she opened her eyes, Gavin was still watching her, and still holding the panties out. She walked toward him, but when she would have taken them from his hand, he caught her wrist instead and pulled her close.

"I'm sorry."

Struggling against him for a mere instant, then giving up, Sara said, "There's no reason to apologize. It wasn't your fault."

"I started things this morning, when I knew my family was coming. And I'm the one who invited them here in the first place."

"No, I started things." Then she peered up at him, giving him a weak smile. "And we both forgot they were coming."

"True enough." He tugged her closer and bent to kiss her neck. "You make me forget everything."

"I can't face them, Gavin."

"Of course you can." He framed her head with his palms and forced her to meet his gaze. "My family loves me, and that means they'll love you, too. No matter what. You have nothing to be embarrassed about."

Pressing her forehead to his chest, she groaned. She didn't understand him, or his reasoning. Surely his family wouldn't care about her just by association. "What did they think when you got my underwear?"

"I explained. It was no big deal."

"But they're all still laughing, right?"

"Naw. If I know my sisters, they're probably figuring some way to blame me entirely, while working up a good dose of sympathy for you."

"Why would they blame you?"

"Because I'm the baby brother, remember? They've always blamed me for everything."

Sara knew he was only distracting her, but she appreciated his efforts. "Even when you were innocent, I suppose."

"Of course. I got blamed the time Pam's bra ended up in the pool when she had her first boy-girl party. And Gina blamed me for scaring her boyfriend away one Halloween night." He said in an aside, "The guy was a real wimp."

"And what about your other sister?"

"Carol and I are closest in age. She just blames me for stealing all her girlfriends away."

"And did you?"

He shrugged. "I let them steal me away a couple

of times." Then he chuckled. "But I never let any of them keep me for long."

"Maybe that's what Carol objected to."

"Yeah. They wouldn't come around her again after that."

"They were embarrassed. I can understand how they felt."

Gavin kissed her ear this time. "I'm letting you keep me, remember?" Then he added in a rush, "Besides, you're made of sterner stuff than they were. You're an iron woman. Shoot, I still remember the way you swung that rake..."

"Stop it, Gavin." But she was grinning. "All right. I suppose I can face them. But it won't be easy."

"You don't know my family."

Five minutes later, Sara discovered Gavin was right. He made the introductions with haste, barely giving Sara time to acknowledge each person.

"My oldest—nay, ancient, sister Pam, and her very brave husband, Gary. The two little rug rats who look alike are their six-year-old twins, Stevie and Stephanie. Then there's Gina, who's very obviously pregnant again, and her stallion of a husband, Sam." The other men cheered Sam and his potency in high good humor. Sara laughed with them. "The curly-headed seven-year-old is their son, Chris. And last is Carol, only two years older than me. She's married to Roy, and they have the little redheaded girl, Laurel, who's four. And standing in the corner, smiling at me like

I was still twelve, is my mom, Nora. The guy shaking his head—he does that a lot—is my dad, Hank.''

There was no mention of her earlier entrance, and his sisters appeared to accept her easily enough. They weren't the kind to crowd a person, but they were open and accepting and as ready to grin as Gavin always seemed to be.

The brothers-in-law appeared devoted to their wives, attentive and loving. And the children were a boisterous handful. It was interesting for Sara to see the way they all seemed to work as a family. There was no real dissension, but the jokes and teasing were constant. Gina was especially tended to, her husband barely leaving her side, and Sara realized it was because the woman was pregnant. Sam strutted around her like the typical proud papa-to-be, never letting her out of his sight.

Sara knew it would take her a while to get all the names straight, but she found she was already looking forward to it.

Having Satan and the dog, which the kids lovingly named Tripod, gave her instant popularity with the children. And the animals seemed to wallow in their attention. Sara gave the kids a cat brush, and before long, Satan writhed on the ground in blissful ecstasy while they attempted to groom him. She saw the children chasing Tripod around a tree, but moments later they circled back, and Tripod had changed from the pursued to the pursuer. The kids squealed in playful excitement, and Sara could have sworn there was a smile on the little dog's furry face and a look of sheer rapture in her brown eyes as she flashed past.

"They're wonderful animals. How long have you had them?"

Sara turned to Gavin's mother. Nora was the kind of woman who never aged. Though there were lines on her face, and a few gray hairs mingling in with the dark, she was still attractive and still energetic. She made the perfect counterpoint to her Hank, who seemed an older version of Gavin. Both father and son shared a similar height and strength of build.

"I got them both from the shelter about a week ago. I knew the dog was wild, but I didn't think Satan was still this frisky." They both watched as the cat began chasing the dog and the kids.

"Cats are like men, honey. They never stop being frisky."

Sara chuckled, thinking of Gavin. "Amen to that." Then she caught herself, remembering that it was his mother she spoke to. Heat climbed up her neck. "Ah, I don't…"

"You're still embarrassed, aren't you? Please, don't be. We're all just so happy to see Gavin happy. Not that I ever doubted he would be. He's a hedonist by nature. Always has been. But his idea of happy and ours is very different."

Feeling uncertain, Sara said, "You want him to settle down?"

"Gavin told you? Never mind. Of course he did." Nora looked across the yard to where Gavin stood, tweaking his sister's hair, then dodging away from her playful slaps. "I was nothing short of shocked when he called to say he'd moved in with a woman."

Sara chewed her lip. Nora didn't exactly sound disapproving, but still... "He's lived with women before," Sara pointed out, subtly defending their living arrangements.

"Yes, but he never called to alert me to the situation, or to tell me about the woman he was living with." She turned and smiled at Sara. "This is different. You're different."

Yeah, right. Gavin isn't sleeping with me. But no sooner had she formed the thought, she had to shake her head. Sleep, yes. Sex, no. But that might have changed if the Blake family had arrived an hour later. Gavin had definitely been ready to give in. And she was more than ready for the momentous occasion. Past ready. Desperate. On the verge of... Ah, but there was still the coming night, and Sara intended to force the issue, if it proved necessary.

"Great news, Sara." Gavin sauntered up, interrupting her thoughts with a warm kiss to her lips. Her gaze darted to his mother, who stood there wearing an indulgent smile for her only son. "The guys are going to help me move the rest of my stuff down here."

"The rest of your stuff?" She knew what that meant, but she could still hope.

"Yeah. My bed and dresser."

Her hope died. Gavin grinned at her crestfallen

look, then gave her another kiss. "We'll be back in a few minutes."

Disappointment changed to chagrin when she caught his mother's amusement. Good grief. Fumbling through her explanations, Sara said, "He, ah…"

Nora waved away Sara's concerns. "I know my son very well, Sara. He's a rascal. Don't let it bother you." Then she added, "What do your parents think of your house?"

"They haven't seen it."

Nora merely blinked. "Oh?" But it was a very maternal inquiry, and Sara found herself drawn in.

"We're not really…close."

"Oh, that's too bad. They live far away?"

"No." There was something about Nora that invited confidence. Her questions were genuine, prompted by concern, not idle curiosity. Sara bit her lip, then blurted, "My parents live close, but they're not really interested in me or what I'm doing."

Nora studied Sara's face for a moment, then she shook her head. "Sometimes parents do the dumbest things. But you know, it's only because we're human. I can't tell you the number of mistakes I made with my children. Why, you could fill the Taj Mahal with my goofs."

Sara did a double take. "Gavin told me he had a wonderful childhood!"

"Oh, I'm sure he did. Still, there were plenty of times when he thought I was picking on him. All the kids have accused me of having a favorite, or treating them unfairly at one time or another. That's all part of being a child, I suppose. Kids view the world through a narrow lens, never noticing all the outlying problems that parents might have to deal with. Their feelings get hurt, and they think we don't care, when actually, we didn't even realize how they were feeling.''

Sara thought of her parents' divorce, and how distracted they both became after that. Then she shook her head. ''I understand what you're saying, Mrs. Blake. But my parents really didn't care.''

''I can't believe that. No, you're a very nice girl, and children seldom get to be that way without some love and guidance.''

The grin tugged at her lips, but Sara held it back. ''What makes you so certain I'm a nice girl?''

''Gavin's with you, isn't he? And even though I have to admit to making mistakes, I know I didn't raise any dummies.'' She softened those words by asking, ''Have you ever told your parents how you feel?''

''Well…no. There would be no point to it.''

''Have you called them and invited them over? Do you try to go see them?''

Again, all Sara could do was shake her head.

''You know, honey, they could be thinking back on the past, seeing things now that they couldn't see then, and wondering if you could possibly still love them.'' Nora patted her cheek. ''I have no idea what problems you had with your parents, but why don't you think about it? And remember that nobody's perfect, parents least of all.''

Sara remembered those words the rest of the day. They kept coming back to her, over and over again. She realized she wanted to believe there might be some chance. She wanted the kind of relationship she'd just witnessed between Gavin and his family. That would be stretching it a bit, but perhaps there would be something, some closeness, to work with if she only initiated it.

She understood now why Gavin was so special, so understanding and accepting and confident. And seeing all that only made her want him more.

GAVIN HELPED BUCKLE his youngest niece into her car seat, then allowed her to give him a wet smacking kiss on his cheek. Carol stood on the sidewalk, saying her final goodbyes to Sara. Being closest in age, the two of them had really hit it off, and Gavin knew Carol would come calling again. All in all, he was pleased with the way Sara had been accepted.

His family had spent most of the afternoon with them, and each of his sisters had taken a turn grilling Sara for information. But Sara hadn't seemed uncomfortable with them. In fact, he'd seen her laughing out loud several times.

Lunch had consisted of takeout chicken, and they'd eaten picnic style on the back lawn. Satan had wandered from person to person, glutting himself on tidbits of food, then amusing everyone with his dexterity as he faced a mock battle with a chunk of chicken. He rolled on the ground, throwing the food in the air and then swatting it around. For a while there, it had seemed the chicken might actually win, but in the end, Satan proved the victor.

Tripod was just the opposite. She found a lap and refused to leave it. She was pampered and petted and hand-fed until Gavin feared she might pop.

When Sara had apologized for not having any lawn furniture, Gavin saw his mother's eyes light up and knew some would be arriving soon. He wondered how Sara would receive the gift, if she'd understand the spirit in which it was given.

The cars began driving away in a loud farewell ceremony of honking horns and cheerful children and waving hands. Carol embraced Sara, who looked somewhat startled by the gesture, but she returned the hug. Then Carol came to the curb with Gavin.

"Don't blow this one, brother."

Gavin grinned. "I don't intend to."

"Ah. So it is like that. Mom said so, but I wasn't sure."

Gavin looked back at Sara. She stood on the sidewalk, watching him and Carol. She was keeping herself apart, he realized. She refused to accept all of him. He hated it.

Smacking Carol's backside, he said, "Go on and get out of here. I have things to do."

"Uh-huh. In that big king-size bed you had Roy help you move?"

"Despite being married and a mother, you're too young to know about such things."

Carol merely snorted, then climbed into the car. She waved to Sara and Gavin as Roy pulled away from the curb.

When Gavin reached Sara's side again, she said, "Your sister is nice."

"Carol? She's a pain in the ass, but I love her." He put his arm around Sara's shoulders and started her toward the house. "So what about the rest of my family? Did they overwhelm you?"

"Of course. But then, you knew they would."

They passed the animals lying beneath a tree. Satan was sprawled on his back, his mouth open, snoring loud enough to scare away every bird in a five-mile radius. Tripod had her head resting on his belly. She watched lazily as the humans walked by, but didn't bother to follow. Gavin chuckled. "They look pooped."

"I think they both had more fun today than they're used to."

"And what about you?" They had reached the porch, and Gavin urged her up the steps. "Did you have fun?"

They stopped in the doorway. Sunlight slanted over the porch, diffused through the thick leaves of the tree Satan rested beneath. Gavin still had his arm around her shoulders, and he felt as much as saw her small shrug.

"Sara?" He felt concern, wondering for the first

time if he'd done the right thing by bringing his family around so soon. It had seemed a perfect gambit, a way to prove to Sara that happy marriages did exist, that families could and should be a wonderful thing. But now, he wasn't so sure.

Sara took a small step toward him and he automatically put his arms around her, giving her comfort if that was what she needed. Maybe his plans had backfired. Maybe his family had only reminded her of what she didn't have, of how little her parents supposedly cared.

Hugging her tighter, feeling her body pressed to his from knees to chest, he stroked her hair. "What's wrong, honey? Did someone say or do something to upset you?"

She nodded, and Gavin felt his stomach tighten. "Tell me what happened." If one of his sisters had said something stupid to upset her, he'd...

"It was the men."

"My brothers-in-law?" Now that surprised him. They were all such laid-back, easygoing guys. He couldn't imagine them treating Sara with anything less than friendly respect. It had to be a misunderstanding. He cupped her chin, then tipped her head back so he could see her face. She wore the most wicked smile he'd ever seen on a woman.

"Your family is wonderful, Gavin. But I didn't appreciate the men fetching your bed. I hope you weren't actually planning on using it, because I'll have to say right now, up-front, I won't stand for it."

God, she was good. How any woman could look so innocent while she blatantly seduced a man was beyond him. Her cheeks were pink, but her eyes were direct, proving she didn't intend to back down.

That suited Gavin just fine.

"I wanted you to have a choice, babe." He searched her face, trying to read her expressions. He needed her to understand, to know how important this was to him. Sara wasn't just another convenient woman, she was *his* woman. Forever. "I didn't want you to make love with me just because circumstances had thrown us together."

"Circumstances didn't throw us together, you threw us together."

"I, uh, it wasn't exactly like that."

"Then why do you insist on sleeping with me every night?"

He ran a hand through his hair in vexation, then tried again to explain. "Because I wanted you to want me. But I don't want you to do something you'll regret later, and—"

"Gavin? Shut up." She went up on tiptoe to kiss him, and his lungs shut down. He was already hard, had been hard since she'd mentioned the damn bed, and the feel of her soft body shifting against his as her warm tongue stroked into his mouth nearly buckled his knees.

Pulling away a scant inch, she drew a deep, shaky breath, then swallowed. Her eyes still held his, and her tone was a husky, warning growl. "The only regrets will be yours when I murder you for being a tease. Please. Make love to me.''

Gavin stared a moment, stunned by her blunt plea. ''Now?'' *Please, let her mean now.*

Without looking away, Sara slammed and locked the front door. ''Right now.''

His breath left him in a loud whoosh. He trembled. He shifted. He grinned. ''Okay, woman, you've convinced me.'' Gavin grabbed her hand and started down the hall at a trot.

And as he tugged her down onto the bed, his body covering her, she groaned in relief. ''It's about time.''

8

SARA CURLED INTO GAVIN, feeling his heat, his hardness. His mouth was hungry on hers, his breath coming fast and uneven. His hands seemed to be everywhere at once, but it wasn't enough. She clutched at his back, holding on as he rolled on the bed, positioning her firmly beneath him, working himself between her thighs, thrusting against her.

His hands slid down to her hips and his fingers dug into her flesh. He panted in excitement. "I'm sorry, Sara. Too fast."

"No!" She was so afraid he'd draw back, quit again, that she wrapped her legs around him. "Stay with me, Gavin."

"Oh, I intend to." But he pried himself loose, pinning her arms over her head and levering himself upward. "We have to slow down. I don't have any protection in here and…" His head fell forward and he groaned.

"Gavin?"

"Don't move, sweetheart. I swear. This time I'll be right back. Don't you dare move." He shoved himself off the bed and jogged out of the room.

Sara lay there staring at the ceiling. One. Two. Three. Four... Gavin was back. He set a box of condoms on the nightstand then turned to look at her. She remained perfectly still.

Fascinated, she watched his gaze going over her from her tangled hair to her feet. One of her sandals had fallen off, the other dangled from her toes. They had taken turns showering after his family arrived, and they were both dressed casually in shorts and T-shirts, but now Sara's shirt bunched up beneath her breasts and her shorts were unsnapped.

Gavin knelt on the bed, one large, hot hand coming to rest on her bare midriff. He stroked her, his hand trembling, his nostrils flaring as he struggled for breath. When he began slowly lowering her zipper, she brought her hands down to help him.

"No." Gavin caught her wrists and returned her arms to rest over her head. "Don't move. I mean it, Sara. You move and I'm done for."

"I can't just..."

"Yes, you can." He sounded very positive. Then he caught her T-shirt and pulled it up until he could twist it around her wrists. He held it there with one hand while he deftly unhooked the front closure on her bra. The material parted and her breasts were exposed, her nipples tight, a light flush heating her skin.

Gavin stared, then closed his eyes with a guttural groan. "Don't move."

"You already said that."

"I know."

He went back to her shorts and Sara, though more excited than she'd ever thought imaginable, had to fight her embarrassment. "I had no idea you were so kinky, Gavin."

"This isn't kinky, babe. It's survival. I've wanted you for so damn long I can't remember not wanting you. And I've been disgustingly celibate for too many months. I'm working on a hair-trigger libido here. One wrong move, and..."

Stunned by his admission, Sara forgot to be embarrassed as he stripped her shorts down her legs and removed her one remaining sandal. She hadn't been with anyone, but then, there was no one she'd wanted. She'd never considered that Gavin had remained alone, too, since his breakup. She was amazed, and for the first time, she started to believe how much he might care for her. It seemed *un*believable, but also undeniable.

He traced his finger along the edge of her silky panties. Her breath constricted, her stomach muscles tightened. "Gavin? You've...you've really been celibate?"

"As chaste as a schoolgirl." His hot, intense gaze swept up her body, then settled on her face. "I didn't want anyone but you. Even before I broke things off with Karen, I was waiting for you. Just you, Sara."

Sara smiled, feeling oddly touched. She didn't know what to say, so she mumbled, "That's so sweet."

Gavin wasn't amused. He yanked her panties

down, causing Sara to yelp. But before she could move he was over her, his mouth covering hers again, his tongue sliding in, hot and wet. His large palm smoothed over her breasts, pausing to lightly abrade her peaked nipples, then coasting down her belly and cupping over her mound.

"This is sweet, Sara." His fingers pushed inside her and she groaned. "Oh, yeah, very sweet."

For long, agonizing minutes Gavin tormented her. He wouldn't let her touch him at all, and that frustrated her. But how could she protest while he was making her squirm and beg and pant?

Gavin's mouth slid over her throat to her shoulder and then to her breast. He gently sucked her taut nipple into the heat of his mouth, and Sara felt her entire body clench. His fingers were still stroking over her, inside her, and she felt a wave of sizzling sensation begin. She fought it, but Gavin was relentless.

"Yes, honey." His tone was low and guttural, insistent. "Don't fight me, Sara. Not now."

Since she seemed to have very little choice in the matter, Sara gave in. Her climax was blinding, and she arched and twisted, hearing in the back of her mind all the soft, sultry words Gavin uttered to encourage her.

Limp, Sara was only vaguely aware of Gavin standing beside the bed removing his clothes. She opened her eyes a crack and surveyed his body. "That wasn't fair."

"Who ever told you love was fair?"

Love? Her heart skipped a beat and her emotions shattered. She didn't know if it was hope or fear or relief she felt, and since Gavin continued disrobing, she decided not to dwell on it. More than likely, it amounted to mere pillow talk. She wasn't overly familiar with the type of conversation appropriate at such a cataclysmic time.

Gavin's body demanded her attention, and her eyes widened as he shucked his shorts down his legs, taking off his underwear at the same time. She was sated, but she'd have to be dead not to be moved by such a sight. He was strong and powerful and pulsing with arousal. She could have looked at him all day and been deliriously happy. But Gavin wasn't very accommodating. He faced her, his hands fisted at his sides, and gave her only a scant second to soak in the sight of his nude perfection before he climbed back into bed with her and reached for the condoms.

"Let me," Sara said.

But Gavin gave her a horrified look. "Not on your life. I'd never live through it."

"I wouldn't hurt you."

"No, you'd kill me." She frowned and he added, "I mean it, Sara. You keep those little hands to yourself. Maybe later, after the box is nearly empty, I'll let you play touchy-feely. But not right now."

He seemed so serious, she couldn't help but chuckle. "So you can play, but I can't?"

"Damn right." He slid the condom on, then turned

toward her. "I'm sorry, babe, but I'm short on control right now."

"Then I'll hold you to your promise of later. Because I really am looking forward to touching you, Gavin."

His expression stilled with her words, his chest heaving, his jaw tight, then he growled suddenly, "Dammit!" And Sara knew she'd said too much.

She loved his loss of control. Gavin was like a wild man, starving for her. And here she'd thought he didn't want her! Ha! She had wasted a lot of time, she decided.

But then she couldn't think anymore. Gavin pulled her legs apart and said in a rough whisper, "Please tell me you're ready for me," and before she could answer, he pushed inside.

Frantically she tried to remind herself that sex was just sex, not love. But it didn't seem that way now. Not with Gavin staring down at her, his eyes so hot and filled with bursting emotion, his fingers twined with her own, gripping her, almost painful in their urgency.

"Sara," he breathed, and began to move.

Unbelievable the way the tension built again so soon. She cried out, but Gavin kissed her, his tongue deep in her mouth muffling the sound. When he came, he threw his head back and yelled like a crazy man. Sara touched him everywhere she could reach, stroking, kneading, then as he gave a great shudder she looked at his face and felt her own raging orgasm.

Very slowly, Gavin sank down onto her. She felt the harsh pounding of his heart against her breasts, felt his breath gusting against her sweat-damp skin as he tried to regulate his breathing. She was amazed. She was stunned.

Calm, confident, even-tempered Gavin was a wild man. Sara closed her eyes and hugged him close. She loved it.

MORNING SUN CAUSED his eyelids to twitch, and very warily, Gavin peered over at Sara. She was asleep, thank God. He felt numb all over, especially weak in the legs, and he wasn't certain he could do more than manage a shallow breath.

He'd planned, for so damn long, to make love with Sara and overwhelm her with his touted finesse.

Instead she'd damn near killed him.

She'd taken him seriously when he'd carried in the box of condoms. There couldn't be many left, probably only the ones he'd thrown beneath the bed, hiding them from her so she'd give him some rest. The little witch had been voracious. She certainly had more faith in his stamina than was warranted.

Many times he'd drifted into a deep sleep, only to jerk awake moments later, already hard, with her small hand stroking him or her mouth teasing him, or... But it had been wonderful. Exhausting, but wonderful. He muttered a quiet curse when he realized he was hard yet again.

He glanced at Sara's sprawled body and knew escape to be his only option. He had an hour before he needed to be on a job, and Sara had to go into work today, too. He sincerely hoped she had more energy than he did. His knees shook when he stood.

Satan and Tripod came together to the bedroom door when Gavin started out. The two pets had made a vicious ruckus last night when he and Sara had forgotten to let them back in. It had been the only reprieve Sara had given him, allowing him to feed the animals in the kitchen. But once that was done, Gavin found himself dragged back to the bedroom.

He grinned and shook his head. It hadn't taken Sara long at all to lose her inhibitions, and she was a glorious sight when she became demanding. He'd gladly play her sex slave again, just as soon as he had recuperated.

Picking up Satan and whistling softly to Tripod, he tiptoed out of the bedroom and into the hall, silently closing the door behind him. After giving the cat a few affectionate pats and rubbing Tripod behind the ears, he went into the bathroom to shower. He had just finished washing and was leaning back against the cool ceramic tile when the shower curtain opened and Sara stepped in. He gawked.

Sara slanted him a disgusted look, then stepped under the water. "Forget it, Gavin. I'm zonked."

Seeing that he was safe enough, he gave in to the urge to grin. She really did look exhausted, poor thing. He couldn't resist teasing her. "First wine, and now sex. You really do have this thing about over-indulging, don't you?''

She pushed wet hair out of her face and glared at him. "Me? You're the one who wouldn't stop—"

"Oh, no, you don't. I was asleep, woman, and you—"

"You said I could touch you! But every single time I bumped you during the night you turned into a sex-crazed maniac!"

His fatigue miraculously disappeared while he watched the water sluice down her naked body. He picked up the soap and idly began working up a lather. "You have a way of *bumping* that sets a man off."

"*Everything* sets you off!"

"Well, what did you expect? I'd been deprived for too long. If you hadn't been so insistent on waiting…"

"Me!"

"Hush. Let me wash your back."

His hands went around her, then settled on her slick, wet skin. They smoothed over her shoulders, down the length of her spine, then lower. Sara said, "Gavin! That is not my back."

"That's okay." He kissed her throat, licking off a drop of water. "I dropped the soap anyway."

"Gavin…" Her voice dwindled to a throaty, demanding moan.

Twenty minutes later, they were both running late. Gavin finished dressing first, and he stopped on his way out the door to kiss Sara goodbye. She sat at the kitchen table, only half-dressed, still nursing a cup of coffee, and she barely managed a pucker.

He chuckled to himself as he headed for the office. He had papers to pick up, a few phone calls to make, he needed to meet the finishers at a house in less than an hour. His knees were shaky, his eyes burned from not enough sleep, and his heart felt full to bursting.

At this rate, Sara would cripple him within a week. But it was a week he anticipated with a good deal of excitement.

SHE WAS LATE, more than an hour and a half. Gavin was probably furious, since he had expected her home by six. Still, she sat in the car a few minutes longer, not opening the door, not looking at the house.

She heard the pitiful whining in the back seat and winced. Three pets was two more than Gavin had agreed to. Not that she felt she had to gain his permission for every little thing...but then, this wasn't a little thing. This was a very big thing. A very big, furry thing. With problems. *But what else could she have done?*

Sara saw the front door open, and then Gavin filled it. It was his habit to greet her at the front door each night after work, and she realized she'd already gotten used to it. He looked so good standing there, his hands on his hips, his brow furrowed in concern. He'd been worried about her? She hadn't considered that possibility. No one had worried about her in a very long time. He started down the steps, so she quickly came out of the car and met him on the sidewalk. She wrung her hands, trying to order her thoughts.

"Sara? What is it, what's the matter? Do you have any idea what time it is?"

His tone was sharp, a mixture of annoyance and worry. It was the first time he'd lost his temper with her since the day she'd brought home Tripod. She opened her mouth, ready to launch into her well-rehearsed explanations, and instead, she burst into tears. She was horrified by her own actions, but it had been such a horrendous afternoon.

Gavin grabbed her shoulders and shook her. "What the hell is the matter? Are you hurt? What happened?"

She shook her head, hiccuped, then tried again. "I'm sorry I'm late. I had to go by the shelter, and…Gavin, I have to tell you something."

He seemed to relax all at once. He pulled her close against his chest, and she didn't want to admit, even to herself, how wonderfully safe it felt. "Shh. Calm down, babe. Whatever it is, it'll be okay."

Then the sound of the sad, mournful whining reached their ears. Gavin froze for several heartbeats, then with a resigned sigh, he looked over her head to the car. Holding her shoulders, he pushed her back a ways to see her face. Sara bit her lip, knowing she looked guilty as sin, knowing she looked upset, but dammit all, there was nothing else she could have done. Gavin moved around her. Sara started talking ninety miles a minute. The problem was, she only had a fifty-mile-a-minute tongue, so most of what she said was garbled and nonsensical.

"It was the most terrible thing. Tragic. Just tragic. And so sad. You see, the old man died, and then the woman—his wife—just couldn't bear to go on without him, and she went into a decline. She's well over eighty, and she couldn't take care of herself, much less a dog. The family has its hands full looking after her, and the dog was simply wasting away. She misses everyone so much, and she's so unhappy. God, Gavin, I've never seen a more unhappy creature, and…"

Sara's explanation came to a screeching halt. Gavin opened the rear car door, shook his head, then began talking so softly, so calmly to the dog. When he lifted the collie out, holding her weight easily in his arms and started toward the house, Sara was speechless. She trotted after him.

"What are you doing?"

Gavin never slowed his pace. He crooned to the dog, but he turned his head enough to say, "She's upset. I'm taking her inside." The dog looked up at him, and Gavin asked, "What's her name?"

"Maggie."

He said the name, softly, slowly, making it sound like a compliment, and the dog stared at him as if captivated. Sara stepped through the doorway, holding the door for Gavin, and Satan and Tripod walked to her with rapt looks of curiosity. She took a brief moment to pat the animals, then rushed after Gavin. He took the dog to the kitchen and sat her on the floor by the sink, in the spot where the late-day sun coming through the window made a warm, golden pool on the tile.

Gavin knelt in front of Maggie, rubbing her laid-back ears. Maggie curled into a small semicircle, her entire countenance one of wary disbelief. "What's the matter, old girl? This is all pretty new, isn't it? But you're okay here."

His understanding, the gentle tone of his voice, brought on a fresh rush of tears. Sara felt her bottom lip begin to quiver and pulled it tightly between her teeth. Tripod sat back to watch the happenings from a distance, choosing to lean against Sara's leg. But Satan observed the situation with a jaundiced eye, then walked over and regally placed himself over Gavin's knee. The look he gave the dog was filled with possessive warning. Gavin chuckled, stroking the cat.

"Be nice now, Satan. You can see she's scared. Make her welcome."

Satan blinked, gave one of his rumbling, rusty purrs, and brushed against the dog. The dog's head snapped back as if startled, but Satan was relentless. Within moments, Maggie was splotched with Satan's yellow hair. But she didn't seem to mind, especially since Gavin was still petting her. Tripod moved closer and sniffed the dog, then flopped down beside her. She looked ready to go to sleep.

Sara sniffled, so touched by the scene she could barely keep her tears in check. Gavin heard the small sound and turned to her. ''Why don't you go take your bath, honey? I'll look after Maggie, get her settled down for the night. In the morning, she'll feel better.''

That did it. Sara wailed, covering her face with her hands. Only a second later, she felt Gavin pull her close. ''Shh. It's all right now.''

''I... I...know.'' She hiccuped, then made an effort to calm herself, but it was impossible. ''I didn't know what to do. When Jess called me at work to tell me about Maggie, I just had to go and see her for myself. She wouldn't eat and she kept whimpering and she...well, she was so alone. So scared. You can't imagine what that's like, Gavin.''

''Shh. It's all right now.''

''I just had to bring her home.''

''Of course you did. And now she'll feel loved again and everything will be fine.''

After a loud, disgusting sniff, Sara wiped her eyes with the back of her hand. It was then she realized the kitchen smelled of cooked chicken. She looked around and saw a variety of pots and pans on the stove, and the table was set, complete with a lit candle. Or at least, it had been lit some time ago. The wick had long since burned down. Oh, no. Gavin had cooked dinner and she'd missed it. Again. He'd wasted another special meal on her.

''I'm so sorry.'' She wiped her eyes again, trying

to rid herself of the insistent tears. She put her hands on his chest and looked up at him. "You went to all this trouble, and I wasn't even here in time to appreciate it."

After a long, intense look, Gavin glanced over his shoulder to where Maggie was allowing Satan to curl into her side. The dog gave a single, loving lick to the cat, leaving Satan's entire head damp and his fur ruffed in the wrong direction. Satan closed his eyes and rumbled a ragged purr. Tripod never stirred. Gavin turned back to Sara and kissed her. "I'd say you were doing something more important. And dinner isn't wasted. We can eat the chicken cold. In fact, take your bath and I'll set us up a picnic outside. The animals could use the night air."

Suddenly she couldn't breathe. Sara took a step back, appalled, frightened, amazed. It wasn't a slow awareness, but a burst of realization that nearly brought her to her knees. *She loved him.* She didn't want to, didn't want to set herself up for another disappointment, another hurt. But he gave her no choice, damn him. How could she not love a man who'd put the needs of an animal above his own?

The words felt choked as she forced them through her throat. "Why are you doing this?"

Gavin knelt again by Maggie's side and stroked along her back. This time the dog lifted her tail in a one-thump wag.

Gavin seemed to take an inordinate amount of time before answering. Finally he looked up, his expression blank of all emotion. "Did you really expect me to play the tyrant and demand you take the dog back? Only a real bastard would refuse to give that dog a little love. Ah, and you were late, too. Should I have thrown a tantrum because dinner was ruined? Would you have dealt better with that?"

Sara shook her head, even as she said, "I don't know."

"You don't know me. Yet you keep comparing me to Ted and your parents and every other person who ever let you down, and I don't mind telling you, it makes me mad as hell."

"I didn't—"

"Yes, you did. Why would you think I'd feel any less compassion for that dog than you do?"

"Because…" Sara swallowed. She drew in a ragged breath and started again. "Because you don't know what it means to be alone and scared and—" Her voice broke, but Gavin didn't make a move toward her. He continued to stroke the dog, and occasionally Satan when the cat demanded it. But his gaze never left her face, and through her tears, Sara saw his understanding. It was humiliating, because she had a feeling he knew her better than she knew herself.

"I'm going to go take my bath now."

Gavin nodded. "I'll get our dinner together. And Sara? When we're done eating, we're going to talk."

It sounded closer to a threat than a mere statement. Gavin watched her closely, as did Satan and Maggie.

Even Tripod managed to stir herself enough to give a quick glance. Sara felt outnumbered, and after a huge sigh, she nodded agreement.

As if relieved by Sara's decision, Maggie laid her head on Gavin's thigh. The dog no longer looked so cautious or forlorn. And Satan seemed to be taking the addition of yet another pet in stride. That is, until he stood up and decided to mark Gavin as his own territory in the time-honored tradition of all male animals. Gavin jumped to his feet, but not in time.

Sara realized she no longer felt like crying. In fact, she had to hold her mouth to stifle her laughter. She had just turned to leave the kitchen when she heard Gavin mutter, "I'll put ten bows on you, dammit! Do I *look* like a tree?"

9

FOR MOST OF HER LIFE, Sara had felt hollow. She hadn't realized that until now, when she felt ready to burst with an incredible wealth of emotion. She'd lived with emptiness so long, it was almost alarming to acknowledge the difference now. But feelings she'd never encountered before filled her, making her whole. She wanted to cry, she wanted to laugh.

She wanted to tell Gavin that she loved him.

But she didn't dare.

This was all too new and too fragile to put to the test so soon. As she sat through the dinner that Gavin had prepared, on the tablecloth he'd spread on the ground, she couldn't help but smile. He coddled Maggie, he calmed Tripod and he reassured Satan, all without thought. Simply because he was that kind of man—so different from any other person she'd ever known.

That, too, was frightening. How could a man like Gavin ever really care about her? She was so used to people turning away, or in Ted's case, running away. She wanted to surround herself with things that would be permanent. Like her house, her pets. But she couldn't make Gavin permanent. He would only stay if he chose to.

He looked up and caught her staring. She smiled, a sappy smile, she knew. Then she leaned over the food and kissed him. "Thank you."

He didn't question her sudden gratitude, or want an explanation for what she was thankful for. He merely nodded. "You're welcome."

"You're too good to me."

Gavin shot her a look, growled low enough to startle all three animals, then hauled Sara over the food, scattering plates and chicken and knocking over drinks. She found herself facedown over his lap, with his hand hovering over her backside.

"Gavin! What in the world…"

"What did you say, Sara?"

"Uh…" She wasn't certain what had prompted this barbarian mood of his, so she didn't know how to answer. But she did giggle.

His palm thwacked lightly on her upturned derriere. She tried, but couldn't quite stifle another giggle.

"That was what I wanted to talk to you about."

"My backside?"

"No, this damn habit you have of thinking I'm being too good to you."

"Oh." Her tone softened. "You really are— Ouch!"

"Did that sting?"

"You don't sound the least bit remorseful." She

tried to rub her bottom, but he caught her hands and held them away.

"I'm not remorseful. Now let's try this again. Repeat after me."

"Yes, sir." She started to giggle again. She doubted, in her present mood and her newly acknowledged love, that Gavin could do anything to dampen her spirits or make her angry.

"Say, I deserve the very best there is."

"You are that, Gavin."

"My palm is itching, Sara. I think I may have a propensity for this type of thing. Don't tempt me."

"I deserve the very best."

"Much better." He began to massage her bottom. "Now say, I will stop keeping track of every nice thing Gavin does and accept his affection without remorse."

His roving, caressing hand made speech difficult. Sara squirmed over his knees. "Yeah, what you said."

"I want you to be happy, Sara."

All the teasing had gone out of his tone. When she tried to turn over, he helped her until she was cradled in his arms. She kissed his chin, his cheek. "I *am* happy. Very happy." She kissed his mouth, and the next thing she knew, she was lying on her back on the soft grass, with Gavin's weight pressing into her.

"You make me happy, too, babe. Believe that, will you?"

She didn't answer him. He didn't give her a chance to.

HE WAS READY TO KILL HER.

One animal had been enough. Two, he could have tolerated. Even three, given the circumstances, he'd have handled just fine. But five? He stared at the old, shivering poodle she held in her arms and felt his temper ready to snap.

"What's the matter with this one?"

Sara flinched slightly, and she had a little trouble meeting his direct gaze, but she finally muttered, "He's deaf."

Deaf. A deaf poodle. Just ducky. "Sara, I thought we agreed after the last dog—"

"I had to bring Melon home! No one would have wanted a pregnant dog. After she has her puppies, we'll find a home for them."

"And for this…this decrepit old soul? You know you won't want to part with any of them, Sara."

She hugged the poodle closer to her chest. "It's a good thing he can't hear you. And he's not decrepit. Just a little…"

"Ancient? Hell, I see gray hairs on him."

"That's the natural color of his coat."

"Yeah, right. What about his double chin? I swear, I've never seen a dog with a double chin before."

"He needs to be treated gently."

That was the thing about Sara. She seemed to have taken his words to heart two weeks ago. She was more relaxed around him, more accepting of him. But she still wanted to save every single animal that came into the shelter. Luckily the backyard held up, but they had to take regular duty with the scooper twice a day, and the pet-food bill grew daily. Gavin honestly hated to stem her enthusiasm for helping the animals, but enough was enough.

"Sara, this is not a halfway house for socially challenged animals. The last two you brought home weren't at the shelter long enough to be adopted."

"Because I know whoever took them wouldn't have been as good to them as we are." The poodle lifted his grizzled head and gave Sara a slow lick on the chin. Gavin winced.

"Babe, listen to reason. When Melon has her pups we're going to be overrun with dogs. Poor Satan is liable to run away, Tripod will go into a nervous decline, Maggie will hide—"

He stopped abruptly when the poodle turned watery eyes in his direction, looking wounded to his very soul.

Dammit all.

He fought the inevitable for another three seconds, then stomped forward. "Here, give him to me. He's probably cold, even as warm as it is. I'll put him in on Maggie's blanket."

Sara's grateful smile wobbled. "Thank you."

Gavin managed to point an accusing finger, and his

frown was downright mean. "That's enough out of you, lady."

She took his warning to heart and turned away, but he still caught sight of her smile. She trusted him now. But she still hadn't told him she cared.

He was about at the end of his patience.

After getting all the animals settled, Gavin located Sara in the laundry room and announced he had work to do. "The finishers are still up at the house. I want to go check on them, make certain they're on schedule. Tomorrow we'll be getting a new shipment of drywall and now that three of the houses are almost complete, I don't want to fall behind."

"It will be strange having neighbors, won't it?"

Gavin grinned. He knew Sara liked having the street to themselves, but she was also extremely proud every time he sold a house. So far, all the lots had been taken, with plans for the house styles already chosen. Within a year, all the buildings would be complete, and the street would become a neighborhood. Maybe, Gavin thought, someone moving in would want a dog.

He gave Sara a quick kiss. "We'll eat out tonight, okay?"

"I could cook if you want."

"No." He hoped he hadn't sounded too anxious, but in truth, Sara's cooking was almost inedible. "We deserve a night out."

"All right. I'll have all the housework done before you get home."

She was always so eager to please him, working extra hard to uphold her end of their bargain of sharing the chores. He shook his head, knowing better than to argue with her again. She was adamant that she always do her share. She worked so hard at making the relationship work, but she never gave him what he really wanted—a declaration of love.

SARA HURRIED THROUGH the house, making certain everything was tidy, sparing herself enough time to get ready for dinner. She wanted to look extra nice tonight, since Gavin was taking her out. She did her best never to look frumpy around him, though there wasn't anything she could do about her hair, which would always have a tendency to go its own way, regardless of her coercion. Gavin had told her once that he liked it for that very reason.

She was dabbing on a touch of makeup when the doorbell rang and all four dogs began barking at once. She had to shove animals aside to reach the doorknob, and when she opened it, she wished she hadn't bothered.

Her ex-fiancé, Ted, stood on the front porch, his hands shoved into his pockets, a suave smile on his handsome face. She took two steps back.

Her simple movement jump-started the outraged barking. All the animals seemed to vie for the greatest show of bluster, growling and snarling and forcing the hair on their backs to stand up. All but the poodle, who couldn't get his hair to oblige. But he made up for it by taking small, snapping bites of the air very near to Ted's leg.

"What the hell! Where did you get all these creatures?"

Sara had her hands full trying to calm the animals. "These are my pets. Hush, dogs!" They ignored her. While they had each openly accepted Gavin, not a single one of them seemed inclined to allow Ted past the front door.

Except for Satan.

Satan just sat and watched from a padded chair arm, his round eyes unblinking, his expression suspicious.

Ted tried to shout over the noise. "I'd like to talk to you, honey."

"I'm not your honey." Sara made a grab for Maggie, who was behaving in a very un-Maggielike manner. She caught the dog's collar and began dragging her toward the kitchen, at the same time urging Tripod forward with the edge of her shoe. Ted stepped inside and stared.

"My God. That dog's missing a leg."

She ignored him and whistled for Melon, the only one of the bunch who would respond to such a command. The heavily pregnant animal lumbered behind, but she kept looking over her shoulder and growling at Ted. Since Melon was a singularly ugly bulldog, it was a sight to cause awe.

Ted called out, "The damn poodle is still threatening to bite me. Whistle for it."

"Won't do me any good," Sara yelled between bouts of barking. "He's deaf. Can't hear me anyway."

Ted stared at her in amazement. Then his expression suddenly softened. "My poor baby."

Sara closed the low gate to the kitchen and admonished the dogs to quiet down. Gavin had purchased the spring-action gate after having a night with Sara interrupted. Tripod and Maggie had decided to sleep with them, and Satan, of course, had refused to be left out. In truth, Sara wondered if Satan might not have led the troop.

She picked up the poodle and set him gently over the gate then turned back to Ted. "Now, what exactly did you need, Ted?"

He maintained his tender expression and pronounced, "You. I need you, Sara. And obviously you need me, too."

Sara stared. "What in the world are you blathering about?"

"It's plain to see, sweetheart." He shook his head in a pitying way and smiled again. "You're surrounding yourself by these pathetic creatures because you miss me. You need to be loved."

Sara felt as if someone had poleaxed her. *She*

needed to be loved? It wasn't just permanency she craved? No, of course not. She did want to be loved. She wanted that so desperately, she'd been afraid to admit it, even to herself. She'd been doubly afraid to admit it to Gavin.

Then she stiffened her spine. No more. She wouldn't remain a coward. She loved Gavin and he deserved the truth, despite what his reaction might be. If he didn't care enough about her, if he couldn't learn to love her, then he might want to go now before her feelings began to suffocate him.

Sara paced. How to tell him? She couldn't very well just blurt it out...

Ted cleared his throat. "Sara?"

She glanced up, surprised to see Ted still standing there. He moved closer, and all the animals were quiet, as if waiting. Sara blinked at him in question.

"I'm sorry I hurt you, sweetheart. It was never my intention."

"No? That's strange. Did you honestly think I would appreciate having my fiancé in my bed with my neighbor's girlfriend?"

Ted made a *tsking* sound. "It wasn't exactly like that, Sara. I just got carried away. We both did. But we realize now what we might have thrown away by acting so—"

"We?" Sara felt her insides freeze, her lungs constrict. Ted took a step closer. Satan made an agile leap from the chair and sauntered slowly toward them.

"Karen and I." Ted glanced at the cat, then back to Sara's face. "I want to make it up to you, Sara. I want to come back to you."

A bubble of laughter took her by surprise. "That's absurd." She flapped her hand, dismissing the mere suggestion of such a ridiculous thing, then asked, "Did you say, Karen? She's here?"

"Yes, of course." This obviously wasn't going the way Ted had intended. "Listen to me, Sara. We can make a go of things. I'm ready now."

"I'm not." She forcibly kept her tone one of polite inquiry. "Where, exactly, is Karen?"

He heaved an impatient breath. "She went up to the empty house that worker boyfriend of hers is at. She saw him go inside the garage just as we turned on the street. She's hoping to patch things up with him."

Sara felt every protective, possessive instinct she owned come slamming to the surface. Karen with Gavin? Beautiful, tall, sexy Karen. Good grief.

She started to move around Ted, her steps anxious. "Excuse me, I have to go."

Ted turned, startled. "Go where?"

"After Gavin."

"Who the hell is Gavin?"

"The man you'll never be. Let yourself out, will you?"

"Now, wait a damn minute!"

With his raised tone, all the dogs howled in outrage. They leaned against the gate, snarling and yapping and doing their best to get through. Sara tried to ignore them all; her only thought was to get to Gavin and tell him her feelings before Karen had a chance to work on him. Not that she didn't trust Gavin, but this was too important to leave to chance.

But then Ted stupidly grabbed her arm to halt her exit, and all hell broke loose.

Satan roared out the most ferocious, menacing, hair-raising growl Sara had ever heard from him, and the gate in the kitchen collapsed from the combined weights of four enraged dogs. Ted flew from the house, high-pitched screams of fright signaling his terror. The animals took off in furious pursuit, Satan leading the way.

Sara watched it all in mingled amazement and horror, then she remembered Gavin. And Karen. And her love.

She thundered after the group, every step echoing her resolve.

GAVIN DID HIS BEST to free himself from Karen's grasping hold. The woman had no shame, especially given they were standing in the open garage. Twice now he'd told her it was over, that he'd meant it when he'd broken things off so long ago. Even without Sara in his life, he wouldn't take Karen back. She wasn't the type of woman he wanted or needed to be with.

He tried to be gentle, but Karen was deliberately obstinate about the whole thing. She refused to listen.

Gavin sighed in disgust as she once again threw herself against his chest and wrapped her arms around him. He propped his hands on his hips, allowing her, for the moment, to have her say. It wouldn't matter. He wanted Sara, and he'd have her eventually on his terms, no matter how long he had to wait, or how many pets he had to put up with. Sooner or later the woman would realize she loved him.

He could feel Karen cuddling closer and once again he clamped his hands on her forearms and prepared to pry her loose. Then they heard the noise.

Karen looked up just as Gavin leaned around her.

Racing down the middle of the street, looking much like a bizarre circus parade, was Sara's ex-fiancé Ted and every pet Gavin had recently acquired. They made a huge amount of noise—a mixture of human horror and animal determination. Gavin started to chuckle.

Good old Satan led the group, galloping at full speed, his heavy body stiff with anger, his bent tail sticking out like a broken lance. All the dogs followed, even the aged poodle. As Gavin watched, Ted made a leap for a skinny little tree and hoisted himself upward.

Satan followed.

Ted wailed as the cat perched on the same branch, then sat back to watch. The cat didn't make another

move, but he looked down at the loudly yapping dogs
with faint approval.

Sara appeared.

She took one look at Karen draped in Gavin's arms
and began a forceful, determined stride in their direction. She was breathing hard, and she looked as enraged as the animals.

Karen stiffened. "Oh my God."

Gavin allowed her to jump behind him and use him
as a shield. Sara looked ready to explode with righ-
teous anger. Gavin couldn't have been more pleased.
There was no way he could mistake the jealousy in
her eyes. Her lips were pulled back in a snarl and he
could just see the tip of her crooked tooth.

He wanted very badly to kiss her.

When Sara got close enough, he grinned and
reached into the garage for the plastic rake leaning
against the wall, then offered it to her with a flourish.
It was a subtle reminder, giving Sara the chance to
collect herself before she did something she might
regret later.

To his surprise she smiled, but it was a smile with
evil intent. "I love you, Gavin."

For a long moment he couldn't move. Hell, he
could barely breathe. Sara looked so stern, so forbid-
ding. Her arms were held stiff at her sides, the rake
in one fist, her legs braced apart. She'd said it like a
command, and he nodded. "It's about damn time."

She took a step back, stunned. "Then I don't need the rake?"

"You don't need the rake."

She glanced at Karen who dared to peek over his shoulder. "You have about three seconds to make yourself scarce before I sic the animals on you."

Karen screamed, causing Gavin's ears to ring, and then she ran. Gavin started laughing and couldn't stop. Ted hollered for someone to help.

He and Sara both ignored him.

After fidgeting a moment, Sara took a small step closer. "I've been afraid to tell you."

"I know." Overwhelmed by tenderness Gavin touched her cheek. "I would have waited awhile longer before getting insistent."

"Insistent about what?"

"About hearing a declaration. About getting married." He didn't like his own feeling of insecurity, but he acknowledged it. "You will marry me, won't you?"

"I'll insist upon it."

Gavin pulled her close and began kissing her. It was only the honking of horns that forced him to pull away. "Oh, hell."

Sara followed his line of vision and then blinked in surprise. "Your family's coming to visit again?"

"Sort of. You see, you mentioned to Mom that you needed lawn furniture. That's probably what's in the truck."

Sara was stunned. "I can't accept lawn furniture from her!"

"Trust me, honey. She likes giving things. The whole family does. Do you think you'll mind being married to the spoiled, youngest child of the family?"

She gave him a slow, blinding smile that nearly melted his heart. "Are you kidding? I get you and lawn furniture? What more could any woman possibly want?"

Epilogue

THEY ANNOUNCED THEIR intent to marry an hour later over coffee and cookies. It hadn't been easy to explain Ted, especially since he'd refused to come out of the tree. When he did come down, he had no way to leave; Karen had taken the car.

Gavin called for a cab, then explained to everyone that Ted preferred to wait on the curb—with Satan—until the cab arrived. Not a soul questioned that decision.

Sara had even more relatives to meet this time. It seemed his mother thought Gavin could use the extra support of the elders in the family, so there were two sets of grandparents tagging along. When the oldsters discovered Gavin had managed quite nicely on his own, they each claimed good genes as the deciding factor in his victory.

After Ted was finally picked up, the animals all wandered back to the house. Sara retold the story of how the pets had rallied together to come to her defense, and everyone was suitably impressed. Grandpa Blake showed a special fondness for the sweet-tempered Maggie. He claimed to have had a dog just like her in his youth.

Gavin's grandmother on his mother's side ended up with Tripod in her lap, throughout the entire visit praising the animal for her courage. And as Gavin watched them all interact, an idea came to mind.

"Does the retirement village allow you to have pets, Grandpa?"

"They do, and I know a lot of the folks in the village would love to have a good, dedicated dog. But most of them are on limited incomes and pets cost money."

Sara picked up on Gavin's train of thought immediately. "I have two friends who run a shelter. I bet they'd be willing to give the shots and checkups for free if the animals had a good place to stay. And Gavin and I could build a run of sorts right off the back door of each condo, so all the owner would have to do is hook the dog to a leash in the morning."

Gavin nodded. "It could be done. The village is set up with only ground-floor condos. If Jess and Lou would agree…"

"I'm certain they would." Sara looked so excited by the idea, Gavin knew she would be comfortable with the animals' living arrangements. They could personally select which homes the dogs and cats would go to.

All the elders agreed to take a pet from the shelter.

They even seemed anxious about the idea. Sara promised to go first thing the next day and see what animals were available.

Gavin bided his time until he could get Sara alone in the kitchen for a few minutes, and then he pulled her close. She snuggled into him with a sigh of pleasure. "Thank you for coming up with such a wonderful plan, Gavin. It makes me so happy to know that a lot of the animals won't have to be alone anymore."

He squeezed her a little tighter. "They remind you of how you've felt for much of your life."

She nodded, then laid her cheek against his chest. "But at least I understand that now. And I think, if you don't mind, I'll try inviting my parents to the wedding."

"Of course I don't mind. Why don't we drive over and see them together? We can ask in person. You said they didn't live all that far away."

"Not too far." She stared up at him and sighed in wonder. "I really do love you, you know."

And he did know. He'd known all along she could give him what no other woman could. Herself.

He was just about to kiss her when he heard the rushing steps of a small army of children. They squealed in delight as they raced past Gavin and Sara in the kitchen, Satan hot on their heels. And as the cat flew past in graceful, playful pursuit, he looked up, and Gavin could have sworn he was grinning.

Sara laughed. "Your mother's right. He's just like you."

Gavin merely grinned.

CATHY YARDLEY

The Cinderella Solution

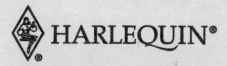

HARLEQUIN®

TORONTO • NEW YORK • LONDON
AMSTERDAM • PARIS • SYDNEY • HAMBURG
STOCKHOLM • ATHENS • TOKYO • MILAN • MADRID
PRAGUE • WARSAW • BUDAPEST • AUCKLAND

Dear Reader,

I love fairy tales, but my sense of humor won't let
me leave them alone. For example, what if Cinderella
didn't *want* to change? What if she decided to go to
the ball just to get a pushy fairy godmother off her
back?

Enter my Cinderella—tomboy Charlotte Taylor.
On the one hand, she's got two relentless "fairy
godmothers" determined to get her married no
matter what she wants. On the other, she's got her
best friend, Gabe Donofrio, who will do anything to
make sure she stays "one of the guys"! Throw in a
thousand-dollar bet, some makeover madness and an
irresistible attraction between two best friends, and
you get *The Cinderella Solution*.

I hope you enjoy reading this as much as I loved
writing it. Drop me a line at P.O. Box 1239, San
Leandro, CA 94577, and let me know what you think.

Cathy Yardley

To my family and friends for supporting my insanity. And to my critique group: Alyssa Ganezar, Ruth Barges, Rose Murray, John Lovelady and Christina Crooks. Thanks for believing in me.

1

"I'M GOING TO KILL HIM," Charlotte muttered, hitting the accelerator on her car awkwardly in her satin high heels. "I'm going to get through this wedding without throwing up, and then I'm going to kill him."

The tires squealed as she tore into St. Mary's lot, cutting the curve just a little too close. She whimpered. Her morning-after headache punched at her brain like a prizefighter.

Of all the days to be hungover, this was the red-letter worst.

Her car screeched to a stop and she yanked up the emergency brake. She took a quick glance in the rearview mirror, grimacing at the pale greenish cast to her face. "I'm going to kill him," she repeated.

She groaned as she wriggled out of her car, no small feat in her constricting pale-pink bridesmaid dress. She slammed the door shut, then gagged as the sound rang through her head. She rarely drank and had only experienced a hangover once before. She didn't remember how bad that had been, but it couldn't have been as bad as this. *Nothing* could be as bad as this.

"There you are, Charlie," a male voice boomed from the front steps. "We've been waiting for you!"

She was wrong. There *was* something worse. "I am going to kill you," she whispered.

Gabe Donofrio smiled mischievously at her from

the top of the stairs. He looked handsome, as usual, she noted with disgust. That gorgeous summer tan he kept all year long held no tinge of post-party green. His gray eyes weren't bloodshot, but lit with devilish humor. His dark hair and bright smile made him look as if he ought to be on the cover of a magazine. He looked as if he'd passed the previous evening curled up with a book and a glass of warm milk, when she knew perfectly well how he'd spent his night. He'd spent it making sure she'd be miserable this morning!

"Well, well, well." Gabe eyed her curiously, meeting her halfway down the stairs but wisely staying out of arm's reach. "Feeling a trifle ill this morning, are we?"

"Shut up. This is all your fault." She gripped the cold steel banister as if it were a life preserver, while her stomach did a queasy little dance step. "What in the world possessed you to con me into crashing Brad's bachelor party, anyway?"

"What were your options? If you'd stayed at my mom's house with my sister the bride, and her side-kick, Dana, you'd have gone crazy. Now that Bella's getting married, you're the last one." Gabe laughed. "You realize, of course, that now they're not going to rest until you're hitched."

She wished he were lying. The headache exploded dully behind her eyes, and her stomach constricted. "So you thought, say, the best way to prepare Charlotte for the grilling she's going to get tomorrow is...I know! Having her watch a half-naked exotic dancer freeze her butt off on a beach!"

"Actually, I just figured I'd pour ten tequila poppers down you, and at least cheer you up for a few hours," he said with a grin. "Come on, Charlie. Nobody held a gun to your head and made you drink."

"You bet me!" She poked a finger at him. "You

bet me a month's worth of car washes that I couldn't keep up with you. In the name of female honor, I had to pop that inflated ego of yours.''

"Female honor? Oh, right, that's it,'' he said, laughing. ''You've been this way since we were eight. You can't turn down a wager with me to save your life.''

"Wanna bet?'' She glanced over her shoulder at him, then stuck her tongue out.

"And, I might add—'' his quicksilver eyes twinkled with amusement ''—I've been beating you since you were eight.''

"Shut *up*.'' She eyed him balefully. ''Or I'll throw up on your Armani suit.''

"And wouldn't that go gorgeously with the decor,'' he quipped, glancing into the church. ''I think Bella's got every gardenia in Southern California crammed in there. Honestly, I don't know how someone as girly as my sister wound up with a nice, normal friend like you.''

Charlotte stepped into the small foyer of the church and stopped dead, assaulted by the overpowering floral scent. In her hungover state, the smell almost knocked her off of her feet.

"Oh, no.'' She started taking quick, shallow breaths. ''Oh, God.''

"Huh? Oh, *nuts*. Hold on, angel.'' Gabe was at her side in a flash, the teasing look replaced with one of serious concern. He anchored her with one strong arm. ''Take it easy, you're going to be fine. They can wait a few more minutes,'' he assured her, his voice low and comforting.

Charlotte fought the urge to sit down on the step and ride out her wave of nausea, knowing that if she sat down, she'd never get back up. ''How does Bella look?'' she asked, more to get her mind off her stomach than anything.

Gabe shrugged. "Like she was caught in a lace factory that exploded.''

Charlotte chuckled appreciatively. Slowly, the pounding in her head and the churning in her stomach receded. "If her dress is half as uncomfortable as this one, I pity her.''

"She's getting married. I pity her already,'' Gabe said, but his face still showed concern. "Feel better?''

"Not tremendously,'' Charlotte said, sighing, "but it'll have to do. My only goals for today are not throwing up on anyone, and avoiding the killer question.''

He snickered. "You mean,'' he said, mimicking a nasal feminine whine, "'So, when are *you* getting married, Charlotte?'''

"Exactly.'' Charlotte tried to ignore the pang the question caused, even asked as a joke. It seemed as if she'd been facing questions like that forever.

When are you going to find a nice boy, Charlotte?

Why can't you be more like the other girls, Charlotte?

How do you expect to catch a man looking like that, *Charlotte?*

She was single by choice, she reminded herself. She'd said the words so often, she ought to have them tattooed on her forehead.

"You know, you wouldn't keep getting hit with these questions if you'd stop saying yes to being a bridesmaid. What is this? Three times?''

"Four,'' she corrected him, pulling herself stiffly upright.

"Oh, right. After four tours of duty as a bridesmaid, you know my family is going to hassle you into becoming a bride yourself. Besides, I know you.

You're not exactly the type who swoons over china patterns and floral arrangements. Why not sit one out?''

"It's *Bella,* Gabe," she said crossly. "I probably should have turned down the earlier weddings, but Dana and your sister... I had to say yes. They're like my family." She lurched up to the foyer of the church. "Your family has actually *been* my family since Dad passed away."

"I know," Gabe said, subdued, then he chuckled. "I think I figured that out when my mother asked when *you* were going to give her a grandchild."

Charlotte felt it again, that little pang, but it was different this time. It wasn't just frustration, she noticed. It was suspiciously like envy. "The point is, I'd do anything for my friends, Gabe. You know that. The only reason I haven't murdered *you* is the fact that you're my best friend." She smiled at him weakly. "But I swear, if you pull another stunt like last night's bet, I won't be responsible for my actions. Got it?''

"Of course, of course. I wouldn't dream of it." Gabe nodded solemnly, but a smile still haunted the corners of his lips.

When they stepped into the church, she saw ten pairs of eyes snap toward them eagerly. All of Gabe's aunts homed in on her, calculating smiles on their faces.

"So I guess you won't bet me a month's worth of laundry that you can successfully avoid my aunts at the reception?" Gabe whispered gleefully. "Before you got here, I sort of suggested that you might be interested in their advice in the man-hunting department."

"Make it two months," Charlotte said through gritted teeth, "and remind me to kill you when this is all over."

"I'M LOOKING FOR CHARLOTTE," Gabe yelled over the din of the speakers and the laughing, boisterous couples on the dance floor. "She disappeared on me right after we took pictures. Have you seen her?"

"Nah, I haven't," his friend Sean replied, looking at the crowd of guys near him for a response. They all shook their heads. "If you see her, though, tell her we're having a poker match tonight at Mike's."

Gabe nodded. "If anything would get her out of hiding, it's a good game of poker. Thanks."

He continued his slow tour of the large ballroom. He was so intent on tweaking Charlotte out of her gloom and giving her something to do at this reception other than focus on the "killer question," that he'd forgotten he was the target of that same question himself...and not from his aunts. He'd been circling the reception hall for more than an hour, looking for Charlotte, while trying to avoid being singled out. Emphasis on "single."

Ordinarily, he wouldn't mind a room filled to the rafters with pretty single women. But this was a wedding, and that changed the rules. Suddenly, asking a woman to dance was tantamount to handing her a ring. It was a dedicated bachelor's nightmare, Gabe reflected. If he had Charlotte by his side, at least he'd have a better chance at fending off the hungry stares and blatant invitations. It figured that the girl he was searching for was the one girl in this whole sea of single women who wasn't looking for matrimony in general, or him in particular!

He sighed. She might say she was ready to kill him, but that wasn't what was keeping her hidden. He sensed that there was more to Charlotte's avoidance than just being frustrated with his family's gentle pressuring, or their inability to accept her tomboy ways. It went deeper than that. Whatever it was, it tripped warning lights in his head. For all their pranks and high jinks, the bottom line was, she was his best friend on earth. If she avoided him for this long, she wasn't angry, she was upset. And he was going to find out why if he had to drag it out of her...or bet it out of her.

He felt a hand on his shoulder and tensed.

"There you are, bro'."

Gabe turned, grinning his relief. "Hey, Brad. So, how does it feel being married to my sister?"

Brad smiled, his light brown eyes lighting up like candles. "I've never been happier in my life."

"So you say now," Gabe joked, giving his new brother-in-law a friendly punch on the arm.

"Trust me," Brad said, "when you find the right girl, there is nothing in the world that feels more perfect. Nothing at all."

"I'll take your word for it." Gabe shifted his weight uncomfortably. "It seems like I'm surrounded by women who would like to be *anybody's* 'right girl.' Weddings seem to cause some weird chemical imbalance in women. If I asked any one of the single women here if they'd run off to Vegas to get married tonight, I think they'd do it in a heartbeat." He gazed around the room, shaking his head. "And they don't even know me!"

"Which is the only way they'd agree to it," Gabe heard Charlotte mutter darkly behind him.

He spun around. "There you are..."

But she wasn't. He caught a glimpse of her weaving away from him, disappearing into the party guests. Before he could follow, Brad spoke up.

"Was that Charlotte?" Brad craned his neck to

squint at her disappearing form. "You know, this morning when I saw her walking up the aisle, I barely recognized her. It was probably all those curls...and I don't remember the last time I saw her in a dress."

"The hangover didn't help," Gabe added, trying in vain to track her. "I dragged her to the bachelor party last night and bet her she couldn't drink as much as I could."

Brad scowled. "You brought a woman to my bachelor party?"

"No, I brought Charlotte. There's a difference." When Brad didn't look mollified, Gabe shrugged. "I kept her off in the corner, Brad. Besides, she's been one of the gang for years, and we didn't do anything even remotely shocking."

"It's the principle of the thing, Gabe. You know, No Girls Allowed?" Brad shook his head, finally laughing a little. "And Charlotte's not a bad-looking girl, either, when she gives it a shot. I can only imagine what she looks like when she's not green. Of course, it might help if she didn't look like she was plotting your murder, either."

"She'll get over it. It might take a while, but she always does. Hell, half the time her practical jokes are worse than mine." Gabe laughed. "Did I tell you what she did last week—"

"Hi, Gabe."

The two men turned to see a lush-lipped blonde, staring at Gabe with deep blue eyes. Her voice was husky, but slightly overdone.

"I've been watching you run around all night, Gabe. You're missing out on a great party. Want to dance?"

Gabe sighed. "Sorry, I'm looking for someone right now. Maybe later." *Like in twenty years.*

"You sure?" she drawled, making a seductive little

shimmy that did nice things to her dress. "Whoever you're looking for could probably wait a little while."

Gabe sighed even harder. *Charlotte, where the heck are you?* "Really, I'm sorry."

The woman pouted. "Suit yourself."

"Whoa." Brad watched her shimmy back into the crowd, then turned to Gabe. "You're out of your mind! How could you turn down an opportunity like that?"

"She had 'husband-hunter' written all over her, and I don't play that anymore." Gabe shuddered. "No, thanks."

"Aw, come on. It was one dance. You could find Charlotte later...."

"Let me explain something," Gabe said seriously. "When I was younger, I had a few serious relationships. One even came close to marriage. All of them ended like train wrecks."

"Ouch." Brad shook his head. "But what does that—"

"My friends were the only thing that got me through them," Gabe said seriously. "That's when I figured it out. I don't do commitments anymore. Why should I? I party with the guys whenever I want, I have a job most men would kill for, and I have a best friend who knows me inside and out, who's there for me twenty-four, seven. Women come and go...."

"With a rather high turnover rate, in your case," Brad interjected.

"But friends are forever." Gabe smiled smugly. "If I just stick to that, I have, literally, the perfect life."

Brad laughed. "I've got to admit, it sounds attractive. But there's just one problem."

"At the moment, it's Charlotte," Gabe conceded.

"But she never stays mad at me for long. She'll feel better as soon as she gets even."

"The problem is," Brad continued, "you're going to fall in love one of these days. And that's going to throw your perfect life for a loop."

"Never happen." Gabe winked. He'd caught sight of Charlotte, speaking with some young women over by the side of the dance floor. "I've got it all under control."

Before he could make a move toward Charlotte, the women swarmed over to where he and Brad were standing.

"Oh, I think it's wonderful," one of the women gushed.

He blinked at her. "What is?"

"That you want so desperately to adopt a young child to love, you're going to ask someone to marry you tonight!"

Surrounded by beaming, hopeful faces, he looked over to the other side of the room to see Charlotte grinning at him from ear to ear.

"Yup," Brad said, patting him on the shoulder. "Obviously. You've got it all under control."

CHARLOTTE WOULD HAVE BEEN enjoying her revenge on Gabe a lot more if his sister and Dana hadn't finally cornered her. Reluctantly, she went up to the hotel room the Donofrios had rented, flanked by the two girls, as if she were a prisoner. While she had managed to avoid the aunts, these two could not be dodged.

"I'm telling you, Charlotte," Bella wheedled, "this book will solve all your problems."

"Why are you punishing me?" Charlotte groaned, throwing herself on the king-size bed. "I got here, even though I was green as spinach and my head was ready to explode. I even wore pink, for pity's sake! What do you want now? My blood?''

''We just want to see you happy…and we want you to read one little book,'' Bella said, calmly taking off her wedding veil. She grabbed her dark-rose traveling suit off a low chair in the corner. ''Don't let her get away, Dana,'' Bella instructed, her eyes glinting mischievously as she held up a wispy little nothing of white lace. ''I have to get into Brad's surprise gift.''

''No problem,'' Dana said, her eyes never leaving Charlotte.

Charlotte sighed. There was no escape.

Dana tossed the slim paperback on the bed. Picking it up, Charlotte read the cover out loud. *''The Guide… How to Go from Miss Wrong to Mrs. Right in One Year.''* She groaned again, pushing her face into a pillow. ''You have *got* to be kidding me.''

''It worked for me,'' Dana said, tugging Charlotte into a sitting position. ''And it worked for Bella. You can't argue with success. Bella's practically glowing. Don't you want to be as happy as she is?''

''Bella got the last good man on earth,'' Charlotte muttered, eyeing the pillow. She would have made another dive for it, but for all of Dana's petite, sophisticated looks, the woman had the grip of a wrestler. ''Why is it when your friends get married, they suddenly expect you to?''

''You're twenty-eight, Charlotte,'' Dana said firmly. ''Hear that ticking? That's your biological clock.''

''I'm hitting the snooze button.''

''Denial,'' Dana announced, grabbing Charlotte's chin and angling her face until they were eye to eye. ''You've been out of the dating scene for too long. Ever since you graduated from college, you've been burying yourself in that design firm and hanging out with those guys...what do they call themselves?''

"The Hoodlums," Charlotte said.

"Right. I don't know how many sets of baggy jeans and grubby sweatshirts I've seen you go through."

"Everybody wears casual clothes at work," Charlotte argued. "I'd look stupid in anything else!"

Dana rolled her eyes. "You can dress casually and still dress like a female, Charlotte. As much as you complain about it, you look good in a dress. And your hair looks cute curled."

"Dana, you know I can't curl my own hair to save my life." She gestured to the ringlets that were now sticking haphazardly around her head. "I look like I've been electrocuted."

Dana huffed. "It's not that bad, and you know it. What's really bothering you?"

Charlotte just sat there for a minute, silent. There *was* something bothering her. It had all started when she got to the church and Gabe had reminded her: four tours of duty as a bridesmaid.

Always the bridesmaid.

She glanced at the book. *Miss Wrong...*

As much as she touted that she was "single by choice," the truth stared her in the face whenever she looked at her friends. Beside Dana and Bella, Charlotte had always felt like a dull brown wren standing next to exotic birds. They were beautiful and sophisticated. What's more, their beauty was complemented by flirtatious, sparkling personalities. No, Charlotte Taylor was about as sparkling and mysterious as a glass of milk.

She didn't want their arguments, or worse, their pity. So she couldn't tell them all that. She wouldn't.

"I just don't see what the big deal is," Charlotte

finally answered. "I know I've only had one serious relationship, but it was a really convincing experience, believe me. Now I'm enjoying my life. I've got a great job and great friends. Please, couldn't you just let it go?"

Before Dana could respond, Gabe popped his head through the doorway. "Hey! The car's revving, and so's the bridegroom," he yelled. "Where's Bella?"

"Getting her traveling suit on," Dana answered, obviously irritated with the interruption.

"Good grief," Gabe said, walking in and rolling his eyes. "What is it about women that takes them so long to get dressed? It's never taken me that long to get clothes *off* of a woman."

"And Lord knows, you've had practice," Charlotte muttered, clambering off of the bed.

"You and I need to have a little talk," Gabe said, his eyes glinting with dark promise.

She grinned. "We can discuss it when you do my laundry for two months, O unlucky one."

"Gabe, you're not helping," Dana complained, glaring at him. "We were discussing important things before you breezed in and brought your…your Hoodlum, 'just one of the guys' vibes with you."

"What are you talking about?" he asked.

"I was talking to Charlotte about her future," Dana said, offhandedly gesturing toward the book on the bed. "You're distracting her. Can't you just wait in the hall?"

"Distracting her from what?" Gabe asked, then stopped as he glanced to where she'd gestured. "Oh, no. Not that."

"Not what?" Charlotte said, frowning.

"Tell me you're not going to read that!"

Charlotte saw where he was pointing and quickly

made a dash for it. Gabe dove onto the bed, grabbing the book at the exact moment she did.

"Let…me…see…this," he said, tugging stubbornly.

"Like hell I will!"

"I'm ready," Bella sang, opening the bathroom door, only to gasp in horror as she caught sight of her brother and her bridesmaid tussling. Dana simply shook her head. "What is going on here?"

Taking advantage of Gabe's momentary distraction, Charlotte made one last yank at the book. She managed to tug it away from him, but overbalanced. In a cloud of watered silk, she went flying over the edge of the bed, landing with a heavy thud.

"Got it," she crowed triumphantly, then rubbed her head. "Ouch."

Bella sighed. "When are you two going to grow up?"

"Never," Gabe replied. "We're going to be chasing each other with squirt guns when we're in a rest home together. Come on, angel, I'll give you a hand up."

With muscular grace, he helped her off of the floor. Then he promptly snatched the book out of her hand.

"You dirty…"

"*The Guide.* Oh, good grief," he snickered, thumbing through pages and reading passages aloud. "Be dramatic, but be demure. You're a woman. *Be* a woman." He guffawed, ignoring the trio of women glaring at him venomously. "What else would you be? A hamster?"

"Oh, give me that," Charlotte snapped, yanking it back out of his hands.

"You don't want to be Mrs. Right in one year, anyway," Gabe said with certainty, then narrowed his eyes. "Do you?"

"Of course not," Charlotte replied by instinct, then stopped. Well, it wasn't really a matter of wanting to be. It was a matter of knowing she *couldn't* be. Still, did she want to be?

Yes, a tiny voice inside her whispered, surprising her. In one year or one decade, she wanted to be right for someone. She wanted to find someone right for her.

"Charlotte might not think it's what she wants, but she hasn't had enough experience to say definitively," Dana said firmly. "She's got a lot going for her when she tries. If she'd just put her mind to it, she'd be a knockout. A real head-turner."

"Given a little time and a little effort," Bella added, crossing her arms, "I doubt it would take a whole year to find some guy who would fall all over himself to marry her!"

Charlotte felt a sudden burst of panic.

"And a gorgeous one, at that," Dana added enthusiastically, building momentum.

"She'd have him at her feet in a month," Bella said.

"Now, let's not get crazy here," Charlotte interjected, not liking the direction this was going at all.

"And she'd get a proposal in a matter of months, if she really went all out," Dana said, nodding. "Three months, easy!"

Gabe shook his head, throwing a casual arm around Charlotte's shoulders. "Why push her? Charlotte's my best friend, and I know her better than anyone. You can't tell me that she's going to read one stupid paperback, get a new hairdo or something, and suddenly turn into a *wife*. That's ludicrous."

Charlotte had been about to protest, also, but not in those words. "Not that I have any interest—"

"She's not even from the same planet as those

women that do *The Guide* thing,'' he continued. ''I mean, the women who use that as a game plan go at it like pros. They've got the looks, the moves, the whole nine yards. They turn men into putty.'' He grinned at her. ''We both know you're not like them, Charlie.''

The three women stared at him in silence for a long moment. Charlotte was the first to recover.

''Thank you,'' Charlotte said, her voice frosty. She pushed his arm off of her. ''Would you like me to turn the other cheek, so you can hit me with another backhanded compliment?''

''What? Oh, come on, angel,'' he said, tugging at one of her cockeyed curls with a look of amusement. ''We're talking about a marriage proposal in three months. Let's get back to the same zip code as reality.''

''I'm not saying it's what I *want*,'' she said, trying to maintain as much dignity as she could. ''But if I really wanted Mr. Right, I could get him. I'm just happy with my life the way it is now, that's all.''

''Really?'' Gabe's eyes lit up, and Charlotte immediately mistrusted them. ''And you actually believe that?''

Charlotte's temper flared, hot and dangerous. ''Try me.''

''No, thanks,'' he said, chuckling. ''If we're going to bet, I'd like at least a minor challenge.''

Charlotte's blood began to boil. She privately didn't think she was some skilled seductress, granted. Hearing him announce so easily that he *knew* she wasn't was something else entirely.

''You're on. I'll bet you ten bucks I could.'' It was stupid, but her pride pushed her to it. She was *single by choice,* and that was the lie she was swearing to. How dare he turn on her like this!

"Ten bucks? Seriously?" Gabe's eyes widened, then that damned amusement grew more pronounced. "Come on. It's not like we're betting on football here. Or who can hold their liquor better, for that matter."

Now her head was pounding. She wanted to smack that smug grin off his face. The words tumbled out before she could think about them. "One hundred dollars, Casanova. And I'll be wearing things that would make even you blush."

"That in itself would be worth betting on. Sometimes I think you were born in a sweatshirt," he said, his grin growing. "One hundred dollars is still child's play, angel. Maybe make it two months, and we'll talk."

"Two months," she agreed, her voice low. "And two hundred dollars."

Finally, some of his amusement slipped. "Charlie, come on now. You're getting in way over your head."

His patronizing tone threw gasoline on the fire. "Five hundred."

He was no longer smiling. In fact, his face looked grim. "This is ridiculous. I'm not going to listen to one more—"

"One thousand dollars."

Dana was staring at her, speechless. Bella's mouth had fallen open.

"One thousand dollars says I get a marriage proposal in two months," she repeated, staring at Gabe's face as if there was no one else in the room. Her hands bunched in fists at her sides. "One thousand dollars says you don't think I can do it. That no man would have me."

He paused, then looked at her shrewdly. "Only if you make it one month."

He waited for her to back down.

She didn't waver. "Deal."

"You don't want to do this, Charlie," he said, giving her a little shake. "You're losing your mind!"

"And you're losing your nerve," she said, smiling coldly. "Put up or shut up, Gabe."

They stood toe to toe for a long, maddening minute. Gabe studied her, not blinking. Then he smiled, a megawatt-bright smile.

"You're bluffing...and I'm calling you." Battle lit his eyes, and he held out a hand. "You're on."

With a swift motion, Charlotte grabbed his hand in a hard shake.

He stared down at her for a moment longer, then shook his head. "Fine. I'm going to go downstairs and tell the men you're taking your time," he said to Bella. "I'm sure you're going to want to stay a few more minutes to work on a game plan. That is, before Charlotte drops a grand in a month."

Giving Charlotte one last smug wink, he strode out the door.

"Oh, my God," Bella breathed. "I can't believe you did that!"

"What's done is done," Dana said, nodding with approval. "We've only got one month. A shopping trip, first thing. No, wait. My hairdresser! And maybe a facial..."

"Facial, nothing. Full day of spa treatment," Bella said, diving for her purse and producing a business card. "I'll be back from Hawaii in exactly two weeks. You guys take care of clothes and makeup. I'll work out a strategy."

"One thousand dollars," Dana said, glancing at Charlotte with a curious gleam of pride. "Unbelievable."

Charlotte gritted her teeth. "I've never lost a bet with Gabe without a fight. Now, pipe down," she ordered, a viselike grip on the paperback. "I'm trying to read here!"

EIGHT O'CLOCK the next morning, the persistent sound of her doorbell jarred Charlotte from a restless sleep. She stumbled out of bed, muttering and rubbing at her sleep-sandy eyes. "If it's Gabe, you might as well know I decided to forfeit," she called. "I must have been insane. Would you just leave me to wallow in my singleness in peace?"

"Not a chance," a muffled female voice countered. "It's Dana. Open up."

Charlotte groaned. Dana. Even worse. She unlatched the chain and cautiously pulled the door open.

"Well?" Dana looked far too enthusiastic about being up this early on a Sunday morning. "Today is the first day of the new you, Charlotte Taylor. Are you ready?"

"What are you? Captain of the matrimonial cheerleading squad?" Charlotte shuffled over to the kitchen and turned on her coffeemaker. No way was she facing one of Dana's makeover speeches without caffeine. "Besides, I'm not going through with this. I did a lot of thinking, and I'm going to get Gabe to just drop the whole thing. I don't really need to prove anything...."

"Oh no you don't," Dana countered, frowning at Charlotte as she unslung a fair-size bag from her shoulder. She started piling small jars, bottles and tubes on the kitchen table. "On any other bet, I'd probably be trying to stop you myself—you two manage to come up with some fairly idiotic ones—but this time, I'm all for it. I've waited ten years for you to do something with those buried gorgeous looks of yours. There is no chance in heck I'm letting you off that easily.''

Charlotte eyed the supplies warily. "What's all this for?''

Dana smiled. "This is step one.''

"Step one?'' Charlotte picked up one of the bottles. The label was in Norwegian and most of the ingredients had eighteen syllables. "How many steps are there?''

"That depends on how cooperative you are.''

Dana proceeded to get a box of oatmeal out of the pantry, then mixed some with water in a bowl.

"I wasn't planning on eating breakfast,'' Charlotte groused, pouring herself a mugful of coffee, "so I hope that's not for me.''

"This isn't for your insides. This is for your outsides.'' Dana grabbed one of the bottles, added some of its green liquid to the bowl, then studied the resultant mixture. "It's also going to get a little messy. Here, stir this.''

Charlotte stirred, then gaped as Dana produced a clear plastic tarp from her bag and laid it out on the living room floor. "What is *that* for?''

Dana didn't answer. Opening the front door and walking to the deck, she grabbed one of the forest-green plastic chairs and dragged it inside. "Here you go. Sit down.''

Charlotte took a quick chug out of her coffee mug before Dana plunked her down in the chair, ignoring Charlotte's startled yelp. Charlotte tried to frown at her friend, but wasn't able to turn far enough in the chair to see her. "Okay, this has gone from annoying to painful, Dana."

Dana took a breath, and Charlotte could feel that intent, "helping friend" stare of hers. "Listen to me. I don't mean to be pushy, or rude, but I'm going to flat-out say it. Honey, you need help…and for the first time since high school, we're going to make sure you get it."

Charlotte gritted her teeth. Apparently, the time for wheedling and not-so-subtle nudges from her friends had passed. Dana and Bella had gone to war. "I know I haven't seemed—"

"Hush. Let me finish." Dana's voice was firm. "I don't mean to play amateur psychologist here, but being raised by your dad alone all those years couldn't have made it easy for you. Bella and I did everything we could, but even I know two girls aren't going to replace a mother."

"You both loved me and did what you thought was best at the time." Which Charlotte had really appreciated, even if she often chafed under their efforts. "It wasn't easy, but see? I managed just fine."

"But you're *not* managing. That's my whole point." Dana sighed with obvious frustration. "You've tolerated us, you've humored us, but you're stubbornly convinced that you're not pretty and that you're not going to find a man who will fall in love with you. You're just hiding behind that 'just one of the guys' facade. Well, your days of hiding are over." Dana craned her head to stare directly into Charlotte's face. "And don't do that chin thing at me, either."

Charlotte blinked. "What chin thing?"

"The 'I'll tune back in when she says something I want to hear' chin thing."

Charlotte sighed. "Okay. I'm listening. What exactly is it you want me to do?"

"Really try at this. Give it your best shot."

"I'm not hiding, Dana. I…okay, *maybe* I could be a little braver in the social arena. But frankly, I'm happy with my life as it is. I don't *need* to date. I don't *need* to change my appearance. Why can't people be happy with me the way I am?"

Dana sighed. "Someday, a man is going to love you for just who you are, honey. I promise that. But if you're so happy with your life, why were you so sad at Bella's wedding?" Her eyes bore into Charlotte like lasers. "And don't tell me it was your hangover. We've known each other much too long."

That was the problem with having childhood friends. They read you like a book, Charlote thought, resigned.

"We'd leave you alone if we knew you were really happy," Dana said, giving her a quick, hard hug. "But we're not letting you just settle for a life of mediocrity without a fight. If you'd let that outer beauty catch up with your inner beauty, I know you'd find the right person for you. I just know it."

"Beauty? Me?" Charlotte's voice cracked. "What have you been smoking?"

Dana huffed impatiently. "One step at a time. Right now, the body comes first. We'll work on attitude soon, though."

She lifted the bowl in front of Charlotte, then grabbed a handful of the oatmeal mixture.

"Dana," Charlotte warned, "no way am I letting you turn my face into cooked cereal…arrrgh." She was silenced as Dana mercilessly glopped the thick, pasty stuff on her face. She shut her eyes and faced the inevitable.

"Sit still. This is just the beginning. I've got a hair appointment for you at twelve, and get ready for a full afternoon of shopping.…"

Dana continued to burble on happily as she outlined her grand scheme for Charlotte's transformation. Charlotte fought tears as the list grew longer.

There was no way she could turn down their help. If it had been anyone else, she would say exactly where they could stow their bright ideas and makeover agendas. But it was her two oldest friends... friends who had made room for her at holidays, friends who had clapped and cheered at the college graduation her father had missed, dying two years earlier of cancer. She loved them enough to put up with their pushing, prodding and relentless mothering. She'd die for them if they asked.

But dying was one thing, her mind countered stubbornly. Making a complete fool out of herself for the second time in her life was something else!

"Charlotte, have you heard a word I've said?"

Charlotte was jolted out of her thoughts. "What?"

Dana chuckled, then walked to the kitchen to put the bowl down in the sink. "I've been outlining your beauty agenda. I'm sure this is overwhelming to you right now, but I know you. You're going to work harder at this than at anything in your life."

Charlotte turned, only to have her head spun as Dana grabbed her hair and made thoughtful noises. "What in the world gives you that impression?" Charlotte asked, puzzled.

"That bet," Dana said, reaching for another jar. "You've never done less than two hundred percent to win a bet with Gabe. When you two shook hands, I could have kissed him!"

The temper that had gotten Charlotte into this mess sprung to life. "Oh, me too," Charlotte said acidly. "My best friend tells me in no uncertain terms that I not only lack the looks but the outright talent to get a man. Yeah. What a pal."

Dana laughed, then smoothed a fistful of clay onto Charlotte's head. It felt cold and squishy, and dribbles of it crawled down her neck. She squirmed uncomfortably in her seat.

"Well, now's your chance to prove him wrong. Really go all out. Honestly," Dana said, massaging the clay into Charlotte's scalp, "forget the bet. If you don't get a guy in one month, I will not only be shocked, I will throw in the towel for good. I'll give up my title as both matchmaker and makeover-er."

The sharp retort that Charlotte had been about to make died on her lips. "Really? You'd give it up?"

"Full money-back guarantee, and I'll never bug you on the subject again," Dana said, popping a clear plastic shower cap over Charlotte's mud-laden head. "I'll make sure Bella doesn't, either. I have that much confidence in you."

Charlotte didn't say anything. A diplomatic way to get her friends to leave her alone? After only one month?

Suddenly, the bet with Gabe didn't seem like such a horrible thing after all. Sure, she'd have to figure out a way around the thousand dollar part, but otherwise the rest of it was a piece of cake. She'd let the girls curl, crimp, color and coordinate to their hearts' contents. Then she'd lose, they'd concede, and she could finally get on with her life with some modicum of peace. It was perfect!

Suddenly, *she* felt like kissing Gabe. This backhanded bet was just what she was looking for!

"Well, then," Charlotte said, beaming her first real smile of the morning. "Let the transformation begin!"

"What transformation?" Gabe's voice called from the front door.

Dana let out a startled little yip. Charlotte, on the

other hand, made a break for the bathroom as soon as she heard him. Unfortunately, her foot slipped on the slick plastic tarp. She sprawled out on the floor, facedown and bottom up.

"Well, well," Gabe drawled, grating on every single one of Charlotte's nerves. "There's a sight you don't see every day."

"And thank God for that," Charlotte muttered, getting up slowly. "Don't you knock? And what are you doing here this early in the morning, anyway?"

"In all the years I've known you, I've never knocked if your door is open," he said, shrugging. "As far as why I'm here, there's a football game on in half an hour. I haven't gone food shopping yet, and I thought, my good buddy Charlotte always has something…"

"Please. Just help yourself," Charlotte said sarcastically, rolling her eyes.

"Don't mind if I do," Gabe agreed, helping himself to a mug of coffee and rooting through her refrigerator for a bagel. "You seem particularly grumpy this morning. Could it be because our good friend Dana here got you up early, or because she spackled your face?"

Dana and Charlotte both glared at him, and he laughed. "Sorry. I guess it's a girl thing."

"It's more like a bet thing," Dana snapped, gathering her makeover supplies and piling them back into her bag.

"Bet?" Gabe pretended to mull it over. "I seem to remember something about that. One grand, one month, and from the looks of it, a whole lot of oatmeal." Gabe winked at Charlotte. "Think you'll be able to wash all that off by Thursday? We've got one serious poker night going on at my house, and I don't want you covering your famous poker face with that goop. You'll scare the guys.''

''The only thing they'll be scared of is making their rent after I've cleaned them out,'' Charlotte boasted.

''Oh no you don't,'' Dana cut in, frowning at Gabe before turning back to Charlotte. ''From here on out, Thursdays through Sundays are designated date nights. You're booked.''

Charlotte took a deep breath. Just one tiny, minuscule month, she reminded herself. ''Okay, coach.''

The teasing look washed off Gabe's face. ''Okay?'' His gray eyes widened. ''Just like that? You'd ditch poker night to wait for…for some *guy?*''

''No,'' Charlotte corrected him sweetly, ''I'm ditching poker night to *go out with* some guy.''

Gabe scowled at her, but Dana laughed. ''That's my girl! Now, I've got to confirm that massage and full body wrap I've got scheduled for you tonight at the spa. Where did you leave your phone?''

''It's in the bedroom,'' Charlotte said absently. Dana made a beeline for it, reciting her makeover to-do list as she went.

Now was the perfect time to maybe negotiate the bet from a thousand down to something more reasonable. She might have to swallow a little pride, but it would be worth it. With Gabe's help, the four weeks could fly by. Without it…

''You can't be serious about this,'' Gabe muttered before she could say anything.

It wasn't so much what he said. It was the *tone* that immediately put her back up. ''Why not?''

''Because it's insane!'' Gabe said, running his hand through his hair in a trademark gesture of frustration. ''I was just kidding, for pity's sake. I figured even if you did agree, one week with the makeover fascists would have you crying uncle.''

Charlotte almost smiled at that one, until she heard his next sentence.

"Besides, you don't really want to find Mr. Right. You wouldn't know what do with him if you found him. You're not like those *Guide* women at all." His voice rang with certainty. "Think about it. You, trying to snare some unsuspecting man and drag him home by the hair?"

"Actually, I was planning on just wearing something see-through at my front door and luring them in," Charlotte snapped back, irritated by his amusement. "The kind of men I'm after would probably be too heavy for me to drag."

Gabe growled, then took a deep breath, apparently deciding to try a different approach. "There's nothing wrong with the way you are, and you shouldn't let them try to change you," he said, his voice more serious. "I thought you liked your life the way it was. What's so wrong about hanging out with us guys, anyway? We never hassle you about changing. We don't care *what* you look like!"

Translation: she could be the ugliest mud-beast to walk the face of the earth, but she'd always be "their Charlie."

"So you dress grubby…" he continued.

"Okay, stop right there." Swallowing her pride was one thing. Choking to death on it was another! "Before that foot becomes permanently lodged in your throat, stop trying to convince me. My mind's made up. *I'm going through with this bet.*"

This was not the way to convince him to help her, she realized. But the way he was acting, she didn't *want* his help. He wasn't pitying her, exactly, but he was…excusing her, somehow. It was worse than being pitied by the girls. He deserved a little payback, even if she knew she couldn't win. She might not ever look "beautiful," but he'd definitely think twice before he used the term *grubby* again!

"I may not look like much now, Gabe," she said, with anger-induced bravado, "but I swear, I'm going to look like the goddess of love when you're signing that check."

"Better watch that mud pack, Venus," he countered, leaning closer to her, a wicked grin on his face. "I hate to tell you, but you've got terra-cotta coating your neck. And there's a cozy scoop of oatmeal between your..."

He started laughing too hard to speak, cutting off his sentence, and he raised a finger to point.

Charlotte saw red. Snatching up one of the pillows from her overstuffed couch, she side-armed it at him, catching him straight in his chuckling mouth. He grabbed the little plastic chair as a shield as she pelted him with the rest of her ammunition.

Still steaming, she glanced around for something else to throw. Then she noticed the unholy gleam in Gabe's eyes as he put the chair down.

She felt a brief pang of panic as she realized his intentions. "Gabe," she protested, holding a hand up. "Now, let's not be hasty here. I'm your best friend...."

He picked up an armful of pillows and grinned.

"Ga-a-a-abe!" She gave one last, desperate cry as he began to bombard her. He was blocking off the entrance to both her room and the bathroom, and his aim was wickedly on target. With a scream, she bolted toward her front hallway, with Gabe in full pursuit.

"Dammit, Gabe!" Trapped, she threw open her front door and ran out, his deep, rolling laughter dogging her every step. She made a dash for the side of the house. She hoped the garden hose was out so she could give him a nice cold blast, when instead she ran smack into a broad, muscular chest.

"Oof," she uttered, landing on the soft grass of the side yard with a thump.

"Oops! Sorry," a deep male voice intoned, with an undercurrent of amusement. "Are you all right?"

She looked up. A golden, gorgeous Adonis was staring down at her. His bare, golden tanned chest emerged from what looked like a low-slung pair of Dockers. She gaped, horrified.

"Are you all right, miss?" Adonis repeated, looking less amused now and more worried. He also looked vaguely familiar. She shook off the thought. If she knew somebody this good-looking, she'd remember it! "I didn't mean to knock you over," he apologized. He offered her a hand to tug her up.

She stared at it. Of all the days for this sort of thing to happen to her, why *today,* when she looked like this?

Gabe suddenly emerged, pillows in each hand, yelling like a Comanche. He stopped, mid war cry, as he noticed the new participant and saw Charlotte on the ground.

"What happened?" Gabe asked, quickly dropping the pillows and falling to his knees by Charlotte's side. "Angel, are you all right?"

She grimaced at him. Did she *look* all right?

Adonis cleared his throat. "I'm sorry. I...she was running around the house, and I didn't know she was coming, and we bumped into each other. I think maybe she got the wind knocked out of her."

Charlotte groaned and pushed herself up to her feet, glad that at least the oatmeal covered her blush. "No, I'm fine," she muttered. *Of course I'm fine. Adonis moves in next door to me, and I run at him like a stampeding wildebeest.* "I guess I should have been more careful of where I was going, but I didn't know anyone lived here.''

Adonis smiled, dimples pitting his cheeks. ''No problem. I just moved in. A friend of mine owns this place, but he's subletting it to me for a while. I've always liked Manhattan Beach. It's fun.'' He winked at her, a gesture that reminded her of Gabe. ''Always something crazy going on.''

''This isn't what you think,'' she protested weakly.

Gabe was obviously enjoying the predicament she'd landed in. ''What, exactly, do you think he thought this was?''

''You...'' she began, only to be stopped by Adonis's laugh.

''Do you two live next door, then?'' Adonis glanced curiously at her house.

''I live there,'' Charlotte answered, giving Gabe a quick glare. ''The comedian over here doesn't. He just stopped by to make my life miserable.''

''Oh,'' Adonis said slowly, looking back at her. ''I thought you two were married.''

''Us?'' Charlotte's eyebrows jumped up, causing crackling oatmeal to sprinkle into her eyes. She blinked hard.

''Not just no, but *hell* no,'' Gabe said. ''Marriage is miserable enough by itself. Why would I compound it by marrying her?''

This time, she aimed a kick at him. He dodged it, still grinning.

''Oh,'' Adonis said, smiling broadly. He offered his hand to her. ''Then let's get introduced. I'm Jack Landor.''

''Jack Landor? *Society* magazine's Most Eligible Bachelor in America?'' She laughed. ''Sure you are. And I'm Glinda, the Good Witch of the North.''

He laughed, a deep, rough laugh that appealed.

When he smiled, he *did* sort of resemble Jack Landor, she noted.

"Well, Glinda, you can just call me Jack."

"Hi, Jack," Gabe said, stepping slightly in front of Charlotte and putting his hand out. Jack had to release Charlotte's hand to shake Gabe's. "I'm Gabe Donofrio."

"I'm Charlotte Taylor," Charlotte added, nudging Gabe a little. He didn't budge.

"Hi, Charlotte," Jack said, smiling. He added a nod to Gabe. Charlotte smirked when Gabe finally moved aside a little.

Gabe smiled back at her, too smugly for her peace of mind. His gaze shifted downward a little, and his smile widened, amusement dancing in his eyes. She tried to track his line of vision. What was so funny?

Abruptly, she remembered the comment that had started all of this. She had oatmeal between her *what?*

"Well, welcome to the neighborhood, Jack," she said quickly. Hoping that she wasn't nestling cereal between her breasts, she smiled sheepishly and added, "I've got to go slip into something less, er, edible."

Jack smiled back, this time with a hint of heat. "Oh, don't bother on my account."

She paused for a moment.

That sounded like a come-on.

Shaking her head, Charlotte laughed, waved and walked back up toward her house. Of course it wasn't a come-on. Adonis, hitting on the oatmeal mud girl? She'd been out of the dating scene way too long if she could entertain a crazy idea like that!

Gabe trailed behind her, pillows in hand, but with no obvious intention of throwing them, thankfully. They walked into the house together. Dana waited for them in the living room, a horrified expression on her face.

"I can't believe you just did that," Dana said, her fingers tugging at her short red hair. She'd obviously been spying from the bedroom window. "Did you see that guy?"

"Couldn't miss him," Gabe said sourly, before Charlotte could answer. "He's Jack Landor."

Dana's eyes bugged. "No way."

"Way." Gabe plunked down on the couch. "And he was hitting on Charlotte."

"No *way!*" Dana threw a quick hug around Charlotte's shoulders, then just as quickly pulled back, rubbing at some clay that had gotten on her sleeve. "He hit on you? Looking like, um, that?"

"Coated in oatmeal and mud, you mean?" Charlotte gave an exasperated sigh. "He couldn't take his eyes off of me. I'm literally like no other woman he's ever seen before…or ever hopes to see again, I'm sure." She frowned at Gabe, kicking at the feet that he'd propped up on her coffee table. "Gabe's just pulling your leg, Dana. Jack Landor wouldn't be interested in me in a million years, and besides, I'm not even convinced that Adonis really *was* Jack Landor. Either way, that guy was not coming on to me!"

"Adonis?" Gabe repeated, frowning.

"What do you mean, he wasn't Jack Landor?" Dana persisted.

"He wasn't that good-looking," Gabe interrupted, standing up. "Are you interested in him or something? Because I think he's a little out of your league, Charlotte. I mean, I know you're taking this bet seriously and all, but you don't want to rush into anything."

"Right. That does it." Charlotte tugged the plastic cap off of her head. "Dana, I'll see you at the hairdresser's. Gabe, go to the supermarket, then go home. I'm going to take a shower. And we are not going to talk about oatmeal, mud packs or Jack Landor ever again, are we clear?''

Dana smiled. "See you at twelve."

Gabe got up, following Charlotte to the bathroom door. "Need help scrubbing off your back? I'm sure I could dig up a volunteer next door."

She slammed the bathroom door in his face and turned the shower on, full blast. Feeling the oatmeal run off her face under the pounding spray, she had one thought...

She might not win *this* bet, but the next time Gabe saw her, he wouldn't know what hit her. She'd stake her life savings on it.

3

By Thursday, Gabe was sick of being put off for Charlotte's "makeover agenda." She wouldn't see him, barely even had time to talk to him. Now he had only one goal: getting her to give up this stupid bet, for her own good.

He pulled his sleek black Mustang convertible into the parking lot of Howes Design, jetting into the nearest parking space. Getting Charlotte to do anything was difficult. Getting her to do something for her own good was damn near impossible.

"I am such an idiot," he muttered under his breath, retrieving the bouquet of white roses he'd gotten for her. Charlotte was a sucker for flowers. Two dozen red roses had saved his butt when he'd accidentally cracked her car's back window last year with a practical joke, he remembered with a smile.

Somehow, he doubted he'd get off the hook that easily this time. Once he and Charlotte shook hands on a bet, she was like a ton of cement: hard, completely set and impossible to budge.

He had handled Saturday badly, he realized. Even if she wouldn't believe it, he had been trying to help her. He knew how pushy his sister could get, and she had been after Charlotte for years, trying to "girl-ify" her. He was just trying to help Charlotte stop them, he thought logically. Then she'd gotten that fire in her eyes, and he'd indulged in pricking her temper. He knew he shouldn't get as much of a kick out of it as he did, but when Charlotte sparked, he couldn't help but react. He loved watching her go to any lengths to beat him at whatever it was they were shaking on. Besides, he'd thought she was bluffing, and he wasn't about to knuckle under if she was. It wasn't until he'd seen her the next morning that he realized everything the bet entailed.

What if she did meet some guy, like that jerk she'd dated in design school? The guy had turned into a psychotic Pygmalion, trying to turn Charlotte in as his final project. Gabe had just graduated himself and was looking forward to spending more time with Charlotte...they hadn't been close when he was in high school, but when he'd moved away to college on the East Coast, he realized he missed the tomboy brat who lived around the corner. But instead, she'd spent all of her time with her boyfriend until the jerk dumped her, and she'd wept on Gabe's shoulder and told him the story she couldn't tell the girls: how the guy had been trying to change her, how he'd said he'd given up because "the project was only as good as the materials...and you're not good enough."

She'd then made Gabe promise not to kill the guy, a promise Gabe still regretted.

If Charlotte went all out on this crazy bet, who knew what sort of lunatic she'd hook up with, just to show him she could.

And if she got married, where would that put me in her life?

He ignored the tiny voice that had been poking at him since Sunday morning. He'd make her see reason, no problem. From what he'd seen, she wasn't unhappy with her life. She always seemed happy when she was with him, anyway...except for the wedding. But that was probably just a fluke, a mood thing. As he'd said to Brad, weddings did weird things to women. And if he knew Charlotte, he knew she didn't want to be anybody's Mrs. Right.

He'd make sure she remembered that.

"Say" came a woman's voice from the front door. "Are you going to come in, or are you just going to loiter for the rest of the afternoon by our front door?"

"Huh?" He was startled out of his thoughts. "What?"

Wanda, the receptionist at Howes Design, smiled at him as she held open the door. "Those flowers for me, handsome?"

He smiled back. "No, they're a peace offering for Charlotte. Is she in?"

A strange look crossed Wanda's face. "She sure is." Gabe followed Wanda through the door into the air-conditioned lobby. "So. Are you what happened to her?"

"What happened to her?" he echoed. "What do you mean?"

"She looks strange, Gabe," Wanda said conspiratorially, leaning a little too close to him. "I mean, I've never seen her look like this before. It's weird."

He groaned. "Oh, no."

Wanda shifted gears, her smile turning seductive. She was close enough that her red curls brushed against his shoulder. "So what are you doing this weekend, handsome?"

"Penance," he muttered. Then he added more clearly, "Thanks, Wanda."

He hurried down the hallway. What could Charlotte have done now? God, he hoped she hadn't unearthed those bizarre designs that jerk had concocted…pastel granny dresses with combat boots. Or was it worse? Pinstriped straightjackets with sensible shoes? Leopard prints? Lederhosen? Or had she just given up completely and shaved her head?

Taking a deep breath, he courageously slapped on a big smile before throwing the door open and entering, flowers first.

He froze.

Charlotte barely glanced up, smiling tiredly. "Hey there. Come on in. I just need to finish up this sketch…this client is a nightmare. I've been working like a demon all morning."

He felt like somebody had punched him in the stomach. "Um, sure," he said slowly, wishing he could stop staring. "You look…good."

She looked up at him for a second, with a little smirk. "Damn me with faint praise."

Whatever he had been expecting, it wasn't this. She looked strange, all right. Strangely alluring, strangely striking. Strangely beautiful.

Her straggly long hair had been cut to her shoulders, falling in graceful waves. Something else was different about it, he noted. It was darker, more chestnut, maybe. She wore it pushed back a little, showing off that swan's neck of hers. It suited those high cheekbones nicely.

He blinked. When the hell had he noticed she had high cheekbones?

Her hazel eyes were huge, glowing with life. "Gabe? Hello-o-o, Gabe." Her smile was shy and self-conscious. "That bad, huh?"

It was the smile that snapped him out of it. No matter what she looked like, that smile was pure Charlotte…that little softness that took the sting out of her sharpest, hippest remarks. "Nah," he said, regaining his equilibrium. "I was just mentally balancing my checkbook to see if I could clear a grand, or if I'd have to raid my savings."

She laughed, showing off a rosy little blush that added life to her clear porcelain complexion. If this kept up, he thought desperately, he'd start writing a sonnet about her. He thrust out the flowers almost aggressively. "For you," he muttered.

The blush deepened a little. She was wearing some kind of dusty rose lipstick, and her lips looked full and generous as they curved into a delighted smile. "I didn't get anything for you," she joked, her voice low and husky.

Her voice had always been like that, hadn't it? So why did his pulse suddenly rev up like an engine at the Indy 500?

Then she got up and took a vase off of the tall bookcase behind her worktable.

He thought he'd been shocked. Now he was beyond shocked. He felt like someone had taken a sledgehammer to his chest as he tried without success to take a breath.

She wasn't wearing her usual baggy jeans. Instead, she wore a short, flirty sundress in a fragile pastel pink that floated like a cloud around her body. The neck scooped to reveal the gentle swell of her breasts. And she was wearing strappy white sandals. With *heels*. He wasn't sure what weird equation of physics made heels do what they did to women's legs, but they were acting in overdrive on Charlotte's. Her legs were long and luscious, just the way he liked…

This is Charlotte you're ogling.

The thought brought him up short.

She paused in her impromptu flower arranging, pulling out the little white flag he'd tucked into them. She turned, tapping one foot as she smirked at him. "So what's this for?"

"Unconditional surrender," he murmured, wrenching his gaze up from her legs and wondering just when the hell he had lost control of the situation. "On both our parts. Let's just call this stupid bet off, Charlie."

He watched as her face turned hard, and sighed. It just wasn't going to be that easy.

"So what brought this on, Gabe?" She walked over to the drawing table, her heels clicking viciously against the hardwood floor.

"What do you think?"

One of her finely arched eyebrows quirked up. "Let's see. Because you don't think I have a prayer of doing anything but making a fool of myself with this bet?"

"I never said that," he interrupted. "I just don't want you to get hurt."

"Translation—you think I'm going to get hurt because I'm not the sort of woman that men go bonkers over."

Until today, he thought. He couldn't remember exactly what he'd thought before today. "I never thought you were ugly," he said instead, more sharply than he'd intended.

"Oh, really? Then what did you think?"

He opened his mouth, then shut it, reconsidering. "You're sweet, and nice, and funny. You're a mean poker player and a great quarterback. You're brilliant at your job...."

"Oh, and all that keeps my organizer filled with dates," she said, breaking in sarcastically. "My looks, Gabe. How did you think I *looked?*"

He sighed. "You're my best friend. How am I supposed to know? I don't think of my friends that way!"

"That is the biggest cop-out I've ever heard."

"I knew it. You've only been doing this for a few days, and already you're turning all girly on me," he said with asperity. "Looking at you, hearing you talk, I know this is a bad idea. Besides, do you know the kind of men that are prowling around these days? You don't know what you're getting into!"

Her eyes blazed. "I can take care of myself, thanks very much. I have for years. You don't need to worry about me!"

"I've been worrying about you for years," Gabe raged back at her. "And that was when you were still in your right mind!"

They stood there for a long moment, their words like fallen swords between them. Before either could break the silence, the phone rang. They both jumped, startled.

Charlotte snatched up the receiver. "Yes?"

Gabe took a deep breath. Okay, he'd botched that one thoroughly. He'd meant to be convincing, suavely persuasive. Then he'd taken one look at her and his well-laid plans went straight out the window. Hopefully, he could still salvage the situation. Once she got off of the phone, he'd try to be a little more smooth.

"Glinda, Good Witch of the North?" Her eyes widened, bewildered, then closed. "Oh, my God. Hi, yes, I'm sorry. This is Charlotte Taylor. I didn't mean to snap like that, I'm just in the middle of something. Is this Jack?"

Any thoughts Gabe had of peacemaking disappeared. Jack Landor? What was he doing, calling Charlotte here? And what did he want?

Gabe stopped himself, midthought. Oh, he could guess what good old Jack wanted, all right.

"Hi, Jack. Yes, I've recovered fully from this weekend. You're a brave man, not to run off screaming at the sight of me. I'm sure I was something to see." She chuckled, halfheartedly. "What? Oh, that."

238 The Cinderella Solution

She laughed again, and Gabe saw a deep red blush creep across her face. "You weren't supposed to notice that blop of oatmeal there."

Gabe saw purple. Suddenly, he felt the overwhelming urge to hit something, preferably Jack. That lech!

"Hmm... So, you want a local person's advice on what the hot spots are in Manhattan Beach, huh? Well, I guess I could help you a little. I know several excellent restaurants, a ton of sports bars and a few dance clubs...what?" Gabe suppressed the urge to hit the speaker button and hear what was causing the shocked look on her face. "Um, I'm, uh, not sure. Today's Thursday, right? No, I don't have any other plans tonight...."

Gabe clenched his fist. The man was railroading Charlotte into a date. The nerve of the guy!

"What? Your other line? Sure, I can hold," Charlotte said. She looked over at Gabe, covering the mouthpiece. "It's Jack Landor. I'm holding."

"Breathlessly," Gabe growled. "You're not thinking of going out with that character, are you?"

"Well, I hadn't..." she started, then stopped, her eyes flashing. "Why shouldn't I?"

"He could be an ax murderer for all you know!"

"He's Jack Landor!" Charlotte exclaimed. "At this point, he's getting so famous he's lucky to go to the bathroom with privacy, much less kill anyone!"

"My point exactly!" Gabe yelled back, then stopped. No, that wasn't his point at all. Normally, he had a lot more logic on his side, but his anger had seriously shorted out the better part of his brain. "All I'm saying is, you're not thinking this through. He's big-league, he's famous...and you've got that damned bet on your brain. Why would you want to go out with some celebrity freak show otherwise? Think about it!"

Her eyes narrowed, like shards of hazel ice. "Or, more to the point, why would he want to go out with me?"

Gabe grimaced. "Don't go there, Charlotte. I swear."

"Jack? Hi." Her voice rang with an edge of steel. "I'd love to go out to dinner with you tonight. I think we should try Blue Moon, over on Manhattan Beach Boulevard. It's sort of nouveau Italian, and the food is terrific. How does seven sound?" She paused for a moment, listening. "Perfect. Well, yes, you *do* know where I live. We can just walk there, it's very close. Sure. I'll see you then." She placed the phone gently in its cradle, then stared at it. "I have a date with Jack Landor. Tonight."

"How did he get your work number?" Gabe asked pugnaciously. "Answer me that, why don't you!"

"Gabe, I don't have to answer you one little thing." She pointed to the door. "What's more, I think this conversation has gone about as far as it can go. Get out, Gabe."

"We're not finished," he warned.

"We will be if you keep it up. Out!"

"Fine!" He couldn't resist slamming the door, an action that caused several heads to pop up like gophers over the low cubicle walls in the main room. He scowled at them. They disappeared rapidly.

So she was going out with Jack Landor tonight, huh? Thought she could "take care of herself." Well, he'd just see about that. In fact, if she was so hellbent on proving what a *Guide* girl she was, he'd show her exactly how insane those women could be.

Tonight, he planned on showing her that nobody knew more about dating—or winning—than Gabe Donofrio.

HOURS LATER, CHARLOTTE was still raw from her exchange with Gabe. Imagine him stomping in here like a caveman and claiming that she couldn't take care of herself. And the ridiculous accusation that she wouldn't be safe with Jack. If that was the best he could do to win that stupid bet, she'd win by default!

She threw her design stuff in her catchall basket, too stressed to indulge in her usual calming ritual of organization. Now, thanks to his meddling, his pressuring and his big mouth, she was going on a date in two hours.

Suddenly, the thought hit home.

Date.

She was going on a date.

In two hours.

With the most eligible man in America.

Oh, no. What had she just agreed to?

She walked out, dazed, not surprised to see that most of the other designers had taken an early Thursday to enjoy the Indian summer weather. A lot of them had been working weekends to land the Kensington account and deserved a little break before the next big project. A project she'd still be working on if she hadn't agreed to this dinner date with Adonis, she thought, getting more anxious. Maybe she should cancel. He'd understand if it was for work, wouldn't he?

Or maybe she could call him and tell him she was sick. He'd have to understand that. In fact, she felt like throwing up right now.

Wanda was just shutting down the switchboard for the night when Charlotte walked through the lobby. Wanda surveyed Charlotte, her lips bowing into a tiny, pointed smile. "That friend of yours went tearing out of here this afternoon like he wanted to kill somebody. What happened?"

Charlotte sighed. Wanda was the biggest busybody in the building. She also went through men the way kids go through Pez candies. "He doesn't approve of my taste in dates," she muttered darkly.

"You've got a date?" Wanda's ultramarine eyes rounded. This was probably the juiciest gossip the woman would get all week. "Well, that explains it."

"Explains what?"

"The changes." Wanda's well-manicured ruby nails gestured to Charlotte's dress. "The get-up. You know."

"Maybe I just wanted a change," Charlotte protested.

Wanda gave her a pitying look. "Come on, now. It's just us girls here." The two walked out of the building, Wanda punching in the alarm code as they left. "Nobody goes through all that trouble unless there's a manhunt involved. It's not like you'd look like that normally."

"Is there something wrong with the way I look?" Charlotte said, half-defensive, half-worried. She gave herself a surreptitious glance in the reflection of the glass doors. Dana and the woman at the store had said that the dress was flattering, but she herself hadn't been that crazy about it. Pastels weren't her thing. Darn it, she just wasn't sure about this stuff!

"Oh, no, of course not. It's sort of... well, it's very different," Wanda said graciously. "And I've often said that you needed a change. I just wasn't expecting one quite so radical."

"Radical?" Charlotte didn't think it was that big a deal. Okay, maybe she did, but she wasn't expecting everyone she knew to think it was that big a deal.

"But maybe radical is just what you need," Wanda continued. Her skyscraper heels clacked on the asphalt as they walked to their respective cars.

If I walked that way, I'd dislocate one of my hips. Charlotte shook off the thought. "What do you mean?"

"From the extreme change, I'd say you must be on a husband-hunt. And that calls for the heavy artillery." Wanda smirked as she strutted over to her red convertible. "Desperate times call for desperate measures, right?"

Charlotte stopped by Jellybean, the nickname she'd given her roly-poly purple VW Bug. Unlocking the door, she murmured, "Been there already, huh?" She glanced skeptically over Wanda's chartreuse linen suit, with its micromini hemline.

Wanda laughed, not insulted in the slightest. "Not on your life. I need a few more years of fun before I settle down. But if you need any help with hints, you just ask your girlfriend Wanda. You're taking a step in the right direction with the makeover, but when you're really ready to step up to the major leagues, you just let me know and I'll see what I can do to help, okay? Good night!"

"Good night," Charlotte replied weakly. She watched Wanda zoom out of the parking lot, her red hair floating behind her. She looked like some ad in a fashion magazine.

Charlotte didn't realize she was still gripping the door handle with a choke hold until long moments later. She opened the door and sat down, then took a quick glance in her mirror. While Wanda's face had still looked porcelain-doll perfect, she herself had lost her lipstick and she had a smudge of pastel high on her right cheek. Where Wanda's red tresses were carefully coifed, her own unruly brown waves were pulled haphazardly in a scrunchy white elastic band, to stay out of her way while she worked. She tugged the band off, watching the locks bounce in front of her eyes. With a deep sigh, she started the car.

Desperate times call for desperate measures.

If she canceled on Jack, she would just be prolonging the agony. She needed to stop these makeover attempts, once and for all. Just one month, she reminded herself. Just one lousy dinner date. She could do this. She *had* to do this.

Well, at least she wasn't going to be under too much pressure. After all, she'd known going in that she would lose the bet, she tried to comfort herself.

Then she decided not to comfort herself. It hurt too much.

4

CHARLOTTE WAS FRANTICALLY dashing around her bedroom when the phone rang.

"Hello?" She tugged her panty hose up to her waist with one hand, tucking the cordless phone between her head and her shoulder with the other.

"So is it true?" Dana asked with no preamble. "You're going on a date with Jack Landor?"

"Bad news travels fast," Charlotte groaned, wondering if Gabe had sent out a press release on it or something. She stalked to her closet. "Yes, it's true. I'm getting dressed, *oof*—" she juggled the phone, buttoning her silk blouse "—as we speak."

"What are you wearing?" Dana's voice held the sharp tone of an interrogator.

"White silk blouse, pinstriped charcoal trousers, low heels, black blazer."

"Are you going on a date or an interview?"

"You're already on my list for putting me in pastels," Charlotte warned, tugging on her pants. "Don't start with me today, Dana. I mean it. I'm on my last nerve."

"Why don't you wear one of your new dresses?" Dana continued, ignoring Charlotte's annoyance.

"Well, A, I wore one of them to work today, B, it's going to be chilly tonight, and C, I don't want to wear anything that screams 'Take me, I'm yours!' to

Jack Landor, who probably has more scantily clad groupies than the Rolling Stones.''

Dana sighed in frustration on the other end of the line. ''If he does have groupies, it's for a darned good reason, Charlotte. The man gives Brad Pitt a run for his money.''

''Did you have something constructive to tell me, or are you just trying to give me an ulcer?'' Charlotte yanked on her blazer impatiently. ''Because if you *don't* have any helpful information to share with me, I'm going to hang up and attempt to drown myself in the bathroom sink.''

''Relax, honey. Breathe,'' Dana said soothingly. ''In through the nose, out through the mouth.''

''Easy for you to say,'' Charlotte replied, trying to take a deep breath. ''You're not having dinner with the most eligible man in America.''

''Well, you must be pretty attracted to him,'' Dana pointed out. ''You said yes to the man, didn't you?''

''Well, yes. But I'm not sure that I would have if Gabe hadn't been hassling me about him.'' Charlotte frowned, then gave her makeup a quick glance in her bedroom mirror. The face there frowned back at her. She'd reapplied her cosmetics carefully, just like the lady at the spa had instructed. It probably worked…it was like looking at the face of a stranger, and it made her uncomfortable. ''I feel like an idiot, Dana. My palms are sweating, and my heart's beating like a jackhammer.''

''Sounds like love,'' Dana suggested in a singsong tone.

''Sounds like terror,'' Charlotte retorted in the same tone. The next time she saw Gabe, she'd strangle him. She wasn't sure how she could prove it, but she was positive this was all his fault!

The doorbell rang, and she jumped, tripping on a

pair of sneakers she'd left lying on the floor. "Oh, no. It's him."

"Remember to take a condom," Dana advised.

Charlotte sighed. "I was thinking more of a cyanide capsule. Good night, Dana." She hung up the phone before Dana could offer any more helpful hints.

Taking a deep breath, she went to the door and opened it slowly as she tried to hold on to her smile.

Jack was waiting, wearing a pair of black chinos and a dark green cable knit sweater that matched his eyes. He looked good, she thought, and her smile curved a little more naturally. "Hi, Jack."

"Hi." He smiled back. "I barely recognized you."

"You're telling me," she said with feeling, grabbing a light jacket and her purse. "I barely recognize myself these days."

When she turned back to face him, he was staring at her strangely. "Why?"

"Why, what?"

"The only time I've seen you, I didn't get a good look at your face," he explained, his smile broadening but his eyes still puzzled. "So it's a surprise to me. But I'm sure you've seen your own face without oatmeal before."

She blushed. *Nothing like starting the evening off feeling stupid!* "Oh, the oatmeal." She laughed self-deprecatingly. "Well, the oatmeal is doing wonders. I'm a completely new person, which is why I have trouble recognizing myself." Somehow that sounded lamer out loud than it did in her head.

"Really?" He gave her a complete once-over. "What did you look like before?"

She smirked at him, putting on her jacket. "I used to be a six-foot-tall Scandinavian, for one thing."

He laughed, and she grinned back weakly. How

long was it going to take him, she wondered, to realize he was going out to dinner with someone completely inept at being a girl?

Oh God, let me survive tonight.

Half an hour later, she was still surviving. Barely.
She had managed to order without embarrassing herself, and there had only been three uncomfortable
pauses. However, she had already managed to knock
over her water twice, and had come perilously close
to setting her menu on fire with the romantic tea-light
candle in the center of the table.

"Sorry," she said, trying to smile. His eyes were
kind, but she felt sure it was a sort of "taking pity
on the handicapped" smile. "I'm not usually this
clumsy."

"At the risk of sounding immodest, I've been
around people who get nervous around me." He
shrugged. "You get used to it."

She frowned. "Well, you *are* gorgeous. I guess I
figured other people must get pretty blasé about that
after a while."

They both blinked at what she said, and she stammered, almost knocking over her third glass of water
that night.

"I'm sorry...that wasn't...oh, God. That sounded
really stupid, didn't it?"

"Actually, that was really cute." He laughed. "I
meant that people usually get nervous about the
money thing. Of course, there is that stupid 'Eligible
Bachelor' thing...."

"I remember reading about that," Charlotte said.
She also remembered Wanda pinning a picture of him
at her desk for about two months.

"Ever since that went into print, I've had women
literally tongue-tied when I wind up going to dinner
with them. Or else chatting their heads off trying to

convince me they're the greatest thing since sliced bread.''

"Ick." Charlotte rolled her eyes, laughing. "No problems here. I am definitely not the greatest thing since sliced bread.''

"I don't know," he said, a hint of laughter in his voice. "It's really easy to talk to you, and you're disarmingly honest, Charlotte." His eyes glinted with mischief. "Or is it Angel? I heard that guy—what was his name?—call you that.''

"Oh," she said, feeling a blush heat her cheeks yet again. "That. My friend Gabe. He just calls me that nickname because he knows it annoys me.''

"Why would being called 'angel' annoy you?''

She sighed. Well, it had been a sort of comedy of errors all night. She was just about getting the hang of being permanently embarrassed, so why not? "It's stupid, really. When I was little, my dad used to call me Charlie, and Gabe and I used to watch *Charlie's Angels* all the time. Gabe's sister even tried feathering my hair once, with that little flip…you know, like Farrah Fawcett. It was a disaster," she said, laughing ruefully at the memory. "Gabe teased me mercilessly after that. I'm Charlie, the bad hair Angel.''

Jack's smile was warm. "Well, you don't qualify for bad hair, and you don't really look like a Charlie. The angel part fits well enough, though.''

She smiled, flustered, uncertain of what to do next. It was just a simple compliment, but she wasn't sure how to react. She fell silent, and he waited expectantly. She wished she had anything, absolutely anything, to talk about.

Then she saw *him*.

Gabe sauntered in with a sly smile. He didn't look at her. He was instead riveted on his dining companion for the evening.

The woman was perhaps five-ten with platinum-blond hair and a huge chest that didn't bob when she walked. It was easy to tell, too, in that painted-on dress she was almost wearing. Jeez, Charlotte thought, Gabe had better taste than this, didn't he?

You haven't seen him out with a woman in forever. How are you supposed to know what his taste is? And what do you care?

The woman was draped over Gabe like a shawl. Charlotte felt her blood pressure rise a little.

"Speak of the devil," Jack said. "Isn't that your friend?"

"It would appear to be," she said tightly. "I don't know the woman, though."

"She doesn't seem to be the sort of person one would forget," Jack said with a little cough, looking at the woman skeptically.

Charlotte immediately graced Jack with a radiant smile.

Their dinner arrived as Gabe and the Walking Bust were seated at a table not far from them, behind Jack. Unfortunately, they were in Charlotte's immediate line of vision. She focused on Jack's face and tried not to let her eyes wander to the table where the woman was making playful, teasing gestures with those French-manicured nails of hers. Gabe just smiled as the woman pawed him.

"Something wrong?" Jack asked, frowning with concern.

"Hmm? Oh. Nothing," Charlotte muttered, looking down at her plate. So Gabe was into women who proved there was better living through plastic enhancement. So what? It was a free country.

Gabe leaned forward to catch what his date was saying after they ordered, and Charlotte watched as the woman took an obvious nibble at his ear. Then

Gabe looked directly at Charlotte and gave her a slow, deliberate wink.

Charlotte's breath caught in her throat as something clicked in her mind.

That bum!

It was a setup. She might have guessed! He was showing her the type of woman *The Guide* worked for…the moves, the looks, the surreptitious nibbles. He was rubbing Charlotte's face in the fact that there was no way she could handle this date with Jack. She was outclassed, outmaneuvered and hopelessly out of her league.

She turned to Jack, her heart racing with anger. If Gabe hadn't pushed her into this date, she wouldn't be in this jam in the first place. She'd be damned if he would push her *out* of the same date by making her feel inadequate, by showing up with some hourglass Kewpie doll!

She took a long, slow sip of her water, letting the icy liquid calm her down a little.

You're a woman. Be a woman.

It was now or never. Charlotte hadn't studied that little paperback for nothing.

She let the straw trail on her lower lip suggestively before putting her drink down. "I love this restaurant," she said, her voice deliberately husky.

Jack's eyes widened, and the forkful of rice he'd begun to eat remained suspended in midair. "Really?"

"Mmm-hmm." She smiled, consciously taking a deep breath high up in her chest. "It's one of my favorite places in Manhattan Beach. It's quiet, it has this great romantic atmosphere, and the food…" She smiled, picking up a forkful of her own risotto and tasting it. The delicate blend of Parmesan and the earthy taste of mushroom blended perfectly with the light, crisp asparagus. She didn't have to play up the moan of satisfaction. "Well, obviously the food is heavenly."

He was staring at her as if he'd never seen her before. She beat down the instinct to creep back into her shell. He would react in one of two ways: either he'd think she was absolutely insane, or he'd find it attractive and sensual, just as the book claimed.

His eyes suddenly glowed, a deep, mesmerizing emerald. She'd only seen that sort of look directed at other people, like Dana or Bella, but she knew what it meant. *Full steam ahead.* Now that it was directed at her, she wasn't entirely sure what to do with it. She tried for a sexy smile, and his answering grin was uncomfortably intense.

Gabe's dinner companion broke into the moment with a high-pitched giggle. Charlotte, struggling to keep a grip on whatever she was doing right, reluctantly looked over.

The waiter had delivered a huge salad to Gabe's table. The woman was now feeding forkfuls to Gabe, and he was literally eating it up. The woman's blatant display made Charlotte's subtle little sensual cues look like flirting, Amish-style. She could only imagine what the woman was doing underneath the tablecloth....

Charlotte winced. *Okay. I'm not going to think about* that *again.*

Charlotte forced her focus back to her own table. She glanced down at Jack's plate: poached salmon in a wine sauce. "Could I have a taste of that?" she murmured, looking at him hesitantly. "I've never tried that dish before." She knew she ought to be keeping up the sexy act, but in the face of Gabe's competition, she felt herself losing the battle.

Jack smiled, and he picked up a morsel on his fork, holding it out to her.

Her eyes widened. She'd meant could he put it on her plate. She'd never really eaten off another man's fork before, unless you counted Gabe's, which obviously she didn't. The act seemed too intimate, and she started to protest. One glance at Gabe stopped the protest in her throat.

Gabe was staring at Charlotte again, ignoring the lettuce his date was offering. Amazingly enough, he actually had the nerve to look disapproving!

With a slow smile, she leaned forward, taking the salmon neatly off the fork in one small bite. The salmon was incredible, she noted, and she obligingly let out a long sigh.

"God, if I could find that chef, I'd marry him," Charlotte said happily, her eyes half-lidded. *There. Let Gabe disapprove of that!*

Jack leaned over and took her hand, surprising her out of her feelings of triumph. "How about if I just promised to take you here every night?"

She laughed nervously, wondering if she could tug her hand away without seeming too rude. Jack waited a minute, then stroked the back of her hand gently before bringing his own hand back to his side of the table. She suppressed a sigh of relief and made a more concentrated effort to focus on him, rather than the table across the room. She held up her end pretty well, she thought, as they discussed recent movies and books. She concluded that Jack was a nice man, as well as good-looking.

She kept *The Guide* stuff to a minimum, though. Nice or not, Jack definitely made her nervous. When dessert was finally offered, she was more than ready for the date to be over.

"Everything looks so good," Jack said, glancing over at her. "What would you recommend?"

She gave the dessert cart a cursory glance. "The chocolate raspberry decadence sundae," she said immediately. "That's what I'd get, but I'm not really that hungry. I always share it..." She stopped, before she could say *with Gabe*.

He smiled at her, that sexy smile that was beginning to irritate her. "Then we'll share it. Okay?"

She nodded. At this point, she'd agree if he asked to split a hemlock float. She'd had enough dating for one evening.

"Oh Gabe, I shouldn't! Really. Can't you see this dress? I'm supposed to stick to salads!"

Charlotte glanced over at Gabe's table, the dessert cart's next stop. His date was making a lot of noise, attracting most of the patrons' glances and showing off that bionic-woman body of hers. Charlotte rolled her eyes. Jack alone she could have handled, possibly even enjoyed. But Jack and the poster-girl for *The Guide,* both on her first dinner date in years, was more than she could handle.

"Don't worry," Charlotte heard Gabe say over the woman's squealing. "We can split it."

Charlotte saw red.

"Um, Charlotte?" Jack asked tentatively. "Are you okay?"

Charlotte brought her attention back to Jack, immediately feeling guilty. It wasn't his fault that she hadn't dated in so long, or that Gabe was trying to make a point. "I'm sorry, Jack. I've had a lot on my mind lately."

He nodded, and it seemed as if he really understood. "Want to talk about it?"

"Not really."

"You sure?" He smiled and took her hand again,

without any sexy stares or smiles, just friendly. This time, she let him. His hand was warm and comforting. "I'm a good listener."

"You know, I think you would be," she replied, giving his hand a quick squeeze. "But I'm not a great talker, which I guess you probably figured out."

"You were doing fine," he countered. "But I did notice you were kind of distracted. Could you tell me one thing, though?"

She smiled wearily. "Sure. What?"

He glanced over his shoulder, leaned forward and asked quietly, "Why are you so obsessed with that big-chested woman?"

Charlotte's eyes popped wide-open. "Oh, my God."

"Not that she isn't eye-catching, but you've been sending looks over to that table that could skewer things."

Charlotte put her head down on their joined hands, feeling blood rush to her face. "Oh, no..."

He nudged her head up with the back of his hand, forcing her eyes to meet his. "Come on. It's that guy, isn't it? Your friend Gabe."

"No, it's not like that," she muttered, looking desperately in his eyes for understanding. "You see...well, I've known Gabe since I was eight. He's my best friend. But he, along with about all of the male population of Los Angeles, thinks I'm about as sexy as a nature documentary. And being my best friend, he had no real compunction about letting me know that. After all, what are friends for, right?" Her voice broke and she shut up quickly, before she did something even more humiliating. Like crying.

"I've seen some pretty racy nature documentaries," Jack said, causing her to smile and fend off the tears she felt hovering. "And if this guy, or any of the other guys in this city, thinks that you're not absolutely gorgeous, then they're all crazy. You, lady, are one of the prettiest women I've ever seen.''

She snorted. ''Pull the other one. I like my legs even.''

''I like your legs, too,'' he said, wiggling his eyebrows and causing her to laugh. ''So. What are our friends doing now?'' he whispered, leaning over the table, his face set in a melodramatic look of spylike secretiveness.

She sent over a similarly dramatic glance. ''She's eating ice cream off of a spoon. He's feeding her,'' she reported.

''Aw, we can do better than *that*.''

She smiled, perfectly at ease with Jack for the first time all night. His answering smile was mischievous, and she chuckled.

Suddenly, she and Jack were putting on a display that would have put *9 1/2 Weeks* to shame. He fed her ice cream, and she devoured it outrageously, darting her tongue out, licking her lips. She fed him spoonfuls, cooing ridiculous names like ''Honeybunny'' and ''Pumpkin Blossom'' between bites. It was hysterically funny, especially since no one would expect this kind of behavior from her. Heck, she was surprising herself! It was apparently doing the trick, too… She not only had Gabe's attention, she had drawn the attention of several other tables. It was all she could do not to burst out laughing.

She glanced over to study Gabe's response and was shocked out of her merry state. His date had put aside the spoon and had now scooted her chair closer to Gabe, latching on to his neck like a vampire with her fat pink lips. His eyes were half-closed, like a bored cat's. He barely gave Charlotte a cursory glance as he continued to calmly eat ice cream.

She felt angry, and challenged at the gauntlet Gabe had thrown down. She took one last look at the dish she and Jack had just demolished. The only thing left was the long-stemmed cherry they'd put aside.

"Do you want that cherry?" she asked, glancing at Jack.

"If you want it, it's yours," Jack said, rubbing his stomach and laughing. "I'm going to have a huge stomachache tonight, but it was worth it. I haven't had this much fun in ages!"

"You think that's something," she muttered, picking up the cherry and licking it. "Watch this."

She bit down on the cherry, fiercely ripping it off the stem and devouring it.

"Bravo," Jack said, clapping lightly, but she stopped him with a curt hand motion.

"Not yet," she said, holding the stem. "This is the good part. Watch carefully."

With a quick motion, she sucked the cherry stem in. Her face remained stock-still for a moment, as she moved her tongue in a flurry of hidden activity. Slowly, she smiled, then put her fingers to her lips. With a graceful pull, she produced the cherry stem...only now it was tied in a square knot!

She was gratified by his look of shock. "Party trick," she murmured, shrugging.

Jack's jaw dropped. "I feel like I need a cigarette, and I don't even smoke!"

Applause exploded around her, and Charlotte glanced up.

Two tables of men in business suits were clapping wildly, one man even standing up. "You go, girl!" Wolf whistles emerged from different areas. She even caught several pops of a flashbulb.

Torn between running out of the building and hiding under the table, a gesture that surely would have been misinterpreted, she stood up and curtsied, her face aflame. *The Guide* didn't have a chapter on this one, she reflected. How precisely *did* one look sexy while making a fool of oneself?

Then she looked over at Gabe's table.

Gabe was choking on his ice cream. The busty blonde was hitting him on the back, hard. He only stared at Charlotte, his eyes bulging in shock.

She burst into a radiant smile. *Mess with the bull, and you get the horns, buddy!*

With a flirty little flounce, she turned to Jack. "Well, I guess my work here is done," she murmured, in her best superhero voice. "You ready to go?"

"THAT WAS TOO FUNNY!" Charlotte crowed, feeling drunk as Jack walked her home.

"I think you've pretty much proved your sexiness to the businessmen of South Bay," Jack agreed, ambling next to her. "You sure convinced me."

She sighed. "I can't thank you enough, Jack."

"Anytime." He tugged a lock of her hair gently. "It was my pleasure."

She stopped. "No, really. It...I didn't realize how much it hurt when Gabe said what he did. I know he wasn't trying to be hurtful, but sometimes honesty is worse, you know?"

"He wasn't being honest," Jack said, "he was being mistaken. Why did he say it, anyway?"

She blushed, thinking of the bet. "It's a long story, and it's not really important. I guess he was just trying to make me feel better about being one of the guys. It's not like he really thinks of me as a woman, anyway, so it didn't matter."

"If you're not a woman, what are you?"

What else would you be, a hamster? She smirked

as she remembered Gabe's hooting remark over *The Guide.* "He thinks I'm just like his guy friends. We watch football together, we watch movies together. He's attempted to teach me to surf, but I'm hopeless," she explained, starting to walk again. "He was with me when my father died. I was with him when he got his MBA. He's my best friend, Jack. He wouldn't lie to me."

"Maybe he just can't handle the truth," Jack mused.

"What truth can't he handle?" she muttered, frowning and pulling a flower off of a nearby jasmine bush.

Jack smiled. "Why don't you keep thinking about it, and let me know what you come up with."

Within minutes, they were at their street. Stopping in front of the trellis over the gate to her walkway, she paused, wondering what to do next. She liked Jack, but she didn't want to invite him in. Well, she did sort of want to invite him in, but only to talk, and from the way their conversation was running, they'd only talk about Gabe. Even for a casual date, that seemed tacky.

"Well, I guess this is my stop," she said, shifting her weight nervously from foot to foot. "Thanks for taking me out tonight, Jack."

"We'll have to do it again sometime," he said, his grin like summer lightning. "Um…this is usually the 'good-night kiss' part."

She smiled weakly, taking a half step back. "Would you believe I don't kiss on the first date?"

"Would you believe that's the first time outside of a movie I've heard that?" He laughed. He didn't come any closer, though. "I like you, Charlotte Taylor."

She grinned back, relieved. "I like you, too, Jack Landor."

"Say, I have an idea. What are you doing Saturday?"

She rolled her eyes. "A whole lot of nothing. Why?"

"There's this big party, formal dress thing over in Century City. It'll probably be a crashing bore, but I think I'd have a lot more fun if you were there. Will you come with me?"

Charlotte felt her stomach constrict. "Formal dress? As in, really fancy?"

He nodded, and his eyes were pleading. "I don't know a lot of girls out here...I'm out from New York for only a couple of months. It would be a huge favor to me if you'd come. Please?"

She sighed. He'd been such a great sport about the dinner. It seemed to be the least she could do. "All right, Jack. You're on."

"Super." He gave her a broad grin. "I'll pick you up Saturday at seven. See you then." He kissed her cheek quickly, then whistled his way down to his front gate.

She turned to her own walkway, stepping up to her front door and unlocking it. She walked into her empty house, shutting the door behind her.

Jack was warm, funny, gentle and nice. He was, just as most magazines claimed, everything a woman would want in a man. So why didn't her heart race when he talked to her? Why wasn't she getting all gooey and weak in the knees when he flashed that gorgeous smile? Most of all, why hadn't she invited that sun-god bod of his up to her place, so she could break her several-year streak of celibacy?

Maybe there was something wrong with her.

She was tired, and confused, the little rush of triumph she'd had at the restaurant dissipating. She needed to talk this out, make sense of it somehow.

Not really thinking, she walked over to her room. Flopping on her bed, she picked up the phone and dialed it blindly, completely by reflex.

"Hello?" she heard Gabe's voice say darkly over the crackle of a cellular phone.

She froze. She'd called Gabe, of course, ready to ask him to come over because she needed to talk.

But what was she going to say? That it hurt to hear the truth from him? That she'd made a fool of herself tonight all because of him? That she couldn't ask Jack in, and she didn't know why? What would Gabe think? What would he say?

After a few seconds, he gave an irritated huff and hung up. Listening to the dial tone, she buried her face in her pillow. To her surprise, she felt a tear trickle hotly down her cheek.

Okay, maybe this bet had gone too far. She would talk to him tomorrow, and somehow clear this all up. Having all the men in the world strewn at her feet was pointless if she lost her best friend over it.

5

GABE SAT AT HIS DESK the following morning, staring at his computer. He'd been to two meetings, dictated several memos and reports, and plowed through half a dozen licensing proposals for Lone Shark Licensing dealers. Unfortunately, he hadn't really been paying attention to any of them.

He had been up way too late the night before, but at least he had finally gotten a grip on the situation—and gotten even with Charlotte in the process. It was her fault he was sandy-eyed and unable to focus this morning, he thought. A little revenge was not just appropriate, it was mandatory.

When he'd left the restaurant, his date in tow, he was mad enough to spit nails. The plan had been to show Charlotte just how badly these *Guide* women could behave, how patently obvious their tactics could be, and Terri had filled that teaching position perfectly. What he had not expected was that Charlotte would not only miss the point, but eclipse even Terri's blatant performance. He was so incensed, he'd planned on dropping Terri off, heading to Charlotte's house and having it out with her then and there. When it suddenly occurred to him that Charlotte might not be alone, he all but stuffed Terri in a cab.

Before he could tear off to Charlotte's house, the businessmen who had been having their dinner meeting at the restaurant burst out raucously. With a stroke of luck, he managed to buy a roll of film from one of the men who had taken her picture.

By that point, he had gotten under control. Charlotte wasn't going to do anything with Jack...she wasn't that type of woman, which was fortunate for Jack's chances of survival. Charlotte had acted that way to take revenge on him. She'd turned the tables on him, and done it well. She'd expect him to do the same...and with pictures, he thought, he would do just that.

Taking the film to a one-hour Photomat had managed to produce one dark but distinct picture of Charlotte in the process of devouring that infamous cherry. He could have simply embarrassed her with it. The problem was, she was a master at revenge...like the time she had created a picture of him buck-naked except for an artfully placed party hat, and printed it on his surprise birthday invitations.

He smiled grimly. When it came to bets, he and Charlotte never did anything simply. Sometime in the next few hours, she'd get a nice little volley back in retaliation for her performance last night.

Frankly, her performance had shaken him badly.

He wished he could say it was anger, but he knew better. Just thinking of the episode made his blood heat, even now.

He got up to open his window, hoping that a cool breeze from the ocean would lower his temperature. He could only enjoy it for a second before his door flew open.

"What the hell is this?"

Gabe smiled out the window. He knew that irate female voice well. "Hi, Charlotte. What brings you here?"

He turned to see her, hazel eyes flashing with rage. She was wearing an ice-blue sweater set with a miniskirt that showed off her long legs like an art display. His temperature inched up another notch. Before anything else could inch up, he grabbed the printout she held, focusing on it as if it were the most important document in the world.

"It appears to be a picture of you eating...what's that? A cherry?" He suppressed a grin.

"No," she said, her voice hard enough to shape diamonds. "What I mean is, how did this get sent to *my* computer department?"

He blinked, feigning innocence. "I don't know what you're talking about."

"Oh, don't you?" She advanced on him, the look in her eyes murderous. "Then why is it that Ryan, our poker buddy and my co-worker, popped this into *your* company Web site?"

Gabe bit his tongue. He and Ryan had pulled practical jokes on Charlotte in the past, since Ryan's presence at Howes Design made sneaking things into her office or car that much easier. When Gabe had called Ryan last night, Ryan had jumped at the idea. It was going to be one of Gabe's best pranks yet. "I can't imagine," he said, struggling with a straight face.

"I can!" she yelped, poking him hard in the chest. "Everybody knows that Gabe Donofrio picks the photo for that asinine Lone Shark Babe of the Week page and posts it on the Internet. How dare you take my picture and put it there!"

He chuckled and dodged a hard punch in the stomach. "Now, now, calm down. I got the point across. Besides, it couldn't have been on for more than an hour or so."

"It was on all night!"

His laughter stopped dead. All night? What happened? "I told Ryan about this last night, true," he said sharply. "He told me he didn't come into the office until ten at the earliest, and it's only eleven-thirty.''

"Yeah, well, he thought this was so amusing that it wouldn't wait until morning," she said, her voice dripping with bitterness. "And since everyone *knows* the new girl gets posted on Thursday, your little prank has been open season for any acne-covered horndog who regularly checks your Web site *since midnight last night.*"

He blanched. This had not been his plan at all. "He didn't put your name on it, did he?"

"No, and it's the only reason he's still alive. If Wanda hadn't warned me, God knows how many people would have seen it by now. Our Web site support people say we've been getting hits like crazy, all wanting to know who the mysterious 'cherry girl' is. Can you believe this?"

"Oh, God." Gabe rubbed his hands over his face. "You've got to believe me...it wasn't supposed to happen this way. I thought maybe you'd get ribbed at work, but..."

Gabe's executive assistant walked in. "Um, boss?"

Gabe frowned, wishing Charlotte had shut the door before she exploded. "Yes, Jake, what is it?"

Jake's eyes never left Charlotte's legs. "Um...did you finish going over those memos I typed up for you?"

Gabe walked over to his desk, thankful that it gave him time to try to compose his apology. As he started to sift through the piles of papers, the younger man walked up to Charlotte. "Hi there. I'm Jake. I saw you on the Web site."

"Did you?" She sent a poisonous glance over to Gabe. Gabe quickly shifted his focus back to his desktop.

"Yeah, and I was wondering if maybe you'd be interested in dinner sometime. Or maybe a movie?"

"You know, Jake—" Gabe's voice cut through Jake's invitation like steel "—I can't find them right now, and I'm obviously in the middle of something. I'll get them to you later."

Jake looked ready to continue his pursuit, but a hard glare from Gabe sent him packing. "Oh. Sorry, boss."

Gabe escorted him to the door. Before Gabe could shut it, however, three other men walked up to him, papers in hand. "Is she in there?" one asked quietly, trying to glance around Gabe's chest.

"What do you guys want?" Gabe said shortly.

They shifted their feet, ignoring him even as they thrust documents at him. "We just thought you might have time to look these over."

Gabe took a quick look at one of the sheets. "Dammit, Bill, this is a memo you sent me last *month.*"

Bill smiled sheepishly. "Cut me some slack, Gabe. I needed an excuse to get in here. Is that woman hot, or what?"

Hot? Other men were calling his Charlotte *hot?*

Gabe gritted his teeth, taking a deep breath for patience. "I'm in a closed-door meeting for the next half hour. I'll talk with you later." Without another word, he shut the door in their faces, and locked it.

He turned back to Charlotte. She was still on her feet, eyes blazing. He deserved it. It had moved beyond the playful prank that was so characteristic of their friendship. She had every right to be angry.

But it wasn't the anger that worried him. In all their years of playful warfare, in all their competitions and rough times, he'd never seen this look of pain on her face.

"Charlotte, I'm sorry," he said, knowing that the

words did little and would not erase the anguish he was seeing. "I swear, I didn't mean it to work out this way. It was just a joke. You know how we are, Charlotte. It was just..."

"Tell me something, will you?" Her voice was low and uneven. "How is it an intelligent man like yourself can be so completely clueless when it comes to women?"

"What do you mean?"

"Oh, right, I forgot...I'm not really a woman, not to you." Her voice was as bitter as coffee grounds. "I'm just good old Charlie, one of the guys. Fine for providing food, hanging out with, making fun of."

"You make fun of me just as much as I make fun of you," he argued, wishing she'd turn around.

"Oh, right. Add 'gives as good as she gets' to that list. Did it ever occur to you that just once, I'd like to be able to take it easy? I know I haven't had much practice, but I'd like to try being girly and sensitive. I'd even like to cry once in a while. Did you ever think that what you were saying and doing was hurting me?"

That punctured him. "God, Charlotte. You know I never want to hurt you."

She finally turned around, and her eyes were swimming in unshed tears. "Then why are you?"

"Charlotte," he breathed. He was over at her side in an instant. "Angel, I'm sorry, I'm so sorry." He tugged her up out of the chair and into his arms. "I mean it. I didn't know that dumb prank was going to hurt you like this, I'm sorry."

She cried on his shoulder for a minute, delicate, soft little sobs that ripped his heart apart. He hadn't known. Why hadn't he known?

Because she was right. Until recently, he *had* only seen her as one of the guys. She was so strong, so ready to go head-to-head with him at the drop of a hat. It never occurred to him that she wouldn't say anything until the hurt was so bad she was drowning in it. He was so intent on keeping his "perfect life" intact that he'd failed to see what she was going through. He was such an idiot!

"I'm sorry, Gabe. Last night, then the Web site… I guess it was the last straw." She pulled back, and her eyes were huge and liquid, the hazel color luminescent. "I guess I don't really have the right to be angry at you for speaking your mind. But I have to say this. It's hard to hear from your best friend that you're not pretty, not feminine, that you're never going to get married…."

"Hey, wait a minute," he interrupted, giving her a gentle shake. "I never said anything like that!"

She tilted her head to the side, a sad smile on her face. "Not precisely, but then, did you need to spell it out? I've known you for forever. I knew what you were trying to say." She pushed out of his arms, walking over to the window as she wiped her eyes with the backs of her hands. "Heck. It's impossible to disagree with you. I mean, look at me. What would a man want with someone like me?"

"Are you kidding? Charlotte, you have plenty to offer a man." He leaped to her defense, trying to undo some of the damage he'd caused. "You're smart, and sexy, and funny. You just don't see it in yourself."

"Not you, too," she said, hiccuping. "I thought you of all people would agree with me."

If possible, he felt even lower. "You know I'm on your side, Charlotte."

"You haven't been. Not since this stupid bet got started." She turned on him, her eyes large and luminous. "Do you know why I stuck with it? Because if I lose, your sister and Dana promised they'll finally get off my back and let me live my life, my way. It's the easiest solution. Or at least, it seemed like it was…until you decided to go to war.''

''Charlotte, please. I already feel so low, I could walk under a rattlesnake. Wearing a top hat.'' Gabe rubbed a tear off her cheek. ''I was just being selfish. I was…'' He paused, taking a deep breath, and admitted to Charlotte what he'd never admit in front of anybody else…not his family, not the Hoodlums, not anyone. ''I was afraid. I was scared you'd change into one of those superficial, man-crazy *Guide* girls. And I was afraid I'd lose the best friend I have. How lame is that, right?''

She sent him a watery smile. ''Actually, I kind of know how you feel. I tried calling you last night. I chickened out, because I didn't know how to talk to you about all of this.''

He stuck out his hand. ''Let's make a pact. No matter what happens, we stay best friends. That means we can talk to each other about anything, and whatever else is going on in our lives, we're there for each other. Deal?''

She shook his hand. ''Deal,'' she said, then threw her arms around him. ''Let's not go through this again.''

He returned the hug fiercely, crushing her to him. ''We won't. I'm not going to risk losing you again, angel.''

They probably didn't have to hug quite that long, but one minute seemed to stretch into another, and neither were in any hurry to leave the comfort of the other. She felt compact, fitting snugly against his body. He stroked the back of her head, feeling the silky softness of her hair beneath his fingers, and heard her sigh. He looked down, and she looked up.

Her cheeks were flushed, and her eyes were wide and clear, and looking up at him with that tenderness that he hadn't seen in way too long.

Any woman who looks at you like that deserves to be good and kissed, Gabe.

Damn fine idea, he thought. Finally, his conscience had decided to help out, instead of being such a pill all the time. He leaned down, close, his eyes never leaving hers.

Just a breath away from her lips, he stopped.

Wait a second. What am I doing?

He jerked away as if she were an electrified fence. He put a few crucial feet of space between them, then stared at her. He could feel his heart pounding in his chest like a jackhammer, and noticed that her eyes were huge, almost wary.

"Well. I'm glad we got that all straightened out," he said gruffly.

"Oh. Me, too." Charlotte still stared at him.

"So." He cleared his throat. Boy, that was a close one. What had he been thinking? "I've got an idea of how I can make it up to you."

She sighed. "This ought to be humorous."

"It's my fault you're stuck in this bet. The logical conclusion would be that it's now my responsibility to help you out of it."

"Gabe," Charlotte said in a skeptical tone, "I think you've helped enough, don't you?"

"I didn't know what was going on," he argued. "The problem is, you need to put on a really good show, get a little more comfortable around guys."

"Oh, come on," she said, laughing. "I've been hanging out with the Hoodlums since I could drive. Now you think the problem is I'm awkward around men?"

"But you *are* awkward...when you're being a

woman." He looked her over. "I've got it. We'll do a trial run. Are you busy tonight?"

"You're kidding, right?" She narrowed her eyes at him, then shrugged. "Nope. No dates tonight, and what a shock that is. But it is a designated date night. Dana will probably drop by and drag me somewhere. I hope she doesn't bring her husband with her. How awkward would *that* be?"

"Can you figure a way out of it, and meet me at Sharkey's, around seven?"

"Sure."

"And dress up."

Her eyes widened. "Huh?"

"Just trust me," he said, nodding. "With any luck, it'll make this bet business a snap."

"You're lucky I'm your best friend, because no sane woman would put up with you," she answered, then nodded. "Seven at Sharkey's. Got it."

THE PROBLEM WAS, this had seemed like a good idea in theory. Now, looking at it, it occurred to Gabe that this whole plan would have worked a lot better if the guys hadn't taken their jobs so *seriously*.

"Gabe, this is ridiculous," Charlotte said, laughing.

"I think Gabe had a spectacular idea," Sean said, throwing an arm around her shoulders. "If you want to learn to catch a guy, you gotta go to the source."

"Nobody said anything about catching guys," Gabe said sharply. "I just said she needed to be more comfortable around them when she's dressed up."

And dressed up she was. She looked sharp in a dark lavender dress, similar to the pink one he'd first seen on her when this whole mess started. She was wearing heels again, too. He scrupulously avoided staring at her legs. Or her chest. Or her face, really. He'd pretty much resigned himself to talking to the top of her head.

But the other guys had no such problems.

"Hey, pretty lady," Mike said, beaming his best come-on smile at her. "Come here often?"

"Mike, we were just here last Monday night, remember? Catching the game?"

Mike frowned, nonplussed. "Oh. Right." He brightened, and tried the smile again. "But you didn't look like *this,* gorgeous."

"Gabe, this is insane." She walked over to where he was standing. He noticed the guys riveted to the gentle sway of her hips, and had to stop himself from glaring at them. "It's not like they're really *men.* They're just the Hoodlums."

"I resent that," Sean piped up.

"Yeah, just give us a try, baby," Ryan said, wiggling his eyebrows. "We'll be *plenty* enough love for you, hot stuff."

"Hot stuff? Gorgeous? What, do you guys get handed a manual in high school or something?"

"Gabe," Sean whined. "She's not taking this *seriously.*"

"How can I?" Charlotte laughed. She was wearing a darker lipstick, too, and her eyes seemed even larger in the dim light. Whatever she was doing with makeup was working, big time. "You guys keep clowning around."

"Just pretend you're at some big party or something," Gabe said, trying his best to be focused. He'd promised her he'd get her out of the mess he'd landed her in. He meant it. If he had to help her become the girliest woman on the face of the planet, then he'd do it. "No matter what the guys say, just keep smiling, but throw attitude at them."

"What kind of attitude?" Charlotte asked, bewildered.

"Like they're bugs." He smiled. Teaching her to be girly didn't mean she had to be a pushover, however. He wasn't about to teach her how to catch a guy. "Like you're the most beautiful woman alive, and they're wasting your time. Like they're insane to even *dream* they've got a chance at you."

"Hey, Gabe, no fair," Mike said, frowning. "I get treated like that by every other woman I meet. You're ruining all my fun here."

Charlotte smiled wickedly, slowly getting the idea. "You mean, treat them like dirt, and they'll revere me as a goddess?"

"It's a trade secret, but yup, that's it." Gabe smiled back, savoring the look on her face. This was going to be good.

She sashayed back to the bar stool she'd been sitting on. Gabe couldn't help but be riveted this time, either...the sassy little swing in her hips was mesmerizing.

Mike stepped up to the plate again. "Hey, pretty lady..."

Her eyes were wide and sexy, but her voice was coolly amused. "This—" she gestured down the length of her body "—is not for you." She pointed at him, then smiled and looked away.

Mike goggled. Ryan laughed and nudged him aside. "Excuse me, miss, do you have thirty-five cents?" He grinned. "My mother told me to call her when I fell in love."

Charlotte reached into her purse and produced three quarters. "Here. After you reach her, try calling somebody who cares."

"Ooh, she's good," Sean said as Ryan good-naturedly grumbled and stepped back. "Here's a better one. Are you tired? Because you've been running through my mind all night long.''

Charlotte tried to look bored, but the humor glinted through her eyes. Finally, she broke down and laughed. "Okay. You win. You get one dance.''

Sean broke into a huge grin, leading her off to the dance floor. "Works every time," he called over his shoulder, before pushing his way through the shimmying crowd.

Gabe watched as Charlotte moved, noticing that several pairs of male eyes were watching her with predatory awareness.

He prayed he didn't have the same look on his own face.

He didn't want to be attracted to her. He didn't want to change what they had. All this time, they'd been friends. At first, he could still superimpose the image of her as a bratty eight-year-old over her. When that didn't work, he focused on her grubby jeans and oversize sweatshirts.

Frankly, he'd never *let* himself see Charlotte as a woman before. Now he didn't have much choice. The proof of her transformation hit him in the face like a slap.

He watched as she laughed at some joke Sean was making. She looked incredible. She was happy, vibrant, so alive she almost shimmered with it.

He wanted her.

Want all you want, his conscience chimed in, *but hands off. She's a friend, remember?*

He hated to admit it, but his conscience was right. It was the cornerstone of his life. Women come and women go, but friends are for life. After their massive fight this afternoon, he had gotten a taste of just how painful it could be if he lost his friendship with Charlotte. It might be bad if he couldn't spend as much time with her because she got married. It would be a comparative hell, however, if he couldn't see her ever again.

He was the first to admit that his relationships didn't last long, and those that had lasted a long time had ended with harsh words and no further contact. He wasn't about to risk that with Charlotte. If he did get physical with Charlotte, it would be a relationship. He wasn't so dumb that he didn't realize that.

So he wouldn't get physical with her. He'd just be her friend, and that was that.

The song finished, and Sean led Charlotte away by one hand, grinning like a fool. Before they could make it to the side of the floor, another man stepped in front of Charlotte, stopping her.

Gabe shot to his feet.

Charlotte's eyes widened as the man yelled something to her over the fast tempo of the next song. She glanced nervously at Sean, who shrugged. She bit her lower lip, then shrugged, herself, and accompanied the man back out on the dance floor.

Sean walked over to Gabe, whose mouth had dropped open. "Can you believe that? One dance, and that guy just sneaks in and steals Charlotte out from under me."

Gabe ignored the disturbing thought that phrase provoked. "What were you thinking?" he yelled instead. "She's off with a perfect stranger!"

"So?" Sean shrugged. "She seems to be holding her own. That was the point of this whole exercise, wasn't it?"

Gabe saw the man try to dance a little too close to Charlotte, presumably under the pretext of whispering something to her. Gabe started to stride toward the floor with the intention of beating the man senseless.

"Whoa, whoa!" Sean grabbed him. "Easy, fella. She's okay."

Gabe growled but noticed that Charlotte firmly nudged the man away from her, shaking her head. She wore the same expression that she'd sent to Mike earlier. *This is not for you,* he saw her mouth to the man, frowning.

His breathing eased.

"You know," Sean said perceptively, "if you're not going to sell something, don't put it in the window."

"What the hell is that supposed to mean?" Gabe said, too intent on keeping track of Charlotte to really pay attention to his friend's inscrutable words.

Sean gave him a gentle shove. "It means she looks beautiful, man. Leave her alone."

"I am leaving her alone," Gabe growled.

"Obviously."

Charlotte walked back to the group with her dance partner following her like a puppy. She had a small smile on her face. She turned. "Thanks for the dance."

"Can I have your number?" the man asked eagerly.

She thought about it for a minute. "No."

"Why not?"

"You heard her, buddy," Gabe said, glowering at him as he put an arm around Charlotte's shoulders. "Back off."

"All right, all right. Jeez." The man frowned at Gabe, then sent one last hopeful smile at Charlotte. "I loved your picture on the Web site. I can't wait to tell the guys I danced with the Lone Shark Babe of the Week."

Charlotte's eyes widened as the man walked away.

"It was a great picture, you've got to admit," Ryan said, chuckling at her surprise.

She arched an eyebrow at him, pinning him to the seat with a glare. "Really. And that was what prompted you to post it for twelve hours."

Ryan smirked, unrepentant. "Got a good number of hits, too. The mystery thing really got a lot of guys going. Besides, I think they were starting to get tired of the models we were using."

"Oh, I'm sure." Charlotte's glare intensified.

"No, really. Well, they weren't complaining. A babe is still a babe." Ryan grabbed a handful of peanuts and shrugged. "But most of the babes we had on the site were these 'hand me the cocoa butter' babes that only exist on mythical tropical islands. No average guy is going to run into her in a supermarket."

"So what's your point?" Charlotte asked skeptically. "I'm a 'pass the frozen peas' babe?"

"The point is, you're obviously in real life…you're gorgeous, but you're also available. And that's kind of a turn-on." He grinned lasciviously. "That thing with your tongue was pretty hot, too. I kept a copy of the photo for myself."

She covered her face with her hands. "Oh, God…"

"Hey, can I get a few copies?" Sean inquired. "A couple of guys down at the surf shop wanted to see her, but she got taken off the site too soon."

"No, you can't," Charlotte and Gabe said at the same time.

"All right, all right." Sean looked pained. "Sheesh."

Charlotte took a quick glance at her watch and groaned. "I've got to go, fellas. Thanks for the…education."

The guys put up a chorus of complaints. "It's still

early,'' Sean pleaded, smiling. "What, you got an early date tomorrow or something?''

"Two, actually,'' she said, causing Gabe's eyes to narrow. "The first being a spa date with Dana, starting with an early-morning jog. And since it's Dana, that means *really* early.''

"What's the other one?''

"You won't believe it,'' Charlotte said. "There's this big party at the Century Plaza. Big formal dress thing. If he weren't in such a jam for a date, I'd say no. I mean, you know I'm not comfortable at those kind of things. If I can just get through it without making a fool of myself, I'll be happy.'' She stared pointedly at Ryan. "*Especially* after the Web site thing.''

Ryan had the grace to look embarrassed. Gabe felt an aftershock of the guilt he'd been hit with that afternoon.

She nodded with satisfaction. "Well, I'm glad we both learned a lesson tonight,'' she said, smiling. "I'll see you guys later.''

"I'll walk you to your car,'' Gabe said.

"It's not that far....''

"I'm coming with you,'' he said insistently.

"Don't try to get her number,'' Mike warned, grinning. "Trust me. She's tough!''

They left amid a barrage of catcalls and loud commentary from the Hoodlums. Charlotte just smiled. Gabe didn't.

"Thanks for the help, Gabe,'' Charlotte said, unlocking Jellybean. "I know this can't be easy for you.''

He grimaced. "What can't be?''

"The fact that you're trying to help me stick with this bet.'' She shrugged. "I might have to pay you that thousand in installments....''

"Don't be an idiot," he said, rolling his eyes. "We'll work out something."

She nodded with a thankful smile, then shivered.

"Here," he said, taking off the light jacket he was wearing and throwing it over her shoulders. "You'll catch cold."

"How did I get lucky enough to get a best friend like you?" She gave him a quick hug.

He told his arms not to go around her, but they wouldn't listen.

"Good night," she said casually, obviously not having any of the problems he was having. She got in her car.

"Good night," he replied, and watched her drive out of the parking lot.

He walked back in, frowning.

"Where's your jacket?" Sean asked, glancing at him.

"Charlotte was cold."

"She ought to be," Mike joked. "That was not much of a dress she was wearing. But what she *was* wearing," he said, rolling his eyes heavenward, "was *choice.*"

"So how'd we do?" Ryan asked. "Is she now a kick-butt, man-eating machine?"

"I wouldn't go that far, but I guess we helped," Gabe replied. She certainly looked comfortable enough when she was dancing with that guy. "She's not looking forward to that party tomorrow, though. I wish there were some way we could help her out. That thing with the Web site really got to her." And he'd be damned if he saw her go through that much pain ever again.

"Wait a second…" Ryan said. "There might be a way. She said Century Plaza, right?"

"Right," Gabe said hesitantly. "So?"

"So," Ryan said, "that means it's the Sheffield party."

"Again, so?"

"*So,* I know the printer who makes all the Sheffield invitations," Ryan said, and grinned expectantly.

It took Gabe a second for Ryan's words to sink in. When they did, a matching grin spread across his face.

"Break out your tuxes, boys," he said, snickering and feeling better for the first time that night. "Looks like we've got a party to crash."

6

"I DIDN'T KNOW, CHARLOTTE. I swear to God, I had no idea."

Charlotte didn't even look up from her glass of champagne. "And I still believe you, Jack. Really. Just let it go."

He studied her for a moment, his emerald eyes lighting with warmth. "I can't believe you're being so calm about this. If I were you, I'd be dumping that glass of champagne all over me."

Charlotte grinned. "Now that I've made sense out of that sentence, it really isn't as bad as all that, Jack."

"There must be five hundred people out there," Jack countered, "and they're all staring at *you*. But that's not a big deal?"

She thought about it a second. "Well, it's not your fault I decided to wear red. And it's not your fault that you didn't remember that the Sheffield Ball is also called Los Angeles' Black and White Ball because..."

"Everybody wears black and white," Jack said, shaking his head. "Why didn't anybody tell me?"

"I think it was on the invitation that you didn't really read," Charlotte suggested. "Okay, so maybe it was your fault, a little. And it is definitely your fault that I'm sitting under a spotlight at the head table, but..."

Jack groaned and put his head down on his hands.

Charlotte laughed. "Okay. Feel guilty. You deserve it."

"I owe you for this one, Charlotte."

She shrugged again. "Jack, after what I've been through this week, this is nothing."

When she had walked in with Jack, she had seen the sea of stark, unbroken black and white, and frozen. Five hundred pairs of eyes had snapped on her, staring as if she'd just emerged from a spaceship. It was strangely reminiscent of her old nightmare of showing up for a big class design review in her ratty old underwear. Her initial reaction had been to turn, run back out the doors, steal Jack's keys from the valet and make an escape. But she hadn't. Instead, she kept her chin up, her eyes wide and her smile bright. Even if she had a blush that matched her deep red dress, she wouldn't let them see otherwise how humiliating the experience was.

The fact was, she loved the dress, and it was the first time in her life she could actually say that. She'd put up with the pastel confections that Derek, her ex-boyfriend, had created, and the similarly frail summer dresses that Dana had fobbed off on her. But this, a simple, minimal sheath in a dark burgundy, had practically yelled "Charlotte!" when she stepped into the store. She'd turned down all the peaches and pale pinks that Dana had suggested, and when she tried her dress on, even Dana and the saleswoman had to admit it was fantastic. It fit her like a glove, and she felt like a queen in it.

She remembered that every time she saw someone stare at her with a look of amusement, or worse, contempt. She looked pretty good in her red dress. Pretty *darned* good. So if everybody else was wearing black and white, so what?

She'd been caked in mud in front of the most eligible bachelor in America. She'd practically smeared whipped cream all over herself in a public restaurant. She was the pinup of the week on a national Web site. And she had made grown men weep at a nearby sports bar. Compared to all that, wearing red in front of a bunch of L.A. socialites was a cakewalk!

The funny thing was, she really needed to thank Gabe for his part in her new confidence, even if he didn't realize that he had helped her. If he hadn't pushed her, she never would have realized how much she could take...or how much she had to give. She wasn't sure how it happened, but somehow a lot of things she used to view as "terrifying" were suddenly trivial. She wasn't going to die of embarrassment. In fact, she wasn't even going to *see* most of these people again. The people she really cared about thought she was fine. More than that. They thought she was beautiful.

She was pretty sure Gabe thought she was, at least.

She frowned, remembering that strange moment in his office. He'd leaned so close she could practically feel currents of energy running off of him. For a brief, crazed moment, she thought he might have kissed her.

Not that that was what she wanted. She'd known for years that Gabe was handsome. If anything, he was *too* handsome. Men like that were never interested in women like her, so it hadn't occurred to her to see him as anything but a friend. But for a brief moment, hadn't she hoped...

No. That wasn't going to happen. The things that *were* happening to her were strange enough.

"That's quite a dress," a woman walking past their table said, her voice catty.

"Thanks. I love it," Charlotte said easily. "The

way I see it, red stands out so much better against black and white, don't you think?''

"I certainly think so," the woman's date agreed, giving Charlotte a serious once-over and leering. Charlotte winked at him. The woman gasped in shock before hurrying her date away, hissing at him as they left.

Charlotte looked at Jack, who was goggling at her. "What?" she asked, smoothing her hair.

"Who are you, and what have you done with Charlotte Taylor?"

She chuckled. "I know. It's like the invasion of the pod people, only this time with a sense of humor."

Jack shook his head. "You amaze me, Charlotte. You don't seem like the girl I had dinner with the other night at all."

She sobered slightly, considering his words. "Is that a bad thing?"

"No," he said quickly. "It's just…well, it's like somebody found your volume control and turned it all the way up."

She shot him a skeptical glance. "And that's supposed to be better?"

He grinned and gently stroked his fingertip along her jawline. "It is when you've been whispering for years, beautiful."

She smiled again. If this kept up, her cheek muscles were going to be cramping. But she couldn't help herself.

"I need to go mingle…there are some big fund-raisers here tonight," Jack said. "Want to come with me?"

"Nah," she said. "I've talked to more people tonight than I have in years. I thought I'd people-watch a little bit, maybe sit out on the sidelines."

"Okay, pretty girl," Jack said. "Give me half an hour and I'll take you home."

"Deal."

He gave her a quick peck on the cheek, then headed out toward the milling guests. They clumped around him like iron filings on a magnet. He disappeared into the crowd.

She stood up and started walking toward one of the freestanding bar setups, eager to get a glass of ice-cold water. He was a nice guy, that Jack. After her years of not dating at all, he was an incredibly good "training wheels" date. The only person who had been more sweet and supportive than he was...

She blinked. Was Gabe, now that she thought about it. But Gabe was just a friend, so naturally he didn't count.

There it was again, that flash from Gabe's office. *No, Charlotte. He doesn't count.*

A honey-blond woman stopped her, looking her over. "Great dress," she said. Her tone was genuine, with none of the sarcasm or venom of the woman Charlotte had spoken with earlier.

"Thanks," Charlotte said, smiling. "I have to admit, though, I didn't know about the black-and-white dress code thing."

"Really?" The woman smiled back, and her voice was warm. Charlotte thought she recognized her from a movie she'd seen. "I was sitting at my table envying the hell out of you, ready to rip into my agent for not thinking of trying a red dress last year. You're getting great buzz tonight, so I figured you must be an actress."

"No," Charlotte hastily explained. "I'm a designer."

"That explains it," the woman said, snapping her

fingers. "It's written all over you. Have I seen your fall collection?"

It took Charlotte a minute to figure out what she was asking. Then she quickly shook her head. "Oh, no. I'm not that kind of designer. I'm a graphic designer. I haven't done fashion stuff in years."

"You might want to rethink that. That dress suits you perfectly…it's simple yet smashing. Sort of Grace Kelly does Versace."

Charlotte glanced down at her dress, grinning foolishly. "You know, I was thinking more Audrey Hepburn does Vera Wang."

"Better!" The woman reached inside her purse and handed Charlotte a card. "That does it. If you're up for it, I'd love to have you work with me on my dress for the Oscars next year. I'm always looking for a killer stylist. I have a good feeling about you."

A stylist? *Her?* "Um, sure. I mean, I'll think about it."

The woman smiled brilliantly before moving back into the crowd.

Okay, now this would be the part where I wake up.

But Charlotte didn't wake up. She was still standing there, in her off-the-rack red dress, holding the business card of one of the most successful actresses in Hollywood.

Charlotte felt like singing. She was queen of the world. She was invincible. She was a cross between Marilyn Monroe and Mighty Mouse. Oh, if only the Hoodlums could see her now!

She heard the steady rumbling of conversation slow, then grind to a halt. Curious, she looked toward the doorway.

Speak of the devil.

The Hoodlums were framed in the large doorway, standing resplendent. Gabe, Ryan, Mike and Sean posed like *GQ* sentinels, completely indifferent to the stir they were creating.

It was strange enough to see her poker crew at a Sheffield party, much less their Black and White Ball. But as she glanced over their formal attire, she noticed that something was missing.

Namely, their pants.

They were all wearing brilliant white shirts and black tuxedo jackets. But from the waist down, they wore long, loose-fitting surfer shorts in every color under the sun, paired with black suede high-topped sneakers. Both the shorts and the sneakers displayed a large logo...the distinctive shark with sunglasses that Charlotte herself had designed for Gabe's sportswear company!

In unison, the Hoodlums removed their black Wayfarer sunglasses, tucking them away in their inner coat pockets. They walked down the steps, looking every inch like models on the catwalk as flashbulbs exploded. Guests let out a tentative chuckle and a smattering of applause.

Charlotte made her way through the throng to where they were standing. She loved them for showing up. She just loved them, period.

"Gabe!" She ran up to him and gave him a huge, exuberant hug.

"There you are, angel." He smiled as she distributed enthusiastic hugs to the rest of the crew. "I was just about to send the Hoodlums on a search and rescue for you."

"You could have just stood here on the steps. I'm sure I would have noticed sooner or later." She looked at them, laughter fighting with admiration. Laughter won. "Great gams, guys."

"What do you think?" Ryan struck a *Vogue*-like pose. "I'm too sexy for my shorts."

"You guys are too sexy for this party," Charlotte agreed. "What are you doing here?"

The guys didn't say anything, but stared pointedly at Gabe. Gabe cleared his throat. "Well, we discussed it last night, and we thought you might need a little more coaching."

She raised an eyebrow. "Oh, really."

"Well, we were a little…concerned." Gabe looked slightly red, a fact that caused giggles to bubble through her. She never thought she'd see the day that Gabe Donofrio was embarrassed. "I kept thinking about how you said you felt uncomfortable, and how this was going to be awful, and I thought…well, you know."

She took pity on him. "You guys were trying to help, weren't you?"

They nodded, sheepishly. Then devilish grins broke out. "So, how are we doing?" Ryan finally said.

Charlotte couldn't help it. She burst into laughter. It was one of the sweetest, silliest things she'd ever seen. When she finally recovered, she said, "Well, believe it or not, I really am thankful. You're wonderful. Insane, but wonderful."

"And you, hot stuff, are stunning," Mike said, bending over her hand for a courtier-style kiss. Out of the corner of her eye, she noticed Gabe frowning at the action. "So, do you think you'll give me a dance tonight, or are you going to blow me off again?"

"Dance?" Charlotte said. She glanced out at the ballroom floor. Couples were doing a slow sway to an elevator-music version of some popular song. She frowned. "I don't know. This isn't really my style."

"We'll handle that," Gabe said. "Ryan?"

Ryan grinned broadly. "On my way."

She watched Ryan dart over to the leader of the

orchestra. He said his request, then shook the man's hand. She didn't even want to think how much money Ryan was bribing him with.

The song the band was playing limped to a close. Then, after a few moments of silence, the brass section positively exploded into a lively rendition of "Louie, Louie."

The tuxedo- and evening-gown-clad group was stunned yet again. The Hoodlums, however, were in their element. Charlotte didn't know whether to hide or simply laugh as the four men got out there and shook their stuff.

Gabe smiled, taunting her. "Chicken?"

Chicken? Tonight, she could walk on fire. The man had no idea. "Try and keep up with me," she shot back.

With that, she stepped out on the floor and showed them exactly how it was done.

To her surprise, the faces of the crowd were no longer filled with condescension or disdain. They now seemed to be enjoying the spectacle that was livening up what was obviously a traditionally dull party. She noticed several younger couples moving out on the floor and dancing with them. The Hoodlums were a sensation!

The song wound down with a flourish, and Gabe grabbed her and dipped her on the final note. The crowd erupted into applause. There was no laughter, no mocking, just sheer delight.

Gabe picked her up from the dip, ignoring the response of the rest of the audience. "I don't believe it." His smile seemed to be for her alone. "You're incredible, angel."

He had an arm lightly resting around her waist. She was still breathless from dancing. At least, she thought it was from dancing. She put a hand on his chest and could feel his heart pulsing under her hand through his white shirt. His gray eyes shone like beacons.

Without warning, Edna Sheffield stormed over, her face knit in an expression of fury. "Who are you people?"

Gabe and Charlotte jumped away from each other. Charlotte swallowed hard. "Mrs. Sheffield…"

Ryan, Mike and Sean stood in a united front by Gabe. Gabe cleared his throat. "We're the Hoodlums," he said simply, as if that explained everything.

Edna's eyes widened so far that Charlotte was afraid they'd pop right out of their sockets. "The who?"

"No, the Who is a rock band out of England," Ryan corrected her, tongue-in-cheek. "We're a surf crew out of Manhattan Beach."

"A…*surf crew?*" If possible, Edna's eyes widened even farther. "I don't believe this! I'll give you exactly one minute to get…"

"Gabe! It's great you could make it." Jack's smooth baritone floated over as he made his way across the dance floor. He shook Gabe's hand. Charlotte stifled a laugh at Edna's new look of shock. The woman obviously fawned on Jack Landor, proud of his presence at her society function. Now she'd been insulting what looked like his best friend!

"Jack," Gabe said, grinning. "I just thought that the place could use a little livening up."

"Good thinking," Jack said with a laugh, putting a casual arm around Charlotte's shoulders. He smiled down at her. "You looked incredible out there. I didn't know you could dance like that."

She shrugged. "Another one of my party tricks," she said easily. The crew grinned at her. Edna Sheffield remained speechless.

"Hope you don't mind me dancing with your girl," Gabe said in an oddly neutral tone.

"I don't mind who she dances with," Jack said with an easy smile. "After all, I'm the one who's taking her home." He gave Charlotte a quick squeeze. "Which we can do now, by the way. Edna, it's been a wonderful party. Best one in ages, thanks to these guys."

"Ah, thank you, Jack." Edna clearly looked dazed.

"Take care of my friends, will you? I promised this lovely lady I'd have her home early." He glanced down at Charlotte. "Ready?"

She looked at the Hoodlums. All the guys except Gabe were smiling broadly in approval. Gabe just looked off in the distance, a bored expression on his face.

Well, what was she expecting? A pleading look, begging her not to go?

She glanced at Jack. The most eligible bachelor in America wanted to take her home. And tonight, she was capable of anything.

"Home it is," she said, looping her arm through his. "I'll talk to you later, guys."

They whistled at her, making her exit with Jack a very public spectacle. Flashes went off, people applauded.

She resisted sneaking a peek back at the guys as she and Jack finally walked out the door.

Half an hour later, she was still riding the emotional crest that had hit her at the Sheffield Ball when Jack dropped her off at her house.

"I don't know how to thank you, Jack," she said thoughtfully.

He smiled down at her. "For what? You did me the favor, remember?" He nudged her gently. "I've got to say, it's been a long time since I've had a date that great.''

She shook her head. "You don't understand." How could he? For the first time in her life, she felt…beautiful. She didn't care what the other people thought, or said. She felt like a full-blooded *woman*. How could a man understand that a woman never forgot the first time she felt like that?

"All I know is, you were beautiful out there tonight. You were a sensation." He surveyed her for a moment, silent. "So, here we are again. And it's not the first date." He waited expectantly.

Her post-party euphoria fled in a tiny burst of panic. Now what was she going to do?

Wait a minute. She'd been a goddess tonight. She was beautiful, confident and capable of anything. Why shouldn't she try to see if Mr. Right was Jack, after all?

She took a deep breath and closed her eyes.

After a second, he brushed his lips over hers.

She waited.

And felt nothing.

When it stopped, she opened her eyes. "So. That's it, huh?" she asked in all seriousness.

He laughed. "If you've got to ask, then I'm not doing it right." He dipped his face down to hers again. This time, the pressure was a little more insistent, but it was still more friendly than passionate.

All right, this just wasn't *fair*. She was being kissed by a man who was cute, charming, eligible and apparently interested. And her heart rate barely bobbled!

He pulled away, then studied her face with a nod. "How 'bout that time? Anything?"

She sighed. "Maybe I'm undergoing sensory overload," she ventured in a conciliatory tone. "It's been a long night."

"And an eventful one." He shrugged, giving her a lopsided smile that warmed her heart. "All right, pretty girl, I'm off. I'll call you this week if you want to do something."

"Okay." Did she want to see him this week? She had fun with him, but this was getting a little weird. She waved to him as he turned and walked to his gate.

She walked up to her front door pensively. She didn't know what had happened, and that was part of the problem. She didn't really have a lot of experience with men in the physical arena, but she was pretty sure that what had just happened wasn't a good indicator. Good grief. Dead car batteries had more spark than they'd managed to generate!

She was just shutting the door behind her when she heard a rush of footsteps on the walkway. Praying it wasn't Jack again, she cautiously opened the door a crack.

Gabe gave her a breathless smile that gleamed in the moonlight. "Good," he huffed. "You're still up."

"What are you doing here?" she asked, bewildered.

"Um…" He paused for a moment, a blank look on his face. "Would you believe I'm here to pick up the jacket I loaned you yesterday?"

She quirked an eyebrow at him. "If it's the best you could come up with."

"Then that's what I'm here for."

"Come on in," she said, opening the door for him. "I could use somebody to talk to."

He walked in and sat down, groaning with relief. He surveyed her from head to toe, and sent her a warm but tired smile. "That's a pretty cool dress."

She felt a little pulse of warmth shoot through her. "Thanks. I like it."

"You knocked 'em dead tonight."

"And I have you and the Hoodlums to thank for it," she said. She giggled, remembering the look on Edna Sheffield's face. "So, did you decide you'd just had enough of the party, or did Edna go ahead and kick you out?"

"I'd had enough. The guys are still there," Gabe added, grinning. "And Edna tried to hire us as entertainment for her Christmas Gala." He laughed, tucking his tie into his jacket pocket as he undid the top button of his shirt. He took a deep breath. "God, I hate ties."

"I have no sympathy for you," she scoffed, reaching awkwardly for the zipper on the back of her dress. After the disappointing episode with Jack, she could feel the energy of the evening sap out of her. "This whole outfit is like a tie from your neck to your knees, pal. Not to mention the contraption I have to wear underneath. I feel like I need a team of scientists to get it on and off."

"Looks good, though."

She wriggled uncomfortably, her sudden weariness making her fingers fumble. "Do me a favor and unzip me, will you?"

She turned in front of him and waited.

She thought for a moment he must've fallen asleep on the couch. It seemed to take him forever to get up. Finally, he stood behind her. His breath warmed her nape, and she felt an odd shiver in her stomach.

"How'd you get into this?" he muttered, struggling with the zipper.

"Dana helped. She's got a degree in this sort of thing," she whispered, then stopped on a quick exhalation. He slowly unzipped the length of her dress. She was sure that the way the tip of his thumb brushed down the smooth skin between her shoulder blades was purely accidental. Still, she felt her heart pulse, then double in speed, heat curling through her.

"That better?" He leaned over her shoulder, studying her face for a second.

She gulped, nodding quickly.

"Need help with anything else?"

She glanced over her shoulder and saw his gaze riveted to the back of her hooked bustier.

"Um, no." She bit her lip, confused by the sudden rush of blood racing through her. "I can manage from here."

She bolted to her bedroom before he could sense the rapid change that occurred in her breathing, in her body. There was no way he could have realized that her neck and back were two of the most sensitive spots on her body. They were erogenous zones in their own right, something that always embarrassed her. He certainly hadn't done it on purpose.

She was confused enough right now. This was no time to indulge in some strange, adolescent crush on her best friend!

She quickly and awkwardly shed her clothes, dumping them in the dry-cleaning hamper. She threw on a large T-shirt and flannel boxers, taking a deep breath before wandering back out.

"So what did you want to talk about?" he asked. He'd grabbed a glass of water and was comfortably settled in.

She sighed, flopping down next to him on the couch. "I'm confused, Gabe."

"Confused about what, angel?"

She put her head back, staring at her white ceiling. "It was a lot simpler before this whole bet thing got started. I really thought I was happy with my life."

"I know that one," Gabe said, groaning. "The next

time I suggest something that dumb, just haul out and hit me one.''

"Well, it hasn't been all bad," she said, stretching a little. He put his arm along the back of the couch, and she rested her head on his bicep. "I mean, for probably the first time in my life, I felt *pretty,* Gabe. You have no idea what that's like. I have a long way to go, but…it was nice.''

"You looked great, Charlotte." Gabe's voice was deep and sincere.

"But then I kissed Jack, and it went to hell in a handbasket." She sighed again. "Now I just wish that I was still watching Raider games with the Hoodlums, and wearing my baggy sweatshirts and jeans, and not worrying about finding Mr. Right because I know there's never going to be one.''

Gabe stayed silent.

"But it's too late now," she mused thoughtfully. "It's like I've opened Pandora's box. I don't want to live like I used to, but I don't know what the heck I'm doing. I feel pretty tonight, but I don't want to keep being what somebody else tells me to look like. Derek tried to change me into something I wasn't. How do I know that Dana and Bella are doing the right thing for me?" She rubbed her eyes. "I'm tired, and I just don't know anymore.''

Gabe still didn't say anything.

Finally, she looked over at him. "Are you asleep?''

He was very still, but his gray eyes were wide-open and piercing. "You kissed Jack?''

She rolled her eyes. "Yeah. It wasn't a big deal. Let's just say it was a…chemistry experiment.''

His eyes bore into her. He was quiet for a moment, then nodded, as if he'd decided something. "Are you seeing him tomorrow?''

"No," she said, puzzled. "Why?''

"Because I thought we might hang out tomorrow, but I didn't want to screw up any previous plans."

She punched him in the shoulder. "You're my best friend, Gabe. It's the Hoodlum motto—Friends Come First."

He finally smiled. "Well, isn't tomorrow a designated date day?"

She shrugged. "Apparently Thursdays through Sundays are, according to my scientific dating team."

"Fine." He took a deep breath. "Charlotte Taylor, will you go out on a friend date with me?"

She narrowed her eyes at him. "That's not like a date-date, right?" she said, laughing. "We go Dutch for dinner, there's no small talk and only minimal groping?"

He burst out laughing, then wound down, breathless. "See, it's stuff like that that I've missed. We've been too damn serious since this whole bet started."

"I know." It had bothered her, too.

"How often do we usually see each other in a week, anyway?"

She rubbed her temples, trying to remember life before this dating-or-death life-style. Simpler times! "I don't know. Four times a week, maybe?"

"Exactly. Out to the movies on Tuesday, football on Saturday or Sunday, or Monday night."

"Or all three," she added. "Or you'd drag your laundry here on Thursdays and watch TV."

"My point exactly." He leaned his head back on the sofa. "How often do we see each other now?"

The point struck home. "Okay. The dating thing has gotten a little out of hand."

"Angel, I'm barely seeing you once a week. I feel like you've moved to Tahiti or something." He ran his fingers distractedly through his hair. "I hate to admit it, but I miss you."

She swallowed the lump that was forming in her throat. "Hah. You've probably just got a load of dirty clothes so big, it's impossible to leave your house."

"Well, there's that, too," he said, chuckling. "But I can always buy a washer and dryer. I can't get another friend like you."

She smiled and moved her head to rest on his shoulder. Like a reflex, he curved his arm around her.

"So I figured, if I have to start scheduling dates with my best friend, then that's what I'll do. Whatever it takes to keep our friendship, angel."

"I don't know how Dana's going to feel about this," Charlotte said, snuggling drowsily against his chest. "She knows how bad I am when I'm with you."

"True enough," he said, wiggling his eyebrows. She sent him a sleepy giggle. "But she didn't say she'd pick *who* you were dating, as long as you were dating, right?"

"A date with Gabe," she mused, lulled by his warmth. He rested his chin on the top of her head, and she chuckled. "Hell has frozen over."

She felt his laughter reverberate through his chest, beneath her cheek. She sleepily realized that she was happy. She wanted to stay like this all night, this warmth curling through her, the deep sound of his breathing beneath her, her arms around him.

So invite him to spend the night.

Mmm.

Wait a minute. What was that?

She suddenly shot up, wide-awake, and got to her feet. She was too tired if she could come up with an idea that preposterous. "I'm falling asleep here, Gabe," she said quickly. "Consider it a date. What do you want to do?"

He smiled and stood next to her. Could she actually

feel waves of heat coming off the man? She took a prudent step toward the door, but he followed her.

"There's a Raider game at eleven, which should give you plenty of time to sleep," he said, winking at her. "After that, I don't know. Maybe a video or something."

Now this was more familiar. "Do I get to pick the movie," she teased, "or is it going to be another testosterone fest where we watch two lines of grunting dialogue and two hours of explosions?"

He laughed. "Fine. Be a girl. You can pick the movie, *and* I'll spring for dinner. Pizza okay?"

"You know it's my favorite."

He rubbed the top of her head with his hand, rumpling her hair. "Groping, of course, is optional. I know you can't keep your hands off of me."

She elbowed him in the ribs, gratified by the "oof" he let out. "Get out of here, you bum," she said, trying not to laugh. This was more normal. After all she'd been through in the past three days, it was about time.

Grateful for his caring, she leaned up to kiss him, a quick, typical peck on the cheek. He must have had the same intention, since he was already leaning down toward her face. She just turned a little too fast.

His lips connected to hers like metal to lodestone, unerring, a magnetic connection. Her eyes widened to see his eyes widen, too, with just as much surprise.

Then his eyes closed, and she was lost.

It couldn't have lasted more than a few seconds, but she felt his mouth move, his lips part fractionally. Every nerve ending she had seemed to tingle to life. She didn't mean to, but she felt her body lean forward, her head tilt back.

It was electric.

He must have felt the current jolt through him, because he jerked back, as if shocked from a socket. He blinked twice, then shrugged. "Um, good night, angel."

"G'night." She hurriedly closed the door behind him, locking the dead bolt. She peered through the peephole at his dark silhouette, strolling down her walkway. Then, on shaky legs, she went over to the kitchen and poured herself a tall glass of ice-cold water.

Okay. If that wasn't irony, she didn't know what was.

Legions of hormones had suddenly snapped to attention with one little, insignificant, accidental kiss. With Gabe, no less. How was that for dumb luck?

Well, at least it cleared up one of the more pressing questions of the evening. She knew it wasn't that she was frigid, or that she'd have problems with getting close to a man. If it had been anyone else but Gabe, that kiss would have gone a lot hotter and a lot longer.

But it was *Gabe,* darn it! Where was the justice in that?

Suddenly, an example from work popped into her head. She'd told her toughest client that just because they'd had a bad experience with one designer didn't mean that they'd have bad luck with all designers. It didn't matter how great the concept was: it had to be designed for the client, or it wouldn't work at all.

You have to go with what works for you…not what people tell you to like.

She smiled. In theory, Jack was perfect, Gabe was pointless. Too bad her body thought otherwise.

Suddenly, she blinked.

That's it!

The advice rolled in her head like thunder. *That* had been the problem with all the makeover stuff. When she was younger, she'd been hesitant to go into fashion designing, thinking it too "girly" and obviously out of her realm. So she'd let other people make those design decisions for her, and she'd ended up with stuff other people had told her to like. She had never trusted her own instincts, until the dress tonight. And she had felt spectacular!

She rushed to her design studio, tearing out a huge sketch pad and breaking into her carefully organized tackle box filled with colored pens. She never felt comfortable in pastels, and she didn't like all those fragile, baby-doll designs. If she stuck with what *she* wanted, what could she come up with?

She tore into the paper, drawing hurriedly, all thoughts of Gabe, Jack, the Hoodlums and the girls gone.

It was brilliant, she thought. And it was going to work.

7

GABE WAS VACUUMING his house at ten o'clock Sunday morning.

That was a strange-enough event. Ordinarily, he believed that Sunday mornings were meant for one thing, and one thing only: to sleep in, waking only to take in food or catch a football game. But his eyes had popped open at around six in the morning, and he could not get back to sleep.

Friend or not, he had a "date" with Charlotte.

Not that it was a real date. He'd been very cautious about that, he assured himself, vacuuming around his coffee table. It was all part of a carefully laid-out plan. She'd come over, they'd indulge in all their favorite activities, and it would occur to her that she enjoyed her life just the way it used to be. She would remember how happy she was before she changed her look, before she met Jack, and before Gabe had opened his big fat mouth and very nearly ruined his "perfect life." Then she'd give up man-hunting for good, get back into her old clothes, and things would be just the way they used to be.

He sighed, shutting off the vacuum and grabbing a dust rag. If they could ever be just the way they used to be.

Last night had scared the hell out of him. He'd just about swallowed his tongue when he saw her standing there, a vision in red satin. She'd looked seductive and exotic, and he'd felt an involuntary tug of desire shoot through him before he reminded himself yet again of exactly who she was. He'd had to repeat that little reminder over and over for the rest of the night. When he saw her walk off with Jack, he'd been ready to strangle someone. He'd left immediately after, and gotten to her house with the misguided thought of "protecting" her. If Jack were half as hormonally driven as the average man, he'd have tried anything possible to get Charlotte into bed. Gabe knew that he sure would have.

If he were Jack, that is, he quickly amended. He nervously dusted off his bookcase.

He was relieved to find that Jack wasn't in Charlotte's house last night, but his relief turned to alarm when she asked him to unzip her, revealing all that smooth, creamy skin, and that sexy black bustier. He'd had to get himself a glass of water when she'd been in the other room. He'd almost fled then and there, but by then he'd come up with this crazy "date" plan. At this point, he'd be willing to dress in drag if he thought it might get things back the way they used to be.

He put away the vacuum cleaner and got out paper towels and glass cleaner, heading for his balcony doors. The problem was, as good an idea as this was, he wasn't sure if he could go through with it. His body was starting to boss around his mind, and his conscience…well, frankly, his conscience was always about two minutes too late to really be useful.

He wanted Charlotte. That kiss had come out of the blue, just when he had gotten comfortable. It had sucker-punched him, and he couldn't flee the house quickly enough. He had thought maybe Charlotte had looked dazed, but he hadn't stayed still long enough to really tell.

He'd...well, he'd never really considered her as dating material before. When they'd been younger, she was always that tomboy kid who hung around. When he'd come back from college, she was still grieving over that guy, and he'd felt absurdly protective. He was also still raising hell, and instinctively he knew that Charlotte wasn't that type of woman. She had become his best friend because he could talk to her about things that were too deep to be shared with the Hoodlums, too painful to discuss with his family. When his relationships had gone south, she was the first person he called. When he'd been promoted to vice president at Lone Shark, she was there with a bouquet of cookies on lollipop sticks, of all things. She was the closest person to him on the face of the earth.

No way was he screwing that up because his body had temporarily disconnected itself from his brain. Dammit, it would have been so much easier if she'd just stayed safely shrouded in those sweatshirts and jeans!

He put away all his various cleaning supplies. He plumped up the pillows on his sofa with a vengeance, venting some of the frustration he was feeling. Then he sat down, heavily, sinking into the cushions.

Okay. Obviously, this strange attraction was something they both felt. He knew too much about women not to recognize the bemused look in her eyes and the quickening of her pulse. But he knew that was just because she hadn't really been kissed in years. She was a fledgling, just stepping back out into the sensual world. The idea torched his desire even more, imagining what he could teach her. Brutally, he brought himself back to focus.

One, he thought. She doesn't have these strange

feelings about me, obviously, or she would have invited me to stay.

Two, she is new to this sensual stuff. That made her like a baby rattlesnake: twice as dangerous, because she didn't know about control, and didn't know her own power.

Three, he *did* know how to control himself...and he knew just how lethal she could be.

So what was the answer?

The answer, he told himself firmly, was not to touch her, not get close to her, not do anything that might possibly be misconstrued as *anything.*

He knew what he was doing, he thought, feeling better than he had since this whole thing had snowballed so absurdly. No woman on earth had ever tempted him into turning his back on a friendship, especially one this important.

"Gabe?" He heard Charlotte's voice echo up his stairwell.

"Come on up," he said confidently. It was all good. He could handle it. He was back in control.

She stepped in, arms full of bags and two sketch pads. "Gabe, you have no idea what happened!"

He stared at her. "You're right. What happened?"

"I got hit by the enlightenment stick. Right between the eyes." She dropped the sketch pads on his coffee table, opening them up. The drawings he saw were incredible, but it was fashion stuff. As far as he knew, all she'd ever produced were outstanding logos and corporate designs. These sketches had a vitality he'd never seen before in her work, though.

"Wow." He flipped pages. "These are incredible, angel. What exactly happened?"

"I...well, we don't really need to get into the reason why," she said hastily, "but I finally figured out what was wrong with the whole makeover thing. I'd been going by what Derek wanted me to be, or what Dana wanted or what Bella wanted. Once I figured out what *I* wanted, it was a snap!''

She pointed to the sketch pads. ''I don't like bows, or frills, and I absolutely hate pastels,'' she said enthusiastically. ''If I keep it minimal, and comfortable, I can *still* look good!''

He laughed at her vehemence. ''This should be interesting to see.''

''Wait! I can show you!'' She tore into one of the bags she had lugged up his stairs. He watched with amusement as clothes were suddenly strewn across his extraordinarily immaculate living room. ''I dug out the old sewing machine I used in design school, for exhibit pieces and things, and made up a couple of samples.''

He glanced around. There was a surprising amount of clothes spread out there. ''What time did you finally go to bed?'' he asked, picking up what he assumed was a skirt.

''Huh? Oh. I haven't been to bed yet. I just took a shower and changed into this before I left,'' she said brightly. Then, suddenly, she took off her shirt.

''Hey!'' he said, but before he could stop her, her jeans were unbuttoned and unzipped. They were halfway down her hips before he got to her. ''What are you doing?'' he yelped.

She blinked at him. ''I wanted to show you this outfit. I can't believe I of all people am saying this about clothes, but it's *viciously* sexy. You gotta see it.''

''No,'' he said patiently, trying desperately to stop the blood that had rushed uncomfortably between his legs. Seeing her in a plain white bra and matching panties was viciously sexy enough, thanks very much! ''I mean, why don't you change in the bathroom?''

She laughed. "Have you seen how many outfits I brought over? It would take way too long." She kicked off her jeans and grabbed for a small royal-blue number. "Now, where is the top for this?"

She was killing him, he thought, a protest strangling in his throat. Oh, this had been such a very, *very* bad idea.

She shimmied into the skirt and top. "Now. What do you think of this?" She did a slow turn. "You'll have to imagine the heels, of course, and the cloth is some stuff I was using for color studies for a big exhibit piece I was working on. But it gives the idea."

It gave the idea pretty well, he thought. It wasn't too revealing, but it emphasized her legs and gave a good display of her chest. The color made her skin glow, as if she'd been painted by Rembrandt.

"Very…very nice," he stammered.

"Wait! Wait. I've got a better one in here. Where did I put that?" She tore through the bags again, and he prayed for strength. She started to drop the skirt again and peel off the top.

"Okay, why don't we dump all this stuff in the bathroom, Charlotte?" he said, collecting strewn articles of clothing and averting his eyes. This was more than any red-blooded man could take!

"Gabe, you're holding the dress I wanted to show you.…"

"You know, you're not in any frame of mind for a fashion show," he said hurriedly, still not looking at her. *Remain calm. We can talk her out of this.* "I think you're really on the right track with what you've shown me, but you know me. I'm not any real judge of fashion."

"Gabe," she reminded him, "you're the vice president of a sportswear company."

"Oh." She would have to point out the obvious. "I mean women's fashions."

"Don't you have a women's line, too?"

"On *you,* I mean," he said, finally turning around. Then wished he hadn't.

It was more than a quick glimpse of underwear this time. She was standing there, practically tapping her foot with impatience. Her cotton panties were bikinis cut high on her thighs. Her arms were crossed, and one bra strap was hanging down on her shoulder. Her hair was damp and curling in wavy disarray.

She looked brutally hot. Desire hit him like a tidal wave.

"You're humoring me, aren't you?" she said, eyes narrowed.

It took him a second to form a coherent sentence. "No, I'm not."

She brightened. "Good. Then hand me that deep purple dress you've got in your left hand."

"Charlotte, I *really* think you ought to go change in the other room."

"Why?" she said. "You're just my friend, and there's nothing on me you haven't seen before on someone else."

He sat down. She had summed it all up: he was just her friend. Obviously *she* was having no problem drawing that line. If she was okay with it, then why shouldn't he be? He'd seen plenty of gorgeous babes wearing much less than Charlotte had on.

But he'd never had these kind of restraints on himself, either.

He sat on his couch, trying not to squirm, or even breathe, as she slipped in and out of design after design. She really had a flair, one he would not have suspected, he noticed absently. The clothes she had come up with looked comfortable, amazingly simple, yet they made her look absolutely seductive. The colors weren't at all like the things she had bought when the bet started. They were vibrant, deep colors that made her dark hair and bright eyes look even richer.

Not to mention the effect they were having on his peace of mind.

The worst part of her performance, though, was her little quick changes…a flash of toned muscle, a curve of breast being exposed and then covered by a soft hiss of material. He was being drawn on a rack of self-control, and Charlotte had absolutely no concept of what she was doing to him.

Finally, she got through her last sample and slipped back into her jeans and shirt. He felt as if he was bathed in sweat. His heart was beating as if he'd run a marathon.

"So? What did you think?" she asked eagerly.

What did he think? He thought she'd shaved ten years off of his life with that sensual torture, that's what! "I thought it was…very nice."

"Nice?" She frowned at him, her eyes burning into him like laser beams. "'Nice' is getting a thank-you card. I'm looking for sexy. I'm looking for devastating. Come on, Gabe, work with me!"

"Fine," he said, sighing deeply. "You were incredible. You would make a Buddhist monk pant like a dog. If God had made anything better, he'd have kept it for himself. Now are you satisfied?" He knew he sounded testy, but he couldn't help it. She was just throwing salt on a wound here!

He got up and quickly moved to the kitchen, getting out some ice water. He briefly considered dumping it down the front of his jeans, but settled for taking a bracingly cold gulp instead.

She smiled. "Pant like a dog, huh?"

He sighed. "You're too much, angel."

"That's what I wanted to hear." She yawned, deeply, then settled on his couch. "What time does the game start?"

He cautiously sat down on the couch also, sitting at the far end away from her and grabbing the remote. "Let's see…it's on in about half an hour. I'm sure there's some pre-game stuff on, though. Is that okay?"

"Mmm-hmm." She yawned again, her eyes heavy-lidded.

He smiled tenderly. Now that she was fully dressed again, with no makeup, he felt a little more charitable toward her. She was really cute when she was sleepy like this. She didn't look dangerous at all. "You finally ready for bed, angel?"

She nodded, propping her head up with one arm. "I must be. I was so excited about the design stuff that I felt like I could go on forever, you know? And I had to come over here and show you all of my stuff."

"And you were in such a hurry, you had to show me in my living room?" he asked, trying to laugh about it. To his own ears, he sounded strained.

"Well, it seemed stupid to keep going from one room to the other. You know how I am when I hit a creativity burst." She shrugged, settling more deeply into his couch. "Besides, Gabe, when I hit my break-through, you were the first person I thought of. I wanted you to see it before anybody else."

He felt absurdly touched by her admission. "That's…thank you, Charlotte. I'm honored."

"You're my best friend, Gabe," she murmured. "Without you, I couldn't have come this far. I owe this all to you."

"You don't owe anything to me," he said softly,

watching her drift off into sleep. "You did this all yourself."

The words she mumbled might have been a protest, but in moments, she was sound asleep.

He watched the television screen blankly, unable to focus.

You're my best friend, Gabe.

Easy for her to say, he thought, glancing over at her sleeping form. Now, if he could just keep his hands off her, they could keep it that way.

HOURS LATER, GABE woke up in a darkened room. The TV shone with a blank blue screen. Charlie had woken up briefly for the second half of the game and the first half of the movie. During the second half, they had both fallen asleep. He woke up to find that the movie had run its course and had rewound itself. He glanced at the red clock numbers on his VCR: seven o'clock. He'd been asleep for two hours!

He stretched and started to turn over when his hand fell on a soft, curvy body. Illuminated by the eerie blue, Charlotte was sprawled on the couch next to him. He yanked his hand away.

He smiled. He'd done it. He had spent the whole day with her, doing all of their old favorite stuff. Despite the torturous start, he'd managed to keep his hands off of her, all day long.

He'd kissed her once, he'd seen her half-naked, but that was all in the past. They were just going to be friends from now on. It was perfect.

He felt high with the relief coursing through him. Now all he needed to do was take her out for pizza, and cement the deal. From here on, it was going to be clear sailing.

She was easily startled, so he knelt down next to the back of her head. "Wake up, kiddo," he whispered. "There's a Hawaiian pizza with your name on it."

"Mrmph." She shrugged a shoulder, but she didn't turn to face him.

"Come on, come on. If you sleep now, you'll be up at three in the morning." He gave her shoulders a gentle rub. "You'll feel better with some food."

"Oh," she gasped.

His fingers stopped immediately. "Did that hurt?"

She let out a breathy, half-asleep sigh. "No."

"You nut. You shouldn't have been sewing all night." He increased the pressure, smiling at her groans. "Just call me Gunther, the Swedish masseur...."

"Oh," she breathed again, sharper this time, bowing her back slightly to press against his fingers. "Yeah. Like that."

He looked down to see her body starting to writhe a little on the couch. Her long legs stretched, and her back arched like a cat's.

It was turning him on, he noticed, and stopped abruptly. *We've been doing so well. Don't blow it now!*

"Okay, enough fun," he muttered, turning her to face him. "Charlotte? Come on, wake up."

She blinked for a minute, her eyes half-lidded and slumberous. Her full lips curved into a smile for a second, then she sighed.

"Gabe..."

Before he could move, she reached up and looped her arms around his neck. Before he could think, she had tugged his head down to hers.

By the time he figured out what was going on, he wanted to neither move nor think.

It started out gentle, almost tentative, her lips brushing against his with a whispery caress. He could feel her breathe his name against his lips, and it shot fire from his stomach to his groin. He was struggling for control when she gave him a purring growl and locked more firmly onto his lips.

Whatever control he had left disappeared. He slanted over her mouth, pushing her back into the pillows. She sighed and he could feel a shivery tremor rush through her body. He supported his weight on his arms, half-covering her body with his own. He could feel her nipples through the thin T-shirt fabric, rubbing against his chest. He let out a growl as his tongue swept past her satiny lips.

He heard her inhale sharply before she arched up to rub against him, her tongue dueling with his. Leaning on one arm, he used the other to stroke down the length of her side. His fingers skimmed the column of her neck and she quivered and cried out against his mouth. His kisses grew more insistent as he gently stroked down the side of one smooth, firm breast. She pressed up against him until he was cupping her firmly. He brushed a fingertip over a taut nipple, and she arched up, fitting herself to him with a heated passion that made him gasp.

He wasn't sure how exactly he wound up on top of her, but he was fitted at the juncture of her thighs as she twisted beneath him. She wasn't trying to move him off of her. On the contrary, he could feel her thighs inching higher on his hips as she molded herself against his hardness.

It was intense, intoxicating. It was out of control. His heart was beating so strongly, he could hear it pounding in his ears like a war drum.

Knock! Knock! Knock!

Wait a minute. That wasn't his heart!

"Gabe, man...are you in there?"

He pulled his head away with effort. Both he and

Charlotte went still, staring at the hallway where the knocks were coming from.

"Come on. We know you're home." It sounded like Ryan. "Don't make us break in there!"

The words sent Gabe rolling off of Charlotte and hurriedly getting to his feet. They were both still breathing heavily. "Don't move," he told her, and went downstairs.

He threw open the door. *"What?"*

Ryan, Mike and Sean were standing at his doorstep. "Jeez, man. We just wanted to let you know the surf's up to eight feet. It's perfect out," Ryan said, gesturing toward the beach. "You coming?"

"You nearly pounded my door down to tell me that *the surf was up?*"

"Of course," Mike said, rolling his eyes. "What's wrong with you?"

Ryan studied him for a second, then grinned. "Whoops. I sense bad timing here…if your jeans are any indication."

"Get lost," Gabe growled.

"Really sorry, man," Mike said, quickly backing away. "Really. Do what you've gotta do."

Ryan started laughing, but Sean looked down at Gabe's driveway and looked back at him, eyes narrowed.

"You sure everything's okay, Gabe?" Sean asked quietly.

"It will be when you clowns get out of here."

The three men left and Gabe shut the door, locking it. He went back upstairs.

Charlotte had hurriedly thrown her pell-mell explosion of clothes back into the bags she'd packed them in, and was tucking her sketch pads under her arms. "You know," she said hastily, avoiding his eyes. "I think I'll take a rain check on the pizza."

"Charlotte, about what happened..."

"I'll take the blame for that one," she said, juggling the sketch pads and the bags. "Really. I guess I was just tired, or dreaming, or something."

"It was a California no-fault accident, angel," he said, nudging her chin up to look in her eyes. "Nobody's to blame here."

She still didn't look directly into his eyes. "I need to get home and get some of this stuff in better shape, so I can make real clothes out of them. And I really ought to...um, do some chores. You know. Around the house."

One minute, she's burning him alive, and now all she could think about was tackling household chores?

"Charlotte, are you all right?"

She finally looked at him, and her hazel eyes were dazed. "I didn't mean for...what just happened to happen. You've got to believe that." She took a deep, quavering breath. "I know it was sort of dumb, but we've been friends for so long, you'll be able to overlook it. I know it didn't mean anything."

It didn't mean anything.

Her cheeks reddened. "I'm just really out of practice with this physical stuff," she admitted in a small voice. "Now, with this whole dating thing, and this whole change of attitude...I guess a lot of things are coming up that I didn't expect."

He nodded.

"I'm going to head out, and we'll just pretend that this never happened. Okay?"

"Sure. Okay." That was exactly what he wanted, about both their kisses. Wasn't it?

She sent him a lopsided smile. She got up on tiptoe and looked as if she were about to kiss his cheek, then changed her mind. She walked instead to the front door. He trailed behind her, puzzled.

"See you," she said as he opened the door for her. "I'll give you a call."

He watched her load her car, then drive off.

He shut the door, locked it and went back upstairs. He sat on the couch for a moment.

She'd left. He'd been kissing the daylights out of her, and she'd just…left.

He realized, of course, that he should be happy about what had happened. He'd been telling himself that getting physically involved with Charlotte would mean problems. It would jeopardize their friendship. It would be disastrous. And despite telling himself all of that, he'd let himself get into a passionate clinch with her, anyway, right there on his couch.

And then she'd gotten up, told him to forget anything had ever happened, and *left!*

This had never happened to him before.

Not that his kisses were irresistible. It was…well, okay, yes, his pride was smarting at that one. But the fact that she could obviously write off what had happened as the overfunctioning of long dormant hormones *hurt,* dammit!

He got up, went over to his fridge and pulled out a beer. He popped off the lid and took a long draw.

She was probably right, he reasoned. They were just friends. No more kisses, pretend nothing happened, and he would finally have his wish, right? Things would be just the way they used to be. He wouldn't have to worry about losing her ever again. Just plain old friends. In a weird, roundabout way, his "date" had gone just as he had planned.

He sighed and downed the rest of his beer. Dammit, why didn't that make him feel better?

8

Stupid. Stupid, stupid, stupid.

Charlotte stared at the phone in her bedroom, wondering how she was going to explain to Bella that she couldn't come to her housewarming. "Hi, Bella. I can't show up because I know Gabe is going to be there, and I've been avoiding him for a solid week. Why? Because I shut my brain off, I was half-asleep, and I basically attacked him like an Amazon on his own couch," Charlotte tried experimentally, then stuffed her head in her pillow. "I am so *stupid!*"

She hadn't been thinking at all, that night on Gabe's couch. She certainly hadn't gone over there to seduce him. Seduce Gabe, who had women like that blonde in the restaurant practically tap-dancing naked to get his attention? If anything, he would have been amused by any attempt in that direction.

An image of the kiss flashed across her mind. Images like that had haunted her all week. It hit her in the middle of conversations at work, or when she was grocery shopping, or when she was trying to draw. Or at night, before she fell into a fitful, restless sleep.

It was worst at night.

She sighed deeply. She'd run from his house, apologizing, asking him to forget about the whole thing. By this point, he probably had. But she hadn't, and wouldn't. She knew it wasn't what he wanted. It had probably been pleasant, but he wasn't looking for a relationship with her. And she wanted more than just a relationship, she realized numbly.

She was in love with him.

It was something she should have admitted to herself a long time ago. She was in love with her best friend. When she had no confidence in herself, she had thought just friendship would be enough. In fact, there were times when she felt that his friendship was more than she deserved. But now, with her growing self-awareness, it occurred to her that marriage, family, happy-ever-after were real possibilities.

That is, they were possibilities with men in general. But she wanted Gabe in specific, and that was where the problem was.

She sighed, flopping over the edge of the bed. He wouldn't want to be her Mr. Right. He didn't want to be *anybody's* Mr. Right. Why should he? He could date any woman he wanted. Self-admittedly, his life was "perfect." No, he wouldn't want to throw that all away. He'd never be in love with her.

And that's it? Her conscience sounded indignant. *So now what?*

At any other time, she would have settled for her situation. She would have suffered in silence, just staying friends with Gabe. But she had a real chance now. She felt *pretty,* dammit, and confident. Why should *she* have to be the one to simper and sigh, and wait for him to come to his senses? She had options!

She felt galvanized. She grabbed her purse, digging out a slip of paper, and then reached for her phone.

"Hi, Jack?" She smiled, looking at an outfit she had just finished in her closet. "It's Charlotte. I was wondering…do you think you'd like to go to a housewarming party this afternoon?"

Gabe could do whatever he wanted, she thought, as Jack accepted her invitation. She had her own life to live, and she wasn't going to waste it on dreams that couldn't possibly come true.

GABE HAD BEEN SITTING on Bella's couch, trying to get up the energy to socialize. He was in too bleak a mood since the episode with Charlotte to be very good company.

She'd been avoiding him again, and that was bothering him. They'd talked on the phone a couple of times, but she'd been distant, and he hadn't been able to get her to spill what was going on. Obviously, something was upsetting her, but she wouldn't share what.

She should have been here by now, he thought. He had considered missing Bella's housewarming party, but the lure of finally being able to talk to Charlotte face-to-face had convinced him otherwise. He thought she probably felt awful about what had happened between them last Sunday. She had been embarrassed, possibly even ashamed, at her behavior. She'd even admitted how out of practice she was, as if it were some horrible crime. And all he could do was sit on his hands and take it personally!

Well, he'd straighten her out, he thought, brightening. Granted, they couldn't do it again, but there was absolutely nothing wrong with a few kisses between friends. As confused and worked up as he had felt about the whole thing, it was probably nothing compared to what the poor girl had been going through.

Yeah, right. That's why you've been a hermit since this whole bet started.

Shut up, conscience, Gabe warned. *I don't need your input right now.*

He'd just cheer her up, and they'd go on as usual. She was doing much better, and the clothes she'd designed had seemed to really open a new door for her. In fact, he'd considered asking her if she'd sell a few of the designs for their women's collection. If she'd just *talk* to him for longer than five minutes, if he could…

"Charlotte!" Bella went running to the front door, throwing it open and enveloping Charlotte in a huge hug. "Sorry I haven't seen you since the reception, sweetie, but moving into the house has been such a big production. Besides, I knew you were in Dana's capable hands—"

"Hi, Bella," Charlotte interrupted his sister's usual stream of patter firmly. "I'd like you to meet my friend, Jack Landor. Jack, this is Bella Donofrio…that is, Bella Paulson, now that she's married."

"Congratulations." Jack's deep voice emerged from behind her, and Gabe's eyes shot wide-open. "I've heard so much about you. How was Hawaii?"

Jack Landor was here? With Charlotte? What was *that* all about?

"Oh, just beautiful," Bella said, linking her arm through his. "I'm sorry to have been gone so long and missed all the fun. Charlotte and I haven't been able to talk about *you* nearly enough for my liking." She glanced over at Charlotte, a huge grin on her face.

"Well," Jack said, with a matching grin, "I should be around for a while, so hopefully you can remedy the situation."

Bella laughed, leading the couple to the kitchen. "Can I get you a drink…?"

Great, Gabe thought. Apparently, one of them had managed to put last Sunday behind them as if it were nothing…and it wasn't him.

He got up and slowly made his way to the door of the kitchen, hovering just outside it, by the foyer.

"So this is your new house?" he heard Jack say.

"This is home sweet home," his sister replied. "Brad, why don't you give Jack the grand tour? Charlotte's already seen the house, and she and I need to catch up on some girl talk."

Gabe ducked behind the coatrack, waiting for Jack and Brad to disappear down the hallway before resuming his eavesdropping. He knew he shouldn't, but apparently Charlotte wasn't going to tell him what was going on, and as her best friend, he really had a right to know. At least, that was the justification he was planning on using if he got caught.

"Oh, my God! He is *gorgeous!*" Bella said.

Dana's voice chimed in. "Didn't I tell you?"

"Yes, but it's hard to see exactly how gorgeous he is until he's standing right next to you. A perfect blonde, and that smile! You could tan by that smile!"

Gabe rolled his eyes. If Jack had won Bella's gushing vote of approval, the guy was in for some pressure.

"I love his eyes," Dana cooed dreamily. "That dark, deep green. What's your favorite part of him, Charlotte?" Her voice was amused. "Or can't you tell us?"

Before Gabe could get really irate at that comment, Charlotte broke in firmly. "My favorite part of Jack is that he's sweet and doesn't push me into anything. Unlike you two."

That's my girl, Gabe thought, mentally cheering her on. *You tell 'em!*

"Oh, come on, honey," Dana said, brushing her remark aside. "It wasn't like we put a gun to your head and forced you to take that bet with Gabe, you know. You got into it all on your own. But no matter how you got there, Jack's the sweetest, best-looking date you've ever landed. If we're just trying to encourage you, what's the problem?"

Charlotte didn't say anything, and Gabe strained to hear her response, hoping to finally figure out what was going on.

"I just...I don't want to talk about it. I can't talk about it."

Gabe gritted his teeth in frustration.

"Charlotte? What's wrong?" His sister's voice was concerned. "You've gone all white!"

Gabe started to take a step forward. Sick? Was Charlotte...

"No, it's nothing. I haven't been sleeping well," Charlotte said, and the little irritation in her voice comforted him. If there were something wrong with her, medically, she'd have said something. So what was it? "And I sort of skipped breakfast. I haven't been that hungry lately."

"Well, we'll get you some food, first off," Bella said, switching into maternal mode. "You know what it sounds like? It sounds like you're in love."

In love?

Charlotte, in love with that pretty-boy *Jack?*

"Is Gabe here yet?" Charlotte said instead, and Bella laughed.

"Fine. If you want to change the subject, we'll do it." Dana ignored Charlotte's protests. "If I know Gabe, he's probably camped out in Brad's AV room, watching some sporting event. And no, you can't go find him," she said firmly.

"Honestly, Charlotte, what kind of an impression are you going to make on Jack if you're hooting like a loon with that idiot brother of mine?" Bella added.

Gabe sighed. He was having enough problems with Charlotte. Trust his sister and Dana to make problems even worse!

"I wasn't going to watch sports, and Jack likes me just fine," Charlotte said in an absent tone of voice.

"I just wondered if Gabe was here. I haven't talked to him in like a week."

The room fell silent for a second.

"Okay, what's wrong?" Dana's voice crackled with worry.

"What do you mean?"

"If you're not watching sports, and you're not talking to Gabe, it's an instant code red," Dana explained. "What's going on?"

Gabe leaned forward intently.

"You're not eating, you're not sleeping, and you're…wait a minute," Bella said, slowly. "You're not pregnant, are you?"

Gabe knocked over the coatrack. He caught it just before it hit the floor, in time to hear Charlotte's reaction.

"What? No!" she spluttered.

"Are you sure?"

"Unless you can get pregnant by a handshake and a casual good-night kiss, yes, I'm positive."

Gabe began to breathe again. He didn't mean to feel relieved that Charlotte hadn't slept with Jack, but he did; it was like a weight off his chest. He walked into the kitchen feeling a little bit better. "There you are, Charlotte."

The three women fell silent. His sister and Dana had guilty, cat-and-canary looks on their faces, and small grins. Charlotte just glared at him.

"Anything I should know about, ladies?"

"Just girl talk," Charlotte said shortly. "Nothing you'd be interested in."

"Well, maybe we could talk about something else," he said.

"I've got an idea," Bella said, her eyes snapping with challenge. "How about discussing the fact that

Charlotte's a heck of a lot closer to winning that bet than you gave her credit for?''

"Jack is the catch of the century," Dana said, her voice similarly smug.

Gabe's eyes never left Charlotte's. "Why don't you tell me about Jack, Charlotte?" he said, his voice low. "I don't think I realized how close you two really are."

"There's not much to say," Charlotte said, her chin rising a notch. He knew what that meant: Charlotte's stubbornness was leaping to the fore. "I mean, Jack is a spectacular 'catch,' although I find that really insulting for both of us. He likes spending time with me. I like spending time with him. If he wants more than that, well, we'll see. But for the time being, I'm just trying to spend my time with someone I can actually *envision* having a future with." She arched an eyebrow at him, and he felt a disturbing sense of déjà vu. *This is not for you.* "Does that pose a problem for you, Gabe?"

He gritted his teeth. "Of course not," he replied, his tone just as cool. "Why would it?"

"I think I'll go look for Jack," Charlotte said, smiling sweetly. "I wanted to show him the painting I made for you, Bella. If you'll excuse me?" And without another word, she breezed out into the hallway, disappearing toward the stairs.

"Well," Dana crowed, "I guess she told you!"

"She looks fantastic," Bella said, "but it's not just the new outfit, although it looks like forest green is definitely one of her colors. It's the attitude."

"But I love the clothes," Dana said, smiling. "It looks like our little girl is finally becoming a woman!"

"What do you think, Gabe?" Bella said, smiling.

"I think you two need to stop pushing her," Gabe said harshly, and the two women's eyes widened.

"We're not pushing her," Dana protested. "We're just—"

"You're pushing her. You've never been happy with her the way she is, and now she's changing to please you." Gabe frowned. And he was afraid she'd changed for good. "I'm glad she has more self-confidence, who wouldn't be? But she doesn't need you two nudging her into a relationship she's not ready for."

Bella looked stricken, but Dana's eyes snapped. "She can handle a lot more than you think she can."

"She's a lot more fragile than you think she is," he countered, his voice more gentle. "Trust me, I know. I've hurt her enough. So all I'm saying is, go easy on her, will you?"

Bella nodded. "All right. You know I don't want to hurt Charlotte, ever."

"Of course we don't," Dana said, sighing. "Well, all right, Gabe, but I don't think it's because of us pushing this time. She seems very involved with Jack."

"Maybe." He turned and looked for her in the hallway. He'd just see how involved she was with Jack. As her best friend, it was his responsibility. The last thing he wanted to do was see her hurt...by his sister, Dana, Jack, or even herself.

"THIS HAS BEEN GREAT, Charlotte," Jack said, smiling at her. "Thanks for inviting me."

"No problem." Charlotte took a sip of soda. She was glad he was having such a good time. She, herself, would be having a much better time if she knew where Gabe was. He'd been avoiding talking directly with her, probably from what she said in the kitchen. But it was the truth. Why should she hide from that?

She sighed. It was just that she'd look up and find Gabe staring at her before disappearing. Between that, and the images that would not go away of the episode on his couch, her nerves were quickly getting frazzled.

"You've got a really nice group of friends," Jack continued. "They're like a family. They make me miss my own, actually." He sighed. "They can be sort of pushy, but they love you, you know?"

Her eyes widened. "You could tell that after just a couple of hours?"

He laughed. "I was talking about *my* family, Charlotte. They're always pushing me to get married, that kind of thing."

"I know exactly what you mean," she said with feeling.

"One of these days, I think I'm going to up and elope with somebody, just to get them off my back and get on with my life."

"Hear, hear."

"Charlotte," Jack said, his eyes turning more serious, "have you ever—"

"Excuse me."

Charlotte turned to see Gabe hovering right next to her. "Gabe?"

"Hi. Jack, do you mind if I steal Charlotte for a minute? I needed to talk to her about something sort of private."

Charlotte's eyes widened, but Jack just nodded. "Um, sure. Go right ahead."

Charlotte frowned at Gabe. "I'm sure it's nothing that can't wait...."

"Actually, I have to talk to you *right now*." With

that, Gabe tugged at her arm and started pulling her down the hallway.

"I'll be right back," she said to Jack, then turned to Gabe. "What are you doing?" she demanded.

"Saving your butt," Gabe said, his head craning around. "Bella's got this place filled to the rafters with people, and I need to talk to you in private. Where's...here we go. Come on." He opened a door and led her down the cellar stairs.

She sighed, frustrated. "This had better be good, Gabe," she said, glancing around the darkened room. The air was damp and cool, smelling faintly of lemony detergent.

"Did you hear the line that guy was running on you?" Gabe said, pulling the hanging cord of the lightbulb and turning the light on. "You're lucky I pulled you away when I did."

She blinked in disbelief. "Excuse me?"

"You heard me. That guy was about to make his move." Gabe grinned in smug satisfaction. "Little did he know, huh? You wouldn't buy a bunch of sugarcoated lies about marriage and stuff."

"What makes you think he'd be lying?" she said, anger making her voice sharp. "If he *had* been making a move on me, so what? It's about time somebody did!"

"Are you kidding me?" Gabe replied, his own voice tinged with anger. "Oh, that's rich. Here I am protecting you from a complete lech, and all you can do is give me static about it?"

"Protecting me?" She rolled her eyes. "Please! How many times do I have to tell you—I can take care of myself. I am a full-grown, full-fledged woman who is perfectly able of handling a man who has more on his mind than some casual kissing!"

"Really?" Gabe's voice was sarcastic. "Funny. I

seem to remember a certain 'full-fledged woman' getting distinctly flustered when she found herself just kissing a guy on his couch. I seem to remember her exact words were that she had been 'really out of practice with this physical stuff' for some time.'' His gray eyes were hot as gunmetal. ''Or did I just imagine that?''

Trust him to bring up that episode to use against her, she thought, anger making her clench her hands into fists. ''I *am* out of practice. Jack could be a perfect way to help me get back into the game.''

''Like hell,'' Gabe growled. ''Charlotte, no matter what you think, you don't know what you're getting into. You're way over your head. You don't even know this guy!''

''I do, too, know Jack!''

''After, what, two weeks?'' Gabe took a step closer to her, his eyes blazing. ''So tell me. What's Jack's favorite sport? His favorite movie? His favorite flavor of ice cream?''

Charlotte stepped toe to toe with him. ''He's not a sports fanatic like you, but he'll catch the occasional baseball game. His favorite movie is *Spartacus* and his favorite flavor of ice cream is the same as yours. Mint chocolate chip.''

Gabe narrowed his eyes. ''I don't suppose you could tell me how he is in bed.''

Charlotte gaped, her heart jolting painfully. ''How dare you!''

''Of course, you can't compare us there.'' Gabe smiled coldly. ''Maybe I can give you a hint, though, of what I prefer. So you'll know if Jack likes what I do.''

Before she could move, he laced his hand in her hair and dragged her mouth up to his.

The kiss wasn't like the warm, simmering, sensual

kiss they'd shared on his couch. If that kiss was like a fireplace, this kiss was like a volcano: hot, pulsating and explosive. His lips flowed over hers, molding her mouth to his. She felt his fingers contract at the base of her neck, while his other arm snaked out to wrap around her waist, pressing her intimately to him.

This was wrong. This was out of anger, out of passion, out of control. And yet it felt so right.

With superhuman effort, she pushed herself from him, tearing her mouth from his. Panting for breath, she glared at him. *"Don't you dare!"*

His eyes widened. He was also short of breath, she noticed. The glint was still there in his eyes, but it banked like coals under cold water at her words. There was more steam than fire. He was getting himself back under control.

Charlotte's voice vibrated with the energy rushing through her veins. "Don't you ever, *ever* just grab me and think you can punish me with that kind of thing, just because you've got some macho, testosterone-driven issues. You aren't Tarzan, and I sure as hell am not Jane." She clenched her fists, passions blurring with fury. "When I kiss someone, it's not going to be out of anger, or frustration, or whatever. It's going to be because of desire, pure and simple. When a man kisses me, it's because he wants to kiss me. You got that?"

He drew a ragged breath, his eyes full of remorse. "I got it."

She nodded sharply. "Good."

Without another word, she threw her arms around his neck, lacing her fingers in his hair, and dragged *his* lips down to meet hers.

If she'd thought she could stay in control of the kiss, she was wrong. Vaguely she thought that she was trying to prove a point, but now all she could hang on to was the fact that she needed his lips, his arms. Him.

He stood stiff as marble, probably with shock, before he wrapped his arms around her, his hands clutching at the small of her back. He melted into her, slanting over her mouth hungrily. She parted her lips, wanting more. His tongue traced her lips with fire. She moaned as his tongue swept into her mouth to tangle with hers. Heat speared through her, pulsing like beacons, drawing a median line from her heart to between her legs. She didn't think, couldn't think. She could only desire, and act.

He pushed her against the laundry table, lifting her up to sit on it. She clutched at his shoulders, and her legs parted easily, urging him to stand between them. His hands stroked down her back in long, loving glides. She could feel his fingertips, like trails of flame that only pitched her passion higher.

"Charlotte," he breathed unevenly against her neck, pressing kisses just behind her ear, down her neck, against her collarbone. She arched her back to press her breasts against him. Her legs wrapped around his waist. He pushed forward, and she gasped.

"Gabe," she whispered, guiding him back up to her lips. The kiss was long, drugging, the slow in and out of their tongues reminiscent of the joining they both wanted.

"Gabe? Charlotte? You down here?"

Charlotte gasped, not in pleasure this time, and thought she'd swallowed her tongue. Or possibly Gabe's. The two of them tore themselves away from each other, standing like panting boxers in opposite corners of the room.

Bella peered down curiously. "Are you two all right? What's going on here?"

"We'll be up in a minute," Gabe said. His voice was rough, and his back was to the stairwell.

"Well, when you do, would you bring up a case of root beer?" she said, then shut the door behind her.

Charlotte's eyes glowed at him. "We've got to stop stopping like this."

"Charlotte, this is crazy," he said, reaching for her and kissing her even as the words tumbled out of his mouth. "If Bella comes back, how are you planning on explaining what we're doing?"

"How about, 'Bella, would you mind coming back after we've had sex on your laundry table?'" She laughed, feeling the blush hit her as it occurred to her…that was precisely where they were heading if they didn't slow down. It was followed by a second thought: she didn't care. She kissed him deeply.

He pulled away, backing up until he hit the railing of the stairway. "Charlotte, I can't do this."

She felt his rejection burn her like acid in her chest. "Of course you can't," she said, then blinked when he leaned down and kissed her again.

"It's just really stupid," he said, kissing her neck and causing her breath to catch, "because I know we're just friends, and—" he brushed a deep kiss over her lips "—we both know this isn't going any-where. Right?"

"Of course," she said, pressing a kiss back. "Whatever you say."

"If we just work together, I'm sure we can forget that any of this ever happened." He held her to him, tilting her head back and feasting on her mouth.

She couldn't answer him right away, because she had to catch her breath. "Of course," she finally said, not even realizing what she'd agreed to.

Just as quickly, he pulled away from her, walking

to the far end of the room. "Okay, all right, I can handle this." He took a deep breath, waited a few minutes, closed his eyes. "Steer clear of me, Charlotte. I know you've got something going on with Jack, and I knew I shouldn't have let this go on so long, but I couldn't help myself. I swear, if you give me a few days…no, give me at least a week. I'll get it all out of my system. Okay?"

"Gabe, what are you talking about?"

"You're my best friend in the world," he said, dropping a quick kiss on her already-swollen lips. "Please, for both our sakes, stay the hell away from me."

With that, he bolted up the stairs as if demons were chasing him.

Fanning her face, Charlotte leaned back against the now-infamous laundry-room table. What had just happened was…well, it was unbelievable!

He wants you.

It wasn't a matter of her not being his type. It wasn't a matter of him seeing her as only a friend. He thought that she wasn't interested in him. He thought that she only saw him as a buddy!

She might have a shot at this, she thought suddenly. If she was in love with Gabe, and she knew that he wanted her, she owed it to herself to see if a relationship would work. It was easy to think about, to worry about. It was harder to just go and do it. Now, the time for analyzing was over.

This wasn't about his feelings, or their friendship. This was about love…and about her finally putting her fear aside, and going after exactly what she wanted.

If she recalled correctly, there was a chapter in *The Guide* about how to seduce a man. She smiled wickedly. Now was her chance to try it out.

9

A FEW DAYS LATER, Gabe felt that he had perhaps overreacted at the housewarming. He sat at his desk in the office. It was dark out, but he'd been getting a lot done. Yes, given a week's distance and perspective, he felt quite sure that he'd blown the whole thing out of proportion.

"Boss?"

Gabe looked up from the proposal he was working on. "Yes, Jake?"

Gabe's young assistant shifted his weight nervously. "It's about these." He held up several sheets of paper.

Gabe frowned. "What about them?"

"These letters don't make any sense, boss." Jake put them down on the desk in front of Gabe's briefcase. "I mean, in one paragraph, you're talking about the risks of potentially dangerous mergers. Then you're saying we should throw caution to the wind and sign up tomorrow. What exactly did you want to say here?"

Gabe stared at the letters as if they were live snakes. "I wrote that?"

"The really strange thing is, I didn't even think we were trying to merge with this company. I thought we just wanted to run a couple of co-op ads with them." Jake cleared his throat. "I usually just proof your letters and send them as is, but this was really weird."

"I...thanks, Jake." Gabe sighed, taking the letters and throwing them on top of one of the piles on his desk. "I don't know where my head is. I'll fix them. What time is it, anyway?" He glanced at his watch with tired eyes. "Eight o'clock? What are you still doing here?"

Jake shrugged. "If you're working, I'm working."

"While I appreciate the dedication, are you nuts?" Gabe laughed, standing up. He felt tension in his lower back, signaling he'd been at his desk for way too long. "Just because your boss is becoming a workaholic doesn't mean you have to be chained to your desk."

"I thought you must be working on something pretty important," Jake argued. "You've been here until nine o'clock every night, and you're coming in at seven in the morning."

"I'm just... I've been taking it easy this quarter, and I'm just playing a little catch-up. It won't be like this for much longer," He gave Jake a stern look. "And I expect you to work normal hours unless I expressly ask otherwise, got it?"

Jake grinned. "Thanks, boss." With no further prompting, he bolted from the office.

Gabe sighed, shutting down his computer. He might as well admit it. He'd done everything he could think of to exorcise the ghost of Charlotte. He ran on the beach, worked out in his home gym until his muscles screamed, did paperwork until his eyes crossed. Anything to get his mind off her. But that didn't protect him from his subconscious mind. The minute his head hit the pillow, he was asleep with her taste on his lips, the sweet scent of her hair in his nose and the silky feel of her flesh under his palms. He'd relived that moment in the laundry room every night...and had gone considerably further with it than they had in reality, as if they'd never been interrupted. What was worse, when he wasn't fighting this overwhelming lust for her, he got blindsided by an even sneakier emotion.

He missed her.

He'd tried not to call her, but something would happen and his fingers would instinctively start to dial her number. He had consciously avoided poker night and all the usual Hoodlum hangouts, afraid that she might be there. So far, he'd shuttled to work or home, stopping only for long surf sessions because he knew that was one place she wouldn't be. Out in the pounding waves for hours, he could almost forget how close he was to losing her.

He had inadvertently started this change, by proposing the stupid, shortsighted, damnable bet. Now that the change had started, he didn't know what was going to happen to her, or to them. And he didn't know how to stop it…but at the same time, he knew he didn't want to live without her.

He had done everything but talk about this face-to-face with her. Maybe if he just sat down with her and discussed it, she would understand and come up with some way to help him fix things and make it all right again. He'd tried being around her and it had turned into the episode in the laundry room. Now, having tried not being around her, he found she was still just as distracting in his mind as she was in the flesh.

Okay, almost as distracting, he thought, a quick flash of her flesh burning his memory.

They had to talk it out. It was the mature, adult, rational thing to do. Taking a deep breath, he picked up the phone and dialed her number.

"Hello?"

"Charlotte," he said, clearing his throat. "It's me. Gabe."

There was a moment's pause on the other end of the line. "I thought you weren't talking to me," she said finally.

"It's not working, Charlotte. I need to see you."

Another pause. Her voice came through husky, seductively so. "Okay. Where and when?"

He glanced at his watch again. "I'm still at the office, but I was headed home to change out of the suit I'm in…we had clients, so I couldn't wear casual. Maybe I could drop by after that?"

"I've got a better idea," she murmured. "Why don't I meet you at your house? Say, in…half an hour?"

He sighed. Half an hour. He could pull himself together in half an hour. "Okay. I'll see you at eight-thirty."

"I'm glad you called, Gabe." He could hear the little smile in her voice. "I missed you."

She hung up and he gently placed the phone back on its cradle. "I missed you, too," he said, half to himself. And if this worked out, please God, he'd never have to miss her again.

CHARLOTTE LOOKED AT the phone for a long minute.
This is it. This is your one shot at finally letting Gabe know how you feel.

She stood up, trembling. Confidence, schmonfidence. What she needed was a miracle.

She whipped out her now-worn copy of *The Guide*. "Be what he isn't expecting," it advised. "Men love a break in routine. They want something different and exciting."

She scanned down farther. "Meet him at the door in…oh, my goodness." She could feel herself blushing, and she was all alone in the room. "I don't know if I could do that."

But what choice did she have? He'd seen her as a tomboy, as a Hoodlum, as one of his closest and oldest friends. He was just beginning to see her as a potential lover. She needed to get him to make the transition...add friend to lover, and you had a relationship that was worth trying.

She took a deep breath and headed for her sewing machine. She now had created enough outfits to have a small line of her own, she thought proudly. She had really enjoyed doing something that at one time she would have considered so frivolous, but now found challenging and expressive.

She picked up her latest "creation." It was simple, elegant and to the point. It was a midnight-blue teddy, laced up the front with satin ribbon. It emphasized everything it needed to and was devastatingly sexy. It would take guts to wear it...but then again, it would take guts to do what she was about to do.

She took another deep breath, desperately trying to stay calm.

Operation Seduction. Or, more appropriately, Mission Impossible.

GABE HAD GOTTEN HOME and changed into more comfortable clothes and was waiting for Charlotte to get there. He wouldn't let her talk first, and he wouldn't get physically close to her. He'd lay out the problem as if presenting a brainstorming session and see what she had to say. If he just kept his hands off her, if he could just stay focused, they might get out of this alive.

He smiled mockingly at himself. Okay, he was exaggerating. But not by much. This thing had driven him crazy, and he was dangerously close to the breaking point. He was torturing himself with images of her—at the sports bar, at the housewarming, on his couch. If she wore one of her simple-yet-sexy designs tonight, he wasn't sure what he'd do…throw a beach towel over her, or just flat-out tackle her and take her on the living room floor.

He glanced at his hallway cupboard. Maybe he should get out a beach towel, just in case. Either way, he was close to snapping.

The doorbell rang and he started slightly. "Get a grip, man," he muttered to himself, and praying for strength, he opened the door.

She was wearing her hair pulled back, and her makeup made her eyes look smoldering, her lips inviting. He quickly moved his gaze elsewhere. Thankfully, she was wearing a thick gray wool car coat…apparently over one of her shorter dresses, since he couldn't see the hemline. She was wearing a set of low pumps. He quickly glanced away from her legs, knowing that staring too long at them would definitely push him toward the taking-her-on-the-living-room-floor scenario. "Come on in," he said nervously. "Can I get you anything?"

"Um, a glass of water," she said. Strangely, she sounded equally nervous. Probably in reaction to him. He'd been a complete basket case lately. It wouldn't be a surprise if she were uncomfortable with it. And there was their previous and new physical history. Yes, the sooner they got this cleared up, the better.

"Do you want me to take your coat?" he asked.

She looked at him with wide eyes, as if he'd suggested they go murder somebody.

"Um, never mind. Actually, that's better. Keep the coat on," he said, his words tumbling out one over the other. "I have a few things I need to say to you, and I need you to just listen and not interrupt me."

She nodded slowly, nibbling delicately at her lower

lip. He tried not to let the sweet little gesture distract him.

"Charlotte, we've…" he started, then stopped. "What I mean to say is…" He took a deep breath. *Okay, Gabe, just dive in!* "We've kissed, Charlotte. A lot."

She stared at him for a moment, then burst out laughing. "Um, I know that. I was there, remember?"

Her laughter helped break the tension. After a moment, he chuckled, too. "I keep forgetting who I'm talking to. Charlotte, we really need to talk about that."

She smiled, tilting her head to the side. "Okay. What exactly do you need to say?"

His brain went blank for a minute. This was it. Make-or-break moment. "I…well, I guess I forgot it was you when I was kissing you."

She flinched.

"That didn't come out right," he said hastily. "Let me try that again. I mean, I knew it was you, but I sort of forgot everything that *you* entailed."

"And what exactly does kissing *me* entail?"

He sighed raggedly. "I…what I'm about to say here is, ever since you've changed what you looked like, I haven't treated you like a friend, and that's where the problem has been. I just kept getting side-tracked by what you looked like, and ignored the fact that you're Charlotte. And since you're Charlotte…well, you know what that means."

"I'm not sure. Why don't you spell it out for me?"

How long was this agony going to continue? "It means that I shouldn't do anything like that with you. You're…special, Charlotte," he explained. "You're very special to me just the way you are."

She sighed. Without another word, she got up and went into his bedroom.

He blinked. Well, that had gone worse than he had expected. He followed her. "Are you okay...?" he asked, then stopped abruptly.

She had tossed the car coat onto the floor and was rummaging through his chest of drawers. What she was wearing...

He stopped breathing.

Oh, mercy.

She was wearing a deep, dark-blue teddy, in some shiny material that made it shimmer like a black-blue pearl. What little there was was cut high on the thigh and low down the front. It had a dark satin ribbon lacing it up the front, just begging to be untied. She turned to stare at him, her eyes huge and glowing like hazel crystals.

"Do you have any sweats?" she asked.

He cleared his throat. "I'm sorry. What?"

"Sweats," she repeated, blushing. The pink wash covered most of her body, it seemed, and he could tell...most of her body was deliciously exposed. "I was wondering if I could borrow a pair of sweats and a T-shirt."

His mouth went dry. He tried to look everywhere, all at once, and his pulse beat a hectic tempo in his chest.

She looked down at the drawer she'd opened. "Look, I feel really stupid about this. I should have known...oh, I've just been an idiot. Sure, I've changed a lot, but we've always been just friends. I guess I was starting to buy the hype, you know? Charlotte the Tomboy turning into Charlotte the Sexy. It's like we always say...you know you're in trouble when you start believing your own press."

He barely registered the self-derision in her voice, the embarrassment. A part of him wanted to comfort her, but the rest of him had already started the chemical change that made listening or even rational thought impossible.

The beast was awake, and it wanted Charlotte. Gabe had finally reached his breaking point. He snapped.

"I just want to throw on some normal clothes and watch ESPN until I forget this whole episode ever...hey!" Her words got cut off as in two quick steps he was at her side, spinning her, grabbing her. Taking her.

With an impatient motion, he pulled the ribbon out of her hair, crushing the satiny waves in one hand. His eyes burned into hers. Before she could say anything else, he molded his mouth to hers, branding her. She tasted like some tropical fruit, sweet and tart and exotic. He feasted on her.

When he felt her body melt into pliancy, he gripped her to him, gently tugging at her hair until her closed eyes opened. "I tried, dammit," he said, his voice ragged. "I tried not to do this."

She took a deep breath. "Do you know who I am this time?"

He nodded. "You're the woman I told myself I couldn't want, but the woman that I need more than breathing. You're the woman I crave like a drug." He smiled, his eyes gleaming with ferocious promise. "You're the woman I'm going to make lose control tonight. Satisfied?"

She started to nod. "Well, not yet," she said, and her voice sent sensual shivers from his heart to his stomach, and lower. "But I think I will be."

"Charlotte," he groaned, and took her mouth again.

This was what she wanted, she thought. She returned his kiss with a fierceness she didn't know she was capable of, tangling her fingers in his dark hair.

She moaned, low in her throat, as her tongue dueled with his.

It was only a few steps to the bed, and she laughed as they stumbled over a pair of his running shoes and tumbled onto it.

He laughed, too, a short, harsh gasp. "Okay, I'm going faster than I should," he said, studying her intently. "I've wanted you for too long to lose control now."

"Be careful," she warned, moving her body seductively and grinning smugly when his eyes widened. "You're not the only person who can make somebody lose control." She kissed him gently on his jawline, then lay back on the bed and smiled.

He raised his eyebrow at her challenge. Then he ran his fingers through her hair, his fingertips caressing her face like a blind man, learning with his touch the way he'd only known her with his eyes. "You are exquisite," he said, his voice low and rough. "Don't ever doubt it." He brushed kisses over the trail his fingers had drawn.

He made her feel beautiful. Her fingers went to his shirt. The trembling of her hands made her go much more slowly than she wanted to, but the sensation of material drawn slowly over his now-sensitized skin was having an effect on him. Finally, she tugged the thing off his shoulders and tossed it blindly onto the floor.

She took a minute to look her fill at his broad, muscular chest. Then she skimmed her fingertips over it, taking her cue from him, moving with gentle roughness. The satin smoothness of his skin contrasted wildly with the corded muscles that flexed under her hands.

He smiled that sexy, devilish smile that sent a spear

of fire through her chest. "My turn," he murmured against the base of her throat.

She gasped at the sensation, feeling ripples of it pulse through her chest. He took the ends of the ribbon that laced up her teddy and slowly tugged. The bow vanished. Then he eased the shoulder straps down off her shoulders. "This is nice," he said appreciatively, grinning. "I think you should greet me at the door in this more often."

"Well, you know how it is," she teased, breathlessly. "Laundry day's tomorrow, and it's all I had left...."

He laughed, tracing the low edge of the now-open bodice with his tongue. "Remind me to bring a load of laundry over," he said, his breath tickling her skin. "I think I'd like to know you're not wearing anything when I get there."

She was going to chuckle, but he edged the material lower and she didn't have any more breath to laugh with.

She was amazing. He cupped the undersides of her breasts and teased her through the satiny material. He watched as her nipples grew rock hard under his attention, and smiled tenderly as she edged up to meet his mouth. She was breathing in sexy little gasps, a combination of surprise and arousal. She moved like a dancer, all grace and strength. She pulled her head up and kissed him, nipping at his throat with sharp little teeth. It threatened to send him over the edge, to just grip her and take her.

The glint of sexual challenge in her eyes only encouraged him to take it even more slowly, to torture her the way she was torturing him. He'd take all night and part of the morning if he had to.

He slipped the teddy off her, and revised that thought. He'd last maybe five minutes at this rate.

Her body was perfection. Firm, high breasts over a toned stomach, hips flaring out into curvaceous legs. She twisted a little, obviously unused to being naked to the light of a man's eyes. The little action made him smile.

He stroked her legs lovingly, promising himself that he'd give more attention to them later, when he wasn't under the driving, brutal passion that was grilling him as he caressed her.

She grasped one of his hands. "No fair," she said breathlessly. "It's your turn." She reached for his waistband. He gave her a surprised look. For someone so shy, she took the lead with a look of hunger that tripled what he was already feeling. If this kept up, he might die. But he would certainly die happy.

She was struggling for control as he lay back on the bed, grinning, encouraging her. She undid the button and zipper on his jeans, then eased them off.

He was wearing silk boxers with a dark paisley pattern. She could see the evidence of his arousal springing forward against the slick fabric. She tossed the jeans aside, then paused. "Aren't those the boxers I bought you for your birthday?"

He started to nod, then hissed sharply as she smoothed her hands over them, giving loving attention to his hardness. "Mmm. They didn't feel this good in the box."

He choked.

She laughed, teasing him the way he'd teased her, pressing kisses on his legs, on his chest, at his waistband. Before she could dip lower, he growled, pinning her on the bed. "You keep that up, angel, and I'll be embarrassed. I want tonight to be good for you."

"Gabe," she whispered, pausing to kiss him deeply. "I'm finally with you. It's already perfect."

He smiled, like a man who'd been given the gift he'd always dreamed of, and she shivered as he took her mouth in a kiss sweeter than any she'd ever experienced.

The sweetness converted to hunger, and hunger to fire. She'd always been self-conscious about her body, the first to dive under the covers in her long-ago romantic episodes. She'd never felt particularly confident in bed, for that matter. But tonight was different. Tonight she felt like all those women she'd only read about…temptresses, seductresses. Women men went crazy for. Women men loved.

When he leaned down to kiss her neck, she moaned, wrapping her arms around him, stroking strong, eager fingers down his back. He nipped at her breasts, making her trembling even more pronounced.

"Gabe," she said, clutching at him. "Please. I need…"

He groaned. "Angel, I need you, too."

He tugged off his boxers.

He was magnificent. His skin was gleaming and chiseled. He reminded her of a Donatello bronze that she'd studied in school. Except that his arousal was…

She cleared her throat nervously. *He's huge.*

Something must have reflected in her face, because despite the passion that was clearly burning through him, Gabe chuckled. "Second thoughts, angel?"

"Eep."

He laughed, nuzzling at her neck. She could feel the pounding in his chest, echoing the reckless pulse in hers. He kissed her throat, stroking her back with butterfly-light touches that had her melting into him like butter on toast. When she felt his hardness pressing at the soft flesh of her thighs, a wave of molten dampness answered between her legs. She arched her hips up, cuddling him intimately.

He stopped, poised at the brink of her. His breathing was labored. "Charlotte."

She looked up. His eyes were rings of blazing silver around circles of opaque black fire.

"You'd better want me as much as I want you, because from here on there's no stopping."

It took her a minute to figure out what he was saying, drenched in passion as she was. He was giving her one last chance to stop what they'd started. He was letting her decide.

The fever inside her was beyond reasoning. She arched up against him, kissing him fiercely as she moved her legs to curve around him.

With a groan, he pressed forward, and she felt him fill her with delicious slowness. She gasped, loud. "Gabe…"

"Oh God, angel," he breathed.

He moved inside her, rocking with gentle thoroughness. She could feel the pressure of him, moving over her most delicate flesh, and felt fire roar through her. She pushed her hips up to meet him, wrapping her legs tightly around his.

"Gabe," she breathed. "I can't…I'm…" Her pulse pounded in her ears and she was shouting his name.

He moved against her, and she could feel the slick sweat between them. He was bringing her to the edge, and she could feel that elusive pulse start to ring through her. She pushed against him, and he drove into her, hard.

She was catapulted over into oblivion, every sense overloading. She cried out, clenching him tight. *"Gabe!"*

"Charlotte," he groaned in answer, and his hips jerked hard against hers, once, twice.

He sunk on top of her, their arms twined around

each other, as if they could never let go. After a long moment, he pushed himself up on one arm, stroking her sweat-dampened bangs out of her face. He smiled rakishly.

"I won," he said.

She blinked. "You won what?"

"I made you lose control first." He leaned onto his back, carrying her with him until she was sprawled on top of him. He kissed her quickly. "So, do I get anything? Fabulous cash prizes? A trip to Bermuda?"

She chuckled. Her head was still reeling from what they'd just done. And amazingly, as his fingers stroked down between her shoulder blades, she felt an aftershock of pleasure. She squirmed and his eyes widened as she rubbed against him.

"I think you were cheating," she said, moving seductively, her breathing going shallow. *This is ridiculous. You just had a sexual experience that nearly blinded you! And you're ready to do it again?*

His breathing went uneven, but he smiled. "What are you suggesting?"

She leaned down and kissed him luxuriously, until they were both breathless and gasping. "Tiebreaker," she said, when she could finally speak.

"Two out of three?" he said, moving up with one lusciously rough motion.

She gasped. "You're on."

10

GABE WOKE UP SLOWLY, sensing the sunlight pouring in through his window. He was hot, was the first thing that came to mind. And a little cramped, now that he thought about it. But strangely, he wasn't uncomfortable. In fact, he had an overwhelming feeling of well being, bordering on satiation. Hell, he felt happy. And when was the last time he'd faced a morning with *that* emotion?

He started to roll over and encountered a girl-shaped lump.

He froze.

It was his apartment, his bed. His best friend.

Oh, no.

He had just made love with Charlotte. Several times, in fact.

The shock of what he'd done was nothing compared to the jolt he got as he remembered the night before. He'd told himself, he'd *promised* himself that he wouldn't touch her. He'd just talk it out and be adult about the whole thing! He'd explain what was happening, and then he'd be able to keep his best friend, instead of getting into bed with her, which would lead to a relationship that would be doomed to failure. He *knew* what was at stake and still he had been the stereotypical guy, letting his body do all the talking!

If he had known this was going to happen, he

would have locked himself in, unplugged his phone and sat in his living room with the lights out.

He closed his eyes as more images of the previous night invaded. Or would he?

He tried to calm the unruly response of his body, which even now reacted to the memories of what they'd done. He'd never kissed a woman the way he'd kissed Charlotte. Those kisses weren't a maneuver to get her to sleep with him. He'd kissed her that way because he needed her, because she felt so perfectly right beneath him. And once she'd gotten there, the whole thing had changed. She'd turned into... Well, he couldn't quite describe *what* she'd turned into.

All he could say was, they'd gone five out of seven, and she'd won. And he never would have expected that his best friend Charlotte Taylor would be his perfect sexual complement in bed.

She was sexier than he'd ever dreamed anyone could be, her body like silk and fire. That generous mouth of hers, moving over him...

Now he leaped out of bed. Okay, no more thoughts down that path, or he'd be sure to get into more trouble than he was already in!

He couldn't resist looking at her, though, and the sight made his heart beat unevenly. She was tangled in the sheets, still completely naked. Her body looked lean and graceful. Her hair was tousled and her face was relaxed, her full lips still curving in the remnants of a smile. She had a mark on her neck where he'd kissed her a little harder than he realized.

He leaned down, pressing his lips gently where the mark was. She gave a soft little sigh, turning toward him blindly.

He pulled back as if burned.

He hastily snatched up some clothes and dove into the bathroom. Putting himself under the spray of the shower, he berated himself. Charlotte wasn't a Saturday night pickup or the Babe of the Week. She was, quite possibly, the most important woman he'd ever met. He couldn't use her like this.

Maybe you weren't using her.

The thought was quiet, sneaky, and he growled under his breath. Ah, the ever-helpful conscience. He was wondering when that would show up. And, as usual, it provided no helpful advice whatsoever. He didn't want a relationship with anyone, much less the one woman he knew he needed to keep by him for the rest of his life. If he got into a relationship with her, he'd lose her, it was as simple as that. Honestly, what was his conscience thinking?

Okay, that's it. I'm letting you screw this one up all by yourself.

It's about time, Gabe thought as he got out of the shower and hastily toweled himself off. Then he caught a glimpse of himself in the foggy mirror. His eyes were wild, and he was frowning and muttering.

He was in worse shape than he thought. He was actually arguing with himself!

He got dressed and walked through the bedroom. Charlotte was still sleeping, obviously exhausted. When he saw her, he didn't see what he had in every other relationship. He knew that he'd never ride an emotional roller coaster with her. He wouldn't see jealousy, he wouldn't be forced into little dramas and psychological showdowns. She wouldn't ever hurt him.

As long as she was his *friend.*

But he knew her. She was looking to get married, to be wildly in love. She *deserved* to be in love, even though his chest ached uncomfortably at the thought. She didn't deserve to be hurt because her best friend was an ass. If she had been any other woman, he'd have convinced her to call in sick and they would have spent the day in bed, finding new and exciting ways to enjoy each other. Then, once he'd figured out what it was he couldn't stand, or once she'd played one too many games or thrown one too many tantrums or just gotten a little too clingy, he'd gently break it off and go back to his old life.

He knew there was no way he would feel, or do, any of that to Charlotte. At least, he wouldn't do it intentionally. But what if it did happen? She wouldn't bring in expectations, but she would leave with disappointments. There was no way he could keep her as the friend he needed. And he needed her desperately. God, how he needed her.

Damage control, he thought. *Stop this now, before it gets worse.*

He grabbed a piece of paper and a pen. "Charlotte," he wrote. "Meet me at Hennessy's at seven-thirty. Gabe."

Sighing, he left it on the bedside table. Then, because he couldn't help himself, he lowered his head and kissed her. Even asleep, she stirred beneath his lips, pressing against him. He let himself linger for just a second. *After she sees me tonight, I'll never be able to touch her again.*

He tore himself away.

Got to stop this now, he told himself, locking the door behind him. *Before it's too late.*

"WHAT IS *WITH* you today?" Wanda snapped.

Charlotte stopped, midstride, a dazed smile on her face. "Huh? What are you talking about?"

"You're singing." Wanda's finely drawn eyebrow lifted. "You never sing."

Ryan walked up to her. "You've been dancing in the hallway, too. What's going on, girl?"

"Nothing. I'm happy." Charlotte hugged her folder of sketches to her chest. "Did somebody pass a happiness law when I wasn't looking or something?"

"You're more than happy," Wanda said with some asperity, studying her as if she were a bug under a microscope. "You're glowing."

Ryan squinted, then stopped, his eyes widening. "Oh, no."

Charlotte mistrusted that expression on his face. "What?"

"You got lucky, didn't you?" Ryan crowed with laughter. "Wait till Gabe gets a load of this!"

Charlotte winced.

Wanda snapped her fingers. "That's it! I thought I recognized that look!" She pursed her lips. "I've just never seen it on Charlotte before, that's all."

"Meeeow." Ryan glanced at Wanda, grinning. "Sheathe those claws, Catwoman. So, Charlotte, who's the lucky guy?"

"Remind me again how this became your business," Charlotte retorted, making a beeline toward her office. Ryan and Wanda were hot on her heels.

"Aw, come on, Charlotte. How can you expect me to leave a prime piece of gossip like this one alone? The rest of the Hoodlums have a right to know!"

"Yeah, Charlotte," Wanda said, practically purring. "You can't keep this a secret."

"Right to know? Freedom to gossip is not covered in the constitution!" Charlotte tried to be more angry about it, but the fact was, she was too ecstatic to even care that they were hassling her. "My sex life is private, as in none-of-your-business private. Only one other person is privy to the details." She smirked, winking at Ryan. "And that's only because it wouldn't be any fun if he *didn't* know, you know?"

Ryan roared with laughter as Wanda gaped. "At least tell me this," Ryan hounded. "How was it?"

"How was it?" Hard as she tried, her pulse picked up and she felt the dumb grin she'd been wearing all day broaden. "It was incredible. Out of this world." She stopped, seeing them at the edge of their figurative seats, drinking in every word. "It was just fine, thank you very much. Now, if you'll excuse me, I've got work to do." *Way to be discreet, Charlotte!*

She began to close the door, but Wanda grabbed the door handle. Her green eyes widened. "Oooh! You have a hickey!"

Charlotte's hand flew to her throat, where the makeup she'd so carefully applied must have worn off.

"Charlotte's got a hick-ey, Charlotte's got a hick-ey!" Ryan sang cheerfully.

"Grow up," she groaned, before slamming the door in their faces. She could hear the chanting and hooting laughter for another minute or so before Ryan finally disappeared, his chuckles echoing down the hallway.

She sat down, putting her folder on her desk. She was going to get no work done today, she could tell that right now. Anything she drew would have hearts and flowers on it...or be very, very risqué.

Last night had been more than incredible. She didn't have words to describe the experience. Anything she might have expected was completely surpassed.

And best of all, she'd won, she thought with a wicked grin.

She shook her head, feeling her pulse increase as the heat built in the pit of her stomach. Oh, she wanted him. It had been creeping up on her all morning, no matter what she was doing or who she was talking to. She could not get Gabe out of her mind.

How was she supposed to know that her best friend for twenty years was the man of her dreams?

But he was more than just her best friend now. The image of him would be irrevocably linked to an image of the two of them, tangled in sheets and each other. She would never be able to look at him and just think "weekend football" or "poker night." How could they just share a couch without thinking of what had happened when they'd finally shared a bed?

Not to say that they weren't still friends. To her mind, that's what made it all so perfect. She knew his heart, his secret dreams and fears. He knew hers. There wasn't any awkward getting-to-know-you period, no hesitancy. There was nothing they couldn't share with each other. They clicked so perfectly before; now they were meshed. They were one heart.

She'd always known that she loved him, as a friend. Now she valued his friendship as a lover.

He hadn't woken her up this morning, which was just as well. She would have pounced on him again and neither of them would have made it in to work. She'd never felt that way about Derek, this insatiable hunger. Of course, one man could hardly be considered a control group. If she'd met someone like Gabe to start with, maybe she would have had the hunger sooner.

If I had started with Gabe, I never would have moved on to anybody else.

She glanced down at the note he had left by her bedside. Meet him at Hennessy's. She smiled. Funny that he should pick one of the Hoodlums' hangouts. Maybe he wanted to make their new status public as soon as possible. She'd only been to Hennessy's a few times herself. It was more of a guy's place, a real pickup joint. She seemed to remember they had some nickname for it, but she couldn't recall it offhand. It probably involved "babe-hunting," if she knew the guys.

She smiled, hugging herself as she felt goose bumps crawl up her arms. Gabe wouldn't have to look very far to find a "babe" tonight, she decided. Tonight was the first night of her new future. She shook her hair out of its ponytail, letting it fall in loose waves over her shoulders.

Last night she'd been a goddess, fiery and unconquerable. It had been Gabe's tenderness and passion, and her own confidence, that had finally gotten her there. She couldn't go back to what she was. She didn't want to. Tonight, she was going to show Gabe exactly how sexy he made her feel.

She grinned. And she was going to show him until the sun came up tomorrow morning.

GABE SAT AT ONE of the high, round tables at Hennessy's. It was the height of happy hour, with plenty of men and women laughing, flirting and generally being rowdy as they munched on the buffet and ordered rounds of margaritas. He nursed his beer, glancing at his watch. She would be there any minute. The rest of the Hoodlums called Hennessy's "Heartbreak Hotel," because at one point or another, they had all brought women there to break up with them. It was a perfect setting for it—public, loud, hard to cause a scene in. He had picked it out of habit, and out of cowardice. He wasn't sure how Charlotte was going to handle the news that last night had been a mistake, a poor decision that their overexcited bodies had thrown them into. For that matter, he wasn't sure how he was handling it himself.

He'd rather put a gun to his head than hurt Charlotte. He knew that. But this was the only way to prevent her from getting even more hurt later. He had a chance to catch it now, quickly, before it went too far.

Of course, you're assuming that last night meant as much to her as it did to you.

Ah, my conscience, he thought. He'd been beginning to miss it.

He took a long draw of his beer. Of course it meant as much to her. No one could have gone through what they went through and not have felt the power of it. Just memories of their night together sent pulses of heat through him. He'd been with more women than he cared to remember, but he had never had as intense an experience as he'd had with Charlotte.

But it had to be more than just an experience, dammit. She deserved more. He rubbed his hands wearily over his face. Why in the hell had he slept with her? She was his little Charlie, his best friend, his pal. The tomboy. The one who could play poker or football, help you fix your car or hear you out. She was the perfect sidekick. She wasn't the type of woman you fell in love with, right?

He looked up, midthought, and his breath caught in his throat.

She was standing in the doorway, looking as if she'd just stepped off the Babe of the Week Web site...or better yet, off some runway in Milan. She had on a little black dress with those teeny shoulder straps that made his eyes pop. The dress had a slick, satiny sheen that seemed to take what little light there was in the place and caress it over her curves. It clung to her body like a lover. Her hair was up in a simple twist, framing her face like a work of art. Her eyes looked huge, like hazel-green gems. She looked like a painting, or a sculpture. Or a goddess. She wore deep, dark lipstick, emphasizing the quirk of a smile, and showing just how immensely kissable that mobile mouth of hers was.

He tore his gaze away. *Oh, my God.*

As he glanced away from her, he noticed that he wasn't the only man who'd been struck by Charlotte's entrance. He noted the predatory interest showing on the faces of several of the men around him. It was all he could do not to beat the gleam of lechery off of their smug, beer-guzzling faces. She spotted him, waved to him, her smile growing sexier by degrees. She started walking. She was wearing high heels and her hips swayed hypnotically as she strode toward him.

"Hi, Charlotte," he said hoarsely, leaning forward to be heard over the noisy din of the crowd.

"Hi," she said huskily, then moved in to kiss him.

The urge to kiss back was strong, but he dodged. Her kiss landed on his cheek. She gave him a puzzled glance, looking around. "What? Are the guys here or something?"

He wiped the lipstick off his face. "No. At least, I haven't seen them."

She smiled, sending heat straight to his groin. "I thought about you all day. Thanks for letting me sleep in, by the way." The smile grew more intense. "If you hadn't, I don't think we would have made it in to work today."

Hearing his cowardice interpreted as thoughtfulness, and hearing his own thought from that morning come from her sexy lips, sent pangs of pain through him. He took a deep breath. "Charlotte, we need to talk."

She went still. She reminded him of a nature documentary he'd seen of a gazelle scenting a lion. Her eyes were wary. "Do we?" she asked, reaching over and taking a sip of his beer.

He nodded, taking a deep, aching breath. "It's about last night."

She nodded slowly in return. "What about last night?"

"Last night was...incredible." He hadn't meant to say that, but it was the truth. She deserved to hear it.

Her eyes lit with sultry fire. "Tell me about it."

"But it was probably not a great idea." He saw her eyes widen, and he plunged forward, as if saying the words faster would somehow lessen the blow. "You're my best friend, angel. I don't want to do anything to hurt you, but we've known each other way too long for me to lie to you. You want somebody to fall head over heels in love with you. You want to get married. You deserve that." He swallowed hard. "You deserve better than some fling with me."

She blinked. He felt like he'd slapped her.

"Angel?" Gabe finally said, after a long, pregnant pause. He reached out for her hand, but she didn't take it. He sighed. "Come on. Talk to me. We can always talk to each other, right?"

She continued studying him, shaking her head. Without a word, she began to tremble, putting her head down on the table into her cradled arms.

She was crying. Oh, God, he was such scum. He reached over to stroke her silken, soft hair. "Oh, Charlotte, I'm so sorry...."

Her head popped up, and she wiped at the tears at the corners of her eyes. And that's when it hit him.

She was laughing.

"Oh, for pity's sake, Gabe. You are *such* an idiot," she announced, taking a deep, hitching breath between laughs.

"I beg your pardon?"

"As well you should," she said, between chuckles. "Could you be a little more into yourself?"

Now he felt like *she'd* slapped *him*. Reeling from the shock, he finally stammered, "What are you talking about, Charlotte?"

"Have you taken a good look at me lately?" She stood up, did a slow twirl that caught the eye of every man in the bar. She leaned forward so only he could hear her. "For the first time in my life, I feel *beautiful*. Desirable. It's been a slow, uphill process, but now that I've got it…sweetie, there's no way a rejection from you is going to ruin all that."

He watched the way her eyes shone, and his hand reached out to stroke her cheek before he could stop himself. "Of course not. I never thought that it would."

She pulled away, her eyes flashing. "What I'm trying to tell you is that I'm a big girl now, Gabe. I'm not little Charlotte whom you need to protect. If you feel you can't handle a relationship with me, that's fine. But don't you dare think you can pin this on 'protecting' me, because that just won't cut it."

"But I wasn't—" he started, then cut himself off. Well, in a way, he *was* trying to protect her. He was trying to protect them both. And what was wrong with that?

"We can agree on one thing, though. I'm glad you said something before this went any further. Neither of us needs the drama."

"Well, I'm glad you're not hurt," he said numbly. Funny that his own chest felt like a glacier, tearing a cold path through his heart.

"Are we done with this, then?" She picked up her purse in a businesslike fashion. "I've got to get going."

"Why? Got a date?" He regretted the question as soon as it was out of his mouth.

She surveyed him wryly. "No offense, Gabe, but I've got this whole life *besides* you, you know. And amazing as it sounds, it appears that I *do* have a good chance of getting married and having a wonderful husband and family. In a way, it's all thanks to you." She leaned over and brushed a quick kiss on his cheek. "I'll let you pay me that thousand in installments. Got to run. I'll catch you later."

"When?"

She shrugged. "I don't know. My social life just got a lot more hectic. I'll call you."

She turned to go.

"Charlotte?"

She turned, sighing. "Yes?"

He swallowed hard. "You know I love you, right?"

Did he see the pain shoot across her face, or did he just imagine it? Her face was now a mask of amused tolerance. She shrugged. "Of course I know that, Gabe. But you're not *in* love with me, and I guess we both know that." She sighed. "Maybe we just need a little breathing room. This is all getting too crazy. Steer clear of me for a while."

He watched as she walked slowly across the floor, smiling at various men as she made her way to the door. One man stopped her. Gabe was on his feet before he realized he'd moved.

She simply smiled, patted the man on his shoulder while shaking her head and laughing at something the man said. Then she walked out, every male gaze riveted to her. With her head held high and her hips swaying gently, Gabe could only think of two things.

She was so beautiful, his heart ached to look at her.

She was walking out of his life forever.

11

"CHARLOTTE, HONEY, can we talk?"

Charlotte glanced over at Dana, barely hearing her over the pounding beat of the dance club. "Something wrong?"

Dana turned to where Bella, Brad, Jack, and Dana's husband, Stan, were sitting off to the side. She motioned to Bella, who nodded and hurried over to join them. Charlotte frowned when the two women tugged her outside. The night air was refreshingly cool, and she bloused out the top of her dress.

"Charlotte, we're worried about you," Dana said, in her usual straightforward manner.

"Worried about me?" Charlotte knew from the look of concern etched on both of their faces that this conversation was going to be a doozy. "Why? I'm fine."

"You are *not* fine," Bella contradicted her gently.

"I really appreciate you going out with me as much as you have in the past week, but the truth is, I haven't had a social life this jam-packed since…" Charlotte thought about it. "Actually, I've never had a social life like this." She adjusted the fit of the short cherry-red dress she was wearing. "I've had men stop me on the street and ask me for my phone number. I've been hit on at the grocery store. Somebody tried to pick me up at a stoplight, for pity's sake. It's the most bizarre thing I've ever seen." And it was. Any other time, she would be bewildered by the attention, possibly even frightened by it. But after what happened with Gabe, it didn't matter in the slightest. Very little did. If anything, she was somewhat amused.

"Yes, your social life is skyrocketing," Dana admitted. "But that's not excessive dating that's putting those shadows in your eyes. And have you lost a little weight?"

"Upped my workout a little bit," Charlotte explained, not adding that she'd needed to wear herself out to get a few hours of sleep at night. "And I suppose I've been running myself a little ragged, between work and all of this going out. I'll rest more this weekend, I promise."

"Charlotte," Bella said gently, "nobody could be more pleased than we are that you've blossomed so beautifully. What's more, that you believe in yourself." She crossed her arms. "But we know that you're not happy. Not really."

Charlotte replied impatiently. "First, I'm not paying enough attention to my appearance, and you say you'd leave me alone if you thought I was happy. Now I'm painting the town red and you say you'd leave me alone if you thought I was happy. There's just no pleasing some people!"

Dana and Bella could have been twins, the look of concern and caring on their faces was so similar. They stared at her, waiting for her to speak, ignoring her waspish remark. They also obviously weren't going anywhere until they found out what was wrong.

Charlotte sighed. She loved them for loving her, for trying so hard to help her. But she needed to do this on her own.

"Let me tell you a little story," Charlotte finally said, her voice calm and detached. "Say you take a woman who doesn't have much confidence in her looks, who hides behind being a tomboy. Say you add a man who is kind and loving with a perfect sense of humor. Someone who she could easily spend the rest of her life with.'' She felt her voice catching in her throat, and she focused on the wall of the club, rather than Dana's and Bella's sympathetic eyes. ''That man shows her that not only is she beautiful, she's exquisite and extraordinary. He brings things out of her that she's never felt with anyone else. Say that woman decides she's completely, madly in love and spends the night with him, expecting it to be the beginning of happily ever after.'' She glanced at them. ''Only instead of a relationship, he decides at that point that they would be better off as friends.''

Dana gasped in outrage, while Bella simply nodded sadly, encouraging her to go on.

''The woman now has two choices. She can do what she's always done before…retreat behind her baggy clothes and straggly hair, and never let a man suspect what she's really like. Never let any man hurt her, ever again.'' Charlotte sent them a watery smile. ''Or she can remember one very important thing that the man taught her: he may have shown her how special she was, but he didn't *make* her special. She's special all on her own. And if he can't appreciate that, that's his problem. Not hers.''

''Oh, honey.'' With that, the two women threw their arms around her in a big, comforting hug.

''So maybe I'm not happy,'' Charlotte whispered. ''But for the first time in a long time, I can honestly say that I'm fine.''

They stood there like that for a minute, drawing strength from one another, giving strength to one another. After a minute, they stepped apart, each mopping at her eyes.

"Charlotte, I'm so proud of you," Dana said, wiping at a small blot of mascara. "If I were you, I'd be egging his car right now."

Charlotte laughed. "Well, it had crossed my mind."

Bella looked resolved. "I'm going to tell Gabe that the stupid bet is off. You don't need one more hassle hanging over your head, when you've obviously got so much more important things going on!"

"The bet has been the last thing on my mind. I think Gabe's pretty much decided to forget it, too." Charlotte was glad her voice stayed steady. Even saying his name was difficult.

"Well, I'm so mad I could spit," Dana said, her green eyes flashing with fire. "Who does that guy think he is, anyway? Mr. Most Eligible Bachelor in America! I tell you, if I had him in front of me, I'd make sure his next photo shoot looked like a police report!"

Charlotte stared at her. "What are you talking about?"

Bella sighed. "She's just mad at Jack, Charlotte. We'd have to be blind not to put it together."

Oh, God. Charlotte shook her head quickly. "It wasn't Jack."

Now both women stared at her. "It wasn't?" Dana asked. "Then who was it?"

"I'm not telling you." Charlotte's chin jutted up, determined. "This is my problem, and I'll handle it on my own."

Dana looked ready to argue, but Bella put a hand on her shoulder. "Looks like our little girl has grown up," Bella murmured, smiling.

Charlotte gave each of them a hug. "That, and I don't want you to egg his car."

"WHOO-EE. THE BABES are out tonight!" Ryan said, handing a beer to Mike.

Mike grinned, eyeing the crowd. "Honey alert, twelve o'clock. Get a look at that one, Gabe!"

Gabe swirled his soda around in his glass. He gave the woman a cursory glance, then shrugged.

Mike huffed, nudging Sean. "What is *up* with this man lately?"

Sean studied Gabe intently. "Offhand, I'd say woman trouble."

Ryan gave Gabe a quick glance, then laughed. "No question. Only a woman, or lack thereof, could make a guy this miserable."

"Now that you mention it, he hasn't gotten a lot of action lately. Maybe you should try diving back into the dating pool, bud," Mike suggested helpfully. "This is a target-rich environment. I'm sure there are a ton of babes here who'd love to be your flavor of the month."

"Hah. Of the weekend, maybe, knowing our man's track record," Ryan corrected him.

Gabe ignored them, letting their voices blend into the din. He stared at the tabletop, sighing.

He could remember the past week in crystal-clear detail. His life was a steady routine. He worked out. He surfed. His job was going like clockwork, and he was getting a lot done. Some of what he'd come up with was even usable. He was also going out with the guys every night, something he hadn't done in years. His life was going fine, just fine.

Sure he missed Charlotte. She was his best friend, why shouldn't he miss her? So he'd reached for the phone to call her a couple of times a day. Big deal. And he'd canceled poker night. She was one of the best poker players there. It was pointless to keep playing without that level of competition.

He'd given the football games last Saturday and Sunday a miss, too. There was such a thing as too much football, even for a guy like him. Just because he couldn't watch it with Charlotte didn't mean anything.

"Hello?" Sean nudged Gabe sharply in the ribs. "Check out the redhead coming this way."

Gabe glanced up halfheartedly. A voluptuous woman with flame-red hair was slinking her way to their table, a knowing smile on her pouty lips. The Hoodlums smiled broadly.

She walked straight to Gabe. "Hi there. My name's Melissande."

He nodded.

She smiled, and he felt her chest brush across his shoulder. "You don't seem to be having a good time here. Is there any place I could take you, and maybe help you feel better?"

He could sense the barely concealed glee from the other men at the table. He shook his head. "No. Thanks."

Her eyes widened in obvious surprise. She leaned over a little farther. "Are you sure? I'm very, very good...at cheering people up."

He turned to her, shrugging her touch off of his shoulder. "I don't mean to be rude about this, but I'm not interested. Okay?"

He turned back to his beer, hearing rather than seeing her flounce of indignation.

The guys watched her walk away, then pounced on him. "Are you out of your mind? That woman was hot!"

He glared at them. They ignored his obvious attempt to shut them up.

"Maybe it's Charlotte," Ryan said suddenly.

Gabe's head jerked up. "What the hell are you talking about?"

Ryan shrugged. "Well, the fact that she's finally gotten lucky has got to mean that you're that much closer to losing your bet. But I wouldn't worry too much about it. I mean, she's dating like crazy, but I thinks it's still impossible for her to get somebody to marry her in a week, man."

"How do you know she's 'gotten lucky'?" Gabe asked in a low, chilling voice.

"She had a hickey the size of Cleveland under her jaw, that's how." Ryan laughed. "Happened a week ago."

Mike gasped. "Charlie? Our Charlie?"

"Our Charlie has got to be a lot happier than our cheerful friend here, is all I can say," Ryan said sagely. "Maybe you should take a page out of her book, man, and lighten up. The day after she got that monster, she was so lit up you could have used her for a scoreboard."

"Is she still happy? Shown any more...marks?" Gabe asked, more sharply than he'd intended. Had she found someone that quickly? *That was what you said she deserved,* his conscience asserted. His chest obviously disagreed. The dull ache intensified at the thought of someone else enjoying her luscious body, her bright, sweet smile. Her.

Mike turned to Ryan curiously, but Sean continued to stare at Gabe, his eyes narrowing. Gabe was too intent on Ryan's answer to care.

Ryan frowned. "Now that you mention it, I don't think so. I mean, she's working a lot, but she seems to go out with a different guy every night, and out to lunch with another one every day. While I'll say she's a lot more, er, social than she's ever been, no way is our Charlie easy." On that point he looked adamant.

"So what happened to the guy who gave her the hickey?" Gabe prodded. "She's never mentioned who it is?"

"Well, no," Ryan admitted, shrugging. "But it's pretty obvious, don't you think?"

Gabe held his breath.

"It's gotta be Jack. He was the only guy she was dating around that time that I know of."

"Well, whoever it was, he's one lucky man," Mike said, chortling. "I may have to give her a call, myself…."

Gabe reached across the table and went for Mike's throat.

"Hey!" The other men quickly disengaged Gabe's hands from their friend's neck. "What are you doing, man?"

"Don't talk that way about Charlotte," Gabe demanded, his hands shaking in rage. "Not when I'm around. Not around anybody. If I find out you've said anything about her to anyone, I'll tear you apart."

"I wasn't disrespecting Charlotte, Gabe!" Mike yelled, rubbing at his neck. "What the hell is *wrong* with you?"

Ryan shook his head. "Oh, no."

Gabe turned to face him, ready to take him on, too. "What's *your* problem?"

"I should have realized. You're being sullen, irrational, touchy and hair-trigger violent." Ryan sighed indulgently. "Why didn't you tell us you're in love, man? We could have packed up all your breakables."

"I am *not* in love," Gabe growled. And that was the one thing he could be thankful for. Like he didn't have enough problems right now! "Being in love makes a man crazy. It always ends in disaster, and it's always with the wrong woman. I'm not doing any of that!''

He stormed away, but not before hearing the Hoodlums say in unison, "Yup. He's in love."

JACK DROPPED CHARLOTTE OFF at her house that night. She was glad to see him, but she felt a slight awkwardness after everything that had happened between her and Gabe. Still, Jack had been understanding about her other dates. He'd been downright wonderful about keeping her busy, too. He took her to movies, out to dinner, even on a trip to the zoo once. But she could sense a growing tension from him, a sort of uneasiness that intensified every time she saw him. Whatever it was, it was getting worse, she surmised. He hadn't said anything to her the whole car ride back, and that was unlike him.

He walked her to her door, as usual. "I guess this is good night, Jack," she said, giving him a quick hug. She hadn't kissed him since that disastrous smooch after the Black and White Ball. This time, he kept his arms around her loosely. "What is it?" she finally asked.

"This is sort of rough for me to talk about," Jack said haltingly. "Have I ever told you about my family?"

"No," she said, with some surprise. "Now that you mention it, you've always listened to me, but you haven't told me much about yourself."

"They're wonderful, don't get me wrong," he began, but his eyes looked troubled. "My father is a publisher, you've probably read that much. He and my mother are the greatest, but they've really been pushing me lately. Between them and the press hounding me, I feel like I've been unable to get anything important accomplished, and I've given up meeting anybody who will just care about me for me. I'm at the end of my rope. It's like no one will leave me alone, you know?"

Charlotte smiled. "Actually, I do know. Dana and Bella have been like that for years. You don't want to be pushed around by them, but you love them, and you don't know how to say no."

"That's it. That's it exactly."

She sighed. "I've finally gotten them to calm down somewhat, but now and then, I wonder if I shouldn't just change my name, shave my head and run away to join the circus."

He smiled sadly. "I've got an easier solution, sort of," he muttered, sighing heavily. "But it's crazy."

"Jack, we're friends," Charlotte said, and meant it. "You can tell me. What's wrong?"

"You're going to think I'm insane, but I was just wondering…would you do me a favor?"

He looked so at a loss, her heart immediately went out to him. "Anything for a friend, Jack. What is it?"

"Do you think you could marry me for a while?"

12

"WHERE'S CHARLOTTE?" Mike looked around expectantly. "I thought she said she'd play today. It's the Hoodlum Super Bowl."

"We're sort of...not talking right now." Gabe shrugged, trying to remain cool and ignore the pain the words brought. "But she's fine, don't worry about it."

"Who's worried?" Mike frowned, then laughed as realization dawned on him. "Oh, I get it. You pissed her off again, didn't you? What'd you do this time?"

I lost her. "I didn't do anything."

Sean gave him a quizzical look. "Maybe that's what pissed her off."

Gabe leveled a steely glare at him. "Shut up and throw the damn ball, okay?"

The other guys playing immediately started catcalling and taunting him before settling down to play some serious football. Half an hour later, their jeers had been replaced with groans of pain.

"Dammit, Gabe," Mike muttered, rubbing at his ribs. "This is touch football, man, not the NFL. Go easy, will you?"

Sean grabbed Gabe roughly by his collar. "Time out!" he called to the others, dragging Gabe toward the crashing surf. When they were out of earshot, Sean let him have it. "What is up with you, Gabe?

You almost killed Mike, but you haven't caught a single pass I've thrown to you. Where is your *head?*"

Gabe shook off Sean's grip with a rough shrug. "I don't know."

"It's the girl, isn't it?" Sean gave him a rough pat. "What's she into now?"

"It's not so much what she's into. It's what I'm into. Or not into. What I...that is..." Gabe growled in frustration. "I slept with her."

Sean simply looked at him, nodding. "Like that's somehow a shock."

Gabe blinked at him. Didn't he understand? "I said, I *slept* with her."

"So? Charlotte's beautiful," Sean said, smiling wistfully. "I've entertained some daydreams myself. But she's, like, your soul mate. I mean, the guys are close and all, but that woman knows your heart. So you did something about it." Sean shrugged. "So what's the problem?"

Gabe stood, silent.

"I mean, you told her you loved her, right?"

Still nothing.

"You *do* love her, right?" Sean emphasized his words, as if talking to a child. "I'll kick your ass if you think you don't, because nobody disrespects our girl that way. Least of all an idiot who can't see the truth when it's staring him in the face."

"I don't know what I was thinking," Gabe rasped. "All I know is, I made that stupid bet, and suddenly nothing was the same. She was still Charlotte, sure, but she was wearing those clothes, and we were spending all this time together, like we always do...and then something changed. I did everything I could think of to get us just to be friends again," he

372   *The Cinderella Solution*

argued, "but it just happened. I couldn't stop myself."

Sean sighed. "I sense stupidity ahead. What did
you do after that?"

"I stopped it before it got worse," Gabe said, closing his eyes. The incident still played through his
head every night. If he wasn't thinking of the night
they'd spent together, that is. "I thought maybe I
could catch it in time, that I wouldn't screw up the
friendship completely, but I was too late. Now she
won't see me or talk to me. I don't know what to
do." He opened his eyes, looking over at Sean. "It
was just what I thought would happen. I don't know
what I'm going to do without her."

"Gabe, you're like a brother to me, right? So I'm
going to tell you this from the heart." Sean put a
heavy hand on his shoulder. "You're a schmuck."

Gabe blinked. "Sorry?"

"You heard me. You're in love, man."

Gabe thought about it for a minute. "I don't believe this," he said slowly, even as the truth began to
hit him. "Even if I am...that's not going to help me.
I can't make a relationship work. I never have."

"Those other women you thought you were in love
with. That was bull. You weren't in love with them.
Heavily in lust, addicted to drama, but not in love."

"I tried to make them work," Gabe said. "They
all just fell apart, no matter what I did. That's when
I made the rule—friends over commitments."

"And do you know why?" Sean's dark eyes bore
into Gabe. "Because *you always had Charlotte*. She
was always the first person you called when one of
the women you believed you were 'in love with' went
haywire. If you had a problem, or good news, or if
she needed you, then you two were together, no mat-

ter who you were dating. They had your body, but Charlotte's always had your heart.''

Gabe stopped, started to speak, then stopped again.

''This time, you've got a shot at the whole thing—marriage, kids, the whole nine yards. And you're scared.'' Sean shook his head. ''Scared of all that, but even more, scared of screwing up the most important thing in your life and losing her. So what did you do?''

Gabe sighed. ''I screwed up and lost her.''

''Bingo. So what do you think all this means?''

Gabe stood for a minute, staring at the waves. He never wanted to see Charlotte with another man. He couldn't stand all the time he'd spent without her. He needed her smile, her laughter, and most of all, her love.

''It means I'm in love with Charlotte, and I'm going to do something about it.''

''All this time together, and you're just figuring it out.'' Sean sighed. ''It's things like this that convince women we're idiots, man.''

Suddenly, Ryan came running down the beach, crowing and waving a newspaper.

''Ryan, don't you wear a watch?'' Mike yelled as Ryan approached the group. ''You're two hours late!''

''You've gotta see this,'' Ryan answered, puffing from his run. The guys crowded around him, and he pushed a tabloid into Gabe's hands.

''What the...'' Gabe gaze fell on a full-color picture of Charlotte and Jack in a tabloid. The lurid headline jumped out at him: Lady in Red to Wed Jack Landor?

''Isn't it a scream?'' Ryan's face broke into a wide,

foolish grin. "Our honorary girl Hoodlum, getting married to the Most Eligible Bachelor in America?"

Gabe watched, detached, as his fingers twisted the paper, practically ripping it in two. He barely heard Ryan's yelp of protest.

"You've got to go, Gabe." Gabe looked up, and Sean's face was solemn. "It's not too late."

Gabe made a break for his car, praying Sean was right.

CHARLOTTE WAS EATING LUNCH outside at Martha's Café with Dana and Bella. She wasn't looking forward to her conversation with them, but it had to be done. They would notice when she suddenly, after a few weeks of mad socializing, stopped dating anyone at all and disappeared from the scene.

What she really wasn't looking forward to was explaining *why*.

"So I finally told him, I don't care whose wedding you're working on, you promised me two hundred orchids for tonight's banquet and I don't want to hear another word about it." Dana nodded sharply, and Bella laughed. "Honestly! Like I'm going to let him put me on the hot seat at work because some Arabian prince needs centerpieces!" She glanced over at Charlotte, winked. "Now, if it were Jack Landor's wedding, that would be something else...."

Before Charlotte could question that, Bella sent her a piercing, inquisitive look. "Speaking of, is there anything you'd like to tell us?"

"Well, yes..." Charlotte said, then frowned as the tone of her question sunk in. "Wait a minute. What are *you* talking about?"

"Charlotte, it's been in all the tabloids," Dana said in a rush. "There's a picture of you in that red dress, and there are all these rumors that you're going to get married!''

''We wanted to wait until you told us,'' Bella said with a brilliant smile. ''But you were taking so long, we just couldn't hold out! So what happened? How did he propose to you?''

''And when's the wedding?'' Dana asked, jumping in. ''I'm so excited, I could pop! Imagine, just like you thought, a proposal in under a month!''

''Now, hold it just a second,'' Charlotte said firmly. ''Jack did propose, but I need to explain a few things....''

''Charlotte.''

She stopped, midsentence. Taking a deep breath, she turned. ''Hello, Gabe,'' she said quietly. Her fingers tensed on her glass of lemonade.

''Ooh, Gabe, have you heard?'' Dana's voice was bright and, to her credit, only a little smug. ''He proposed! Jack proposed to her!''

''So the papers claim. I thought I'd find out for myself what the story was.'' His voice was low and dangerously husky. ''It took me a little while to track you down, but I need to talk to you, Charlotte.''

He looked like hell, Charlotte thought, her heart aching. He had a rough day's growth of beard, and his hair was windblown and careless. It would have made him look more rugged, like Indiana Jones, if it weren't for the shadows in his eyes. He looked like a man fighting demons.

Every fiber in her being wanted to stand up and throw herself into his arms. But she just sat there. ''Couldn't believe it, huh?''

''I didn't want to, but yes, I believed it.'' His eyes gleamed silver and lightning. ''I just wanted to hear the truth from you.''

She struggled to keep her voice calm. "If you must know, yes, Jack did propose to me."

"I see," he said, his voice low.

She barely noticed the excited sounds from Dana and Bella. It was as if the world had narrowed to encompass just herself and Gabe.

With a slow, deliberate motion, Gabe reached into his leather jacket pocket and pulled out his checkbook. "I guess you win, angel. As it happens, I have the check right here."

Dana and Bella high-fived.

Charlotte's heart broke, splintering like glass. She showed no outward signs. Her face remained impassive and her eyes were glued to the check in his outstretched hand.

"It's yours," he said. "Just come here and get it."

Like a marionette, she got up and walked to where he was standing. On the front of the check, in his bold handwriting, was the amount: one thousand dollars. And written in a scrawl on the memo line was a small sentence.

"'Congratulations to the winner'?" she read aloud.

He nodded.

She would rip it up and throw it in his face, she thought. Then she'd leave and never see him again.

She reached for the check.

With a quick motion, he grabbed her wrist, pulling her to him, molding her to him. She looked into his tortured eyes just before his mouth dipped down to hers and she felt the inferno that built whenever they kissed.

"Double or nothing," he whispered against her lips. "I bet you that I can make you happier in the next fifty years than that guy could have ever made you. I swear."

She felt a wild surge of happiness but pulled back a little, tugging against the hands that caressed her back and looped her in his embrace. "Gabe..."

"Yes?" His voice was tender yet rough.

"Are you saying this because you love me," she asked carefully, "or are you just a sore loser?"

His eyes widened in shock, just before a chuckle emerged, growing into the rich laughter that she loved so much. "Okay, I deserved that one. But let me explain." He pulled back enough to look into her eyes, his gray gaze level and sincere. "I didn't know that this was what being in love was. I always thought that love was this big production, with all the drama and screaming, and everything that went with it. But then I figured out that I was just scared. Scared of screwing up and losing the most important woman in my life. So what did I do? I went ahead and did just what I was most scared of."

"You know, this is why women think men are idiots," she teased.

"What? Am I wearing a sign?" He laughed softly, nuzzling her neck, then turned serious. "Even when I thought I was in love, I never shared myself with those women the way I did with you. Nobody knows me like you do." He stroked her cheek, his smile like the sun. "And nobody matches me as perfectly as you do. I love you, and I'm in love with you. Say you'll marry me, Charlotte."

"I told Jack I was too in love with you to marry anybody else. There wouldn't be anybody else I'd marry," she said vehemently. She leaned forward and shared a passionate kiss with him, relishing the feeling of his arms tight around her, as if he'd never let go again.

"Um, excuse me?"

Gabe and Charlotte turned and looked over at the lunch tables. Women all over the café were misty-eyed, and several were sighing deeply. Bella looked as if she were in shock. Dana, on the other hand, simply looked flabbergasted.

"Would somebody like to explain what's going on here?" she asked.

Charlotte looked up at Gabe and smiled. "We decided to make another bet. And this time, we'll both win."

Looking For More Romance?

Visit Romance.net

Look us up on-line at: http://www.romance.net

Check in daily for these and other exciting features:

Hot off the press

View all current titles, and purchase them on-line.

What do the stars have in store for you?

Horoscope

Hot deals

Exclusive offers available only at Romance.net

Plus, don't miss our interactive quizzes, contests and bonus gifts.

PWEB

Mother's Day is Around the Corner...
Give the gift that celebrates Life and Love!

Show Mom you care by presenting her with a one-year subscription to:

HARLEQUIN
WORLD'S BEST
Romances

For only **$4.96**—
That's **75% off the cover price.**

This easy-to-carry, compact magazine delivers 4 exciting romance stories by some of the very best romance authors in the world.

Plus each issue features personal moments with the authors, author biographies, a crossword puzzle and more...

A one-year subscription includes 6 issues full of love, romance and excitement to warm the heart.

To send a gift subscription, write the recipient's name and address on the coupon below, enclose a check for $4.96 and mail it today. In a few weeks, we will send you an acknowledgment letter and a special postcard so you can notify this lucky person that a fabulous gift is on the way!

Yes! I would like to purchase a one-year gift subscription (that's 6 issues) of WORLD'S BEST ROMANCES, for only $4.96. I save over 75% off the cover price of $21.00.   MDGIFT00

This is a special gift for:

Name

Address   Apt#

City   State   Zip

From

Address   Apt#

City   State   Zip

Mail to: HARLEQUIN WORLD'S BEST ROMANCES
P.O. Box 37254, Boone, Iowa, 50037-0254 Offer valid in the U.S. only.

Back by popular demand are

DEBBIE MACOMBER's

Hard Luck, Alaska, is a
town that needs women!
And the O'Halloran brothers
are just the fellows
to fly them in.

Starting in March 2000 this beloved series returns
in special 2-in-1 collector's editions:

MAIL-ORDER MARRIAGES, featuring
Brides for Brothers and *The Marriage Risk*
On sale March 2000

FAMILY MEN, featuring
Daddy's Little Helper and *Because of the Baby*
On sale July 2000

THE LAST TWO BACHELORS, featuring
Falling for Him and *Ending in Marriage*
On sale August 2000

Collect and enjoy each MIDNIGHT SONS story!

Available at your favorite retail outlet.

HARLEQUIN®
Makes any time special ™